SILENCED DREAMS

By
Analiesa Adams

Silenced Dreams

Copyright © 2019 by Analiesa Adams

All Rights Reserved. Please do not participate in or encourage piracy of copyrighted materials in violation of the author's rights. All characters and storylines are the property of the author and your support and respect is appreciated.

This book contains mature content and is intended for adult readers.

This is a work of fiction and any resemblance to persons, living or dead, or places, events or locales is purely coincidental. The characters are products of the author's imagination and used fictitiously.

Cover by http://thebookcoverdesigner.com/designers/betibup33/

Acknowledgement

Through it all, there have been few who have stuck by me. Some have passed on from this lifetime, others are still with me. My appreciation goes to my good friend, Toni, for sticking by my side. I will never forget your kindness. My heart will always be with you.

TABLE OF CONTENTS

Copyright
Acknowledgements
Prologue
Chapter 1
Chapter 2
Chapter 3
Chapter 4
Chapter 5
Chapter 6
Chapter 7
Chapter 8
Chapter 9
Chapter 10
Chapter 11
Chapter 12
Chapter 13
Chapter 14
Chapter 15
Chapter 16
Chapter 17
Chapter 18
Chapter 19
Chapter 20
Chapter 21
Chapter 22
Chapter 23
Chapter 24
Chapter 25
Chapter 26
Author Bio

PROLOGUE

The War Zone D-compound of the 1st Battalion, 7th ARVN Regiment was positioned at one of the strong points over the battlefield at Dong Xoai, Veitnam. Every soldier, able to walk, was assigned to take part in an effective 24-Hour watch at one of the four corner lookouts. So far, they hadn't seen the enemy for days. In fact, they'd been briefed that morning there weren't any Viet Cong for miles.

Yet, all of a sudden, a rampage of heavy mortar and small arms tore through the camp, killing many and wounding others within minutes of the attack. A deluge of flame throwers and human waves from the enemy came through to pick up anyone who may have escaped the first round of gunfire.

It was as if they'd come out of nowhere. They seemed to be everywhere. The battle was devastatingly bloody, wiping out the whole area in the blink of an eye. Retreat was the only answer for anyone still alive. Few units were able to hold on, but not without cost. Bodies lay where they'd fallen, lives taken away before their time, for reasons no one really understood.

Once inside the bunker, they were able to hold on for a short time with only a few more minor attacks from the enemy. They received orders to evacuate at day break, when air transportation would pick them up to take them back up to Phuoc Vinh where medical stations had been set up to treat the wounded.

The next morning, already injured soldiers helped others with more severe injuries across the field toward the waiting C-130. The proud and courageous efforts of fellow mates in arms, carrying some who could not walk, guiding others who could not see across the field was braver than they may have suspected. It looked like an evacuating hospital rather than a once whole strong group of young men. Only a handful of soldiers had been uninjured in the surprise attack the previous night. If these young men made it out alive, they would be transported out of this zone to be reassessed for their next assignment.

They could see the air transport through the trees on the other side of the field, each in their own way thanking God for the ability to go back in safety. Then it happened again. From nowhere shots rang out and it felt as if the earth was exploding around them. Sharp stinging points hit their bodies as bits of shrapnel flew around them.

One brave young man, who was carrying the unconscious body of another fellow soldier, felt a sharp painful piece enter just above the eye, causing him to temporarily lose sight in that eye. He fell to his knees at the impact. Ahead of him, his buddy had been keeping up with the pace, but suddenly the ground shook, and he disappeared from sight. The young man got to his feet to search, only to find what looked to be the scattered remnants of a once living being.

Knowing what needed to be done he picked up his keep again and headed for the plane now about ready to take off. In the chaos a few of the injured had been piled haphazardly on the floorboards like sticks being gathered for a campfire. The young man threw his injured man along side of them and grabbed hold of the strap to haul himself up. Then everything blurred and had gone black. He had no memory of what happened next.

Later he'd been told a spray of metal fragments were flying in every direction around him, and one M-16 bullet hit him on the left side, shattering his skull, which was what now affected his motor skills with his hands and arms. Now he was the owner of a six-inch steel plate to protect his brain from further injury. The difficulty now was due to the placement of the shrapnel, which had lodged itself just behind the thalamus and the damage to the cerebral pedundes and occipital lobe, there were no known surgeons available to do this type of surgery. He would need to wait until further assessment could be made.

His only saving grace had been the act of a very disgruntled one night fling he'd had before being shipped off to Vietnam, who showed up at the hospital and dropped off a young toddler, who liked to be called 'Kitten'.

That was 30 years ago.

Chapter 1

Maximilliano Geovani DeAngelo was no coward. The crazed letters didn't scare him. They were just the ranting of some lunatic obsessed with his case.

Right?

The problem was the notes hadn't stopped as authorities expected after his innocence was proven almost three years ago. He didn't kill his wife, but he sure as hell wished they would find out who did, and why this psycho was convinced he'd done it. In fact, the notes he found were getting more and more disturbing, and he wasn't sure how much more he could take.

It seemed as if the writer of these notes knew the exact layout of his house, every move he made, where he'd been the day they were written. He knew he was being watched and he didn't like it at all. Everything about his whole life was some madman's game, which by the progression of the notes, was about to come to an end soon. There was no doubt in his mind someone wanted him dead.

Max drove around the circular drive to the back of the house to pull into the garage. Motion lights shot bright white beams on the car as he pulled forward triggering the light over the connecting utility room door. He sat for a moment to place his forehead on his knuckles clenched around the steering wheel.

Coming home wasn't a joy as it once had been. Now, he never knew what was waiting for him. Notes were placed throughout the house, no matter how often he'd changed the locks. Objects and packages with no meaning were dropped on his doorstep or sometimes on his bed. Things were never in the same place where he'd left them. Pictures looked as if they'd been ripped from their hooks and tossed to the floor. Once he'd found a memento given to his wife, Anna, clear across the room from where it belonged. How her father's silver medal had ended up in his favorite chair, he had no clue.

If that wasn't bad enough, the feeling of being watched really wore his patience thin. He was being watched alright, but this madman wasn't all he had a concern about. Frequently he found himself turning around as a cold chill ran down his back, to find nothing but an empty room. Right after his wife's funeral, once or twice he thought he'd seen a bright ball of light hovering over his piano. Then it would disappear suddenly, as if never having existed before. The odd feeling, she was still there with him, was a little unsettling.

    He desperately wanted to tell someone about what he'd been experiencing, but other than his mother he didn't think anyone would understand. In fact, he wasn't altogether sure he wasn't half crazy himself. Though he didn't dare tell his mother, she was already concerned enough about him. He wouldn't want to add this to her list of worries.

    He'd heard stories of this kind of thing all his life, as Italians were known for their beliefs in the supernatural. But he wasn't sure what he believed, and he found himself trying to convince himself some of what happened was just his mind playing tricks on him. If his Anna was still there with him, surely, it was only to help him when he needed it the most. He hadn't felt anything scary about the feeling she might be watching over him. Maybe that's just what passed loved ones do. But he wished she would let him know somehow it was really her, and not his imagination.

    The same feeling of panic engulfed him, as it did most times when he first came home, and it took a moment before he could draw in a deep breath. The odd quiet gloom surrounding him the night he'd found his wife in a pool of blood in the front room would never be erased from his memory. It didn't matter how much money he had, or how many fans recognized him, nothing could ever make him forget that horrible night.

    A sudden chill ran across his body, as if someone close had breathed down his neck. An intense awareness of being watched came over him, and he jerked his head up. Out of the corner of his eye a dark shadow slid across the side of the house by the open garage door. He grabbed the flashlight lying in the seat beside him and pushed the car door open. Jumping out, he pointed the light in the direction of the shadow. Fast as he could he followed what he thought looked like a silhouette, searching the perimeter of the house for any signs of movement. But found nothing.

He stood in the backyard listening to the crickets chirping and an occasional croak of a tree frog. Stretching his neck, he headed back into the garage. A sliver of light on the cement caught his attention. The crack in the utility room door beamed like a pointer directing him to enter at his own risk. So sure he'd locked it tight that morning when he left, Max shut off the flashlight and gripped the handle in his fist, intending to use it if he had to against an unwanted marauder.

Damn it, Anna. If this is you, it's not funny.

Sweat beaded up on his forehead, as he crept toward the opening. The tickle as it trickled down to the tip of his nose almost made him swear out loud. Irritated, he took a quick wipe with the back of his hand and brushed it away. Holding the flashlight in one hand, he pushed the door open with the other. To the right side, the washer and dryer was piled high with clean shirts he hadn't had time to put away yet. He peered behind the open door to see only his broom and vacuum cleaner where they belonged. Nothing seemed askew—nothing out of the ordinary.

Max's heart pounded hard in his chest as he opened the door connecting to the kitchen. He felt around on the wall for the light switch. As if being hit by a sucker punch, a horrendous stench assaulted his nostrils. He'd never smelled anything so raunchy in all his life. A cross between the sickening smell of a garbage dump and the remains of an octopus he'd seen washed up on the beach once in Italy when he was a young boy. God, that was nasty.

It took him a moment to tamp back the gag he felt coming up. He covered his nose with his free hand and walked further into the kitchen. The dead silence caused his already clenched stomach to churn.

He entered the dimly lit dining area, glancing side to side, and hesitated. The eerie shadows of the high-backed dining room chairs against the wall looked like hooded prowlers waiting for him to come closer for an attack. Out of the corner of his eye he saw the hovering ball of light he'd seen before flash across the room then disappear.

Walking forward, inch by inch, he felt as if Anna were telling him she was there for him. Then unexpectedly the Monet watercolor behind him jerked with an intense slap against the wall. He jumped, about ready to get the hell out of there when a distinct impression of her settled over him. About to take in a deep breath to settle his nerves, he realized the awful odor had gotten worse. He gathered the courage he needed then started again, the dank, rotted stench of decay getting so strong he almost puked. But he kept moving. He had to find the source.

It was there in the soft light filtering in from the kitchen he saw at the far end of the dining room table the rotting carcass of perhaps a small dog or a cat, he couldn't be sure. The sickly-sweet smell surrounded him in its tendrils of death. As he came closer, he saw the carnage, maggots twisting and wriggling their way through what flesh was left. This triggered a gag reflex in Max which couldn't be ignored.

But, with a quick sharp bang, the painting began to flap against the wall again. This time the furious movements of the frame rattled the tiny glass figurines on the memento shelf next to it to the floor. A cold sweep of air, carrying with it a cloud like formation instantly appeared. Startled, Max wasn't sure if he could trust what he saw next.

In the dim light the faint outline of a body began to take shape. It wavered and shifted for a second, then began to develop. He stared, unable to move, his heart pounding in his chest. Then as if in slow motion, the image moved closer to him, drifting across the floor until it stopped a few feet in front of him. He couldn't believe his eyes. There stood Anna, a cloudy gray version of her former self, but it was most definitely Anna.

She smiled softly, pointed toward the corner of the room across from him then slowly disappeared into the bright glowing ball of light he'd seen before. Without fully comprehending what was going on, he glanced to where she'd pointed. In the hazy dim light he saw some type of wire leading from the slightly open window to a strange object, the size of a half dollar, hanging in the corner. Unsure what to do, he turned to go back around the table to investigate, then stopped. Reaching into his pocket he grabbed his cell phone and started walking away from the object. He remembered from before, never to mess with the scene of a crime—and this was definitely suspicious.

At that exact moment, he saw the shape of a man run past the window. The quick loud blast came out of nowhere, like a gunshot. On instinct he dropped to the floor, covering his head with his arms. The single explosion was all—nothing more.

He peered through his arms. A giant hole had been blasted into the wall, the size of a bowling ball, straight through to where he could see into the next room. His heart felt as if it had risen into his throat, riveting in his ears like a jackhammer. He'd stopped breathing. Stars began to float in front of his vision. Unwillingly, he had to breathe in deep or pass out.

The ghastly odor of the carcass took immediate control, inundating his senses with its noxious embrace. He couldn't take anymore, gagging he stumbled to his feet and bolted straight for the kitchen sink. Unable to hold back any longer, he lost the dinner he'd enjoyed an hour earlier. But the stench was still there, causing the waves of nausea to heave up again.

Fresh air—he needed fresh air.

After checking the grounds for any sight of the figure he'd seen through the window, he stood at the corner of the house, sweat pouring down his face. His head felt as if he was underwater, night sounds echoing in his damaged eardrums, but the cool clean air felt good across his cheeks and he breathed in deep. His mind raced over the events of the last few minutes. From the last few months, he'd almost expected someone was going to try to shoot him. But, blow him up?

What the hell is happening?

He realized that wasn't the strangest thing. He'd just seen a ghost. Anna had tried to warn him. She'd shown him what was about to happen and probably saved his life.

A crunching sound came up behind him, almost like he was chewing on a mouthful of Cheerios. Still shaking, Max turned to see his neighbor, Jim, walking up behind him. He was dressed for bed, a worn out dark blue robe hanging off his shoulders, his slippers clapping against the gravel drive.

"Hey buddy, are you alright? Sounds like you're blowing off M-60 shells over here. Had too much to drink?"

Anyone would think he had if he told them about the ghostly images he was seeing. Jim may have been through some of the roughest parts of the last couple of years with him. He was a good friend. Unfortunately, no matter how much Max wanted to blurt out what had just happened, he didn't think Jim would understand he'd just seen his dead wife.

He'd stood by him during the arrest, the investigation, even the times when Max wasn't sure he could continue go on any longer. But this wasn't something you just went around telling people.

"No," Max managed. "The bastard tried to blow me up though, and left me something gross in the house."

Jim's eyes opened wide as he looked at Max. "No. Really? Can I see?"

Max shrugged his shoulders. He didn't think Anna would show up again, so he nodded his head toward the open door. "Go ahead."

He watched as Jim ran into the house and wondered why some people revel at seeing foul and disgusting things. Maybe after having served a couple of terms in Iraq, Jim might have figured nothing could be as bad as what he'd experienced there.

Max dug his cell phone out of his pocket again and turned it on, wishing he hadn't turned it off during the movie he'd gone to see. As he waited for the phone to boot up Jim came out, one hand covering his nose, the other holding out what looked to be a folded piece of paper covered in blood spots.

"I can tell he used the old army kind of C-4. Not enough to do too much harm though. Suppose if you were right up on it you would have a pretty good size hole in you though. Here, I think this was meant for you." Jim said shaking his head. "Boy, he gutted that thing from head to toe, and left if for you to see," he finished with what Max thought was a little too much glee in his eyes.

Max took the note from his friend, not sure how he should interpret the odd, almost joyful shuffle Jim was doing with his feet in the gravel.

"Aren't you going to read it?" Jim asked, as if unable to wait to know what the note said.

With disgust, Max unfolded the paper and read the contents out loud.

"Kaboom! You're next."
* * * *

Max wouldn't let some crazy obsessive maniac ruin his life. Or at least what life he had left. Though there were times like this when he wished he could become someone else—anybody else. It was obvious this madman was taking things to the next level. If this latest incident was meant to scare him, he'd succeeded.

Before, now he'd had it all. Fame and a pretty good start to fortune doing what he loved the most as a musician, a beautiful wife, and a child on the way. In an instant his life had been changed forever. Now he felt as if he was stuck on a scratched CD, the same song playing repeatedly without ceasing. Being reminded day after day, never moving past the single event in his life he wished he could forget.

This newest development kind of freaked him out though. Did he just imagine the ghostly outline of Anna? Was it because he was exhausted and had stopped breathing?

That was all. Right?

No, that wasn't all there was to it. He'd seen her, almost as real as before. She'd come to help him. He felt in his heart she'd always been there to help, though the situation called for her to do something more drastic, like show up.

He sat on the couch at his parent's house and rubbed a tired hand over his face. There'd been no rest since Anna's murder. Since that fated night forward, he didn't feel as if he'd slept a wink. Always waiting, always wondering, never knowing if he would be next.

As he feathered his fingers through the multitude of paper scraps in front of him, he remembered when and where he'd found each one of them. Some were small pieces torn from an envelope, while others were carefully crafted notes, all purporting his predestined demise. Some made sense, others not so much. It was as if the creator of the notes was led to write them in a half-crazed state of mind with some type of fanatical belief in a distorted relationship with his belated wife.

"What do you want to do Max?" his mother, Celeste, asked as she came up behind him to rub the knotted muscles in his neck.

"I don't know, Mama. I can't stand much more of this. I need to get away, at least for a while."

If he didn't get away soon from all of this he would end up in a mental hospital for sure. Maybe that wasn't such a bad idea. Rolling his neck to loosen the tightness, he chuckled to himself. All he'd have to do is tell them he'd seen his dead wife last night.

"That might not be such a bad idea. The situation has progressed to a point where it isn't safe anymore. The threats have escalated, and without putting a watch on you twenty-four-seven, I don't feel it would be advisable to keep living in your house alone," Inspector Warner, advised, giving him an intense look to make his point.

He hadn't told his mother the full story yet. He'd only let her know someone had broken into the house again. She didn't need that type of worry, it would make her sick. His father and Inspector Warren, however, both knew exactly what had happened.

The portly gentleman, a long-time friend of the family, sat across from Max on the mulled wine-colored settee. Every time Max saw him, he was reminded of the nursery rhyme his mother used to tell him. In fact, he caught himself about to call him 'Humpty' at times.

Max had asked for his help not long after the first notes began to show up. There was something not right about the whole thing, and the police had passed them off as not being important to the case. They said celebrities had followers who tended to be a little over the top.

This was different—this was personal.

Now they were saying the C-4 blast had been a prankster's game, not meant to hurt him. They suggested, if he felt the need to do so, to hire a security guard to keep watch. Understaffed, they didn't have the manpower to put this type of prank on the top of their list of importance.

"You can't go back there. No. You need to get back to your music. This is what you were born to do, no?" Celeste gave Max's shoulders a squeeze and moved over to stand with her husband. "Why don't you go back to the stage? You share your voice, your music, it will do you good."

Seeing the two of them together always made Max smile. Even though they'd been in the U.S. for over twenty-five years, they still looked as if they should be featured on the front of a travel magazine for Italy.

"I'm not sure anymore, Mama, I haven't performed since..." Max dropped his head, unable to finish.

"Nonsense, you forget who you are. The opera, the music, it's what is in you. That will never change. Why not come live here? Papa and I, we'd love you to be here with us again. Wouldn't we, Rudolfo?"

"Of course, Max, he is our son. He's always welcome."

Max turned to catch his father's change of expression. A look of concern moved swift and sure into protection as he stood and put his arm around his wife's shoulders. Max knew exactly what he was thinking. His father loved him, but he also realized the risk his sons moving back could have on their peaceful retired lives, not to mention the possible danger.

"No, I won't do that, Mama. I won't put everyone here at risk." Max saw the relief flash in his father's eyes and turned back to face the Inspector. "George, would it be possible to leave the area without anyone knowing?"

Inspector Warner pondered the question, as he tapped his index finger on his chin. "You're no longer a suspect, and the police have suspended any further activity on your wife's case pending further evidence. I don't see why not." He picked up the latest note to look over again. "In fact, it might work to our advantage."

Max raised his eyebrows in question. "How's that?"

"Perhaps in your absence, the killer will become agitated in not finding you, then get sloppy and show up where we can catch him. Didn't you say you had a neighbor you were close to? If you are sure you trust him, you could have him watch more closely, and I can ask one of my associates to stay at your house while you're gone to try and catch this guy snooping around."

"Jim's an all-around good guy, a little weird at times because of what happened during his military stint, but I'd trust him with my life."

"Isn't he the one you refused to let us look into?" Warner furrowed his brows. "I still think we should check him out first."

"Absolutely not," Max insisted. "There's no way he's connected with any of this. Besides, the only reference to the military in these notes has to do with Vietnam."

Warner shrugged his shoulders, "Maybe his father was in 'Nam, and he's reliving his life as a tribute to him, believing you are one of the enemy."

"You're grasping for straws there." Max shook his head wearily. "No, I trust him. I'll ask him if he'd be willing to look out for the place for a while. How long do you think before you know when your associate could take over?"

"I won't know until I ask him. I'll have to let you know tomorrow. When do you want to leave?"

"As soon as possible," Max urged.

Celeste sat down next to her son and grasped his hand. "But, no, where would you go? I won't hear of it. You can't go just anywhere."

Good question. Max puzzled for a minute. Where could he go where nobody would recognize him? Somewhere he could live in peace, at least for a while. Frankly, he didn't care where it was, he just needed to escape for a while.

Hoping nothing would follow him, he started to wonder if he really could get away. Murderers, crazed followers…ghosts.

"Wait, didn't Uncle Estevan need someone to watch his place up in Washington while he was away?"

Rudolfo nodded and smiled. "You are right. This is perfect. He's needed someone he trusts for his stay back in Napoli. He's leaving this weekend."

"I could do some carpentry work while I'm up there. Pick up the family business again, hey Papa?" He didn't care how long he'd been here. His parents would always be Mama and Papa to him.

Inspector Warren cleared his throat. "You might want to change your name up a bit. Maybe you could use something like Geo Angelo. That way you won't be tracked by the full given name you usually use."

Max nodded his head in agreement.

"For a while, maybe, you take your mind away from all of this. But Mama is right. My work is not for you. We worry about you." Max looked up to meet his father's concerned gaze.

"I know."

"Estevan, he has the piano there. Use it. You've lost your smile." Rudolfo reached out to touch Max on the cheek. "Go and get your smile back."

Max didn't feel as if the music was within him anymore. It had been so long. He might have lost his touch. He didn't even know if he'd ever want to play again.

He shrugged his shoulders, and gave a slight smile, "Maybe, Papa."

Chapter 2

"No Evan, I'm not doing this to hurt you." Lauren Roberts sighed as she stared blankly at the wall in front of her.

How many times did she have to listen to Evan blame her for the problems he'd brought on himself? She rubbed a hand over her face to clear the feelings of guilt seeping into her mind. No. She was not going to let him do this to her again. She'd stayed in this God-forsaken place this long, hoping he would develop a good father-son relationship with Josh—or at least as good as one could be when parents were divorced.

"Evan, look I know you don't want to accept this, but the relationship you and Josh have is totally up to you. If you were willing to spend more time with him…" Lauren paused as a rash of words flew through the phone at her. Again, she waited for a break in his comments long enough for her to say what she needed to say.

"We are moving and there is nothing more to be said. It's not like I am moving out of state. We are just moving to another town. You're welcome to come visit him any time you want." She paused to listen to the familiar wave of excuses she'd heard a million times before. "Yes...yes…I know you're a busy man, and you're expected to do so many things…but...," Lauren listened, getting more and more irritated with his explanations of why he'd not been to see his son in over six months—this time. She grabbed a pen and started doodling on a napkin, grimacing at the long list of expectations from his new wife.

His wife, Natalia the swimwear model, was his dream come true. He was expected to take care of her like a princess, which meant time and money. He'd put in so many extra hours at work to ensure *the princess* had enough money to pamper herself and be presentable for their many social activities. Lauren forced herself to breathe and not shout out how much she didn't care.

How often is he going to push that in my face? Oh, how she wished he could have shown her half as much care and commitment when they'd been married.

She turned to look out the tiny kitchen window overlooking the stairway to the second-floor apartments. A butterfly had lost its bearings and was fluttering around in listless circles trying to find a way to freedom. This was exactly what she'd been doing, and it was time to put an end to it now.

"Evan, listen to me," she paused a moment as he finished out his last words. "We need to move. Josh and I have been penned up in this apartment much too long. The house I found is not far away. It's all I can afford right now but will give us some space to breathe."

She paused briefly as Evan began to speak again, only to cut him off in the middle. She'd had enough of his overly simplistic view everything revolved around him.

"Evan, we are moving at the end of the month, and that is all there is to it. I will be sending you all the information you need to contact us. I hope you and Natalia have a nice evening tonight. Yes, I will ask Josh to call you. Goodnight."

Lauren put the receiver back in its cradle on the wall. Taking a deep breath, she turned to face the window. She needed to straighten out her thoughts before letting Josh know his Dad had asked him to call.

Staring out of the window, she saw the butterfly had landed on her windowsill. It was beautiful, with unusual white and black markings, like a zebra. She'd never seen one like this before. It sat for a moment, resting its wings, and appeared to Lauren as if it were looking at her, analyzing her every movement.

She gazed at the beautiful creature wondering why she felt so drawn by its presence. As they seemed to stare at each other for a moment she began to get the distinct feeling this was no ordinary butterfly. It was there to give her a message of some sort.

A quick clear thought rose into Lauren's mind. The kind she'd learned turned out to be important as they came from her inner voice. *"Listen to yourself. Pay attention to everything. Believe in* your *gifts."*

Then the butterfly turned and flew off again, fluttering away with purpose, as if it had known where it was the whole time. Lauren laughed at herself. Now she was really letting her imagination go when thinking a butterfly was sending her messages.

Or was it?

She wrinkled her forehead, raising an eyebrow when the phrase '*pay attention to everything*' popped back into her mind. Picking up the doodle she'd started on the back of the napkin she stared down and saw a medallion of some sort. Without thinking, she'd drawn the same type of thing several times in the last few days. She opened a drawer with other phrases, pictures and words which had come to her recently, and pulled them out. She needed to bring them to her next class at the psychic center, hoping someone would take an interest in them. None of them made any sense to her. But she sensed, they must mean something.

Turning the corner to go into the living room, she almost ran straight into Josh's chest, where he stood leaning against the wall outside the kitchen. He stood a good six inches above her, his chest as broad as his father's. He stuck his arm out to steady her as she nearly lost her balance.

"Josh! You scared me. Don't go sneaking up on people like that," Lauren said with a little more perkiness than she felt.

"Didn't sneak up, Mom, just came in and heard you talking—didn't want to interrupt."

Josh looked at her meekly then headed in the direction of the couch. He sat stretching his long legs out toward the small brown coffee table, which took up half of the room.

As Lauren entered the room behind him, she noted his coat heaped in a pile in the middle of the ugly '70's olive green carpeting. His backpack had been left haphazardly, not far from his coat, as it trailed a path to his room at the back of the apartment.

"Bet you'll be glad when school is out on Friday. Out for the summer! Woohoo!" She hooted picking up his coat to hang on the hook next to the door.

There was no response. Josh was in one of his moods, she could tell. She sat down next to him rubbing her hand across the threadbare material on the arm of the couch.

Lord, she was thankful for the money she'd been able to save. Once they moved, there were quite a few changes she'd planned, including getting rid of this old thing.

"Yeah, I guess," he said simply, picking at the frayed edges of a hole in his jeans. "Mom, what did Dad want?"

Lauren sighed. This must be what was bugging him. "Your father called me back. I left him a message at work to remind him we are going to be moving this weekend."

Lauren looked intently at her son, watching for signs of emotion, or regrets, he might be harboring. As usual, there was nothing but the blank stare she saw so often in his eyes when they talked of his father. He nodded and looked back at his fingers as he twisted and pulled the threads even further.

No wonder she had to buy him new clothes all the time.

"He's not too happy about us moving away. But I told him we won't be that far, and you can spend as much time as you want with him and Natalia."

Stay calm, Lauren, stay calm.

She'd never held Josh back from seeing his Dad, though not ever having to see Evan again would have been a wish she would have granted herself if possible. Every time they talked or met, the hurt he'd caused would well up inside so she'd squelch the negative feelings before letting them come to the surface and taint the relationship Josh could have with his father. Of all things, Lauren didn't want to be the cause of a rift to form between the two of them.

Josh remained silent. Though Lauren's inner voice was telling her something burned deep inside him about the fact his father hardly ever came around. He'd never told her how he felt, and he certainly wasn't letting her in on it right now.

"I will do everything possible to get you out to see them when I can. You know that, don't you, Josh?"

"Yeah, Mom, I know. He just doesn't really want to see me."

Evan had spent some time with Josh as he was growing up, but not much. An effort to see him every couple of months was made, until Josh had turned ten years old. His father's attention was intermittent at best. He'd get involved with someone new and his available time would dwindle down to almost nothing. Then when he'd gotten married Lauren could count the number of times Josh had been to visit his Dad on one hand.

"Well, dear, he is a busy man. He's had a lot to be concerned with these days." Lauren began to stick up for Evan, as she'd done a million times before. Josh turned back toward her. His eyes had turned a dark shade of brown, with a vehemence punching her hard in the gut.

"Don't Mom, I'm not ten anymore. I know he doesn't care. Just leave it alone. I don't want to talk about it." He got up off the couch and leaned over to pick up his backpack. "I'm going out. I think I'll walk to the store and get a soda."

Lauren gave a heavy sigh and nodded. He'd known for a long time now, and she could no longer cover up the fact his father had his sights set on different priorities. There was no changing the situation, though she wished all the pain of rejection Josh had felt over the years would vanish. She knew all too well what it felt like. It was something she wouldn't wish on her worst enemy, and certainly not to the one she loved the most.

She stood up and went to where Josh was standing. Putting her arms around him she squeezed lightly and smiled up into his still burning eyes. "I know Honey Bear, but you know I love you."

"Yeah, Mom!" His half-feigned grimace at the nickname made her smile. "I love you, too." He rolled his eyes and bent down to give her a peck on the cheek. "Be back in a little while."

Lauren nodded and stepped away from her little boy turned young man. She watched as he went down the hallway toward the front door. He hung the backpack on its hook, gathered up his keys and wallet and went out the door, waving a hand at her as he went.

She looked back into the living room feeling the cramped space closing in on her like a vice. The apartment itself resembled a shoebox, with four little compartments. The two bedrooms and the bath took up the better part of living space. This left just enough space for the small front room, where she stood now, and the tiny kitchen off to the side. Each room could only hold a few pieces of furniture she'd collected. The few personal effects she'd squeezed in here and there made it home. But this was not where they needed to be anymore. Life was changing, Josh was growing up, and the change they were making would be a good one.

Lauren placed the scribbled stack of notes and drawings she held in her hand on top of the others she'd been collecting near her notebook she'd take to class the next day. She sat down, ready to start back to edit the short story she needed to submit to her agent for the romance and women's summer and fall magazine editions.

The pounding knock on the door had her jumping out of her chair, heart pounding quick and hard in her chest. *Good Lord, who on earth is that?*

She wasn't expecting anyone. Peering out of the peep hole for safety, she saw her best friend, Rita.

"Oh, my goodness, what are you doing here?"

Rita bustled in with a couple of department store bags and plopped them on the couch. Turning, she gave Lauren a hug. "I was just in the neighborhood and thought I'd drop some things by for you at your new house. I just couldn't wait to give them to you," she said with breathless excitement.

Lauren shook her head. "Rita, you can't keep doing this. I'm not going to have any room left in the truck for all these things. I'm going to have to get a bigger truck."

"I know, I know, but I had to show you what I found." Rita began to pull the boxes and bags out for Lauren to see. "I couldn't resist this. Do you think you could find a place for this?"

Rita held out an intricately carved wooden container and looked around the small front room toward the small area in the corner Lauren called her office. Lauren took the object and gazed down at the beautiful creation. Roses, it was full of roses, as delicate as a flower should be. The deep mahogany of the wood brought them to life, like the tops of a dozen red roses bursting from a vase. Lauren could almost pick up their scent in the air.

She looked back to the area Rita was examining thoroughly. It contained a group of books piled on the floor, and a small laptop set haphazardly atop a flat surface she'd recovered from the garbage out front of the building. She'd washed it up thoroughly and set it on an uneven stack of cement blocks resembling a desk.

As Rita turned around to face Lauren, she knocked the spiral notebook to the floor, along with the stack of drawings and notes. Gathering up the mess, Rita started to flip through the pages of the notebook, obviously unashamed of her nosiness.

"This is that crazy automatic writing stuff you were telling me about. Isn't it?" She stared down at the pages Lauren knew wouldn't make any sense. It didn't make much sense to her either.

"Yeah, Katherine at Crystal believes if I practice enough, I'll be able to receive messages to help me in my stories. She said I might even be able to channel a spirit or two who actually lived in those time periods."

"That would be cool," Rita muttered, staring hard at the markings and words Lauren had felt come through her at the last class. "Look here, I see the word 'mistress'. And this one looks like 'water', doesn't it?"

A little embarrassed, Lauren looked to where Rita was pointing. She hadn't seen it before, but the markings resembled words in some places. Maybe there was something to this Channeling for the Writer group she'd joined. The meditation did seem to clarify her thoughts, and she would come back from the meetings fired up to write again.

"I'm hoping it will help me with my stories somehow."

"Tell me how you do this again. You just close your eyes and let your hand just do what it wants?"

"Basically, that's what happens. We do a meditation to invite our spirit guides, or any spirit of the light who can help us with our question, and we do whatever we are led to do. Some draw pictures or symbols, others can write legible sentences. I haven't quite figured out what works for me." Lauren placed the notebook back on the shelf.

"What about this?" Rita asked shuffling through the scraps of paper and drawings she still held in her hand. "Hey, this one looks like a crest or a medal of some sort." She held the most recent doodle Lauren had placed in the pile a few minutes before.

"It does, doesn't it? I thought so. Looks like a couple of the other ones, too." Lauren took the pile of odds and ends from her friend and placed them back on the desk. "Maybe, Kathryn can help me figure out what all this means. I can't figure out why all this keeps coming up." She gave a crooked smile to Rita. "It might be one of those spirits trying to talk to me."

Rita shrugged her shoulders, but grinned with supportive affection. "Could be, you never know. You always were into that psychic spiritual stuff."

Lauren knew what she meant. Rita never had followed along with her belief in the supernatural.

For Lauren, something about it rang true. After all, it was a proven fact all things were made up of energy vibrating at different speeds to form the items created, including the human body. There was no ending the source of the energy, no matter how the shift happens it just takes on another form. Lauren truly believed this to be true of all things.

She'd just begun to realize the life here on Earth was not the only living energy to be acknowledged. The saying *'when you're dead your gone'* had never made sense to her. All things had a purpose, whether it be a grain of sand, a rock, a small bug, a plant or an animal. There was no way it ended there with human beings. There had to be more to this existence than the short time we had on this Earth. This *'spiritual stuff'* as Rita put it, was real to Lauren, and she believed all things were possible.

She'd even begun to think she had some of the gifts the spiritualists talked about. Everyone had an intuition, but she didn't believe everyone used it as much as she did. She'd always felt things so much deeper than everyone else. The only way to find out was to keep learning and developing these *'gifts'*, whatever they might be.

"I'll let you know if anything weird pops up." She knew this would give Rita a chuckle, which it did.

"A little too strange for me, but whatever makes you happy, I say go for it." Rita reached out to open a binder which held Lauren's latest research notes. "Hey, didn't you have a deadline coming up?"

"It's only a small one. The edits on the short story I wrote for the historical romance magazines are almost done. I haven't heard back yet from the agent if she needs any major revisions on the book. But those can wait until after the move. I need to get out of here first."

"That's for sure." Rita took another look at Lauren's desk. "This definitely has to go. You need a real desk with a comfortable chair. Your new life doesn't have room for crap anymore."

Still holding the gift, Lauren brushed a hand over the top of the box, appreciating its beauty, and knew immediately where she would put it in her new home. She would finally be able to create the home she'd longed for and deserved.

"This is too beautiful to set out here. I'm going to save it as a new treat for my desk at the house. It will look perfect there." Lauren set the box down on the coffee table, her gratitude for Rita's kindness spilling out. "Have I thanked you for finding the house for us?"

"Only a million times," Rita chuckled and gave Lauren a hug. "You're just lucky I found out David's nephew was putting it up for sale."

"I can't believe my first actual house is lakefront property. Lake Wilderness is such a beautiful place. We can enjoy the woods, and still be close enough to come back to the city when we want."

Lauren pictured the two-story home as she'd seen it the first time, sun shining down all around, beautiful trees surrounding the structure, and just enough view of the lake to feel as if she were on vacation.

"It's going to take a lot of hard work to get it back into shape." Rita shook her head. "I don't envy you that part, but it is a great little spot."

"There's no way I could have afforded anything other than a fixer-upper."

"You can always call David over to fix things if you need. I was thinking, some of the furniture they're leaving behind could be actual antiques. You might be able to sell some of them to pay for repairs."

"You're right. But I'm keeping the desk for sure. I can't believe the owners sold the house as-is to your nephew, furniture and all." Lauren agreed.

"I guess they just got too old to care anymore. Their loss, your gain," Rita shrugged. "Come see what else I found for you," she enticed, leading Lauren over to the bags.

Rita's energy was always on a high level, never stopping to let anything get to her. Lauren could feel something was off. She could feel something churning inside her friend. She sat on the couch and patted the cushion next to her.

"Now, why don't you tell me the real reason you've been on a shopping spree. What's going on?"

Rita gave a deep sigh and laughed. "Can't keep anything from you, can I?"

"No, and that's why you came to see me. Tell me all about it."

Sitting down, Rita rolled her shoulders. "It's stupid really. David and I had a fight. I know he didn't really mean what he said, he just did it at the wrong time."

She proceeded to tell Lauren how they'd squabbled over the dinner she'd made. Busy all day with the kids, she'd forgotten to take out the roast planned for that night's dinner, and barely had enough time to make a meal at all. Apparently, she'd already made spaghetti this week. He'd made a comment about her cooking and she proceeded to tell him what he could with his opinion.

Lauren and Rita laughed about the way Rita told the story until they were almost rolling on the floor. It was a good laugh, the kind of belly laughs that clear all the bad feelings which might have been hanging around.

They sat together on the couch, looking through the few gifts her friend had brought for her. Lauren knew she was indeed lucky to have a friend like Rita.

"I'm so happy for you. This is going to be great. A new job, your new house, I'm a little jealous of you." Rita laughed.

"Nonsense, you've got the best husband and the greatest kids. Besides, you can come visit me anytime you want."

"I know. You've needed this change for a very long time. I'm expecting great things for you soon."

"I hope so." Lauren was expecting great things from herself as well. She knew this tiny hole in the wall apartment was not the place she could be her best.

Writing took a special place, where creativity and freedom flowed without restriction. She needed to feel as if the words streamed from within as they should. Sure, she'd been able to publish a couple of short stories and her first regency novel, even snag the attention of a wonderful agent, who was interested in signing her as a client. She knew if she was going to get anywhere with her writing she was going to have to break away from the troubles and pain pounding daily at her doorstep. To create a space where she could spread her wings and just *'be'* Lauren.

She needed to be somewhere her clarity of mind and thoughts could bloom, and then she would finally be able to concentrate on the love of her life. The one thing she'd found would never let her down—writing.

Writing never failed to bring happiness and joy into her life. Never would the words dismiss her as a lowly woman, or let her down as an individual, because they came from within the depths of her own soul. She knew in her heart she'd been given this gift to write beautiful love stories to uplift her readers into believing in themselves again. This was her purpose. Through all the failed relationships she'd experienced in her life, the intimate connection she had with her writing would always be there for her.

There were times when she was writing where the words would fly from her fingertips, without her even needing to think about what she was doing. It was as if she was just a vessel through which beautiful prose would flow. That's what led her to believe there was something true to the spirits leading her to channel their word onto the page. Even if it wasn't their exact words, it seemed as if the ideas and beliefs were coming from another dimension. Lauren couldn't say why, but she felt the words were of pure energy and love, untainted by the ways of this world.

For this to happen on a more regular basis, she needed to be free of her own personal bondage and heartache. It wouldn't happen here. The minute she'd made up her mind to make the change, she'd felt a release of the chains holding her down. Then when she'd seen the house, she knew it was right. This was the place where Josh could grow and flourish as the wonderful young man he'd become. A new life for them both.

Trust yourself, she told herself, *this is the right thing to do.*

Chapter 3

Max stood in the produce section, pondering how many bunches of basil he should get for the pesto he was making for dinner that night. As he reached out his hand collided with someone's arm as they reached for the same thing.

"Pardon me," he said turning to gaze into the greenest eyes he'd ever seen.

"No, no, it's my fault. I should have warned you I was going to reach in front of you." The woman said, a bright blush brushing over her cheeks. The faint scent of apricots and a hint of musk came to him, and he was pleasantly surprised by the warm smile she offered.

"No problem. Just needing to grab a couple of these for my Pesto Chicken," Max said reaching out for the basil.

"Sounds good," the woman said getting her own bunch. "I like putting fresh basil in my minestrone soup."

"You like Italian then?" Max said with a little more Italian accent than he'd done in a while. Then as he saw the blush grow much brighter on the woman's cheeks he realized what that statement must have sounded like. "Italian food," he clarified and even that sounded like he'd just come from his native country.

The woman dipped her head down and smiled, glancing up at him with those beautiful green eyes. "Yes, I do."

"Maybe we exchange recipes sometime?" He didn't know what else to say, but that sounded like a pick-up line too, which was not what he'd intended.

Now what?

She gave him a half grin and nodded, "Maybe." Then made it easy on him and moved past him and down the aisle toward the salad dressings. The scent she wore seemed to linger around him, and he found himself watching her a moment longer.

Intrigued, something about her made him long for the touch of a woman. To gather the soft curves of a woman into his arms, and revel in the feeling of being loved. She glanced up and their eyes met. She held his gaze, almost as if she was thinking the same thing, then turned and slipped around the end of the aisle.

He shook his head. Other than a quick disastrous fling he'd had when he first arrived here, he hadn't thought of being with a woman in a long time. It had been over four years now since his Anna had passed. Was that long enough? If he was entertaining these types of thoughts, well, maybe…

After gathering the rest of his groceries, Max smiled at the teller as he paid for his items. "Thanks, Stacy. Have a great time on your vacation."

"I plan to! Work hard, play hard, that's my motto." Stacy said closing the register drawer. As Max took the couple of bags at the end, she turned to him, "Hey, you're a handyman, right?"

"Mostly a carpenter, but I can do handyman type work, too. Why, you need something done?"

"No, my husband wears that title at my house. But one of our customers put up a flyer on the board over there," she said pointing to the corkboard at the entry. "She said if I knew of anyone, to let them know she needs some help. In fact, you just missed her. She was here a little earlier."

The brief thought crossed his mind. She could have been the woman in the produce section. *Wouldn't that be crazy if it was*, he mused.

Nodding, he glanced toward the corkboard. "Thanks. I'll look."

He'd just finished a small job. He didn't really need the money but found keeping busy helped his mind to clear and refocus. He'd even considered playing the piano some the last couple of months. Just hadn't gotten around to it yet. Maybe something to tinker around with like a handyman job would help. Glancing over the postings for landscaping work, lost dogs, and the next community meeting at the fire station, a flyer caught his attention.

'Wanted – Handyman—Older
home in need of a loving touch.
Small repairs and improvements
needed. Call if you are a small

*licensed contractor willing to work
on a budget.'*

Max looked at the black and white picture of a house, which looked in need of some help. Several of the tags with the phone numbers had been torn off already. Surely, they had settled on someone by now.

He started to walk away when a chilled air brushed past him, making him shiver a bit. It fluttered around the handyman flyer with its precarious placement of a thumbtack holding it to the board.

Oddly, the door had been closed the whole time, and he looked around, almost expecting to see the ghostly image of Anna. There was nothing but the teller at her station talking to the next customer. Shaking his head, he started to move on toward the door. Again, the blast of cold air brushed past him, this time chillier than before. The flyer began to flutter wildly about. Max stared at it for a moment and saw none of the other papers on the board moving at all. His heart jumped up into his throat.

What the hell is going on?

He stepped away, and suddenly felt as if he were being pushed toward the corkboard from behind. The word '*call*' popped into his head and a familiar brush against his cheek made him pay closer attention. '*Call her*,' came to him again, as if someone were whispering in his ear.

This time he knew it was Anna.

Muttering, to himself more than anything, Max reached up and tore off one of the phone number tags for the house repairs. "Alright, but I don't know what's so damned important about my taking on some work."

* * * *

Lauren moved her fingers swift and sure over the keyboard of her computer, deftly putting words on the page. In her heart, she knew she'd been born to do this, and only this. She pounded out the words as if it were to be her last act in this lifetime. The sound of rain coming down outside with a vengeance made no difference. To Lauren the only sound she heard was the story unfolding before her eyes on the page in front of her.

> *"...Lady Merideth wandered through the castle halls from room to room, stopping at the doorway of her father's cabinet. She half expected to see him, quill in hand, writing his thoughts down. He'd always fancied himself being the next Chaucer or Donne. Drifting in she wished she would see him once again in his favorite chair. His treasured copy of Beowulf sat untouched, where he'd left it months before. As she picked up the crystal weight, atop the last papers he'd been working on before falling ill, tears sprang to her eyes, clouding her vision. She sank to her knees in despair. First her mother had been taken from her, and now the apothecary had warned her father was not far behind. What was she to do? How could she make it without them?*
>
> *Maybe, just maybe, she should consider this arrogant nobleman's proposal. Merideth clasped her hands in her lap, a deep sigh escaping her lips. The slightest hint of a smile played at the corners of her mouth..."*

Lauren's thoughts paused, and her fingers stopped tapping on the keys of the computer as she heard the blare of music from her son's room upstairs quit all at once as it had started a few hours before. She shook her head with a smile, the constant hum of bass and drums still thumping in her ears, even though the music had been turned off. How often had she told him to turn that stuff down or it would permanently damage his hearing? Only a zillion times, she thought with a half laugh.

She glanced up, through the window in front of her, and caught sight of the downpour coming out of the sky even though the sun also appeared to be shining. Spring in the Pacific Northwest was such a fickle time, it rained most days this time of year, and in a flash the weather would change its mind and become almost like summer. Then sometimes, doing both at the same time, like today.

It seemed everyone who hadn't visited this beautiful area assumed it was an awful place to live. Lauren chuckled remembering how her new agent had tried to talk her into moving down to sunny California. According to her, Washington had such a dark and dreary climate, there were so many more pleasurable places to live. But then, her agent thought San Diego was the only place on earth where anyone could truly be happy. When Lauren told her about the new home she'd purchased, she was promptly informed she would be miserable and wasting her time and money staying in such an ungodly place.

Lauren was happy in Washington. Born in Chicago, she'd been orphaned at the tender age of nine and moved to Washington to live with her Aunt and Uncle who'd taken her into their family with no qualms. She soon fell in love with the gorgeous atmosphere of the Pacific Ocean on one side, and the beautifully majestic Rocky Mountains close by on the other side. The fresh air and the sound of so many different types of birds chirping their songs to the beauty of their surroundings had melded to her heart as soon as she'd arrived.

This move to the new home hadn't been an easy one. After nine months she was still trying to recover from the financial cost. Most of her savings was spent on the move itself, and she was just beginning to save enough to start fixing up the old place. Even with all the sacrifices she'd made, she still believed this was the best thing she could have done for herself and her son.

There was nothing too major to be repaired, at least not that she'd found yet. The tile floor in the kitchen needed to be replaced. She and Josh had already begun work on installing a new patchwork design, with bright blue and white geometric patterns to compliment this wonderful blue gingham material she'd found at the craft store for curtains.

The home improvements were turning out quite well. Happy to start on anything, Lauren began to purchase some small things like electric outlet covers and drapery rods. She wasn't going to put the new drapes up yet, not until the walls had been painted. But that was not going to happen right away.

There were a few things she could see she would need a professional to do, especially on the outside. She'd wanted someone local and hopefully cheap, that's why she'd put out a flyer at the store. She'd gotten several calls and decided on a local carpenter with excellent reviews to come in to give a good appraisal of all the things needing to be done. Good thing he was a handyman, too.

When she'd talked with this Geovani Angelo she'd gotten an odd urgency to accept his offer to come take a look at the house, as if she was supposed to meet this person. It was one of those inner messages she'd been told take special care to figure out. If nothing else, this would be a good way to test her intuition.

Lauren became aware of another sound. *Plunk, plunk...splat.* It was coming from the kitchen. She must have forgotten to turn the water off all the way again in the sink.

"Stupid knob," she muttered. There was a special way you had to turn the knob in order to get it to shut off. That was another thing that needed to be replaced. This time though, the slow dripping sounded as if it were hitting something other than the bottom of the kitchen sink.

She got up from her computer, giving a long stretch as she'd been in an intense mode at the keyboard for a good part of the morning. As she walked into the kitchen, the sound became faster and more intense.

Why isn't that the gentle drip I normally hear?

As Lauren came around the corner from the hallway she froze with alarm. She saw water dripping down from the ceiling in several places over the newly laid tiling she and her son had installed on the kitchen floor.

"No!" she exclaimed as she ran in, almost slipping as her foot met with the puddle already forming on the tile.

She quickly grabbed a kitchen towel and threw it on the floor where she stood. But that was not going to be enough, the towel thirstily soaked up what water it could hold leaving more to be cleared around it.

"Josh! Josh, bring me some towels from the closet!" she yelled up to her son as she reached into the cupboard for a pot or bowl to put under the constant drips.

"What?" he yelled back from the head of the stairs leading into the kitchen. "What's wrong Mom?"

"Get me some towels!" She threw another pot under the drip coming down beside her.

"What for?"

"Just do it!" she yelled.

She heard him mutter something to himself and move across to the linen closet in the hallway. He came down the stairs slowly, as if he had all the time in the world. Lauren glanced up as he came into view from the dark stairway. His rangy form filled the space from the bottom of the stairs almost to the top of the entrance.

When had he gotten so tall? Lauren wondered as she wiped up water dripping off the countertop onto her foot. *And handsome too!* The dark curls of hair springing jubilantly around his neck needed a trim. The weight set she'd bought him for his last birthday was starting to pay off. He'd lost the boyish pudginess and she could see the rounding of muscles across his chest and shoulders through his T-shirt which hung over a pair of well-worn jeans. She gave an inner grin with a sigh. *My handsome young man*—but he'd always be her little boy.

"Jesus, Mom. What happened?" he asked viewing the water pour out of the ceiling onto the floor.

"We seem to have sprung a leak." She gave him a half-hearted smile and took the towels he handed her.

"I knew we shouldn't have moved into this dump," he grumbled eyeing the mess spreading over a section of the floor he'd helped to put into place.

Lauren straightened herself from sopping up the water and looked at him with patience, though she couldn't help the hurt seep in whenever he spoke about not wanting to be here. He hadn't wanted to leave his friends and his home in Seattle, and it had taken quite a long time to make new friends. At least now he wasn't as angry as he'd been at first.

Guilt began to creep in as she looked at his face. A face she'd loved the first time she'd laid eyes on him in the birthing room. The face had changed over the years, but the eyes had not. They had a close mother-son relationship, and she knew even though things could be tough for them at times they would always know they loved each other—without a doubt.

"It's going to be alright. I'll have the handyman look at it when he gets here tomorrow. I'm sure it can be fixed with no problems." She looked up at the spots where the water dribbled down into the pots and bowls with an almost musical pattern.

Yes, it was going to be okay. It had to be.

This was the house she'd bought, and it was going to have to work out. It was no doubt a fixer upper. She smiled back at him with confidence. If nothing else, she had to show him she believed in what they were doing. She believed things would fall into place soon enough. These were just the growing pains of the transition they were going to have to weather.

Eyeing her, one eyebrow raised, his mood seemed to lighten. He gave a good-natured smile and grabbed another towel to sop up more water beside him.

"Well he'd better get here soon or were going to be swimming around in here."

"You always said you wanted a swimming pool." Lauren smiled, knowing he was doing his best.

"Yeah, but not in my kitchen."

She'd always marveled at how he slipped from anger to amusement in a swift heartbeat. He could make her laugh in the middle of an argument, and they would end up in soul cleansing laughter.

He gathered up the towels and threw them into the laundry room, some landing in a haphazard pattern over the floor. Lauren put her hands on her hips and looked at Josh as he turned around. He muttered under his breath and turned around again to pick the towels up and put them into the washer, tossing in some liquid detergent he turned on the washer and closed the lid.

"Thank you," she said with approval as he came back into the kitchen.

"You're welcome." He wrinkled his nose at her as she brushed a hand across his face. Josh turned to the back door and grabbed his coat hanging on the hook next to the door. "You going to be alright?" He pulled his arms into the denim jacket and snapped it shut.

"Fine, if I can find some more pots." Lauren reached into the cupboard and pulled out some mixing bowls to put under the other leaks which had started. "Where are you going?"

"Robert's got a new engine for the Mustang. He's putting it in this afternoon. I told him I'd be over as soon as I could."

He and his newfound friend had quickly connected over a shared love of cars. Lauren didn't mind him spending time with Robert. She was thankful he'd already bonded with him, taking the sting out of his having to leave his hometown friends. She smiled at him and gave him a kiss on the cheek.

"Alright honey, but don't be too late. I'll have dinner ready around six."

"Okay Mom. Try not to drown while I'm gone." He smiled at her as he opened the back door. Outside water pelted the newly sprouted grass, not unlike spears trying to hit every single blade, as it crashed down from the sky. A swish of cold fresh air came in through the open door putting a chill in the room.

"I won't. If it gets too bad, I'll paddle over on my rubber ducky," Lauren laughed. Josh shook his head at her as he went out the door.

She stood at the door and watched as Josh sprinted to the edge of the property where the line of trees met their back yard. Robert lived on the other side of the forest patch separating the two homes from each other. Theirs was the last house before the lake waterfront at the end of a long gravel road which serviced only four houses. She saw Josh shake himself like a dog as he stepped inside the dense forest covering, trying to shake some of those huge raindrops which had landed on his thick hair.

As he disappeared into the trees Lauren smiled and heaved a sigh. This was home. It might need some work, but this was finally home. There was no place she'd rather be than in this place right now. Things might look a little grim right now, but she knew her choice had been the right one. Josh seemed to enjoy the environment with the surrounding forest and lake. The freedom he had to go where he wanted seemed to agree with him.

She could finally breathe. No more cramped living space and she didn't have to worry so much about Josh. If he wasn't at home, she could usually find him with Robert messing around with an engine or something. A whole new world had finally opened to her, and she loved it.

As she stepped back into the kitchen, her foot encountered yet another puddle forming under a new leak.

"Now, if I can just keep everything from falling apart on me, things will be perfect. I sure hope this handyman can fix everything he says he can for us."

* * * *

The bright, clear sunshine burst through the curtains the next morning, as if the wet and wild storm which had passed by the day before had never happened. Lauren turned lazily over and blinked into the bright golden light streaming over her bed. It was Saturday, so she didn't have to worry about getting Josh out to school. This was a morning she could do whatever she felt like. She knew though, if she didn't stay in her routine of early morning exercise it would be much too easy to start considering it not important enough again.

She stood and stretched her arms toward the ceiling, working some kinks out of her neck to begin her morning routine. As she passed by the oak framed full-length mirror her Aunt Maggie had given her some years before, she took note of the progress she'd made over the last few months. She took a long look to assess how she was feeling about herself.

Not bad looking, I guess. She shrugged. For so long she hadn't even wanted to look at herself in the mirror, so this was a change for the good. At least she didn't repulse herself anymore.

It wasn't easy, but she was bound and determined to drop the weight she'd gained over the last few years. She couldn't blame it on the extremely hard birth of her son anymore, nor could she blame her condition on the waning interest from her husband. Husband no more, Evan was not the reason her health had taken a nosedive when it came to taking care of herself, eating right, and exercising. She just hadn't cared enough to do anything about it. It was her own fault, and she needed to take control.

Can't blame anyone but yourself, nobody has control over you. You are in control of you, she reminded herself.

Evan had delivered a slap in the face when he first told her how he felt about her weight. But the real shock came with a punch in the gut when she found out he'd been sleeping around on her, just like her first husband Ben. Her confidence levels had been battered in more ways than one. She knew her weight was something she could control, and constantly needed to work on, but until a year or so after Evan had left her, she really hadn't wanted to do anything about it. Why would she? He was going to cheat on her anyway.

Exercise was not one of those things Lauren really enjoyed doing. But she figured it was a necessary evil when it came to her getting some of her shape back. She threw on her exercise clothes. A pair of black leggings, and a long over-sized T-shirt in a pleasing spring lavender color, which covered up what she was trying to get rid of with such diligence. She loosely knotted the shirt at her right hip, giving some definition to the curves she was beginning to see again. With some effort she tried to motivate herself into believing she could see a big difference.

Lauren turned sideways in the mirror to study the lines of her figure in the mirror. She'd begun to lose some of the inches around her waist, and the puffiness around her thighs was starting to subside. There was still a long way to go, in her eyes. Being well-endowed, or top-heavy as she was frequently called, was not the easiest thing to handle.

"That's why all the boys like you," Lauren laughed, remembering how her cousins would tease her during high school. They had no idea the challenges, physical and emotional, having this body type caused. The constant struggle to keep the weight off was not easy.

Never again would she have a man say to her the things her two ex-husbands had told her. She was never going to go through the rejection and hurt they'd caused her when they told her she was not what they wanted, and she was too big and ugly to be pleasing anymore.

No, Lauren thought to herself. *I will exercise myself to death before I hear that again.* And if that didn't work, then perhaps life without a man was her destiny.

Pulling her long reddish-brown hair up into a hair tie, it curled lavishly over her shoulders almost down to her hips. The glint of firelight through its strands reminded her of her mother, and she glanced toward the picture she kept on her dresser. She took a few steps forward and picked up the photo, somewhat worn and faded over the years. Though her memories had also begun to fade, in her heart she would always remember her mother's love.

From the clock on her night stand she quickly figured she had just enough time to do her routine and take a shower before the handyman got there to do the appraisal on the house. Her son would probably keep sleeping until noon on a Saturday, so she wouldn't have to worry about taking care of him for a while. After lacing up her tennis shoes, she tiptoed down the stairs, so as not to disturb Josh.

Ready to start planning the changes on the house, Lauren stood for a moment in the brightly lit front room, glowing from the same sunshine which had woken her a bit earlier. The walls looked old and in desperate need of paint. But what she saw were the possibilities. She could see in her minds eye the walls painted a color of soft green that she'd not yet been able to find. Instead of the drab colored draperies hanging over the front windows, wispy cream-colored sheers would be draped like waves across the windows giving the room an open airy feeling. The furniture would be in earthy colors of greens and browns, with wood accents and a splash of orange to give it the look of the great outdoors streaming through the large front windows.

Lauren went to the front door and opened the heavy oak door, bringing in a new stream of light into the front room. The clean fresh scent of morning air came through the opening, making her smile. Yes, this was exactly the feeling she wanted in the front room, as if it was an extension of the living, breathing, outdoors she saw from her front porch.

Breathing in deep, the scent of damp cedar boughs and the natural flora spread over the ground below filled her with a sense of new beginnings. It was almost as if she were a part of the beautiful nature surrounding her. It felt good. She felt the energy of the plants and trees, speaking to her, encouraging her and lifting her up toward the heavens. Yes. This is where she belonged.

    She walked out onto the front porch and envisioned what it would look like by the end of the summer. There would be a bounty of beautiful, colorful flowers landscaped in a walkway up to her front porch, the flowers continuing up the stairs and flowing over in pots to the front door. The classic front porch would be refinished back to its original grandeur, with carved wooden seats along the walls of the wrap around porch.

    The deck on the backside of the house was not yet built, but she could see it clearly. Developing over the last couple of months, her vision was of a large two-tiered deck with room for the barbecue, a smoker, and a cross through window connecting the inside kitchen to the outside cooking area. The other tier would have tables and chairs for dining and family fun. Josh could have his friends over any time to play soccer in the yard as she prepared a meal for the young men.

    It will be amazing, Lauren grinned.

    Her home would finally be a place where her friends and family could come to relax and spend as much time as they wanted. The places where she'd lived before never really felt like home, they were more of a stopping place to get through the part of life she was experiencing at the time. It would bring her indescribable bliss to bring her dream to life.

    Yet, she couldn't shake the disheartened feeling she knew all too well.

    She was happy. Wasn't she?

    Despite what she tried to tell herself, the all too familiar sadness hung over her like a winter storm cloud, just waiting to drench her feelings of joy.

    Damn. Why do you always have to question yourself?

    Still, there was something missing. Deep inside she knew the picture she'd just envisioned was not quite complete. She would have everything she could ask for and more. Why did she always have to yearn for something, or somebody else to be there? Why was it she felt the need to have a man in her life? It had never worked out for her before, why did she always end up wanting to find someone else to be there with her?

And yet, the feeling was there.

Lauren shook her head and shoulders to dispel the loneliness spreading over her. Right now, the only thing she knew to be true was if anything ever were to happen on the relationship front, she was going to have to do something about herself to be ready. Now was the time to concentrate on getting rid of some of this extra baggage she was literally carrying around with her.

Giggling, she thought of the handsome Italian she'd met at the grocery store. Now that was the kind of man she wanted to attract. *Damn, he was gorgeous!*

Her workout was strenuous this morning, for some reason she felt the need to take control. She started out with a lengthy stretching session to loosen up her muscles before getting into the aerobic workout. She'd made one of the rooms in the back of the house into an exercise room, where her treadmill, stair machine and dumbbells set ready and waiting to be used. Today she worked mercilessly on the stair machine, pumping the foot pedals with a determination which would have made anyone gasp for breath.

Forgetting the time constraint for this morning's workout, she'd already spent a good forty minutes working out to her music doing aerobic and stationary muscle-toning exercises. That by itself would have been a good workout. But today she felt she needed to do more.

She let her mind wander and the grocery store hunk came to mind. She wished she could have gotten a better look at him. She'd been so flustered at having someone like him talk with her she hadn't taken the time to study him the way she wished. She did remember though, the way he'd made her feel. As if she was the only one there in the store with any importance. What would it be like to have someone like him put his arms around her, to show her love and affection, to want to be with her as much as she wanted him? Being the romantic she was, she couldn't think of anything better. She started to wonder if she would ever see him again, and if she did what would she do? Would she flirt? That's what she had desperately wanted to do that day.

The strong pump of her heartbeat against her chest told her she should probably start to do her cool down. Her breaths were coming hard and strained as she slowed down her vigorous power climb to a slow and easy stride. Sweat poured down her back and her hair had begun to spring up in moist tendrils around her face.

She took one hand off the handle to grab the towel to wipe across her face as she slowed the movement of her feet on the pedals exercise machine to a stop. Taking a long drink from the bottle of water she'd placed beside her she caught a movement out of the corner of her eye through the open window beside her. As she turned, she almost lost her balance, so she quickly set her water bottle down to grab hold of the other handle. She drew in her breath when she found the figure of the man she'd been daydreaming about outside her window.

He raised a hand in greeting. "Pardon me for interrupting. I'm Max DeAngelo, I believe we have an appointment for an appraisal of work to be done," said her grocery store hunk.

His deep voice was smooth and calming to the ear, sending a tingle down her spine as it had the first time when they'd met at the store. It hadn't dawned on her until now, the handyman from the phone conversation she'd had a few days before, could really be the same man from the store. Then again, how many Italians were there in the woods of Lake Wilderness?

DeAngelo? That wasn't the name of the handyman. It was close, so maybe she'd heard wrong. She was sure though he'd told her before his name was Geovani? What was going on here?

Lauren swore under her breath and looked down at her watch. She'd been at it longer than she'd expected. He was right on schedule and she was not ready for him yet. Taking a deep breath, she smiled and looked out again to the man standing outside her window.

He wore a simple black T-shirt, tucked into a pair of jeans. His gorgeous muscles and handsome face had her almost dumbfounded. He'd had a nice voice on the phone, but she hadn't been expecting someone who looked this good. Handymen were supposed to be middle aged, paunchy men, balding or already bald, without any hint of being attractive.

"I am so sorry. I'll be right out." She ran her hands quickly down her sides, to make sure nothing was out of place. Throwing the towel over her shoulder she locked the stair machine in place for a safe exit. She could just see herself landing on her butt, as she'd done a time or two.

Can't go falling all over myself on the way out.

The man continued to stand on the other side of the window, looking up at her with what appeared to be curiosity on his face, as if he were trying to figure something out. A little unnerved, she knew he must be thinking she made quite a sight, all sweaty and rumpled.

God, how I wish I'd stopped in time to freshen up first.

"I'll meet you out back," Lauren said pointing in the direction of the back door.

He nodded and ducked his head down under a tree limb and headed toward the back. She hurried toward the back door to the small back porch. Lauren stepped down off the steps and turned to him. Out of breath, from the workout and partially because this man could literally knock you off your feet, she gave him a smile.

He was at least six-foot tall if not more, which was a good eight inches above her. His broad shoulders fit snug in the T-shirt, and she could almost see the muscular ripples running down his chest and stomach as he reached out to shake her hand. He wasn't a slim man, but she could tell he worked out frequently. As she reached out in turn to grasp his hand, she looked up through her lashes into eyes almost as black as his T-shirt. So dark brown, they seemed to simmer in a melting pot of secrets begging to be let free. His hair, the color of coal, had a tiny hint of brown shining through in the early morning sun, with a nonchalant wave over his forehead. A touch of gray brushed up through his temples, giving him a very distinguished look. He wore a thin mustache over his lip and a small patch of hair below his bottom lip giving him the look of a swashbuckler. His square chin set off his face in a determined look of a man who was totally in charge.

Oh my God, this is my arrogant nobleman, Lord Calvert! Lauren realized, and almost giggled with the striking resemblance of the debonair rogue in her manuscript. He was the mirror image of the perfect hero she'd created for her heroine—and damned if he wasn't the perfect hero she'd been fantasizing about for herself—right here in the flesh.

At the touch of their hands she felt a jolt run sensuously up her arm. He covered the other side of her hand with the palm of his other hand in an intimate manner, as if they'd known each other for many years. She couldn't seem to pull her hand away and looked down at their joined hands as if she'd never experienced a man's touch before. He had long artistic fingers made to make beautiful music, or magical love she wasn't sure which one it was. She glanced back up to find him watching her, as if he'd felt the same thing. She flushed even more as her heart began to beat in triple time.

"Max DeAngelo," he said, with a slight bow over her hand in a gesture reminiscent of an old English gentleman caller.

"Max? I thought I was meeting with a 'Geovani'," Lauren questioned.

 Lauren thought he looked a bit unnerved as he hesitated to answer. "Yes, yes, I am sorry. I am Geovani DeAngelo. My friends, they call me 'Max'."

"Okay…so, what do you prefer? Should I call you Geovani, or Max?"

He looked at her a moment, his dark eyes expressing thought, "Max. You can call me Max."

Lauren thought it interesting he'd had to ponder the question. There was something about his name which caused him trouble. "Hi. I'm Lauren Roberts. I'm sorry I must not have heard your knock. I get kind of carried away sometimes."

My voice doesn't sound like that, does it? Oh, gosh, all breathy and sexual? Get a grip Lauren.

"Yes, I can see you do. You seemed rather intense when I walked up. Sorry for the intrusion. I wasn't sure you were home, but the front door was wide open." He continued to hold her hand, studying her face. For some reason Lauren felt as if he was contemplating whether to drag her into his arms and kiss her, giving her a reason to be breathless.

Good Lord, it had been too long if she started thinking the handyman wants her!

She disengaged her hand from his, noting that he did not wear a wedding band on his ring finger. When she looked back up, she felt the heat rush up to her cheeks as his intent gaze made her feel as if he knew what she'd been thinking. His smile made her feel a little giddy.

"Oh, right. No worries. There's nobody out here to disturb us. I usually have the door open, especially on a beautiful morning like today."

"Yes, it is a gorgeous day, isn't it?" He looked around the yard, and back to the house. "Where would you like to start?"

"If you don't mind, why don't you look around outside, and make a list of things you can see need to be done. I'm going to run upstairs and change my clothes. I'll be right down." She turned to go back up the stairs then turned, and saw he'd been watching her go up the stairs.

"Will your husband be joining us?" Max asked.

"No, I'm not married." The slight glint of a grin returned in his eyes when she said this. "It's just me and my son to deal with on this project." Their eyes met and Lauren was sure she saw a twinkle in his eyes.

There is no way this man could have any interest in me, especially looking like this! He must want to know who makes the decisions around here.

He gave a silent nod and reached out as if testing the strength of the stair railing.

Lauren couldn't help but smile on the inside—but knew better. "You can start with the front porch. I want to have it refurbished to its original look."

The sudden rustling of the trees overhead had him looking up. But it was nothing unusual, as far as Lauren could tell, just a gust of wind in the warm spring Washington weather. Max looked behind him, and raised his shoulders up and down, as if he'd felt a cold draft, then shook his head and looked back.

When their eyes met, she saw the interest had faded. Almost as if needing to put a wall between them, he stepped away from her and crossed his arms over his chest, guarding himself from further engagement. He looked away from her face, out over the back yard and back again to the house.

He's right, back to business—enough of this nonsense.

But he sure did give her a lot to think about when she went back to writing about her rogue.

Chapter 4

The split-level house had been built in the early 1930's and had been kept up fairly well, until the last few years. Max could see there was quite a bit of work needed to be done to repair safety issues, as well as the work involved for Lauren's plans on the front porch.

When Lauren came back down to join him, she'd changed into a pair of jeans and an oversized long sleeve shirt rolled up to mid-forearm. Unlike her previous attire, the shirt hung down low covering every possible curve. It looked more like something a man would have worn.

Max wondered why she wanted to hide her curvaceous body. He wouldn't mind admiring it a bit longer. She had the body of a full-figured woman which should be appreciated for all its worth. To him she had nothing he could see needing to be covered up in such an obvious way.

She was about the same height of his mother, about five-foot-six inches, just the right height to scoop into his arms for a hug. Her hair was the longest he'd ever seen on a woman. It was pulled back into a ponytail that hung almost down to her hips in wild curls bouncing with every movement she made. Some of the shorter strands had escaped the band holding it back from her face, curling wildly in a halo of color. An attractive face it was, with an aristocratic nose to match the shape of her face. What made things worse was, her glorious set of greenish hazel eyes seemed to smile all the time, captivating his ability to think straight. Damned if he didn't have the sudden urge to drag her into his arms and devour those tempting lips of hers.

Max stood looking at her for a moment as she spoke. Why had he told her his real first name? He hadn't made that slip up since the first time at the hotel he'd stayed at months before. He knew if he wanted to keep his anonymity, he couldn't make that same mistake. Sooner or later, someone would catch on. Interesting though—he didn't know anything about her, but there was something about this woman he couldn't quite put his finger on. Something intrigued his sense of trust, and a curiosity in the definite physical attraction going far beyond anything he'd felt in a long time.

While she'd been upstairs, he'd had to reason with himself the cold chill he'd felt run down his neck before was just a breeze. He'd felt something like it before, when Anna appeared those few times. But surely, she hadn't followed him here. What sense did that make? After all, she'd been the one to push him into calling for an appointment. Hadn't she?

Wondering if he was imagining Anna ever being there, sending him silent messages, he felt the icy fingers of air on his neck again.

Alright, so if it is you, then why the hell did you send me here? You can't expect me not to find this woman interesting.

He needed to focus. It was time to get back to business. He couldn't stand there all day looking at this woman, even though he found he had an intense need to be close to her.

Lauren looked back at him, obviously to make sure he'd been listening, so he nodded his head and pretended to write something down. He made a list of items needing to be replaced or repaired, keeping careful notes of what Lauren described to him as her vision for the house.

"I really should have taken you right in to see the worst of it, shouldn't I?"

"Not really. I like to see the type of plans people have for their homes. Then I can see if I can work some of it in with what they need to have done. Actually, it's my favorite type of job."

"So, you don't think you'd have any trouble in doing this type of work?" Lauren asked with a pensive tone.

Max shook his head. He'd been doing this type of work ever since he could remember. His father was a carpenter by trade and had made his living doing everything from fixing a faucet to creating masterfully intricate cabinets for keeping prized possessions. Max had at one time considered taking over the family business. The one thing he'd learned from his father was everyone's needs and wants were different. No vision was ever the same for any two people. If you listened close enough to what was being said you could interpret the ideas of a homeowner into a beautiful work of art, which they could call home. And home was nothing to be taken for granted.

"I'm not saying there wouldn't be any challenges. But I haven't seen anything I couldn't figure out yet." Perhaps he could regain his passion for life in bringing a dream homes to reality for his customers. He'd once thought his heart belonged to the music he created. Now he wasn't sure where he belonged.

Lauren nodded, thoughtfully. "You haven't heard it all yet. Maybe we should wait to decide until I've told you everything." Her eyes lighted up when she looked toward the steps. "For instance, I've been thinking about putting some stationary flower boxes along the front edge of the deck," she said with excitement.

He listened intently as Lauren described her ideas, and occasionally made suggestions when he felt her vision wavered on what she wanted. Her smile brought him joy, where he'd felt none for such a long time. She turned to direct his attention to a small patch of warped board he'd seen earlier on the porch. Leaning in slightly, he delighted in the scent she wore of apricots and musk, enticing him to nibble at her neck.

"That will need to be fixed first. I've done some drawings of what I think I want for the back deck. It has to have a nice brick barbecue pit where we can all get together on holidays and things," she said dreamily. "Maybe you could look at them and let me know what you think. Tell me how crazy I am. If you have time that is…" She turned to face Max, and he heard her quick inhale at their proximity.

He hadn't realized how close he was to her and found her lips inches away from his. Close enough for him to bend down and take a taste of those wonderfully luscious lips asking to be kissed. He felt as if he'd been here a hundred times before. The feel of her next to him felt so right, as if they belonged together. Curiously he watched a variety of emotions pass through her eyes. The one that ran quickly at the end puzzled him the most. He could feel her breath fluttering over his cheek in quick bursts, and he looked down into confused, almost frightened eyes.

"Pardon me, I was just looking at that railing," he stated pointing behind her, attempting to explain his closeness. He quickly stepped away. "I'd like to see those drawings. Bring them out. I'll let you know what I think." He cleared his throat.

She straightened and seemed to bolster a courage he hadn't seen a minute before. Moving past him, she said, "I'll go get them. It won't take long."

The drawings she brought out were very detailed. He was impressed. As she spoke, he knew this was a woman who knew her own mind. Not one that couldn't decide which way to place a planter, driving the muscle needed to move it a million times crazy with her indecisions. She was very precise in her description, showing she'd thought a long time about her vision.

They talked about the large old giant cedar tree standing about ten feet off the corner of the house on the east side of the property. He suggested he thought it would be a great spot to wrap the deck around the base of the tree, leaving enough room for its continued growth.

"Yes, yes, I thought that too, but wasn't sure if it could be done. Look here. If we can do that, is there a way to tie in a waterfall, too?" Lauren's excitement made him smile.

The running brook-like encasement she described to him would be a challenge, but he could see how they could bring the natural look of running water over rocks in a spot close to the cedar tree that would be a beautiful addition to the home.

Max felt drawn in by the picture she painted for him. Love and comfort foremost, a place to call home, to be enjoyed by all who crossed the doorstep.

An understanding came to him. Without knowing this woman at all, he could tell by her words and descriptions she herself needed approval and reverence. He didn't know where this feeling was coming from, but he knew he needed to transfer it into the work from his hands to develop the vision she described. Just like he used to do with his music, he knew he needed to create again. To create and inspire, in whatever form it took. This was his purpose.

"I'm not even sure why I brought this out to you. I can't do this for quite some time. It's going to cost a lot more than I can do right now." Her wistful smile clutched at his heart.

"Don't worry about it right now. Maybe after we look at the worst of what else needs to be done, we can work this somehow into your budget. I can be pretty creative, when I want to be," he said, smiling down at her.

He really wasn't doing this for the money. It was just something to do while he recharged his own life. Though, he didn't know why, but for some reason he felt he personally wanted to be involved to see the end result.

"Would you like something to drink, before I show you the latest catastrophe?"

"That would be very nice. Thank you," he said as he followed her down the hall into the kitchen at the back of the house.

Lauren let out a giggle as they entered the kitchen.

"Did I say something funny?"

A bit embarrassed to admit why she'd laughed, she tried to explain without saying too much. "Sorry, I didn't expect you to be so polite. You're definitely not what I expected."

It took him a moment to understand what she meant. Then he laughed, too. "I get it, I'm not the stereotypical contractor with a tool belt pulling my pants below the waistline and grunting my responses?" His smile was contagious. "Mama would have my hide if I ever acted like that!"

Glad she hadn't needed to explain herself, Lauren grinned. "You can tell her she trained you well." Looking around the area where they stood, she directed Max's attention back to business. "Actually, the kitchen is the catastrophe. I left the pots where I put them last night, to show you where the leaks were."

Max's eyebrows rose as he viewed the multitude of pots and bowls sitting in odd places around the floor and counters of the kitchen.

"All of these are from leaks that came up from last night's storm?" he questioned.

"Yes. Is it a lost cause?" Lauren reached into the refrigerator to bring out a pitcher of lemonade.

"Well," he said peering up to the ceiling where watermarks, old and new, showed the leaking areas. "I won't really know until I go up onto the roof to see the condition from up there."

"Not a good sign then, is it?"

"I'm not going to say it can't be fixed, but you'll run into a bit more cost if we need to replace the roof."

Lauren poured the lemonade into two glasses, frowning as she realized the cost for all this was going to be way out of her range of what she could do right now. She held out the glass she'd poured for him.

"So, I guess I can forget daydreaming for a while."

"Let's worry about that when we get to it," he said with ease, as if he'd no qualms about getting the work done. "When we get finished, I'll put together a quote for the cost on all the major repairs, and then we can talk about a proposal on the things you would like to do."

The smile in his eyes was one of understanding. Lauren was so thankful he'd seen her vision. Finally, someone understood. It wouldn't hurt to find out what the whole thing would run for her, even if she couldn't do it all right now.

"Okay, that sounds great. Are you ready to see the rest of what needs to be done?" she asked as she put her empty glass into the kitchen sink.

Lauren turned and almost ran right into Max, who had come up behind her to set his glass in the sink as well. He put out his hands to steady her instinctively and they naturally landed at her waistline with a firm grip.

They were so close Lauren could feel the warmth of his body next to hers. He'd been near to her earlier, but not this close, and not this long. The touch of his hands seemed to send bolts of fire into her system. Warmth spread throughout her body as she stopped short of falling straight into his arms. This was the closest she'd come to a man in a very long time.

And, oh what a man he is.

A thought of craziness crept into her mind. To fall into this man's arms and meld her body against his, pressing her lips onto his. Oh, to have that type of connection would be pure ecstasy.

That would be pure insanity. Lauren corrected herself. *No way, someone like him would even want to get close to me,* she thought pulling herself away from him.

"Sorry, I didn't know you were behind me," she offered with a bit of a waver in her voice. The heat she felt rise to her cheeks. As soon as she glanced up at him, the intense warmth became scorching. Confused, she swore she saw the look of a man who was indeed thinking the same thoughts as she.

"My apologies, I didn't mean to startle you," Max responded, removing his hands from her waist. An uncomfortable pause ensued, as neither one of them seemed to know what to do next.

The sound of heavy footsteps from the hallway upstairs jolted Lauren out of her daze. Josh was awake. Bounding down the stairway, his long rangy body came into view as he pulled the worn T-shirt over his head to a pair of his favorite ragged jeans Lauren wished she could throw away.

"Mom, what's for breakfast?" Josh yawned out as he came into sight at the bottom of the stairs. "Oh, sorry," Josh muttered when he spotted Max standing next to his mother. "Didn't know anyone was here." He looked Max over once or twice.

"Please pardon my son for his manners," she said scrunching her nose up at her son. "Josh, this is Max DeAngelo. The handyman I was telling you about."

Max pulled his hand out of his pocket to shake Josh's hand. They shook hands uneasily, Josh looking him over one more time. "Nice to meet you, Josh."

"Yeah, you too," Josh said in a wary tone. He turned and went to the fridge to pull out something to drink.

Well, this is awkward. Lauren realized she'd gotten so caught up in Max and her obvious attraction to him, she hadn't thought twice about her son coming down just yet.

"I'm sorry, I haven't had time to put anything together for you this morning." Lauren frowned.

"That's okay. I can get it myself. Go ahead and finish what you're doing," he said walking over to give her a hug.

Lauren sensed the tenseness in his hug and smiled inquisitively as he pulled back from her. She didn't question him, but found it interesting the feeling she was getting from him. Was he really trying to protect her? He'd positioned himself between her and Max, continuing to look at him with a hardened tough guy demeanor.

She'd never put him in the situation to see another man in their home. For years now she'd felt it best to not be involved with anyone. Never sure of how long anyone would be around. He'd experienced enough with his own father having left so early on. He didn't need to experience it with someone else.

Max smiled, holding out his hand to Lauren. "Why don't we find out what else needs to be done."

"Josh, I'll make you a good dinner later."

"Won't be home for dinner tonight, remember?" Josh said as he leaned up against the counter, arms crossed, an uncomfortable look on his face. "Robert and I are going over to Drew's to play his new X-Box game. His Mom is going to order pizza and then we thought we'd go see a movie."

"That's right, I forgot." Lauren said shaking her head. It seemed like she rarely saw Josh anymore. He was always out with his friends. But it was Saturday night, and he was a good boy. She couldn't keep him home for the rest of his life. "Okay, well then when I'm finished up here maybe we can go over that paper you're writing for English."

Josh rolled his eyes at her and responded with a grunt.

Lauren smiled, knowing exactly what her son was thinking. He'd said so many times before how he didn't need to be like her. She knew he didn't have the passion for literature she did. But she also knew she needed to help him get through his English literature class with some understanding of what it all meant in general, if not what it meant to her.

For some strange reason she felt compelled to take Max's hand to lead him out of the kitchen toward the far side of the house. Without a second thought, she did. The second their fingers touched tiny lightning bolts ran up her arm in a purely sensual stream of heat. For the sheer thrill of it, she left her hand in his temporarily until they got to the hallway.

Little tingling points of fire coursed up her arm from their joined hands. Curious, she glanced up at him before she removed her hand. He was still looking at her with those luscious dark brown eyes, which made her want to melt into his arms and have him kiss her until all thoughts had cleared from her mind.

There was a delicious thought. What would it be like to feel his lips on hers?

Now this is altogether silly, she thought with a little laugh on the inside. *You better just forget wanting to get close to him. That's never going to happen.*

His eyes glittered with a bit of humor as it played across his face. He'd been watching her. Lauren blushed again, realizing her face had shown all too well what she'd been thinking. He obviously must know his affect on women.

Dropping his hand, she led the way into the back room, which served as a storage room and partly as her study. There were boxes still packed, and some half open with the contents having been rifled through, as if someone had been looking for something.

In the far corner was a desk and computer, set up in the only place available. It was a large desk, made of cherry wood, deep drawers on both sides showed their usefulness, and yet the carved handles and curved edges of the surface also showed unquestionable craftsmanship. The deep red tones of the wood were brought out with a fine veneer, enhancing its beauty with a gleam so bright it immediately brought a feeling of warmth and cheer.

Max walked over and gave the carved handle a loving brush of his fingertips. "This is beautiful workmanship."

"I know. I'm so lucky it came with the house."

There were papers stacked neatly in several piles across the surface next to the computer. A sixteenth century history book lay across one of the stacks. Another stack of various books lay haphazardly strewn at the end of the desk. One of the piles of papers had red corrections marked expertly over the writing. A figure on the top right corner of the paper showed 96% and an A+ was written next to it.

"Sorry for the mess. It looks like Josh was looking for something again," Lauren stuffed something back into a box and closed the lid. "This is going to be my room, once we can get it fixed up," she said this with a sigh.

This was going to be her study, a place where she would be able to go and sink into whatever book she was writing. To close out the world behind the door and become part of her storyline for a short time. She could be one of her characters, like the beautiful Allison who had every man falling on their knees at her feet. Or the mysterious and exotic Lucinda who was able to twist the fate of a man's heart around her finger before he even knew what had hit him. This is where she needed to be, in this safe place where she could risk it all, and still come out ahead. At least in her writing she could have the happy ending she longed for with all her heart.

"Teacher?" Max asked, running a finger over the graded paper stack.

"Part-time." Lauren glanced over her shoulder and turned to close another box. "I teach at the community college at Green River—English Literature."

She caught a glance of Max, and the thought of her current hero within arms length, all of a sudden pulled her into the scene of her medieval historical romance she'd been working on the previous evening. To her surprise it was as if her surroundings changed around her and she was standing in the dark halls of the heroine's castle. She felt silly, but it was so easy to imagine herself as Lady Merideth about to be swept into an embrace by Lord Calvert. She couldn't help but see herself clearly as the character, picturing the scene, as if in real life...

... the drop-dead gorgeous hero was telling her they needed to leave or be burned by the fire running rampant through the halls of the castle. She was arguing with him over not wanting to leave her home. Garbed in the long robes of royalty falling to the ground over the voluptuous curves of her body, the colors of burgundy set off the creamy texture of her skin as it glowed in the firelight of a huge stone fireplace. Sparks of red would shoot off the

ends of her hair in a halo effect beneath a crown of jewels, deep with rubies and sapphires...

Embarrassed by her reverie, she quickly came back to the present to find Max gazing down at her, as if he too had been in her daydream. Every point of her awareness had come alive, the air charged with energy. The image remained strong and vibrant in her mind as if it was a memory. This sparked something she'd learned from her teachers at the psychic center. She'd been told to pay special attention to things like this, as they could be visions from a past life. Could the two of them have been together in a previous lifetime?

Nonsense, Lord, why am I letting this man get to me like this? And yet...

"I'm...I'm also a writer, and I have just contracted with my publisher to write a series of period romances of the sixteenth century—hence the history books."

"I thought perhaps you were also a history teacher," Max said picking up one of the books by his hand. He thumbed through it thoughtfully. "So, you write romances?" She'd heard it all before and believed the hint of laughter in his voice as being one of contempt for the art of writing a good romance.

"Yes," she answered putting her hands on her hips. "Yes, I write those ridiculous little romance stories you men seem to hate." Lauren studied him as he looked through the book. She'd never been able to get the approval from either of her husbands. They'd both laughed at her wanting to write about romantic mush.

When he glanced up at her reply and their eyes met, there was more than contempt. It was almost as if a fire ignited between the two of them at the meeting of their eyes. She glanced away quickly, not wanting to show what was running through her mind.

She turned to move over to the window, when she felt his hand on her arm. The powerful feeling which spread through his hand to her made her stop and look back at him. Her eyes widened, mixed with surprise for the unexpected anger she felt, the intensity showing in his eyes.

"Don't categorize me like that," he warned. "I have a great appreciation for the literary and fine arts, whatever forms they might be."

His eyes had darkened to a shiny black coal hinting of his annoyance, and they seemed to look right down into her very soul. She instantly felt she'd hurt him, and immediately wanted to apologize for having put him in the same group as the other men in her life. Lauren began to feel the heat rise to her throat as he continued to look into her eyes.

"I'm sorry I didn't mean to offend you. Not many men appreciate a good romance," she said trying to lighten the mood.

"Romance is not something one should laugh at, especially if you are good at it." A hint of laughter beamed through his eyes as he winked at her in a suggestive manner.

This was the hardest man to understand she'd ever met. Who was he? Carpenter? Handyman? And now a lover of the arts? There was something mysterious about this man she could not quite put her finger on. He had intelligence, far beyond what she'd ever experienced with any other man. She could tell he had deep feelings about things which were as much internal as they were external. His simple statement about the arts showed he had an appreciation for beauty and culture. Not something you would usually see in a man of his field. Perhaps this was what had brought these feelings of intimacy to her. She could appreciate intelligence, and his physique didn't hurt either, she thought with a slight grin. Lauren squirmed a bit as thoughts of getting closer to him came popping into her head again.

"Yes, well, I don't know if I'm too good at it, but my publishers think I put it down on paper pretty good," she said, laughing at herself.

If only she could have the chance again to prove she was all those things she wrote about in her books. She could be mysterious, and exotic, beautiful and captivating. She was, in her heart, she just needed to change her outward appearance and perhaps she could attract someone again in the way her female counterparts did in her stories. Maybe then she could win the heart of a man like Max and keep him happy.

"Don't sell yourself short *ma belle*. Your whole being shouts what you are in your heart."

Her heart thudded with the knowledge that he seemed to understand what she was feeling. She needed to stop this insanity. Allowing herself to feel like this for a man again wouldn't accomplish anything, except maybe a broken heart.

"Yes, well not many can see someone's heart, and not many are very interested," she responded.

"I'm not just anyone." Max's deep voice pulled at her intimately again.

"I can see that," she murmured. Lauren stiffened, trying to ward off another melting of her heart, and turned to the spot where she'd noted the need for shelves.

Max came up close to her and lifted her chin with his fingers, rubbing the side of her jaw with his thumb. Lauren froze, unable and unwilling to do anything but gaze into his deep dark eyes, drawing her into a desire filled pool. He bent slightly and his fingers curved at the back of her neck. She felt his other hand on her waist as he gently pulled her next to him. Lowering his head as if to kiss her, their lips so close she could feel the warmth of his breath brush lightly across her lips.

Suddenly, a quick burst of cool air came through the open window, fluttering the pages of the open book on her desk. Max jerked his head up and drew away from her, looking almost guilty, as he looked around the room. The unusual chill was intense enough to make Lauren shiver. Then another gust of air came through again, this time as warm as it should be this time of year. Motionless, Max stared through the window a moment.

With a skittish gesture of a bird being caught by the swipe of a cat's paw, Lauren moved away quickly to put a distance between them. She didn't know what she would do if he'd placed his lips on hers. As it was, her knees shook, her heart melted as soon as he'd stepped close to her. The hint of an Italian lover slipping off his tongue as he spoke to her had set her mind spinning like a child's top hurling itself into oblivion. She felt like a young schoolgirl who had just received her first kiss. And it wasn't even a kiss.

Don't be an idiot. You are a woman and you know how to act with a man.

But, not this man.

She glanced toward the door, as if looking for a way to escape. No, she would not escape. She would just handle this in an adult fashion and put him in his place. She couldn't just fall into the arms of the first man who crossed her path.

Don't be so willing to fall for another man's advances, she told herself. And he really wasn't advancing he was just being a man.

Taking a deep breath Lauren turned again to face him. "Let's get back to business here, shall we?" Her voice shook with the emotion she still felt, the desire still pumping through her veins.

He stared at her, his eyes, dark and mysterious, swimming with something she didn't understand. Then with a nod, as quick as he'd touched her his whole demeanor changed as if there had been no contact at all.

"Of course." Moving toward the door, he made some notes on his pad. "I'll need some time to put together a quote for you on everything. What do you say we do the roof leak repairs now on a time and material basis? Then I'll let you know what the rest will be later this week."

She nodded slowly. "Fine."

It took Lauren a moment to realize she must have made his simple act of kindness out to be more than it was, and yet marveled at how easily he could dismiss what had just happened. His face had changed back to all business, though his eyes were still dark and tumultuous.

"I'll be back in the morning then."

Max turned and left her standing there stunned. Unable to make any sense of the energy surrounding her, she sat down and closed her eyes. It still seemed to be bouncing off the walls. Finally, she felt it dissipate, leaving her with her usual sense of being calm—and alone.

What on earth just happened? Thinking through the last few minutes, Lauren had a niggling feeling there was something more than just two people sharing an intimate moment. The look in his eyes held so much more.

Was he hurt by her disregard? What did he want from her? And why did she care so much?

* * * *

That night as Max settled back in his easy chair with the plans of Lauren's house spread out in his lap, he took a long sip of the brandy he'd poured himself to relax. He couldn't get her out of his mind. The thought kept coming back how it had felt to hold her next him, their lips about to touch. He would have kissed her too, if Anna hadn't shown up.

Or at least that's what it seemed like. Did he just imagine her being there? The logical part of his mind told him there had simply been a breeze coming through the open window. But the chill had felt like the ones when he'd seen Anna before. He couldn't be sure.

He stared into the amber liquid in his glass as it reflected the flickering yellow flames from the fireplace. Closing his eyes, his thoughts immediately travelled back to the moment he was about to kiss Lauren. Why did this woman stir his blood up so quickly?

He'd caught the faint scent of apricots in musk, and it had almost driven him mad with desire. It kept enticing him to bury his face in the warmth of her neck where he knew the fragrance was emanating. He hadn't been able to keep his mind on anything else.

Sipping the warmth of the liquor, it spread down through his throat sending tongues of fire through his chest. Fire, the same as he'd felt flowing through Lauren as he'd held her for that brief moment. Swirling the liquid at the bottom of the glass, he imagined what it would have been like to taste those beautiful lips of hers. Just like this liquor was doing right now, a raging fire had spread through him, and he'd been unable to control himself.

What had he been thinking? Why had he almost kissed her like that? He'd acted like a fool. There was no excuse for his actions.

Yet, he couldn't deny the fact she'd stirred up feelings he'd thought were gone. The burning desire for intimacy, and the gentle touch of a woman, had come alive again.

His mind began to wander to some of the many scenes he'd portrayed on stage of lovers expressing their feelings for each other, scenes with the desperation of parted lovers. Scenes he was all too familiar with but hadn't thought of in a long while. Scenes from a past life he'd determined never to go back to again. A world with so much pain he couldn't bear to think of again, one which had never left his mind, no matter how hard he'd tried to shove it behind him.

That was until today.

Confused, he thought of his dear, sweet, Anna, the only woman he'd ever really loved. But the feeling had been different with her. They'd been happy. His love for her was the slow-simmering kind, sparking periodically over time. It had been a different type of attraction, he thought, a love holding sturdy and constant. Not like this flash of heat and yearning desire he experienced with Lauren. She'd stirred up something in his blood which felt as if it could be hotter and even more consuming than before.

Max laid his head back on the cushions and closed his eyes again. *I shouldn't be feeling this way*, he thought desperately. *It hasn't been long enough. I'm not supposed to think of another women like this yet*, he thought with disgust at himself.

It had been almost four years now, but a man was supposed to mourn for much longer than this. Wasn't he?

The fact his thoughts seemed to return to Lauren at almost every waking moment since he'd seen her in the grocery store disturbed him greatly. He was going to have to do something about this, and do something soon, or he didn't know what would happen to his sanity. But what he needed to do wasn't clear at all.

Reasoning with himself, Max fought with his thoughts. *Then again, I am a man, and a virile, healthy man at that.* "I'm still young, for God's sake," he said out loud.

He was living proof the normal functions of the male libido didn't stop, even if the one you'd loved recently passed on from this life. His reaction to Lauren was only the male part of him responding to a very attractive woman who was intelligent, yet mysteriously seductive in her hidden looks of desire.

Continued interest was only because he'd gone for so long without female companionship. Though, he had a hard time dismissing the way she'd made him feel. For the first time in a long time he'd felt like he belonged, like he was supposed to be there with her—like he was home.

Something like that doesn't just happen in one afternoon, he argued with himself downing the rest of the brandy. But there was no denying she'd ignited passionate feelings, the kind he'd thought were buried deep inside, passions which were urging him to act upon impulse, where no action was permitted. Pushing aside the papers which had begun to drop out of his lap, he jumped up out of his chair and paced back and forth. Somehow he needed to dampen his growing interest for this woman.

The sudden tinkling sound of piano keys being tapped softly brought him out of his angst. Turning toward the sound, he moved to the piano against the windows overlooking the lake. In amazement he watched a key being pressed down ever so lightly by an invisible force, then another key, and another.

Max looked up toward the skylight, as if to find Anna toward the heavens. "I just wish you would tell me what I'm supposed to do. Why have you stayed? What do you want from me?"

Keys were again pressed on the keyboard. Max laughed. Anna had always known what calmed his nerves.

He sat on the stool and ran his fingers over the ivory and black keys with a deft adeptness he'd developed over time. As he played a light melodious tune, which had been running around in his head for quite some time, the tones and vibrations of the keys seemed to soothe his soul though the notes came forth in a half-hearted attempt. No matter how hard he tried, it never seemed to be the same as it once had been for him. To him it all sounded like garbage.

Anger washed over him, and he slammed the cover over the keys. Fisting his hands at his sides, feeling truly disheartened, he got up and decided to turn off the lights and go to bed. His dreams of creating beautiful moving music had once been his life's sustenance. Now, stripped away by the apathetic actions of this unidentified invader, he could no longer be who he'd once been.

In the darkness, he knew the nightmares would come as they did every night. Tonight would be no different. Every night since Anna's murder, he'd been plagued with the horror of finding her, playing repeatedly in his dreams. He'd tried to put to rest the feelings of guilt and anger, but his failure to be there for her when she'd needed him the most, took away everything which had once brought him joy and passion. No matter how he looked at it, his life had changed, and he had no idea how or when it would ever be right again.

On his back staring at the ceiling, he waited for exhaustion to take over, so he could sleep—at least for a short time.

As he drifted between wakefulness and slumber eyes closed, he saw visions of Anna as she'd been when they first met. Playful and happy, she'd enticed him with her inner beauty. He could see her sitting in her studio, her dark ebony hair swept up in a knot, colorful paint smears covering her smock. He watched as she began to paint her favorite Zebra butterfly, her hand swiftly creating the beautiful markings. She turned and smiled at him, her eyes misty with a wistful sadness. He moved toward her, wanting the heartbreaking tears to be gone. Slowly she disappeared, leaving only the striking black and white image against a sea of green foliage.

In the distance he could hear her laughing, calling his name over and over. He tried over and over to find her. Behind the studio door, in the storage closet, under the drop cloths—but she was nowhere to be found. Turning in frustration he woke from his feverish dream and opened his bleary eyes. From the light of the moon coming through the windows, he could see the outline of a figure in the doorway of the bedroom.

Max swung his legs over the bed and sat up, blinking quickly to clear the sleep from his eyes. He recognized the female figure was his Anna. She held her arms out to him floating closer. As she whispered his name this time her image began to dissipate.

"No, don't leave," Max pleaded, his throat dry and raspy. He didn't know what he was asking he just knew she needed to stay.

The adrenaline rushed through his body felt like a million little tingles rushing over the surface of his skin. The air was cold and thick, as if he were outside on a foggy night. The dense air dampened as his short warm bursts of breath came out like small misty clouds. He felt the edge of the bed press down, the comforter compressed with an invisible force. His stomach was doing somersaults, when he realized the ghostly figure of his deceased wife had just sat down next to him.

Then all of a sudden calmness settled over him. He could almost envision Anna smiling up at him, and he felt a brush of something across his cheek. She'd just kissed him. He knew everything was truly alright. Giving a deep sigh, everything turned back to normal. She was gone.

He shook his head and smiled. Although different from the usual waking from a deep sleep in a panicked sweat, his heart still pounded as if he'd run a marathon. He rubbed his palms over his face, trying to remember what had happened. Something was different. He wasn't sure what had made the change, but anything was better than living through the torment of finding her, night after night.

Knowing he wouldn't be able to sleep again Max stood and heaved a long sigh. He put his arms through the sleeves of his robe and went out into the darkness of the living room. Sullenly he sat down at the piano and began playing notes to soothe his soul.

* * * *

Jeffrey sat on the edge of the bed, his head in his hands, the increasing pain stabbing him at the base of his skull radiating outward into his eyes making a loud ringing sound in his ears. Rocking back and forth, he gulped a mouthful of Jack Daniel's down with another couple of Opioid tablets he'd been able to get hold of this last time. The rolling sickness in his stomach threatened to come up, but he was able to keep it down long enough for the pain to begin to settle. Shit, he hoped Mongo would pull through to get him some more soon. Hell, he'd even settle for some Quaaludes at this point. Crazy hallucinations, be damned. He just wanted some relief from this pain.

He rubbed at several ugly jagged scars running from his temple to the crown of his head, hoping to get some type of relief. He could feel the mixture of alcohol and Opioids starting to kick in, and he lay back down again. His brain bounced back and forth between reality and hallucination, waiting until finally he would drift back into his constant nightmare filled existence.

He reached toward the bedside lamp and his fingers brushed up against the picture frame that held the image of his beloved Anna. Picking up the picture frame beside him, he blinked to clear the haze that had started to set in. He brushed a finger over the face of the young woman in the picture, anger filling him again with the realization he would never see her again.

Jerking the black bag from underneath the bed, he ripped open the zipper to display its contents. Tightly wrapped chunks of C-4 explosive material, cord, and timing detonation devices lay waiting for their ultimate destiny.

"I'm going to get him. I promise you, Anna. He'll pay for what he did to you."

His eyes glazed over as images flitted through his mind. Anna's look of disbelief, fear ripping across her face, and he heard the shot ring out, blood spreading across her chest as if in slow motion. He felt as if he were running, running for his life, until he could run no longer. His memory told him this was the act of a crazed man. Then all of a sudden he was floating in air. He wasn't this man at all. The vivid image of what happened to Anna was all in his dreams.

Abruptly the visions changed. He was running through the mine field again. An unconscious soldier's body slung over his shoulder as he tried to reach the plane about to take off. He reached it just in time to fling the soldier onto the floorboards beside the others who were piled haphazardly like sticks being gathered for a campfire. He grabbed hold of the strap to haul himself up and everything went black.

Shaking his head to clear the pictures replaying over and over in his mind, the pain ripped across his skull like the bullet that had torn away the top of his head so many years before. He couldn't stand this life much longer. There was only one thing left to do.

The bastard had disappeared, but Jeffery wouldn't stop looking until he found him again. He should have taken care of him the last time he'd been at their house. But it was too much fun watching him squirm. The next time they crossed paths would be the last time.

As he took another swig from the whiskey bottle, he placed the picture frame gingerly in its place before the room started spinning too hard. When he looked back up to the star lit sky through the dirty basement window, he almost choked on the burning liquid running down his throat. His vision blurred, then came clear again, and there stood his Anna, a saddened look on her face. She looked the same as she did, the last time he'd seen her, though now he could see right through her.

He tried to reach out to her, "Anna, sweet baby."

The vision vanished in thin air. Then the room started to spin one way and then the other. Laughing hysterically, Jeffery fell back onto the grease stained pillow.

Damned drugs!

Chapter 5

The words were just not coming out right! Lauren scrubbed her eyes with the back of her hand wearily. Why can't I concentrate? She grimaced. All day she hadn't been able to put much more than a couple of pages down on paper. The story had a good flowing line, but for some reason Lauren just couldn't put it into words. Maybe the spirits could give her something.

Grounding herself first, as to not allow herself to drift off to the outer realms, she grabbed the notebook she used for practicing her automatic writing and wrote down a quick question for her spirit guides to answer.

She positioned her hand to receive whatever the spirits would give her and said out loud, "Only spirits of light are welcome here, spirit guides, and angels help to motivate me to write today. Give me direction only for my highest good." Closing her eyes, she waited for the feeling she would get when she'd done this before.

Within seconds, her fingers began to tingle, and she had the urge to start drawing something, instead of writing. Very unusual, as she was not the artist type. The pen began to move quickly across the page, drawing curved lines and arches, the outline of a butterfly began to appear on the page. She deftly began to shade in areas of color, putting detail in where needed. The feeling was totally different than before. It was like she had suddenly turned into a great artist, yearning to get the work of art out on the page. By the time she was finished, she stared in awe of the image which has been created. It was the same white and black Zebra marked butterfly she'd seen before.

Questioning the validity of its origin, surely, she'd drawn this herself remembering from months earlier the butterfly she had seen, and not by the hand of the spirits. Yet, she wasn't an artist. She could barely draw a stick person, let alone this beautiful creation.

This was a question for Kathryn. How had she done this? She'd never remembered to bring the scraps of paper of her doodles in to class with her to ask what they might mean. They never had any real significance to her. Now she had an unmistakable reason to ask questions.

Her fingers began to tingle again, with an undeniable need, so she placed the pen on the paper again to see what would happen. This time a more detailed version of the medallion she'd doodled before came through. Her hand travelled down to the bottom of the page and stopped. Shakily, the definite outline of words began to form, not like the unreadable scribbles she'd experienced before.

...help...death...not him...help...

Still dazed, flashes of a grisly murder scene popped into Lauren's head. She could see the details of the surrounding room where she appeared to be standing. The intricate face of a beautiful Grandfather's clock showed exactly 12:00 o'clock as it gleamed in the partial lighting of the room. Strangely, the pendulum didn't swing but once as she stared, pulled in by the clear image before her. A grimy cloak of deep sadness began to grip her as she looked down to see the figure of a man poised over a young pregnant woman surrounded by the blood red stained carpet around her. She could only see the back of the man's head as he crossed the woman's arms over her stomach, as if she were in peaceful bliss filled sleep.

Then the whole picture vanished from her vision, yet Lauren remained stunned for a few moments longer. As she came back to the present, every atom of her being was moving like thousands of jumping beans. The energy in the room felt electric. She tossed the pen aside and bolted out of her chair.

What the hell was this?

She pushed the notebook closed, only to start pacing back and forth.

Oh, my God! Had some evil spirit taken over?

She forced herself to take some deep breaths to calm herself enough to sense what she was feeling on the inside. No odd changes in her thoughts or what she would normally do in this type of situation. Other than just being shaken, she didn't feel any different. But this was not normal, at least for her. She'd heard them talk about things like this happening down at the spiritual center, though she hadn't really known if she believed it could happen—until now.

Fingers unsteady, mind reeling, Lauren picked up the phone and dialed.

"Hello, Kathryn? This is Lauren. We need to talk."

* * * *

The meeting with Kathryn had eased Lauren's mind a bit. She learned what she'd experienced was something known in the psychic world as being normal. Kathryn was very excited to hear what had happened. Lauren apparently was clairvoyant and was being shown, through something called remote viewing, information which may be important about a crime scene.

Retrocognition. Now, there was a new word Lauren hadn't heard before. This was something generally left to the expert psychics who worked with the police on unsolved mysteries. Wasn't it?

Dabbling in the auto-writing had seemed harmless to her. Receiving needed information from spirit guides and angels was comforting. But she wasn't too sure how she felt about receiving messages from the dead, at least not the scary kind.

Lauren stared out the window of her office. The more she thought about it, what was the difference? The only thing she could see was on one hand the spirit guides and angels were there to help her through her struggles and questions, while on the other hand the spirits who work through psychics needed help to get their message heard. Either way, if we all came from the same energy, helping together in tandem to make a more peaceful existence, who was she to deny her ability to help a fellow spirit in need?

Kathryn had encouraged her to post her vision on her remote viewing website page. She herself had been contacted by some law enforcement agencies about a vision she'd had about a child in Australia they'd found to be surprisingly accurate. It was possible the information Lauren was being shown could help answer some questions in an unsolved mystery.

She agreed to let Kathryn scan a couple of the notes she had drawn of the medallions, and the butterfly, with a description of what she'd seen. If nothing else, it made her feel better to know she was at least trying to help the spirit who had contacted her.

The sudden banging of hammer on nails began again and jerked her out of her thoughts. Lauren rose out of her chair and turned off the gentle sounds of the classical music she'd hoped would help the flow of words as she tried to create her novel. It wasn't just the noise. As she moved toward the kitchen, she knew the real reason for being distracted from her work.

Nothing more had been said about the close intimate call in her office that day. It was as if it had never happened. She noted Max had become rather reserved after their first meeting. He was treating her with coolness, and what she figured was disinterest. As far as Lauren was concerned it was better left alone. She didn't need for any personal relations to get in the way of getting her house repaired. Problem was, she hadn't been able to convince her body the same thing. Her immediate reaction to being anywhere close to Max was undeniable.

He hadn't once made any indication what had happened between them was anything but his response to what she determined were mixed signals. She'd been a little angry, and yes, a bit awe struck by a gorgeous intuitive man. He must have interpreted her reaction as someone in need of kindness. That was it, plain and simple.

There was no way she would allow herself to think he'd shown any interest in a middle aged, out of shape woman, with a teen aged son to take care of, and a fixer upper home. She imagined there might have been an immediate attraction all men seem to get when they ponder someone of the opposite sex. But that was all there possibly could have been.

This morning, Max had been up on the roof fixing the roof tiles and subsequent ceiling damage. Every day that week she'd been listening to the sawing and banging of hammers overhead, disturbing her thought process. Though, what interrupted her thoughts the most, was every time she'd came out of her study, she would run smack into the middle of his broad chest. He'd either be marking the damaged areas to be fixed, or she would find herself looking longingly at the well-built legs, buttocks, and stomach of his lower body coming down out of the ceiling. Just like a tasty Popsicle waiting to be savored.

Those are exactly the types of thoughts to get you in trouble, she thought laughing to herself.

"Want something to drink?" She asked as she found him again spilling out of the ceiling inviting her to reach out and touch. His arms were raised above his head, stretching the muscles in his stomach in a seductively masculine way. The ladder he used was a short six-foot stepladder which came up to the middle of his thighs. He'd removed his shirt, as it was an unusually warm spring day, and hung it over the top rung of the ladder. She could see the light dusting of black curls running down his chest to the waistband of his jeans, against the dark tone of skin.

Oh, Lord.

Lauren took a deep breath, trying to settle the nerves which had begun to jump in her stomach, and only succeeded in filling her senses with the masculine scent of sweat and some type of soap smelling of musk and spices he'd used for his morning shower. Turning, she blew out the breath slowly, wanting to imprint the image and the sensual attack on her senses in her mind.

This will be good for my writing, she thought trying to justify the physical response she felt coming forth from her body.

Max brought his head down out of the ceiling and smiled at Lauren. "Yes, please, that sounds great!" He poked his head back in the ceiling and continued to speak, unknowingly giving her a second chance to sneak a look at his well-formed body. "Kind of hot up here, but I'm almost done securing the insulation. Then I can close it up."

He released the beam he'd been holding onto and stepped down off the ladder. Reaching up he grabbed his shirt and slipped it on.

Watching him as he tidied up his toolbox, she tried to convince herself the physical reaction she felt for him was obviously a strong physical desire for a strong, beautifully shaped male physique, paired with his added seduction of a strong Italian accent and deeply intense eyes. There was nothing more to it than that. And yet, she couldn't shake the feeling he'd come into her life for a reason—more than just fixing a leaky roof.

He was supposed to be there.

As if reading her mind, the intense look he gave her as he accepted the glass of tea had her knees shaking. They stood a moment in a loaded silence while he sipped from the glass. It seemed as if he wanted to say something, then decided not to when he set the glass down on the counter and wandered into the living room, Lauren not far behind. He paused in front of the stereo in the entertainment center. Thumbing through her collection, most of which were in the original vinyl, and it immediately caught her attention how interested he was in her taste in music.

"You've quite a collection here." True to his word, he appeared to have a love of music as well. "Great choice in classical—Beethoven, Tchaikovsky, Mozart and Brahms—and your jazz collection isn't too shabby either. Marsalis, Coltrane, Davis, Bassie." He flipped an album over to look at the cover and gave a chuckle. "You've even got a Thelonious Monk."

He gave an approving nod as he browsed through her few pieces of alternative music and blues. Turning with a copy of one of Stevie Ray Vaughn and Double Trouble in his hand he gave her one of his killer smiles. "Interesting choice in music you have." Max said raising his eyebrow at the selection in hand.

"Well, I'm kind of unusual really." Smiling, Lauren leaned against the arm of the couch trying to look at ease. "I've always been unusual. My Aunt Maggie teaches music at the University of Washington. She taught me everything I know. I learned a little piano, but unfortunately, I don't play any instrument well, not like her."

Max nodded in acknowledgment as he turned to replace the album in its place. She saw him glance over to her special collection of classical and was intrigued when he bent down to look at the titles. Composers who had written some of the finest Operas in history lined this last shelf.

Fascinated by his intent study of several collective highlights of what her Aunt had taught her were considered in technical terms as being Neo-Classicism, Late Romanticism and Post-Verismo styles, she watched silently as he seemed to devour their contents. It was almost as if he'd travelled somewhere far away as he looked through specific pieces from Gluck, Rossini, Piccini and her favorite Verdi. She favored these as they seemed to bring out the creativity in her when she sat down to write. He glanced up at her, his eyes smiling and full of questions, and held her gaze for a moment.

"My Aunt was actually in the first string of the symphony in Seattle," she offered. "She gave it up though when she married Uncle Dan. She said she didn't love the traveling and the long grueling hours necessary to keep it up." Lauren said, trying to explain the odd grouping of music she'd collected. "I guess I sort of picked up her style. She still plays the violin, but mostly at the University with her students."

"And what about your parents?"

Smiling as fond memories came to mind, Lauren looked down to where he'd knelt to look at the remainder of the bottom shelf. "Mom and Dad loved music too, but there wasn't enough time for them to teach me as much," she said wistfully. Seeing the inquisitive look as he glanced back, Lauren explained, "They were killed in a head on collision when I was nine. Mom was the one trying to teach me the piano, but my love has always been for writing. The romantic in me comes out in words, not music." She said with a slow laugh, not wanting to become too heavy or philosophical in their conversation.

Even though the loss had been so long ago, she could still feel the pain and grief almost as deeply as when she'd been told of her parent's accident so long ago. The sadness still came over her at times, especially when she knew her parents would have wanted to be with her. She could almost see the smile in their eyes, as they would hold onto each other in support and love, sharing with her in life's major events.

"It's still tough sometimes, but I'm glad I had my Aunt and Uncle. They're my Godparents. But truth be told, I wouldn't have chosen anyone else." Not only because they'd been named her Godparents, but also because they possessed the type of love only family can have for one another. The unalterable type of love tested time and again to remain unquestionable without fail.

Max rose slowly from the floor. "I am so sorry for your loss." Reaching out he brushed knuckles down her cheek. Compassion seemed to come through him in a wave of emotion she could feel, rocking Lauren down to the very depths of her heart. His sincerity so evident, she sensed immediately he knew exactly what a loss it had been for her. In this moment, she felt drawn to him in a way she'd never experienced before with any other person. Captivated by his eyes, she remained silent looking into the deep pools of his soul, seeing bits and pieces of the pain and grief so deeply ingrained in his being.

"Thank you." She said simply, forcing herself to look away to break the bond which had begun to form between them—a bond she desperately wanted—a bond unquestionably there.

Needing some air, Lauren moved away to open the front door. A soft warm breeze filled with fresh scents of spring wafted in, cooling the heat she'd begun to experience. She saw Josh coming down the path from the woods, a soccer ball in hand, and she waved to him. He waved back and began to bounce the ball against his knee and off the top of his head as he moved along the path in a convulsive type manner only a fellow soccer player would understand.

"Your son plays soccer?" Max asked watching him from the window.

"He's been involved in the school soccer leagues since he was a boy. I try to keep him as involved as I can. But a lot of times he doesn't have anyone else to play with, and I'm not too good at kicking the ball around." Lauren smiled. "He's pretty content to practice by himself, or when his friends come over."

Max turned and gave Lauren a quick smile and a wink. "Boss, can I have a few minutes off the clock to play some ball?" When Lauren gave him a slow nod of her head in acquiescence he strode out onto the porch and called out to Josh. "Mind if I join in?"

Josh stopped in the middle of the path looking toward Max as he came down the wide cedar staircase of the front porch. He nodded to Max with uncertainty showing he was not used to having someone other than his friends to kick a soccer ball around with, especially an adult.

The ball was tossed up in the air and Max took control. He moved swiftly jockeying the ball left and right, back and forth toward the goal set up at the side of the house for Josh to practice. He'd seen it earlier that week and hoped to have a chance to work with it at some point during his job at their house.

Max saw the look of amazement cross Josh's face as he skillfully moved the ball away from him again and again. Then the look of competition came into his eyes, and in a flash, Josh began vying for the ball just as expertly as Max had done earlier. They continued for quite some time back and forth, until finally Max found a hole in the barricaded wall of continual movement Josh had put in front of him. He paused only a brief second to send an expression of pure joy toward Josh as he swiftly sent the ball flying toward the net.

Josh pulled up his next movement to watch woefully as the ball went into the net without a hitch. He turned and moved over to where Max was bent over halfway, his palms on his knees, breathing heavily. Max smiled at him with heartfelt good spirit.

"Good game! Keep it up, you might be able to make the pros one of these days soon." Max watched Josh plop down on the ground and lean back on his hands with his face to the sky, he too was breathing as if he'd just gotten a good workout.

"Thanks!" Josh said happily. "You know that was pure luck, old man."

"Hey, watch it!"

Eyeing him carefully, Josh asked, "Where'd you learn to play like that?"

"I played regularly for UCC a couple of years back. But didn't get picked for a scholarship, so I figured I wasn't meant to be the next national soccer MVP." Max said with a wink as he rose up to stand again. "You've got some good moves there, kid." He reached out to ruffle Josh's curly head of hair.

Max turned and found Lauren standing at the side of the porch watching the exchange between the two of them. She seemed unsure of their interaction, and smiled slowly at him. He couldn't explain why, but it made him feel good inside to make her smile.

The undeniable heat he'd been feeling between them had nothing to do with the fact the temperature had been getting warmer each day. Curiosity had him wanting to know more about this woman. He wasn't sure why his Anna kept showing up, but he was sure she'd brought them together for some reason. Sooner or later he was going to have to go with his gut on this and find out why he felt Lauren pulling at him like some type of fate had brought them together.

This beautifully intriguing woman had so much mistrust, yet so much love and compassion, he could feel it reaching out to him all the way across the lawn. The sudden urge to go tell her exactly what he'd been feeling between them rushed into his chest.

He caught Josh watching him carefully, and the boy shifted uncomfortably. "She can't take much more," Josh said straightening up to look at Max directly.

"Pardon me?" He asked seeing the look of intention from this young man.

"Don't hurt her." Josh said simply. "Or you'll have to deal with me," he said getting to his feet, to be on level terms with Max.

Max understood fully the intention of his words. "I have no intention to," he replied honestly, hoping to instill a trust between them.

Josh paused slightly and nodded. He studied Max a moment longer then held his hand out in proper masculine form of having lost the game. "Thanks for the practice. Next time I'm going to kick your ass!" he said aggressively.

"I look forward to it. But don't hold your breath," Max said with a short laugh.

Nodding back at him, Josh ran across the lawn and up the stairs to greet his mother. He grabbed her and gave her a kiss on the cheek. Max saw Lauren say something, the strong mother's love showing across her face as she smiled. Josh turned and ran into the house.

As he came slowly toward her across the lawn, an aching need ran through him. Her hair flew around her in the breeze, the length weighing it down enough to where it looked like the sails of a ship lazily flapping in the breeze off a sailboat on the Sound. The reddish fiery tints were playing wistfully through the tips like the flames of a campfire just beginning to take hold. Her silhouette was outlined perfectly with the dark forest and the shadows of the covered porch behind her. Then as she came down the steps toward him, sunlight poured down over her in heavenly radiance. She looked like a fairy who had skipped happily out of the woods to greet him, the light in her eyes dancing cheerfully as she watched his careful approach.

"You are a man of many talents I see."

"More than you know," he said playfully, yearning to show her things left alone much too long. He wanted to run his fingers through her hair and bring her close to him, her scent tantalizing his senses to the point of bewilderment. He didn't know whether to reach out and drag her to him or turn and run as quickly as he could to get away from her alluring vibrancy.

The intensity of these feelings became too much for him to handle any longer.

Ah, to hell with right and wrong, Max thought as he reached out to wrap his arm around her waist, pulling her to him with an unmistakable urgency.

Her sharp intake of breath was taken over by the closing of his lips down on hers. At first, she was very still, unmoving and apparently surprised by his impulse. The possessive pressure of his lips pulled a slight moan to escape from her throat, swallowed up by the insistent ravishment of his lips on hers, it caused his kisses to become more demanding. Her hands traveled up the roped muscles in his arms taut with need and desperation.

Max's desire had overtaken him, knocking all sense away, long before he'd even reached out to pull her to him. She was so soft and pliable in his arms, her lips at first were unsure, but then became responsive with as much fervor as he was experiencing. The passion flowing from the sweet taste of her lips poured into him like honey from the tip of a spoon.

Slowly he began to test the reception she'd begun to show by teasing her lips open with the tip of his tongue. She opened to him eagerly and he deepened the kiss, thoroughly exploring long untouched places for the sweetness within. Lauren's response told him the alluring passion he'd seen deep within her had surfaced with his probing kiss. He savored the kindled heat he felt bursting through their lips as he began to impatiently search for the answer he was longing to find.

A slow burning ache began to form in his stomach as he felt his need dive deeper into his body. He craved this woman in ways he'd thought were impossible to reach again. He wanted her like he'd never wanted before. He wanted to feel her skin next to his, to discover the source of the magical scent surrounding his senses. He looked into her eyes, half closed with the sultry release of her will into his. He could feel her trembling against him, causing a rush of indulgent power to be released into his system.

The sudden crash from inside the house brought them both back, down to earth. A stream of curses followed through the open front door in obvious frustration.

"*Dolce Lord,*" he murmured as he held her close for one last moment before letting her go.

Flushed from excitement, Lauren stepped away from him. Huskily she laughed raising her shoulders in apology. Breathless, she turned toward the house.

"*Ma Bella,*" Max said, his voice deepened with the remnants of desire flowing through his words. Lauren turned her eyes bright with the same hunger he still felt. It was all he could do to keep from dragging her back into his arms. "We *will* meet like this again, but next time I may not let you go."

The promises of dark secret passions fluttered through her as she smiled seductively at this perfect image of a tall, dark and handsome man, possible lover.

What was she thinking?

She wasn't, and that was good enough for her right now. This felt too good to be questioned. A smile spread across her lips, a glint sparkling in her eyes as she raised her eyebrows and gave him a provocative wink. She felt the blush rising on her cheeks as she whisked herself away from him up the stairs and into the house as if she had wings on her feet.

No, she didn't need to think this one through, she just needed to feel, and if she continued to feel like this, there was no thought necessary.

As if having watched the whole thing, contented from its restful sojourn, the white and black butterfly fluttered off its perch on a flower nearby, toward the side of the porch.

Chapter 6

"Rita, what am I supposed to do about this?" Lauren asked her best friend as she propped the phone on one shoulder trying to balance two plates, a skillet, and two glasses in her hands as she brought them over to the sink.

Dinner had been a quick Sloppy Joe and salad combo this evening as Josh had plans with Robert to go night fishing down off the dock at the lake to find out what they could catch. Lauren didn't mind because she knew that Josh and Robert were responsible and wouldn't do anything too foolish. Besides, it would be light until almost ten o'clock these days and there were enough people out on the lake shore to help if anything were to happen.

"What do you mean girlfriend? Have fun with it! Lord knows you deserve it. Take whatever he wants to give you, and enjoy it." Rita's bubbling personality came over the lines in a larger than life fashion. Lauren almost felt as if they were sitting across from each other in their dorm room talking candidly about the next fling one of them would try with the newest boy on campus.

Best friends in college, Lauren and Rita became inseparable buddies from the start. Lauren's journey to live in the dorm on campus to discover her self sufficiency had gone askew when she'd been paired up with the party animal Rita. Lauren was not an outgoing person, but she could hold her own in a room full of people. Rita, the life of the party, had given her no choice but to come along for the ride.

But Rita also had a heart of gold and would give the shirt off her back if it meant it would help someone she cared about. She also could listen and become uncharacteristically wise in a heartbeat, when she felt you needed to talk. Together they'd found a long lasting friendship built on trust and kindness. Though, sometimes Rita could be a little annoying with her loud and over active efforts to fix Lauren up with a Friday night date, because don't you know, nobody could be home on a Friday night by themselves.

"Look who is talking, Mrs. Humphries! I don't see you out there flaunting what you've got anymore. Although, you've got an awful lot more happening than I have, that's for sure."

Lauren looked down at herself in disgust. She had to get rid of this extra weight quick, especially if she was going to accept what Max seemed to be offering her. She laughed at herself as she envisioned wild passionate nights and romantic interludes.

"You've always had so much more going for you than me. I wish for once I could be sure that someone was actually interested in me and not just a quick roll in the hay," Lauren said wistfully.

"Look honey, I found my sweetheart early, thank the Lord. You just happened to pick up on a couple of frogs on the way. And don't you go putting yourself down. You have more *chutzpah* than three of me! You have all of the *oomph* you need baby, to drag a man to his knees. Maybe this is the guy you have been waiting for all of your life. Don't pass up the chance to find out if he is a frog or a prince. Just jump in with both feet and watch out for the frog legs, 'cuz there's a whole lot of frogs out there!" Rita laughed wholeheartedly.

"And I married my quota!" Lauren laughed. "No, really, I'm not sure. There's something about it that doesn't feel right."

"Okay. So tell me what's going on."

Lauren hesitated only a moment. She'd always been able to tell Rita everything. Whether she believed her or not, she always had good advice. "You remember those doodles that looked like medallions? Those keep coming to me, and some other things, too."

She proceeded to tell her friend about the butterfly drawing and the sudden scary murder scene popping into her head at the strangest of times. That still bothered her.

"Really? Wow. That's crazy. Retro...what did you call it?"

"Retrocognitive. I might actually be seeing something that happened to somebody."

"Okay, so that's pretty strange. But what on earth does that have to do with the Italian hunk?"

"When we're together I get this weird feeling like someone's watching us. Like I'm supposed to be doing something or seeing something I'm not. Don't ask me how. I don't know why I'm feeling that. It's just one of those feelings I get."

"Do you think this Max has anything to do with this murder you keep seeing?"

Lauren thought hard for a minute and tried to tune into how the question made her feel. "No. I don't get anything bad from him at all. This is all just so strange to me."

"Well, honey, I've always said trust yourself. You've got one hell of a gut instinct. But I'd say whoever's watching you, give them something to talk about! I'd have myself as much fun as I could, while I still can, if you get my drift."

Lauren laughed. "Are you calling me old?"

"Truth is, how often do you get a gorgeous Italian man to come calling at your door, offering sweet kisses and everything you've dreamed of? You aren't getting any younger honey. Better get it while you can."

In the background Lauren could hear the battering of siblings arguing over something that probably wasn't too important. Rita's twins were fourteen and giving her a handful of troubles.

Raised voices became audible over the phone line as one shouted to the other in a high-pitched scream. "It's not yours! Mom, tell her you bought the blue skirt for me!"

"Look, honey, I've got to go right now, or one of the twins is going to be an only sister. Go for the gusto, and if you ask me, I'd jump his bones the next time he looked at me like that! Call me tomorrow and give me the scoop on the next scene in your own personal romance. Smooches……"

Lauren shook her head laughing as she could just picture her friend lounging out by the pool in her neon colored Capri pants and a cool sleeveless shirt, putting the white flag between her ever warring twins.

Lucky to have found the love of her life, Rita and David shared an acceptance for each other and what they could be together. Rita had locked onto him with everything she had the minute she saw him. But she hadn't needed to because David had been lost in her the moment he'd laid eyes on her. Simply they were made for each other. Lauren remembered they'd met up the same time she and Ben and met at the annual campus toga party. Rita had come out with the prince, and Lauren had come back with the frog.

Maybe Rita was right. She hadn't met anyone yet, maybe it was time to stop holding off and actually see if Max was worth her time. But, she would definitely be more aware this time, not to fall head over heels in love like she had before. She'd gotten herself in trouble before, and she knew what to look out for this time. The one thing she needed to do was pay closer attention to everything happening around her, especially if she began to feel as if Max was involved somehow with her visions.

If nothing else, she could just have a good time and see what he was all about—and have fun doing it.

******

Max sat at the piano running his fingers over the keys like the sound of a babbling brook over rocks. He wasn't really concentrating on what he was playing, his mind was on what had happened earlier that day. He knew that it had been a mistake to get so close to Lauren, the brief encounter they'd experienced had soared through his mind all afternoon as he'd finished up the ceiling in the kitchen. Tomorrow he was scheduled to start replacing some of the windows in the back which were leaking, and he wondered if he would get a chance to talk with her again.

As Max sat daydreaming, the only thing he could think about was the way Lauren had felt in his arms when he'd brought her up next to his body. The way her lips had melded to his in that passionate kiss igniting this fire in him. A fire unable to be extinguished. The way the scent of her hair had wafted up to blot out all of his senses, as the silken tendrils had lazily brushed across his arms. The way her eyes had seductively taunted him to take more than he intended when she looked into his eyes.

There was no getting this woman out of his system. He'd told her he wouldn't let go the next time it happened, and the way he was feeling right now he knew it was going to happen sooner or later. There was no stopping it. If they were close enough to touch, he may not be able to stop himself from sampling those sweet tender lips again, if not more of the delectable sweetness sure to be underneath. He hadn't intended to take it any further, but now that he had, he didn't know if he could stop.

Maybe it wouldn't be such a bad thing.

Max lazily got up and went in to fix himself a late supper. He fixed himself a cold submarine sandwich, heavy on the vegetables, not wanting to turn the heat on the stove. Sitting down at the table he began to munch but not even halfway through the first half he realized he'd been going over a new melody in his head repetitively since he'd gotten home that evening. It sounded really good. He jumped up and rushed over to the piano to pick up a pencil and some score paper and began writing out the notes playing in his head.

He sat up until well after midnight working on the melody and chords of the aria he'd been creating. Not even noticing, he hadn't thought of Anna all evening, he stretched himself fully from head to toe, feeling more relaxed than he'd felt in almost six years. Knowing he needed to get up early the next day to start back to work on Lauren's house, he flicked off the lights and wandered into the bedroom where he passed out promptly once his head hit the pillow. Not once did the dread of going to sleep and the recurring horror of his past come into his dreams. In fact, he dreamt of the purity of soul and mind of a lovely red headed fairy who had whisked away his thoughts into pleasant images of clouds and soft petals and scents of flowers to soothe his tired soul.

* * * *

Aware Max was working on the back of the house where he'd just removed the old wood-framed single-pane window from its space in the wall, Lauren hated the fact he could see her from where he stood. She'd decided it didn't matter. She couldn't let anything deter her from the workout regimen she'd set for herself. Hopefully he couldn't see what she was trying so hard to work off. Today she'd dressed in her workout clothes, sporting a pair of black leggings hugging her shapely legs and a large man's T-shirt made to be more comfortable by cutting the sleeves out and the neck in a V-shape showing the gentle swell of her breasts against the tight black body suit underneath.

As she worked her body rigorously with the pace of the treadmill, she set her mind on a subject to take away the boredom and feelings of uselessness she tended to get when working out. Her first thoughts were of the handsome carpenter outside her window. She watched him measuring and marking the opening for the new window, being careful to be exact before cutting into the outside wall. She began to wonder if she were kidding herself in thinking anything more than friendship could happen between them.

They'd begun to become friends, over a short lunch here and there or a glass of lemonade on the porch in the afternoons. They talked about both of their lives growing up. Neither she nor Max spoke much about their adult life. Max especially seemed to avoid anything of a personal nature.

He shared with her he'd been born in Naples, Italy, and lived there until he was about ten years old. Lauren loved the way his eyes brightened with the memory as he spoke of the beautiful countryside and the gentle laid back atmosphere of his grandfather's vineyard. His grandmother was still in Italy, but his Poppa had passed away a couple of years back.

His older sister Carmine had gone back to live with her after Poppa's funeral. They laughed as Max told Lauren how his sister had met and fallen in love with a young Italian man who was working hard to take over the family pizzeria business. Apparently, the young man had been so taken by Carmine's beauty he'd delivered the wrong pizza to her table three times before getting the order right. They were planning to be married in the fall.

He spoke about his Father's decision to move to America, the land of opportunity, where he could prosper as an entrepreneur. His mother, as he described had the beautiful soprano voice of a gilded whippoorwill, and had begun a promising career in opera. Her dream had been to sing in the most notable opera houses in the world. Italian stages knew her well, though her dreams were cut short when she decided the love of her man and raising a family was more important. The way in which he spoke of the various operas his mother had performed in, his eyes seem to glow in his appreciation and deep love for the art. Lauren hadn't heard his mother's name before, but she would definitely look into the production of the arias and duets he'd named. Though she wasn't sure how much information she could find from so long ago.

The way, in which he described the performances in detail, was as if he had performed them himself. In fact, at times as he spoke, she could see him as the devilish antagonist, or the handsome hero of the story. Lauren couldn't shake the feeling he wasn't telling her a vital piece of information to his stories. She actually saw flashes of him in costume. But this must be her imagination, Lauren told herself. Not once did he give any indication he had ever been on stage.

While they talked, Lauren was pulled into his descriptions of family. They meant the world to him. Yet in all of the stories he told, there was something missing. He was nowhere to be found, as if he were intentionally leaving himself out of his family history. Puzzled, Lauren tried to get him to open up, but every time he would start to say something that sounded as if he were to tell something about himself, he would close up the story quickly with a reference only to what had happened.

Lauren had shared with him things about her childhood, and various parts of her adult life, carefully avoiding anything which would bring back the pain she'd felt with her two husbands. She carefully avoided any mention of their infidelity, not wanting to answer any probing questions about what had happened. She felt almost as if she could tell Max anything, but she held back not wanting to cloud their friendship with anything to remind her of the past.

She pondered the fact she felt it necessary to hide certain things from him. Perhaps, he as well had a past much too painful to remember.

Lauren reached out to brush the sweat from her brow. This was her second workout of three, the most strenuously planned for the day. Sweat poured off her brow, fatigue beginning to take hold. She reached out to grab the bottle of water on the tray beside the treadmill. Lifting it up and shaking it gently to find there was no water left, she set it back down again and grabbed hold of the handles of the machine for support.

Just a few more minutes, Lauren thought, *I can make it through a few more minutes.*

Heat poured off her body like fiery waves coming across the parched sand of the Sahara Dessert at mid-day. She didn't care. *No pain no gain*, she kept telling herself as she blinked the sweat out of her eyes.

This horrible image she'd allowed herself to become was the only thing holding her back from considering Max's subtle hints over the last couple of weeks. He hadn't come right out to say it yet, but she could tell he was trying to find a way to ask her if she wanted to go out with him. But, she'd brushed him away with excuses of not enough time, or needing to finish some unidentified duty. In reality, she was afraid of what would happen if they were to get too close too soon.

Lauren stepped off of the treadmill and began a slow routine of stretching exercises to allow her muscles to cool down. Her back was toward the door as she stretched her arms toward the ceiling, rolling her shoulders and turning from side to side. When she bent down to ease the tension in her lower back she caught sight of someone in the doorway. Jumping up she turned quickly to find Max leaning against the doorjamb watching her intently from behind. He held in his hand a bottle of spring water.

"What are you doing?" She asked suspiciously. When he held out the bottled water for her to take her heart softened. His kindness melted her heart as she looked up to see a grin on his face and a twinkle in his eyes.

"Enjoying the view." Mischief twinkled in his eyes as he raised his eyebrows suggestively.

Lauren rolled her eyes at him and gave a laugh, pleased at the compliment he was giving her. She took the bottle of water from him and screwed off the top, taking a long thirsty drink. "Thanks. You didn't have to." But she was glad he'd noticed her. She wasn't used to anyone paying much attention to her, but she had to admit, she liked it.

"Glad to do it," he said with sincerity. "Lauren why do you work yourself so hard?"

Taken aback by his question, Lauren looked up at him with a slow inquisitive gaze. In front of her stood the most amazing specimen of a man she could think of, and he wanted to know why she was working her tail off to try to be something he could want with as much desire and intensity as she wanted him.

His eyes were as kind and giving as his question was honest, which unsettled her a bit that he hadn't figured it out himself. Maybe he really had no intention of being anything more than friends.

"Just something I need to do," she shrugged it off.

As she bent down to pick up her towel off the stool next to the treadmill, Max reached out and put his hand on her arm. The thrill of his touch shot straight up her arm.

"Don't do it for me," he said as if reading her mind.

She turned with purposeful intensity. "No, I do it for me."

He had to know she didn't want to be out of shape. Even more for herself than to become what he might want her to be in the end.

"Just don't hurt yourself doing it. That wouldn't do any of us any good." His brows knit together.

She appreciated his obvious concern. If only she could turn his compassion and concern for her into the touch of a lifelong mate and companion. He made her want to be held in his arms, encouraged and strengthened by his reassuring words.

Lauren shook herself out of the dreams she'd conjured up in her head. This man probably had no more than a thought of a quick affair in mind. There was no way she was going to be able to lose all of the weight she needed before he was done with the job and out of her life for good. If something did happen before then, she would be nothing more to him than just that—a nice lay.

Laughing lightly she come forward to move past him to the hallway.

"Sure you want to run away? Why don't I just take you here and now? You know it's going to happen sooner or later *Ma Bella*."

Max reached out to circle her waist with his arms, drawing her closer than they'd ever been before. The warmth of her body, still burning from the workout, turned into a fiery inferno as he brought his lips to her throat. Sending chills down her spine in a torrent of desire, he began to explore the length of her neck with his lips, nuzzling a spot just behind her ear, enticing a throaty moan. Without thought, she threw her head back, arching her throat and her chest toward him urging him to taste and to feel.

No thought was possible—she would just experience this heart pounding sensation.

The texture of her skin reminded Max of the finest silk, pale in color, warming at the touch of his lips, begging for more. He let out a soft moan as he buried his face in her hair. The humming in his head all but wiped out every cohesive thought from seconds before. An urgent need to touch every inch of her body was overwhelming. The scent of woman invaded his senses, her unusual musky scent mixed with sweat poured over him, urging him to take her to the next step.

Right here, right now.

But he couldn't. Not yet. Although the desire was almost unbearable, he knew he needed to take it slow. He didn't need her son, Josh, to tell him. She'd been hurt before, he could tell by the look in her eyes when they flirted. If he moved to fast she could be hurt, and he did not want to hurt her again.

He eased away slightly. As she brought her head back up, the flushed hue of her skin, and the dazed look of excitement brewing just under the surface, fed his ravenous hunger for her even more. The fervor there was so strong, if let loose he wasn't sure he could handle it. This was a woman of strength, one with deep seated passions screaming to be released.

One had only to look into her eyes to see she had the capacity to love with no questions asked, to give without taking, and to feel deeply every emotion possible. Max had prided himself in being intuitive and sensitive. He'd brought it out in his music and his own life. And now he held in his arms a woman who was willing and able to give him back what he'd locked away for so many years.

But was he able to give back what she needed as well?

The doubts and pain he'd held so long began to seep into his thoughts. Could he love again like he had before? He'd loved before. Everything he'd known had been stripped away exposing the raw wounds to fester without resolution to the cause, his heart shattered and blown away in the wake of his murdered wife and child.

Was he willing to risk the chance of his heart being exposed like that again? It could happen again, just like it had before. The murderer hadn't been caught yet. Memory of the myriad of those horrible notes, which had plagued him after the funeral, flashed before him. Notes which had made him feel helpless and exposed. Threats to his own life, threats which made him run like a spooked cat. Scattered visions of that horrible night came shooting through his mind, taunting and urging him to dispel any reasons to feel pain again.

Forced to withdraw, in an attempt to regain his composure, Max lowered his head to Lauren's forehead, willing the visions to disappear.

Would it end? Would he ever be able to live again without fear?

His breathing quickened, with sudden intakes of air and short breaths out. His arms went limp around her, as if he'd become void of any feeling whatsoever. Lauren opened her eyes and looked up into his face. Her immediate reaction made him feel like a scared child, seeking the comfort of his mother when he'd had nightmares when he was younger.

Unquestioning, she moved closer and took him into her own arms, stroking the hair on the back of his neck. She muttered soothing words, calming the fears which had risen so quickly in his mind. After a minute the tension started to release, and his breathing steadied, as he willed himself to calm down. Lauren's loving soul calmed him sooner than when he'd had to deal with the waves of fear by himself time and again.

Normally he was able to restrain his emotions during the day, it was only at night when he slept and his defenses were down did these thoughts come creeping back in to haunt him.

This was unusual to have these visions come over him while he was awake.

Not willing to succumb to the fears which had surfaced, he remembered the loss of control over his life was like an anchor pulling him back, its weight never allowing him to be free of his nightmare. When he'd come to Washington, he'd been determined not to let what had happened to him continue its barrage of pain and imprisonment over his life.

He was the one in control here—not his fears or his invisible assailant.

He realized he'd let his guard down and allowed this deep emotion to brush his heart again. Passions and desire stirred up his heart in a way he'd not allowed himself to feel for a very long time. Until now, he'd thought locking these feelings away from sight and thought was the best action to take. Now, it seemed impossible to do. Nor did he want to.

This was a woman who could obviously stir deep feelings, a woman who deserved his full attention, and that was exactly what he was going to do. It was time for him to move on from the pain. Yet, he couldn't do so without her knowing everything about him. She deserved to know who he really was, and the risks she might be in if they were to go any further. He needed to plan this out. This wasn't the kind of thing you just blurt out to someone.

Lauren moved away slightly, continuing to hold him in her arms. "Hey there, are you going to be alright?" Her eyes were full of concern as she caught his gaze. "Didn't mean to scare you," she said with a half laugh.

"Sorry, you just kind of knocked me off my feet." Disengaging himself from her arms he moved away allowing her room to move past him.

"I'm sure I did!" Her laugh was light, almost too light. Max knew his sudden withdrawal had hurt her, but it couldn't be helped. He would find a way to make it up to her.

He didn't know what to say, so he said nothing, feeling sheepish.

She gave him a long hard stare, followed by a slight nod. The awful way this made him feel had his heart rolling up to his throat. He followed her as she moved past him into the hallway and continued down the hall into the front room.

"I'm going to go take a shower and go for a while. I'll be back later. You may not see me before you leave." Lauren's voice sounded pinched, as if she were holding her feelings in check. "Tomorrow we'll have the picnic lunch like I promised."

Max nodded. "I've got to get that window in before nightfall, so I better get back to work." He said trying to cover up for his feeling of inadequacy. Max moved past her to go out the front door. Willing his determination to not let fear rule his life again, he took a breath and turned with a smile showing a smidgen of his former confidence. "Don't think this is over. You will be mine at some point, *mia dolce amano*."

Noting the look of confusion on her face, Max strode over to where she stood and swept her again into his arms. Almost in defiance of the fear which had taken over before, he brought his lips down onto hers in an almost savage crushing move.

"It's just a matter of time," he said, then was gone, out the front door and down the steps.

From his perch a couple rungs up the ladder, Max heard the water start for Lauren's shower. He stopped his work to take a minute to lean his head against his arms across the ladder. With his eyes closed he made his heart slow down to a normal pace. It hadn't stopped thumping since he'd taken Lauren into his arms the first time that afternoon.

How could she make him feel this way so quickly? Part of it he knew the fact he'd not been with a woman for over four years, but there was something more to it. This feeling seemed to have taken over him the first time he'd laid eyes on her. Unexpected emotions had been stirred up and exposed, which on one hand made his heart sing and his body seem invincible, and on the other caused him to be afraid of the outcome, fearing vulnerability.

Shaking the doubts forming in his mind, Max raised his head and began shaping the opening for the new window. He was not going to become a sniveling wimp of a man. He would not allow what had happened to control him or what he did in his life. He was in control, and there was nothing that was going to stop what was happening between Lauren and he. If it were going to be something on a deeper level, then they would just deal with it when it happened.

Anna would have wanted it that way for him. Suddenly a cold breeze whipped around him. Max smiled and touched the ring that hung from the chain around his neck. He was beginning to think her showing up at times was not a bad thing. Maybe she was just being supportive.

Yes, she would have wanted him to be happy.

The humid scent of a freshly showered woman came wafting down out of the open window above him. The sound of light Irish harps came floating out to tickle his ears and the scent of flowers and springtime all but took his senses away again.

There is that woods fairy again, he thought with a smile. *Come dance around me and make my heart sing again.*

He stepped down off the ladder with a happy jig, and glanced up to catch a glimpse of the fairy he dreamed about through the sheers. Too bad he couldn't see much of anything but the faint outlines of movement from within.

Pangs of desire came welling up from deep within as he imagined her smoothing lotion over her wonderfully supple body, running her hands up and down her legs. He fought the urgency to run up the stairs to her and pull her into his arms again. She'd invoked sensations and emotions in his heart which could not be ignored. He had to have her. His heart began to pound thunderously in his chest as he watched her faint outline through the opaqueness of the curtains.

Then, too swiftly for his taste she began to dress, covering those voluptuous curves with clothes that hung down to cover what he thought was a beautiful piece of art. She reminded him of the Rubenesque shape of the women in the early sixteenth century artist's paintings. Ruben's depiction of wanton scenes, representing the female as a purely sexual being, spread out on lounges and across satin laden beds, flaunting their shape without fear of contempt, or self-inhibition was an attraction in itself.

Here was a woman who deserved the unreserved attentions of a man, and yet seemed totally unaware of her appeal. Her full shape enticed him beyond words. He had an unexplainable urge to touch and caress the very curves she tried so hard to cover up. She'd drawn out of him an inexplicable need to show her the attraction he held for her.

Max looked back down, not wanting to get caught taking advantage of the view. He began humming to himself, thinking of all the ways he could accomplish this, his mind so intent he didn't realize he'd begun to sing out loud the words to an aria he'd once performed. It made his heart happy to know this beautiful woman was attracted to him as well. Unsure what this meant to them longterm, he knew soon he would be enticing the enchanting Lauren into sharing her innermost passions with him.

Grinning, he bent down to begin his work again with images of those soft lovely curves in his arms, naked and filled with need and ultimately washed in unquestionable satisfaction.

Chapter 7

Lauren sat relaxed, the dim light enough for her to see the page in front of her. Soft music played in the background to help them in their silent meditation. The question she had posed to the spirits of light wasn't specific to her writing this time. She'd felt like she needed more from them today, so she'd asked for any information she needed to know for her highest good. The pen she held in an upright position didn't move at all. Not like it had in the past.

The other writers in the room seemed to be having much more success. She could see them writing and drawing busily over their pads of paper. Feeling as if she hadn't gone through the meditation right, she tried again to go through the steps herself.

That's right, Kathryn had said you needed to be specific in your questions. *Maybe I'm not asking the right question*, she thought. She wrote down the first question that came to mind. *What do I need to know about Max?*

Tiny little tingles began to run over the tips of her fingers, and she felt the urgency as the pen begin moving across the paper. She didn't focus on what was being written, only on the energy that was coursing throughout her hand. At first, she could sense the usual scribbling marks being made, so she asked for the messenger to slow down and write clearer words.

The pen hesitated, and she could feel a more purposeful message come across. Then it began to draw the same medal she'd felt before, in a cruder form.

All of a sudden, she felt the need to ask *"Should I trust Max?"* The answer that came back was a definite *"YES."*

Lauren needed to know where this was coming from, so she asked silently. *"Who are you?"* and the pen began to move.

"Anna" clearly came through.

"Why have you come to me?" Lauren questioned, hoping to get some answers. More words came forth, and then stopped. She stared down at them, unable to piece them together in the hazy illumination of the room.

Then too soon, Kathryn began to bring them out of their meditative state, and Lauren felt the energy swiftly leave her. It gave her a small head rush, and she needed to take a few deep breaths.

"It is time to come back now. I would like you all to start your journey back to the present. Take your time."

Soon the soft lights were turned back up to their normal levels, and Lauren looked down at the page on her pad. Her eyes first landed on the medal she'd drawn many times before. Then she started seeing the words jump off the page. They had never been so clear before.

"How did everyone do?" Kathryn asked.

Lauren sat silent, listening to what the other writers had discovered. She didn't really hear much of what they said, she kept staring down at her own channeled piece. Finally, it came to be her turn to share.

"Lauren, do you have anything you would like to share with us today?" Kathryn asked.

Lauren glanced up at her, then back down to her page. "No." She felt everyone's eyes on her. "There's nothing more than I've gotten before." Lauren said, trying to appease their curiosity. She could tell Kathryn knew better.

"Okay. Well good job everyone. I think we are out of time now. I've got a client coming up here soon. I hope to see you all next class," Kathryn said, opening the door to her little office. She followed her students out into the hallway, chatting a little more about their experiences.

Lauren stayed where she was. She needed to talk to Kathryn alone, even if it was for just a minute. As she waited, she gazed around the room. Crystals of many shapes and colors were placed here and there reflecting the flames from candles placed nearby. Beautiful blues and mauves seemed to emanate from a large round crystal in the middle of the table.

Kathryn had called this her Scrying ball. It wasn't clear, like the crystal balls depicted in movies, where witches hover over them to see into the lives of others, to bring havoc and destruction. This crystal had many glistening facets appearing to swim around, constantly forming something new for the one who gazed upon its beauty. Spirit might use the crystal to show messages to questions being posed. Kathryn had explained, the crystal itself was not evil, it held only the intention given to it by its owner. This crystal's purpose was only to bring the highest good to those who used it.

Lauren tried gazing into it to see if anything came to her now. Bright as can be, the white and black butterfly popped into view, for only a second then it was gone. Lauren blinked a few times, staring into the globe willing the image to come back. But it didn't. A few times she thought she saw a group of the beautiful creatures flying around in the middle, but she couldn't be sure. Then all of a sudden, in her peripheral vision she saw the same butterflies dancing happily over the candle in the corner of the room. When she turned to look directly at them, they disappeared.

Kathryn came back in and closed the door behind her. "What do you see?" She asked as she came around the table to sit down.

Lauren felt silly asking this, but she'd been meaning to find out. "Does it mean something if you keep seeing butterflies around you?"

Nodding softly, Kathryn smiled. "It is said when butterflies gather, spirits are present." She reached out to pick up one of her decks of Oracle cards and began to shuffle. "And there were many spirits here with us today."

"If you see one in particular all the time, does that mean it is one spirit?"

"Could be," Kathryn assented. "You are beginning to see symbols of spirit communication. It might be time for you to think about doing some psychic development to enhance your discoveries."

The thought was a little to much to handle at the moment. Lauren nodded absently as she looked down at the channeled paper in front of her. Realizing she didn't have much time, she wanted to find out what Kathryn felt about what had come through.

"I'm sorry, I know you've got someone coming," Lauren rushed out.

"You are my someone," Kathryn reached out to pat her arm, the smile in her eyes warming Lauren's heart.

"Oh," Lauren stumbled unsure of what to say. She hadn't thought she'd been so obvious.

"Now why don't you tell me what's on your mind."

Lauren placed the paper in front of Kathryn, who studied it a moment, then sat back.

"I see your question at the top. This is not very specific. Tell me what you wanted to know about Max?"

Looking at the drawings and words, Lauren wasn't sure now why she'd asked the question. "I'm not really sure. I guess I wanted information to understand him better."

"Okay, then that may explain the reason for some of these answers. Look here," Kathryn said pointing to the words *'need rest'* and *'DAD sick'* then to the words *'not him'*, then sloppily as if her hand was getting tired *'gun'* and *'MONGO.'*

"That's sort of what came to me before, when I saw the murder scene. Do you think Max has something to do with that?"

Kathryn closed her eyes to intuit what she was feeling from spirit, then shook her head. "Not in a bad way. Somehow, he is involved, but I can't be sure how. I believe the real question is how you feel about him. Do you trust him?"

Lauren didn't need to think very long. "Yes, I do. I'm not sure why, but there is something about him that makes me feel safe. I don't understand much about him. But I do feel safe around him."

"I've told you before to trust in yourself. Your gut instincts will never lead you astray." Kathryn took the sheet from Lauren to gaze at the markings. "May I mark on this?" She asked picking up a pen.

"Go ahead," Lauren responded, hoping there was more to be seen. When Kathryn handed the sheet back, she'd underlined some markings which were not so clear. Now the words *'love'*, *'music'*, and *'you'* stood out now.

"What does this feel like to you?" Kathryn asked.

"I'm not sure," Lauren hesitated. "But apparently this Anna is trying to tell me something."

"Any idea who she is?"

"No clue."

* * * *

The previous day had been a whirlwind of emotions for Lauren. Ever since the little scary scene when Max seemed to loose it, she'd been trying to figure out just how to ask him what had happened. For a change she wasn't running off to her classes at the community college, or taking Josh to some of his activities.

She'd invited Max to join her in a leisurely picnic lunch under the big leafed oak tree out back. The light chicken salad with some fruits and vegetables to compliment the dish was her way of showing how much she appreciated what he was doing for her.

As she peeled the cucumbers and carrots for dipping, she wondered how to come out and ask who this '*Anna*' might be. She wanted to find out more about him, not only his family. She needed to know what type of secrets he was holding onto causing him to pull back like he did earlier. Did it have something to do with this Anna? What drove him to do the things he did, and why was he not pursuing the things he obviously loved. Reminding herself worrying about it wouldn't solve anything she gazed out the window as she washed her hands.

"*Trust yourself,*" she heard in her head. Then as if on cue, she saw in the distance a butterfly, dancing around in the air over an Asian Lilly she'd planted earlier in the year, its vibrant red flowers fluttering in the breeze. Lauren gave a little laugh. Maybe this was Anna she kept seeing hanging around.

"I sure wish you would tell me what you need. It would make things a lot easier," Lauren muttered, drying her hands on the dishtowel.

She heard the back door open and close, and instantly knew Max was in the house. Up the hallway he came, his serene presence soothing to Lauren's soul. She turned as he came into the kitchen.

"Lunch is ready. I was just about to bring it out."

Max's smile brought joy to her heart. "Thought I would come see if you need any help. Guess I'm too late."

"Not at all, you can help me bring the plates to the table out back. I'll grab the iced tea and glasses."

They sat on the blanket she'd spread out on the ground, the house to their backs, and a view of the lake in front of them. It had cooled slightly and a gentle breeze swept through the leaves of the trees with a relaxed rustling sound. Sparrows happily chirped their songs of happiness, bringing a connected unity with nature to float down around them as they sat in silence.

Lauren had changed into a long flowing broomstick skirt made of a light cotton material which brushed her ankles above bare feet. The pretty pale blue flower pattern matched a light breezy shirt that hung down over her loose fitting chemise of the same color. Her feet were slim with beautifully shaped toes she'd painted with a light frosted pink.

This was the first time Max had seen her in clothes more fitting to a female than the baggy jeans and loose fitting shirts she normally wore. Even her more dressed up clothes she wore to her classes in the evening were overly pronounced with the intention to cover and hide things beneath.

Max marveled at the way she'd made herself even more appealing than before. The alluring scent she wore made him want to taste her all over. He watched as she got up to set the empty dishes on the back steps going into the house. The sway of her hips pulled at him to tell her how she was making him feel.

Sitting back down on the blanket, near enough for him to feel her presence next to him, she smiled with eyes bright and glowing. Eyes so expressive, he could almost tell what she was thinking. She was nervous, he noted as she rubbed the texture of the skirt between her fingers. But she had something specific on her mind, and she was trying to figure out how to say it.

Patiently, he waited.

"What happened in there before? And don't tell me I scared you. There is more to it than that," she said, turning to give him an intense serious gaze.

He'd been waiting for her to ask him this question all afternoon. Wincing a bit at the suddenness of her curiosity, he dropped his gaze and looked out toward the water. How would he explain his fear of getting to close? He needed to handle this very carefully.

Someone had murdered his wife and had turned insanely psycho on him. It had made no sense to him then, and certainly wouldn't make sense to someone for the first time hearing about it now. Why would someone who had come to rob and steal, murder his wife, and then risk being caught by threatening him. There was still a fear for his life. How could he explain to her he was hiding out from a crazed murderer and still expect her to remain calm and receptive? And why shouldn't she be scared, he was a live target concealed temporarily by his cover.

In all reality, he should go, never to come back. By staying he would only put Lauren at risk too. Somehow, though, he couldn't bring himself to leave the only thing to produce such a feeling of happiness within him. He just couldn't do it, not now that he'd discovered her. There had to be another way.

Taking a deep breath he answered in the only terms he knew how without causing her to fear being with him. "Something happened a long while ago between me and a woman I cared for very deeply. It haunts me sometimes and scares me from wanting to feel again."

"Was it Anna?"

His head shot up and he stopped breathing. The blood drained from his head, making him dizzy. He felt like he'd been punched in the gut. "What...how do you know this?"

Lauren looked down at her hands, then back up again. "I sense it. Things come to me sometimes."

"How?"

She shrugged her shoulders. "When I'm writing. It's like information comes to me in different ways."

"Like a psychic?" He asked, curious now.

She looked almost embarrassed. "Yes, something like that."

"What else have you seen?" Max began to wonder if she knew more than he'd thought.

"I'm kind of new at all of this, so I really don't have much. I've been seeing and feeling more lately. I think I need to help in some way, but I'm not sure how. The name Anna came through yesterday. Then something about Mongo, does that mean anything to you?"

Could Lauren possibly be hearing from his Anna? That's what psychics do, talk with dead people, right? Though, she'd never said anything about being a medium.

Looking into her expressive eyes, he saw concern, and innocence, nothing more. Unsure of what he thought about mediums and their ability to see and hear from spirits. Were they real or were they just tricksters?

He tried to reason out other ways Lauren might have known Anna's name. Giving it a minute, he was sure he must have said the name without realizing it, which would explain her knowing. Of course, that must have been what had happened.

"Yes, it was Anna. But that was a very long time ago," he said continuing on, not wanting her to ask to many more questions, he needed to steer her away from the past and toward the present.

"Something bad happened to her, didn't it?"

He wanted to tell her why he was so scared, he wanted to open up and tell her everything, but he knew he couldn't. The investigator had told him to be discreet about telling anyone what had happened. The killer was still out there somewhere. This was the time for him to get away from the incessant notes which were streaming into his already upturned life. He didn't need his fans to find out where he was, or worse the writer of those harassing notes.

"Let's not worry about the past anymore and just concentrate on right now."

"But, I want to help."

"Nothing can change what has happened. We can only be in the present and take care to recognize what we have. Lauren, *ma bella*, you have made me feel things I thought would never come alive again." Reaching over he gently pulled her to him, needing to feel her next to him, needing to feel it was indeed possible to love again.

The smile in her eyes was infectious, coming straight from the heart. Max could almost feel the waves of emotion flowing out from her. This was right. From his being, he knew this was what they both needed to feel and discover together.

Lauren lay her head on his shoulder without further comment, and they watched in silence as the gentle breeze rustled through the tree leaves, the far away motion of children laughing and playing in the lake causing ripples to fan across the lake.

On impulse, Max pulled away from her to look into her face. "Go out with me on Friday. The Seattle Symphony is performing the works of the greatest musicians, Mozart, Beethoven, and Brahms. They call it '*A Symposium of Love.*' I want you to go with me."

Oddly, she took a moment to answer, a variety of emotion playing in her eyes. He couldn't tell why, but it seemed as if she were weighing her options. Then finally, rolling her eyes she gave a smile, and said, "I would love to go with you. But I haven't got a thing to wear!"

Relieved, and happier than he'd been in a long time, he laughed out loud at the comical look on Lauren's face. He lifted her hand to brush his lips over the palm in an intimate manner. He could feel the heat from her palm energy intensify as his lips lingered, making her even more adorable.

A playfulness came over him, and Max glanced up to catch her eyes in a fiery gaze. "I wouldn't mind if you wore nothing at all, but then we more than likely would never make it to the Symphony."

She smiled softly and broke off the gaze as a blush rose up her throat to her cheeks. He brushed his fingers over her cheeks, intrigued by the inexperienced reaction of her blush. She obviously had not received many compliments, and now here he was rushing forward with comments like that. Perplexed, his brows knit together.

Why hadn't this woman been given what she so deserved?

She laughed lightly, and began to play nervously with the napkin in her hand. "Yes, well, *that* won't be happening!"

Wanting to dispel her nerves, he made sure to make eye contact with her again. "I don't know why you try to cover yourself up, *ma bella,* you have a beautiful body. You should be proud of the gifts you have received."

Then without thinking, boyishly he let his gaze wander slowly down to the pinks of her toes, and back up again. Max's eyes lingered on the curves of her breasts temptingly peeking out of the lowered neckline of her chemise. When his gaze returned to Lauren, the hardened look she gave him was unexpected.

Moving away from him, in what seemed to him to be defensive, she started to get up from the blanket. She confirmed this with a self-disparaging look at herself. "No doubt, I do have more than most."

Aghast at how she had taken his remark, he reached to place his hand on her arm. "Please forgive me, I did not mean to hurt you with my words *bella.*"

She'd set her face in an unemotional stance. "Well when you have hips like these, its hard not to notice the ample supply I've been given." The sour smile and the hard look in her eyes disturbed him greatly.

Max jumped to his feet quick enough to grab her arm before she could get away. "*Bella,* don't do that to yourself. Don't put yourself down. I didn't mean anything by it." She turned to meet his eyes in an intense look of past pain and current uncertainty.

Bringing her hand up to his lips he made sure she was looking directly into his eyes. "What I meant to say was you draw me to you like a bee to a flower. The scent you wear encompasses my very spirit with its sweetness. I cannot lie. I am enticed by your curves and your female sexuality. But I am just a fool. My mind wants to know you and woo you into wanting to find out about me, yet my body urges me to take you and fulfill the needs you stir up inside me every time I see you."

She looked up at him with as much cynicism as anger in her eyes. Dismissing the words he'd just said, she raised an eyebrow and gave a wary smile. "You do have a way with words. I bet you tell all the girls what they want to hear, don't you?"

Her cynical look of disbelief broke his heart. How would she ever believe him if she couldn't believe in herself? Puzzled by the turn of their conversation, he shook his head, feeling almost defeated.

"No, *bella*, not in a very long time," he sighed, hoping she would feel his sincerity.

They stared at each other in uncomfortable silence. The battle Lauren was fighting within herself showed in her beautiful green eyes, and Max wondered if she would ever look at him the same as she had before. Then she appeared to come to some sort of decision, the kindness he was so drawn to returning.

She dropped her gaze. "Sorry, that was just one of those left over things from the past. Don't worry about it. I'll get over it. I guess we both have some things to work on."

"He must have hurt you very badly."

Her expression changed back to what he felt was a hardened protective front. "As you said, we can't change the past can we. We can only deal with what we have in the present. I agree."

Max studied her, searching for some insight as to what she was thinking. The only thing he could see was she'd closed herself off to him and put up a wall too thick to breach. He nodded silently, continuing to study her, unsure of what more he could do.

She turned to walk away and then turned back suddenly. "Why do you want to go out with me? You could just continue to woo me here, and not go to all the trouble."

Her statement shouldn't have surprised him, but it bothered him greatly. She obviously thought he was only after the one thing all men were after—sexual satisfaction. Although, this was something sooner or later he hoped they would both want, he knew what he felt was something much deeper.

"Finding someone to share life's joys is not easy. I wanted to share with you something that touches my heart. You intrigue me, Lauren. I don't bring many close to me, but I would like to find out more about you and find out why I am pulled to share these things with you."

The warmth returned to Lauren's face, and she smiled again nodding.

When he saw this had been exactly what she'd needed to hear, his smile deepened and he chuckled. "And I haven't been able to get you out of my mind since the first time I saw you."

Lauren looked at him thoughtfully. "It's only because you've seen me almost every day for the last three weeks."

Max paused for a moment, not understanding why she couldn't accept a simple compliment. He would find out what had happened to her to make her so skeptical. But now was not the time.

To drive away the continued self-doubt and fear he felt bubbling inside her, he raised her hand to a whisper away from his lips. Turning her palm upward as he bent his head, he secured her eyes seductively with his, and brushed her wrist with his lips where he could see the rapid pulse of her heart beat.

"Yes, but don't you owe it to yourself to find out if that is all it is?"

****

From his viewpoint, Jeffrey could see everyone who came in and out of Max's house in Chicago. It had been months since he'd seen him. He saw an occasional suspicious looking person go in and out, but never Max. His neighbor, Jim, frequented the Veteran's hall where he would stop for breakfast most weekends. He was hoping this neighbor might know something about where Max had gone. So, the more jovial they could be, the better. They'd talked a few times, about sports and politics, not much more.

Jim was out watering his lawn this morning, then he saw him walk over to start watering some of the plants along Max's driveway. Nobody else was there, so tis might be the perfect time to pry some information from him. In a stealth like manner, he popped out onto the sidewalk, as if he'd been there the whole time, and started walking up the driveway where Jim stood in his flip flops.

He pulled out his keys and flipped to the one he knew was the one for the current lock. Jim stopped his watering, looking at him with a suspicious frown.

"Hey, Jim, got lawn duty I see." Jeffrey said with a smile that hurt his head.

The frown slowly started to turn into a smile. "Oh, yeah, Jeffrey isn't it?" Jim said in final recognition of who he was talking to. "I didn't know you knew Max."

"Of course, you do, you saw me at the wedding." *Dumb fuck*, Jeffrey thought. Well, maybe it's a good thing he doesn't remember who I am. "Friend of the family."

Jim furrowed his brows in thought. "Yeah, yeah, I saw you there. You were in your dress greens, weren't you?"

He nodded and then looked down at his feet. "Such a shame what happened to his wife." Jeffrey shook his head, hoping to stir up sympathy.

"Yeah, he's had a hard time of it. Then there's the crazy guy threatening him too. What is this world coming to?" Jim shuffled his feet.

"Good question. Hey, let me go grab this stuff Max asked me to send over to him." He hoped by showing Jim he had access to Max's house it would build Jim's confidence in him. "I'll be right back."

Jim watched him as he went straight to the front door and opened without any trouble. Jeffrey had to figure out in a hurry what would look important. Grabbing some papers out of the office, he saw a small box on the shelf with a lock on it. Looked important enough to him. As he turned, a pain shot through his head, but he couldn't stop now. He had to work through it.

He felt one of his episodes about to come on. He stopped short when he saw the dark shadow of dried blood on the carpet in front of the couch. As if in a slow silent movie, he saw a cloud rise from the floor and start to form into a shape. Coming toward him, he saw the faint outline of his beloved Anna. He stared hard at the image, praying this was just another hallucination. Beside her, floating in air, suspended by nothing, the medal he'd given her as a reminder of who he was came to him and dropped to the desk beside him with a clinking sound. Her image disappeared as quickly as it had appeared. Leaving only the medal as proof this had really happened.

Grabbing it, he stuffed it into his jacket pocket, and rushed toward the front door. He had to get the hell out of here. Sweat had begun to pour down his back. He needed to get some air. As he came back out to the front porch, Jeffrey swiped a quick hand over his forehead, and walked out to where Jim was still watering the flowering plants.

He hoped he was right in thinking Jim knew where Max had gone. He started searching through his pockets, pulling out receipts and slips of paper, then shoving them back into his pockets. "Looks like I forgot his address. Must have left it on my kitchen table."

Making a show of it he transferred the items he held to his other arm, and searched through his other pockets, turning up nothing.

"Damn, that's a hell of a long way to have to go back for his address. I was on my way out to the VA to visit an old friend," he said making up lie after lie. He started to walk away, then looked over his shoulder to Jim. "You wouldn't happen to have Max's address, would you?"

Jim looked at him a moment, as if weighing his options, then tossed the hose down. "Yeah, hold on a minute." He shuffled off toward his own home and came back with a folded notepaper.

Jeffrey glanced down at the address. It was only a PO Box. But it was one step closer than he'd been before. At least now he knew where he was headed and how much money he had to come up with to get there. He didn't know how big a city Maple Valley was, but now all he had to do was figure out exactly where he was hiding out.

"Thanks, man, I owe you one. See you at the VFW?"

"Sure thing." Jim said picking up the watering hose again.

As Jeffrey walked down the pathway toward the sidewalk, he mumbled to himself, "Dumb fuck!"

Chapter 8

As Lauren drove to work the next day, her thoughts moved back to her afternoon with Max. It's not like she hadn't already gone over every inch of the conversation with a microscope a zillion times already. Maybe this time she would remember something she hadn't before.

He hadn't answered any of her questions about Anna. For most, that would bring up more questions about his involvement with her death. But, for Lauren, she had to go with her gut feeling. She knew in her heart he was innocent. She sensed the deep hurt he felt when she'd brought up her name. A pain so intense the sincerity couldn't be questioned. He couldn't possibly have been responsible for this Anna's death.

She chuckled to herself. After all, even Anna had told her she could trust him. The problem was, Lauren didn't know whether that pertained to everything, or if it only meant she could trust he didn't have anything to do with the murder? At the time, her intent with the question to spirit had more to do with the vision she'd seen of the murder scene. She'd learned from Kathryn, spirit knows what you mean and answers accordingly, and not necessarily how you pose the question. So, until she had time to ask more questions, she would interpret the answer as Max had nothing to do with the murder. On a personal level, she would trust her feeling about him and see what unfolded from here.

Oh, lord, he asked me on a date. A nervous tightening at the pit of her stomach caused her to take in a slow, even breath. How was she going to handle a date? What would she do, and for goodness sakes, what would she wear? She hadn't been on a date in well over a decade.

She couldn't think of it as a date, she'd to think of it as two friends just going out to enjoy something that they loved. A light of excitement entered into his eyes whenever they spoke about music. This might be the chance she needed to find out more about why it was so important to him. She felt deep down there was more to this story. A man, who enjoyed the symphony as much as she did, didn't come around every day.

No, this is a first, she thought with a grin. *But a date, oh no!*

Anguished by the thought they may end up in a situation where he might want to take her to bed, she'd been uncomfortable not knowing how to accept the compliment he'd given her. He seemed to be sincere. His eyes had no hint of criticism at all.

There was no question he wanted to end up in bed with her. *It isn't time*, she thought nervously. *He can't see me naked, not yet, not like this!*

What had bothered her so much was his change in approach. He'd startled her when he looked at her in that way. Like a hungry wolf about to devour his dinner. She'd seen the look before. It reminded her of her past bad relationships.

At first, she couldn't help but think, *"Here it is starting again. First they notice your full figure, and then they act on it, because they figure you are an easy target. Finally, they get tired of you and toss you away like you never existed."*

So, regrettably, she'd acted on what she thought he'd meant. Reacting in the way she'd learned in the past by voicing the reason for criticism about her own self-worth before hearing it come from someone else.

But then she'd realized he didn't deserve to be slashed to the ground like her former husbands. He hadn't done anything more than give her an off-handed compliment at first. It wouldn't do any good to blame him for her past problems. And yet she was troubled by his actions.

Was he following the same pattern as the rest of them? Was he just after her body for a quick release and playful bout of romance? Would it wear off like all the others had done?

What bothered her even more was his words had changed to something much more. In not so many words, he'd spoken of love and commitment. She didn't know why, but she almost believed his heartfelt words. Words making her believe in the impossible. But her mind was quick to question the plausibility of such a thing.

Did he really believe there was something between them? Could this be more than just a casual physical attraction between two people? What would happen if this turned into something more serious? Is it possible a man like Max could really find her attractive? This could turn out just as disastrous as her other relationships. Only this time she wasn't sure she could handle the pain of someone using her and then leaving again.

She parked the car in a space not far from Building B where her class was held every Thursday evening. She absently pulled the things she needed from the back seat and closed the door, her thoughts still pondering over Max. She walked for a bit trying to figure out how all this was making her feel. Luckily she was early, so she didn't have to bother with small talk with students or fellow teachers. Out of the corner of her eye she caught a butterfly fluttering around the red Rhododendron bush at the corner of her building.

She stopped and watched for a moment as is touched down on several of the blooms, then landed to rest, its beautiful wings spread out wide. This made Lauren smile. This must be Anna. The unusual Zebra markings reminded her she needed to look up this beautiful creature to find out its origin. She wondered if she could tie it somehow to Anna, to prove it was her.

"I sure wish you could help me out," Lauren said to the butterfly as it flew away.

Should she trust Max and his words of love?

No, not yet.

She hadn't seen anything yet to prove his words to be true. She would wait and see what this man was really all about first.

Familiar words popped into her head, and she smiled.
Thank you little one for reminding me, Lauren thought.
Above all, she would trust in herself.

****

Lauren heard the gravel sputtering under the tires of Rita's SUV as she pulled up the long driveway. As she came out to the front porch, the sun was shining down through the beautiful maple and birch trees, their leaves fluttering softly in the gentle wind. Rita hopped out, and then bent down quick to peer closely at the side of her shiny red Escalade. Lauren could hear Rita muttering as she rubbed something on the back panel.

Grateful Rita had come over the first chance she'd had Lauren knew of anybody, Rita wouldn't let her do anything to bad to mess this up. They'd talked at length about Max, and without her even having to tell Rita, she'd guessed this was not your run of the mill date. Even though she questioned herself, she could tell this was different somehow.

"Hi! You made it." Lauren said as Rita came up the front steps.

"As you know, no small feat, girlfriend," Rita exclaimed. "The twins were on a rampage this morning...again." She wrapped her arms around Lauren, looking curiously around. "Hey, looks like this handyman of yours is doing a great job. I'm not afraid of falling into any holes this time."

"He's been working hard to get all the safety items done first," Lauren confirmed as she pulled out of the hug. She didn't know why, but for some reason she felt proud for Max in that moment, knowing he was doing such a good job. "It's really starting to look nice, isn't it?"

Rita nodded walking to one side of the wrap around porch, looking toward the back of the house. Lauren was amused as she watched her friend walk quickly over to the other side of the porch to do the same, but knew she wouldn't see much as there was a huge Japanese Lilac tree impeding any clear view to the back.

"Ok, so where is he?"

Lauren laughed. "No beating around the bush for you."

"I'm here on a mission, my friend. There's no way I'm leaving this choice to date or not date up to you. You haven't had the best of luck so far."

Lauren grinned. She really didn't need convincing. What she needed was another female's support, with her best friend's perspective.

"For sure, that's why I called you." Lauren bent down and picked up a stray marker that must have fallen out of Max's tool belt. "Max went out to get more supplies. The railings and a few boards need to be replaced on the back staircase."

Rita placed her hands on her hips. "Well, when will he be back?"

"Soon," Lauren giggled. Coming back to the reason she'd called her friend to come all the way out, she felt the weight of her concerns wash over her again. "But really, I need your help. I can't figure out what to do. Maybe I should just call the whole thing off."

"No way!" Rushing forward, Rita took her by the arm and started into the house. "I haven't even met him and I can tell if you're this worried he must be worth being worried about. Let me work my magic, and I'll have you looking your best."

"Oh, thanks a lot. I guess that means there's work to be done."

"You said it, not me," Rita shot back.

Their banter back and forth continued all the way up the stairs to Lauren's bedroom as they began the daunting task of going through every stitch of clothing she owned. Most of which were bought for the purpose of her classroom wardrobe. Black, brown and grey made up the majority of her outfits, with an occasional dark blue or maroon thrown in for some color.

She really hadn't had any reason to try and dress up. Her figure didn't need flaunting. In her eyes everyone knew what she looked like underneath. There was no reason to point it out to them. She'd lost a good portion of the weight she'd put on after Evan had left her. But there was still a long way to go. If she didn't watch it though, she could still hear him telling her how unattractive she was to him.

"What am I supposed to wear Rita?' Lauren insisted pulling clothes out of her closet then tossing them on the bed, the floor, and over the chair in the corner of the room. "I don't have anything to wear!"

Rita, who had been watching in silence, held up a classic navy-blue suit and a pair of navy pumps. "This is...nice?" she exaggerated.

Lauren's gasp of exasperation as she rolled her eyes had Rita tossing it onto the bed without further question.

"Are you kidding? I'd look like an old spinster who'd paid for the escort on my arm."

"Good one," Rita snorted out with a laugh as she rummaged through some of the clothes on the end of the bed. "If you ask me, I don't know how you wear any of these."

Lauren turned to see Rita viewing herself in the full length mirror. Dressed in her usual flamboyant style, her neon-pink Capri pants showed off her slim long legged build. The tips of her toes peeking through a pair of Gucci sandals had been painted to match the color of her pants. While the electric green tank top displayed tanned skin and her voluptuous curves over a tiny waist. To Lauren she was a picture of perfection, even if she did have somewhat of a gaudy choice in the colors she chose. Nobody would ever guess she was the mother of three boisterous children and been married for twenty years.

"You need to toss most of these clothes out. They're all so dull, and believe me they don't do your figure any justice at all." Rita ruffled through the items they'd already tossed to the floor. "I don't understand why you don't just go buy yourself something new. You deserve it. Treat yourself."

Lauren smiled absently with a half hearted nod as she brought a flared black skirt up to her waist. "I know. I just can't do it right now."

She knew Rita's financial means to buy anything she wanted, anytime she wanted, clouded her ability to see why she couldn't even buy one thing without planning first. Lauren wished she could afford to buy a closet full of new clothes, but also knew Josh needed new jeans and another pair of tennis shoes, too. The last time she'd bought anything new for herself was the blue suit she'd used for her interview to become a faculty member at the community college.

Rita reached out and grabbed Lauren's hand with her beautifully manicured fingers. "Good God, when was the last time you had a manicure? Oh, this just won't do, you've got to start taking care of yourself honey."

Embarrassed, Lauren pulled her hand away and hid it behind her back. She was right of course. How could she even imagine Max would be attracted to her looking like this? She certainly didn't want him to regret having asked her out. She seriously began to ponder whether she could spend the money to buy a new dress for the night out.

"Where is he?" Rita paced over to the window. "I can't wait to set eyes on this hunk you keep talking about." She looked back at Lauren amidst the pile of clothes on her bed. "This bad boy better not keep me waiting. I've got to see what all this fuss is about."

As if willing it to happen, the sound of tires on the gravel driveway could be heard from the open bedroom window. In anticipation they both waited for the driver to get out of the truck that pulled up next to Rita's flashy red SUV. Lauren grinned when she heard Rita's quick intake of air as they watched him stand up and stretch his back, his brawny muscles flexing.

"Hey, is that the stud?" Rita asked excitedly as she peered out the window. "Oh momma!" She confirmed for herself before Lauren could answer her.

They watched Max carry several large pieces of wood on his right shoulder, his left hand filled with a couple of bags and a can of stain. He easily handled all of the items, the muscles of his chest rippling under his black T-shirt. The waves in his hair curled wildly over his head as a breeze blew against his face. The tone of his skin was enhanced by the slight flush of exertion, making him look unquestionably sexy.

He came back to the truck to grab something off the front seat, and when he turned back around he glanced up and caught them both staring down at him. With a grin that lit up his face, he gave them a little wave of his hand. Giggling like school girls, they both pulled back away from the window at the same time, bumping into each other, which made them burst out in laughter.

"Yes, that's Max," Lauren sighed. Every time she saw him the nerves in her stomach would jump around like Mexican jumping beans. Turning, she pulled Rita into a hug, and gushed, "He is a hunk, isn't he?"

Rita rolled her eyes and said dreamily. "Honey, if you don't sweep him up, I'm going to have to snatch him up and tell David to take a hike."

Suddenly, the sound of Max's tenor voice came wafting through the open window. They both stood perfectly still, as the

Italian words were sung with fervor. Though unrecognizable by either one of them, there was no doubt this was a love song he knew well. The magnificence of his voice settled over them like a warm soft blanket. Lauren had never heard anything so beautiful.

"Tell me why you haven't jumped his bones?" Rita put her hands on her hips. "I'd be on him in a heartbeat."

"Rita!" Lauren exclaimed, shaking her head.

Dramatically Rita grabbed Lauren by the arms and began hoping up and down like a teenager. "This is the guy. I know it. I can feel it!"

"What are you talking about?" Lauren said laughing at her friend.

"You know how I can tell things sometimes? This is the one for you. I can feel it in my heart. He is your man, the one you have been waiting for all this time."

"Rita, you haven't even met him. You can't possibly know that." Lauren shook her head. But her interest was peaked. Rita did have an uncanny way of predicting when a couple would end up together.

"I know, I know, but you've got to trust me. I know about these things. Remember Katy and Donald, and Theresa and Justin? I knew they were made for each other the first minute I laid eyes on them." Animated, Rita excitedly ran over to grab her purse from the chair. "Come on, let's go. We're going shopping. You've got to get something new for Friday night, something daring and provocative. Something that's going to knock his socks off."

"Rita, I can just find something I already have." Partly laughing, Lauren turned to pick up a dress she'd thrown across the end of the bed. "Besides, he's probably just feeling sorry for me since he's never seen me go out."

"No chance my dear. You are going to get something new and amazing to show him what you are made of. Besides, if that's all it is, then at least it will be a chance for you to get out and enjoy yourself."

Grabbing Lauren by the hand Rita pulled her out of the closet and shoved her though the bedroom door. All the while trying to convince Lauren she needed to do exactly what she was telling her, Rita continued to nudge her until they'd reached the bottom of the stairs where Lauren ran directly into Max's chest.

He reached out and steadied Lauren on her feet. "*Attenta, bellissima,*" the Italian rolling quickly off his tongue. "Came up front to find out what all the commotion was about."

Rita bent down and whispered in Lauren's ear, "That voice, oh my God, that voice is delicious."

Max looked back and forth between them, a curious smile spreading across his face. Lauren had seen this look before, and she had to admit herself, the two of them did seem like an odd pair. Not many would match the two of them together as friends.

"Hello there handsome!" Rita said with a flirtatious laugh.

Lauren couldn't blame her when she sensed Rita's heart jump a beat when Max gave her a warm smile, his distinct features outlined by his dark intense eyes.

"Hello yourself." Max replied, with what Lauren hoped only mimicked the played up seductive suggestion in Rita's voice. Quizzically he looked her friend over taking in the vibrant colors and the upswept curls of blond hair tumbling over her back.

She is definitely a sight to see, Lauren thought, patiently waiting to be released from his hold. Her own heart was giving a tremendous beat as he continued his comfortable hold of her against his chest.

"Maybe, I should let you two get to know each other." She stepped away from Max.

Rita gave her a nudge and a wink, which was a sign that she was going to have a little fun. It helped knowing her friend's playful seductive manner was all a game. They'd done this many times in college just to see how serious the approaches of men were about their friends. She tried hard to dismiss the playful message in her words, though it did rub a raw nerve this time. Lauren looked again at Max, wondering if his reaction was truly as playful, or if he meant he was truly interested in her. She felt a wash of relief as he glanced back down at her with a perplexed look as if trying to figure out what she was thinking.

He does care.

"Are you going to introduce me to this gorgeous man or what?" Rita asked with a low sultry laugh, offering a hand to him.

"This is Max DeAngelo. He's helping us fix up the house. " Lauren's outward casual answer was meant to dismiss the inner jealousy she'd begun to feel as Max took Rita's hand and lifted it to his lips.

Rita rolled her eyes at Lauren in exaggeration, raising her other hand to her heart as if it were fluttering out of her chest at his attentions. Lauren shook her head with a laugh. The dramatics of her friend were unquestionably humorous at times.

"And this is my flirtatious friend Rita Madson, who is married and has three children." Lauren wrinkled her nose at her friend.

"You are always such a party pooper Lauren, I thought maybe I could get Max to come back in the study and we could get to know each other a little better," she intimated with her throaty bedroom laugh.

"Nice to meet you Rita. As inviting as that sounds, I don't believe I'm interested in getting my nose broken," Max returned as he let go of her hand.

"Honey, David wouldn't hurt a fly, but he might give it a valiant try when it comes to me." Rita looked Max over once more, shaking her head. "I'm afraid my David wouldn't measure up to a fine specimen of a man like you."

Max appeared to be humbled as he grinned and turned toward Lauren. "What are you ladies up to this fine afternoon?"

Rita grabbed Lauren's hand and began pulling her toward the door. "We are going shopping. You are not going to recognize this woman when she comes back. Be prepared, it's going to be a transformation."

Lauren looked over her shoulder at Max. "Help me!" she moaned.

Max furrowed his brows as he watched them both. "I kind of liked her the way she was."

"Oh, isn't he sweet," Rita gushed. "Don't worry, she'll be stunning."

Lauren grabbed her purse from the end table and sent an equally fearful look his way. "Just lock up if we aren't back before you need to leave. Josh has his keys, but I should be back before he gets home."

Laughing and carrying on as they got into Rita's SUV, Rita stopped and looked at Lauren as she started the engine. "Girlfriend, that man could be the cover page in the next Beefcake calendar!"

Lauren sobered up and looked down at her clasped hands. She glanced back up to her friend with a huge grin, "I know."

****

Jeffrey sat in his car at the corner of 4th street, watching the house on the corner where Max's parents lived. He'd gotten the address from the list he found in the closet where Anna had kept wedding invitations and memoirs of what Jeffrey considered was the worst day of his life. Though, he couldn't remember much of it, his brain had been in a fog the whole day. Nothing had made sense to him. He didn't know why he'd been forced to wear a tie, but she'd insisted, and he could never say 'no' to his Anna. She should never have married Max. He'd taken her away from him.

Rubbing the pain from his eyes, Jeffrey straightened up fast when he saw the front door open. Both Celeste and Rudolfo came out, each carrying an item to go into the recycling bin. Celeste began rummaging around for something in the purse on her arm as she spoke to Rudolfo. Jeffrey couldn't make out what they were saying, though it seemed to be a deep discussion. Rudolfo shook his head, which produced a stern look from Celeste. He looked down at his feet, then up to the sky, as if asking for help as Celeste continued to talk. He nodded in agreement and took the keys Celeste held out for him. They both got into their SUV and pulled out of the driveway.

"Bingo!" Jeffrey said out loud. "It's about time."

He'd been sitting there all morning, waiting for them to leave. After devising several ways to go about this, he'd determined going in, when neither of them was home would be the best. That way if he made any noise, there wouldn't be as much of a chance in being discovered.

As they passed his car, Jeffrey turned away to look as if he were searching for something in his passenger seat, not wanting to be seen by either of the two. They kept driving, so he must have avoided any recognition. Making sure nobody was in their front yards, or walking down the sidewalk, he slowly he got out of the car, checking his pockets for what he needed. His casual gait, as he went across the street, wouldn't have looked like a man about to break into someone's home. As he passed the house on his right side, he sauntered across the back yard along the tree line. This way he could sneak into the man door at the side of the garage without anyone seeing him walk up the front lawn.

Testing the door knob, he smiled as the door opened easily. Slipping through the opening he snapped the door shut behind him. Sunlight streamed through the windows at the side making it easy to find what he was looking for once his eyes adjusted to the light.

He'd done his research to figure out the best way to make this happen. It wasn't too hard to figure out, once he'd found Rudolfo was a carpenter by trade. Just as he'd imagined a retired carpenter might have, there appeared to be several small projects in different phases of completion. Paint and cans of stain lined the back wall of the garage, a few sitting beside the projects being work on. Pieces of a birdhouse cut from plywood were stacked on the workbench, not yet ready to be assembled. The door to a cabinet lay on top waiting to be repaired.

He couldn't believe his luck as his gaze rested on the bentwood rocking chair in the middle, sanded and ready for stain. On the floor was a can of stain, paint brush and sponges on top. Next to them sat an empty container and a can of paint thinner to clean the brushes when the project was finished. This was going to be easier than he'd thought.

If this doesn't bring him back I don't know what will.

Opening the top to the paint thinner, he then reached into his pocket for the small container of clear liquid. Careful not to splash, he poured the liquid into the paint thinner can, and quickly closed the lid over the top before the toxic gases could escape. He got a slight whiff of the concoction and his vision blurred for a moment.

As he grabbed onto the back of the rocking chair for support he heard the engine of a vehicle shut off followed by two car doors and realized they'd come back sooner than he'd expected. Jeffery stumbled to the side door and opened it slowly. The fresh air he breathed in helped to clear his head. He peered out toward the driveway and was glad to hear them both entering through the front door. As quickly as he could, he ran to the far corner of the backyard with the intention of disappearing into the woods.

"You there, what are you doing?" shouted the homeowner in his heavy Italian accent. "Come back here."

Jeffery knew better than to turn around, so with his back still turned he slipped through the trees. Far behind him, the snap and crack of dried tree branches as Rudolfo attempted to catch him, reminded him he'd been trained to escape, and could easily hide where he couldn't be seen. He'd worn his camouflage jacket for just this purpose. He ducked down behind a large fir tree, and dropped to his knees, crawling on his stomach until he reached the deep ravine at the backside of their home. Sliding down the undergrowth, he clung to the side of the hillside out of view from above.

"Rudolfo, come back here. He might have a gun. I've called the police," he heard Celeste call out frantically from the tree line.

Rudolfo had reached the ledge and was walking up and down just above Jeffrey's head. He peered up through the roots of the overhanging trees and saw Rudolfo searching the other side of the chasm.

Rooky mistake, Jeffrey thought.

He felt a deep pang in his head, sharp enough to have him shout out. But he kept his mouth shut and ground his teeth together. Droplets of sweat were pouring down his neck as the pain got sharper. Visions started popping into his head, and he had to try to hold on best he could. He began to see himself in the jungle back in Dong Xoai, Vietnam, heavy mortar and small arms flying past him everywhere. He could almost hear the screams and shouts from his unit members.

He blinked his eyes furiously to make the visions go away, reminding himself he was safe now. But, it would be dangerous for him to go into one of the full hallucinations he'd been having lately. This wasn't the time or place. He needed to get out of there fast. If the wife had called the police, they would be there soon, and then he'd be in a whole mess of trouble.

Thankfully, the husband turned and started back toward the house. Jeffrey could hear him stop a couple of times, and imagined he was turning around to see if there was any movement. So he waited. He waited until he could hear him and his wife's frantic words. Slowly, he began to move along the dirt wall just below the ledge. As he reached the road, he peered up toward the house, out of view, and saw nobody was there. He threw his leg up over the side and hauled himself up from the ravine. Staying low to the ground he went to the edge where the road met the gap. Flashes of red and blue lights on the front lawn meant the police had arrived, but he didn't see any officers scoping the place yet. So, he turned the opposite way and went up the hill away from the house, moving as quick as he could.

He'd taken the precaution of swapping his plates with a junk yard car, so nobody could track him that way. Until the commotion had settled down he couldn't go back to his car. He would have to come back for it later. So he walked, and walked, battling the pain seeping into his brain. Walking, in what seemed to be circles, he finally settled in on a vacant home with a small shed out back he'd seen on his drive earlier that morning. Breaking the lock on the shed door, he found a corner to hide in the dark—and wait.

****

As Lauren put the final touches to her make-up, she thought of her son. He'd been showing his concern for her all afternoon. Asking if she needed him to do anything for her and offering to do the laundry so she wouldn't have to worry about it today. She took in a deep breath and shook her head in awe. Josh was such a good young man, down to his very soul, and she was proud to know it had been as a result of a lot of hard work and the bond they'd formed between the two of them. She didn't know what she would have done if he hadn't been there for her to care for and love all these years.

Turning to look in the mirror again, she gave a little chuckle. Yes, she had to say she looked damn good tonight. The dress and the hours she'd spent at the beauty salon today had all been worth it. There was no mistaking, she definitely looked feminine. All the way from the subtle red polish on her fingers and toes, to the henna the stylist had talked her into running through her hair. She was determined to look her best for Max tonight. And perhaps she would do some things she wouldn't normally do.

She was feeling rather feisty and wanted to see just how far she could entice Max into wanting her. She knew what she wanted, and right now it was for Max to want her back. Perhaps she would get lucky, if she allowed it to go that far. She hadn't decided if tonight was the night or not. Like he'd said they were heading in that direction. Sooner or later they might end up in bed. She wasn't sure if she was ready yet, all she knew was she wanted this feeling of utter thrill and passion to continue as long as it could before it ran dry. But for now, she sure would have fun enticing him tonight.

Meanwhile, Josh sat on the edge of his mother's bed waiting for her to come out of the bathroom. *She's been in there forever. What's the big deal? He's just the handyman fixing the house. Don't know why she's going to all this trouble over a stupid date with this guy.*

Finally he heard the door opening and his mother stepped out. She put one arm up to touch the door frame, the other hand she put on her hip in a sassy Mae West fashion.

"What do you think? Am I looking good or what?"

She'd gone into the bathroom to take a shower and get ready for the evening looking like she normally did, in her baggy shirt and jeans, and had come out looking like a movie star. Josh made a whistling sound and got up to take a good look at his mother. This was not the woman he knew. She'd brought her hair up to the top of her head, letting the long curls cascade down her back in a wild profusion of ringlets. The dress she'd picked out was a black number which made him look at her in a totally different way then he ever had before. She was definitely an attractive woman. He didn't even want to think what some other guy would be thinking about the way she looked tonight.

"Mom, you certainly are a sight." He stood to take her extended hand in his, twirling her around in a circle. "I'm going to have a talk with Max and give him the low down on the rules of this house when it comes to dating," he said with a laugh.

Lauren bent and gave her son a kiss on the cheek. "That is so sweet, but I think I can take care of myself. I'm a big girl."

Giving her a big hug Josh resigned himself to the fact she was an adult and could take care of herself. But that was not going to stop him from telling Max what was what regarding his mother. He needed to let him know if he even thought about hurting her, he would have to deal with him. Even though he might not be able to take him on himself he had a few friends who would help rough him up if he were to do anything wrong.

The sound of Max pulling into the driveway had his mom rushing to the mirror to take another look at herself.

"Oh dear, there he is now. Go down and let him in and tell him I'll be down in a minute."

"Alright Mom. You look fine. Don't worry so much. I'll see you in the morning. Robert and I are going to watch horror flicks and order pizza. Have a great time and don't do anything you wouldn't want me to do!" As he went to go out the door, he stopped and turned back around. "Mom, I love you."

Lauren had turned to take one last look in the mirror before going down to meet her Friday night date. Her hand stopped mid-way up to fix a sprig of curls wildly dancing around her face. Her eyes met her son's in the mirror.

"Oh stop that now, you are going to make me cry!" She turned to face him and blew him a kiss. "I love you too sweetheart."

Acknowledging she knew what he meant from his heart he nodded his head and turned to go downstairs to have some words with Max.

Downstairs Josh opened up the door and stood on the front porch watching Max park his car next to his Mom's. *Nice car*, he thought with a hint of male acceptance. The gold Jaguar gleamed in the early evening sunset as if having just been pulled off the showroom floor. Max stepped out and took a long look at the set, grim look on Josh's face. He walked slowly toward Josh not intimidated.

"Evening Josh. Your mother ready to go?" He asked lightly giving him a nod of his head. Josh noted he also had dressed for the occasion in a dark charcoal gray suit and what looked to be a black silk shirt and tie. The handkerchief showing in his left-hand breast pocket matched his tie and had been meticulously folded to show just the right amount of color to be considered stylish. His shoes were made of soft Italian black leather topping off the whole look as being one of great style and elegance.

If the car hadn't been enough, the man's style impressed Josh to take a little different look at how he would approach him with what he needed to say. He nodded his head slowly showing his acceptance in his eyes. "Just about. She told me to tell you she would be down in a minute."

Max didn't take the first move to go up the front stairs. Josh appreciated the respect he was showing.

"Mom doesn't do this often," Josh said slowly, not exactly sure how to tell him what he had on his mind. He paused and then decided to just put it on the line. "She is really special, and she doesn't deserve to have her heart broken. Don't do anything stupid or I'll have to take care of you, my way," he said with a touch of defiance.

Max listened quietly. "Josh, what happens between your Mom and I is just that. It belongs between us and only us. But I will tell you, I have no intention of doing anything to hurt her. I promise. She is very special and means a great deal to me, too."

He paused and put out his hand to offer his word. Josh took it tentatively, but shook firmly to show he meant what he'd said.

"And I certainly don't want to have to deal with you on any terms other than friendship. I don't think this old man could stand up to you if you were to want to kick my butt," he said with a laugh in his voice and a gleam in his eye.

Josh took his hand from his and smiled, feeling as if he'd gotten his point across. "You can bet on it old man." As he went on past Max toward the path in the woods to Robert's house, he turned around running backwards and yelled back, "Mom said to go on in, she will meet you downstairs."

Max raised his hand to Josh in acknowledgment and turned to go up the stairs to wait for Lauren in the front room. She'd begun to do some subtle changes to the room. The walls had yet to be painted, but the windowsills had been sanded down to the original oak, where she was going to stain them with a clear finish. A can of paint in a light ethereal green sat next to a roller and pan. She'd pulled up the old worn carpet to reveal a beautiful oak floor which needed to be sanded and finished as well. There were swatches of colors and prints hanging across the chairs in different shades of greens and browns. He could see the evolving picture she'd told him as her dream for the room.

He heard the click of heels on the stairs and turned to watch as Lauren came down to greet him. In the shadows of the unlit stairway he could see the definite shape of a woman coming down the stairs. She slowly came into view at the bottom step in the light from the front windows filtering in the evening light, not with brightness, but with a dreamy sort of haze. Max could barely keep his jaw from dropping down to the floor as he gazed at Lauren. The woman who stood before him was not the gentle subdued woman he'd begun to care deeply for, but the picture of a vibrant seductively sexy woman who was confident about her self and the view she presented.

The gown she wore was stunning to say the least. The black satin material ran down her body in a sleek sensuous manner, revealing all of the curves she possessed. The billowing neckline curved gently in soft waves as it fell softly from her shoulders showing just enough skin to tempt his senses. Suggestive long black sheer sleeves were anchored at the wrist to reveal her beautiful hands, the skirt sweeping down to her ankles. There was a flounce discreetly rippled around the hips just enough to hide what she needed to hide, but the slit up the side of the leg came up far enough hinting for a view of the treasures hidden beneath. She wore a pair of high-heeled sling back black sandals showing just the tips of her painted toes, just high enough to enhance the shape of her leg through the slit in the skirt.

    She smiled coyly and turned in a circle for him to get the full view, the low V-cut back of the dress peeking from beneath her hair. Max was speechless. Before him was the vision of a goddess. He stood perfectly still in awe of the vision before him. She was a goddess, disguising herself in her day-to-day attire as having no shape and no thrills to entice a man. But this was a beautiful and abundantly curved woman standing before him now. Her hair pulled up to the top of her head spilling wild curls down her back, almost begging him to pull down the clips and to run his fingers through its silkiness. The color was a little different though. It seemed to have much deeper reddish tones than he could remember before. But at the moment he couldn't remember much of anything. This was like looking at a new woman, one he'd never seen before.

    Obviously pleased with the response she'd gotten, Lauren sauntered over to Max who continued to stare. Her scent came over him gently, enticingly as she put her arm up to curl her finger in the hair at the back of his neck.

    "Going my way big boy?"

    Max could barely speak, his throat had become terribly dry and he felt like heat had begun to pour off of his skin. "Ah, *ma belle*, you are a most beautiful sight. And if you keep that up we won't be going anywhere."

    His arm slipped around her waist and he drew her slowly against him. His eyes looking deep within hers, he brushed his lips against hers, so lightly it felt like butterfly wings. Lauren's breath caught in a hitch.

    Knowing he had to step away quickly or there would be no date to speak of, he held out his hand to take hers.

    "Shall we go *bella?* We are going to be late if we don't get started."

Chapter 9

The drive into Seattle was a pleasant one. Max talked lightly of some of the sights he'd been able to get out to see since he arrived in the area. They talked of the Pike Place Market and how fun it was to watch the vendors showing their wares, especially the fresh fish market tossing fish back and forth in gay revelry for their customer's delight.

Before long they'd parked across the street from the Seattle Opera House and were walking in the night air across the sidewalk to their destination. The night was clear and beautifully warm, with a light breeze coming from of the water. Max reached out and held Lauren's hand as they walked in the dusky night air. Her heart melted in pure enjoyment, feeling an intense security in the warmth of his hand in hers. They walked hand in hand toward the opera house, silently enjoying each other's company.

"So, I never did ask you why you wanted to come to the Symphony," Lauren said lightly, remembering she'd meant to ask him earlier.

Max smiled. "I have an appreciation for a great many things," he said with hesitation. "There is a lot about me you do not know, *bella*. I am not just the simple carpenter you might expect."

Lauren turned to look into his face as they approached the steps leading up to the open doors to the ticket booths.

"Yes, I know," she acknowledged. "But how can I learn if you won't tell me?"

"You have only to ask, Lauren," he replied, returning her gaze. She could feel a million questions stirring up to be asked.

So simple, yet so complex, Lauren thought.

He took his fingers from her hand and brought the hand up to settle in the crook of his elbow in support as they went up the stairs. Placing his other hand over hers, he led her up to the entrance.

"Do I? Then you better watch out, I have more questions than you might be able to answer!" Jokingly she squeezed his arm with her hand for impulse.

But when she looked up into his eyes this time they were swimming with uncertainty. She suddenly felt from him the same type of fear he'd shown before, questions needing to be answered, and doubts to be resolved. Then it was as if he shut the door tight. They were still there, but he stuffed them back down. If they were going to get to know each other, sooner or later he was going to have come clean with what he was dealing with in his life which made him fearful. This she knew for sure.

"But, let's wait to later for all those questions. I want to enjoy the evening with all of its wonders, including the beautiful woman on my arm," he said tightening his hand over hers. "There will always be time for questions later."

Max had gotten them front seats in the opera box above stage right. It was a perfect setting, with only a few other attendees having joined them. It was almost as if they had the whole performance to themselves. Nobody was passing by them to get to their adjoining seats. There was a full view of the whole stage without having to look over someone in front of them.

Lauren settled back in her seat to find Max had stretched out his arm behind her so she could settle into his arm close to him. Longing to turn into his arms and have him hold her there in the perfect embrace of a lover, she settled back and ventured to place her hand on his knee in a gesture of hidden intimacy she hoped he was sharing. He reached his free hand forward and grasped her hand and gave it a squeeze bringing her hand up a little further on his thigh for a more comfortable reach for them both. Lauren could feel the butterflies in her stomach flutter, in response to the unspoken bond being formed. As they waited in anticipation for the curtain to rise, she turned to find him smiling at her, a gleam in his eyes. It was as if he understood what was happening between them. There was something in his expressive eyes which showed more than desire. A flame of energy had ignited between them, with a power greater than she'd experienced before.

Sure, she was no virgin. There had been other men before him. His energy was much different than she'd ever experienced before. It seemed to shake her down to the depths of her soul. It didn't scare her in an unpleasant way. It scared her she could have such feelings dwelling so deep within her. Feelings of brazen sexuality were calling to her to throw caution to the wind and give him what he wanted. A sexuality she'd never explored before, at least not to the depths she felt would surface with him. With a small giggle of enjoyment, she settled back into his arms to savor the moment.

The music was a perfect selection of classical composers including Beethoven, Brahms and Mahler for instrumental versions of operatic love songs. Each one endearing you to the next, ending in a finale by Schumann entitled "Dichterliebe", which was worth the full admission. Its heart wrenching melody and love-laden notes made the heart race and cry out for more. By the end the entire audience was on it's feet giving heartfelt appreciation for the performance.

Three standing ovations brought another selection from the artists to play with as much feeling as the first. After the last of the curtain calls, Lauren reached down to get her clutch and instead found Max's hand. She turned to look up into his face and saw something she'd not expected. There was the glint of tears in his eyes, and when she began to question him he shook his head and pulled her down to sit again.

"Why don't we just sit here for a moment until the crowd passes, so we don't have to be hurried," he murmured in her ear.

Lauren didn't question him outwardly. She nodded her head in agreement and settled back into his arms to wait until he was ready to go.

Max's heart beat thunderously in his chest with the realization of what he'd discovered that night. He knew Lauren had questions, and at some point he needed to answer them all. How was he going to tell her what she needed to know? *There may be more things to tell than she may want to hear*, he thought with consternation. But he knew the only way was to tell her the truth and see where it led them. He would find a way to deal with it when the time came.

During the performance, the realization had hit Max hard. He had to perform again. He needed to write his music and perform again to audiences, who he now remembered had shown their appreciation just as they'd done here, in awe of this gift he'd been given. There was no doubt this was what he was meant to do. Max's heart was filled with such joy it was all he could do from jumping up and dancing.

The night had brought back to him the bliss he'd previously felt on stage. He'd sat imagining himself performing some of the soloist piano spots, and singing the beautiful words to the love songs in his own tenor voice. So moved, he'd almost stood up to sing out from the balcony.

He was not going to be able to brush this away like some unwanted burden any longer. It had been to long since he'd gotten the urge to get back onstage to perform. He'd been shocked by Anna's death into not caring about the things which meant the most to him. But now he knew it was time he broke out of this prison he'd set himself into, and become again the man he was meant to be.

It would take some time, but he was going to contact the Investigator Warner and let him know what his intentions were. There might be a need to hold off for just a short time more, but he needed to come out of hiding and take hold of what was his to claim. Nobody was going to make him hide like a coward. If this nut case wanted to kill him, let him just try.

Max was filled with such glorious triumph. He felt as if he'd won a victory—a victory worth winning. He also knew in his heart without this wonderful woman beside him he may never have broken free to overcome his entrapment.

So thankful, he held onto Lauren tightly, overjoyed by his discovery. She turned her face up to his and he caught her in a surprise kiss, with an outpour of feeling. As he lifted his lips from hers, she'd all but melted into his arms with the passionate intensity of his kiss.

Breathless, she smiled. "Goodness, remind me to let you take me out more often."

"You will be the only one I would want to have on my arm for a presentation like this." He rose from his seat and held a hand out to her. "Come, let's go enjoy a walk down at the Pier. It's much too nice a night to end so early."

****

The evening had been perfect. Lauren enjoyed herself thoroughly with Max. He was the most intriguing man she'd ever met. He was a professed carpenter, yet had an obvious wealth stream coming from somewhere. The car, the clothes, the shoes were all definitely beyond the means of a carpenter. She couldn't believe it had all come from repairing homes. But she didn't feel comfortable yet asking where he got his money.

During their walk along the Pier she'd found out quite a few things about him. Though she already knew this, he confirmed for her he had an awesome appreciation for quality and the more refined things in life. His interests were widespread including music, art, and drama. That in itself was astonishing. Most men she'd met would turn up their noses at the mere thought of attending the Symphony or going to a ballet. Max had told her any time she would like to go to see a play, or the ballet, he would be more than happy to escort her.

He'd talked about how his father, who had recently retired, was a highly renowned and brilliantly creative woodworker with a very successful business in Chicago. Max had worked with his father in some high profile custom homes, hence his knowledge of carpentry. His father's business had become one of the most requested shops known for its authentic Italian workmanship.

His mother had passed her love of music down to her children, hence his interest. Unclear in his meaning, Max had started to tell her how much he followed in his mother's footsteps. But, when Lauren asked more about this side of his life, Max changed the subject and steered her away from any further questions. There so much more to be asked, but she didn't want him to feel as if she were grilling him. The night had been too perfect.

Now, she sat beside him in the Jaguar, the sounds of Tchaikovsky's *Fifth Symphony*, Second Movement, floating over her senses as she dreamily looked out the window into the evening. Lauren could not remember a time when she'd had such a good time on a date. She'd been so worried they would be tense, or the feel of the evening would not be right. But the whole evening had been spent as if they'd been long time friends and lovers, enjoying each other's company, reveling in the awe of being together. Lauren smiled in comfort wanting to remember this night forever.

They drove in silence most of the way home. There was no need for words. It was as if it was already understood there was no need to question its existence. Max reached out and pulled Lauren's hand into his, lifting it to his lips for a kiss on the tips of her fingers. Lauren felt a tremble of excitement pass over her when his lips touched her skin. She couldn't help the quick little intake of breath when he brought her hand down to his lap. She wasn't even embarrassed when she glanced up to find he must have heard, as his lips were turned up at the corners into a grin.

"Thank you for such a lovely evening," he said, his deep voice making her heart skip a beat.

"No, thank you, Max! I don't know when I have ever had such a wonderful time on a date before," Lauren said truthfully, turning to look at Max's profile. His dark, almost perfect profile stood out against the lights flashing by from passing cars.

He seemed to be in profound thought, then as he turned briefly to meet her gaze, his smile came to her in a wave of warmth, spreading his amazing way of making her feel so comfortable.

"The night is young. How would you like to come share a drink with me at my place? I don't live very far from you, only about ten minutes around the other side of the lake. I promise not to take advantage of you, though I can't tell you the feeling isn't there," he said with a laugh.

His smile had turned to a humorous glint in his eyes. Lauren blushed knowing the full meaning of what he was saying.

This might be a chance for me to get to know you a little better, she thought. *You can always find out more about a person by the way he lives.*

"I think I would like that," she almost purred, with the contentment she felt. The earlier spunk had returned. Now was the time to see just how much he really wanted her. "But I'm not so sure I can promise I won't take advantage of you," she returned flirtatiously. Max raised his eyebrows in a cross between surprise and anticipation.

"Well, well. We will just have to see about that."

****

"Madame." Holding out his hand, Max took Lauren's hand as she got out of the car.

They'd pulled up into Max's driveway, as he'd said not too far from Lauren's house. The driveway had gone up a hill and just over the rise she saw what she could only say was the homiest looking log cabin she'd ever seen. It wasn't a large home, but it was a good size for the type of architectural style it was. From the front she could see it was all one floor, the front porch came up only a couple of steps off the ground to the front door.

As she got closer she could see the authentic old stem fir logs which had been used for the outside structure. From a large chunk of fir, a wood carved black bear crouched next to the staircase as if ready to pounce, protecting its inhabitants from unwanted guests. Flowers of all kinds happily bloomed in their place against the house in a splash of reds and orange, some pinks and white interspersed along the way. It instantly charmed her by its warmth and comfort.

"This is beautiful!" She exclaimed turning to Max.

Max said nothing he only smiled and led her up the stairs, unlocked the door and brought her into the entrance hall. To the right there was a sunken living room, royal colors mixing together in rich tones of blue and red, jade and purple. It was almost out of place from what was expected from the outside. But it was done in a tasteful way, encouraging one to lounge in its richness, drawing from its aura of luxuriant royalty.

Beyond the living room, almost as if set on a pedestal against the huge bay window looking toward the lake, stood a baby grand piano in all it's grandeur. The black sheen of its finish glimmered in the moonlight, enticing one to come play on its ivories an enchanting tune. Lauren was almost beside herself as she stood looking at the setting before her. This was not what she'd expected at all. This was the home of some famous person on the inside, not something she could see a working man, such as a carpenter, would have. But then, he wasn't just a carpenter, was he?

She turned and looked at Max as if to question if they were in the right house. In his eyes, she could see some type of war being fought. It was as if he wanted so badly to tell her something, but couldn't. Whatever it was, it was serious.

As he seemed to do more often lately, he brushed this off, too. "What, you didn't expect me to live like a King?" He smiled, leading her into the living room.

"I didn't really know what to expect. But it certainly wasn't this. This is wonderful Max. How….where…?" Lauren stumbled on the words to ask the questions forming in her mind. Leaving the words unsaid, she began looking around her at the collection of fine art which lined the walls. Moving from pictures to sculptures and then again to a collection of books sitting comfortably in a beautiful wall mounted display case, Lauren could see these were authentic collectibles not many people would have in their possession.

She turned and looked at Max, who was standing close behind her viewing her intent review of the collections. Lauren was not sure what to make of this man. He worked as a carpenter, yet lived like a king. And looked and worked comfortably in both settings. He had a smile in his eyes now, as if he must have found her reaction to be humorous. Before she could speak, he raised up his hand to prevent her from saying anything.

"Before you ask your million questions, how about if I were to get us a drink?" He grinned as he bent forward to brush his lips across her forehead.

Lauren, knowing he was pulling back for a reason, let her questions rest for the moment and decided to enjoy the feeling of just being with him. She brushed her hand up his arm, marveling in the feeling of his well-shaped muscles. This was a night for dreams and enchantments to be real. Lauren wanted to know more about this curious man, and she would find out in time. Tonight she wanted to see exactly what he was feeling for her, and now was as good a time to start as any. Brushing her curves up next to him in a sultry way, she returned the kiss by brushing her lips next to his ear and giving a low tone of agreement.

"Oh yes, I think that would be wonderful." She pulled back enough to see the darkening of his eyes with a look of surprise at her advancements, then the unquestionable mark of desire.

"Watch yourself, *mia dolce*, you play with fire." He pulled her against him, brushing his lips against her neck and nuzzling below her ear where she'd left a trail of perfume. "*Buon dio, ti voglio.*" Pulling away from her, he took a deep breath.

She had no ideas what he was saying, but the look in his eyes was one of tremendous restraint. There was no longer a question of how much he wanted her. It was how long she could keep this up without succumbing to his desires.

"Brandy is my liquor of choice. But I do have most anything you might like. What shall it be, *bella*?"

"Brandy sounds wonderful. Do you have any apricot brandy by chance?" Lauren asked tracing a finger down the front of his unbuttoned jacket, stopping just at the top of the waistband of his slacks. She could feel the twitching of his stomach muscles beneath her finger as Max snatched her hand and brought it up to his lips. He brought up his other hand and wagged a finger at her.

Lauren could see the glimmering of laughter in his eyes as he raised his eyebrow at her. "No, no, no..." he warned. He laughed out loud. "Why doesn't it surprise me you would like apricot brandy? It goes with the whole picture. You are a sweet ripe fruit waiting to be picked and sampled. You enchant me with your smile and my senses go wild when you come into a room. What is that scent you wear? You smell like an apricot orchard." Leaning in far enough to nuzzle her neck again, he let out a low moan.

"That's for me to know and you to find out!" Lauren teased.

His purposeful restraint was impressive. He pulled himself away from her and shook his head and smiled. "Fire, *mia dolce*, fire."

Not far from having to restrain her own self, Lauren sauntered across the room to the piano. Sitting down at the bench she noticed this too was not what she'd expected. There were several scores of sheet music laid haphazardly over the closed lid of the piano. But these were half written pieces of music, notes hastily written in places, scratched out bars in others. She picked up one laying on the music stand and looked at it curiously.

Having played the piano while growing up she recognized the makings of a sonata. Opening the cover to the keys she began playing the notes hesitantly, then more intently as she became more accustomed to the style. The notes which came out were reminiscent of raindrops tapping lightly on a window. Beautifully light and airy notes making her smile, and want to get up and dance around the room.

Lauren's fingers danced over the keys, bringing to life the stillness of the black notes on the page. The tempo changed from a light pattering of notes to a more intent barrage of sounds which made her think of the sudden downpours one could only relate to if you lived in Washington. But it was so much more than that. The music had an intensity and passion of a complex need, a searching of the soul. The music from the keys came to an end, as did the written notes on the page.

Having sensed Max behind her Lauren dropped her hands to her lap and drew in a deep breath. The comprehension of what this was dumbfounded her. This man was a musical genius. There was no doubt in her mind he had an unquestionable gift, a precious gift which needed to be shared. This was the kind of music to last for generations upon generations as a classic.

She lifted her eyes to meet his, and found him looking back at her with a mixture of pride and humbleness. Lauren was at a loss for words. What she felt could not be expressed. Before her stood a wonderfully gifted man, looking rakishly handsome in his Italian suit, his hair slightly mussed from the breeze on the car ride in.

"You wrote these, didn't you?" she asked laying her hand lightly on the scores of music. Without needing an answer she patted the piano bench next to her and said, "Play for me, please."

He only nodded, and handed her snifter to her. Setting his own glass down on the window seat beside him, he reached across and searched through a few unfinished sheets to find another score of music.

Lauren saw he found the one he wanted even without titles, or notations, as to which one it was, and brought it to the stand. He placed his hands on the keys and took in a deep breath and let it out.

Slowly his fingers began playing a mystical melody with notes starting slow and deep, moving into a crescendo of tones which seemed to pull Lauren from the very depths of her soul. As she listened, she could envision a spark turning into a slow moving flame, spreading into a fan of flames reaching higher and higher up to an invisible beckoning from above. She watched Max's fingers as they danced over the keys bringing forth a passion only he could bring out in this way.

Lauren could almost feel her heart begin to pound in time with the music, building faster and faster until it felt as if it would beat out of her chest. She could see he'd closed his eyes and was playing now from his heart. The notes he played feathered down to almost nothing as the piece came to an end, as if the passion had been spent and was now basking in the afterglow.

Max sat, his hands resting lightly on the keys. The feeling of pure joy Lauren had felt pouring out from him had settled into contented peace and fulfillment. He opened his eyes and turned to look at Lauren who was now looking at him in awe.

"That was the most...beautiful thing I have ever heard, " she said simply. Her heart was still pounding, a mixture of feelings running through her. She was feeling joy and pleasure, heat and passion summoned by this man's music. This wasn't just music. What he'd played was a piece of his heart and soul. This utterly complex man had the hardness of a construction worker, yet the heart of an artist. The beauty coming from within him was astounding. She could literally feel the electric energy still dancing through the air.

"That was you." Max turned and picked up his glass from the window.

Her look brought humbleness to his heart, and an urgent need to show her what had been locked away for so long. He'd needed to show her what he was feeling. She was more to him than just an attractive woman. This piece of music he'd been working on was not just a piece of music, but one he could only attribute to the feelings he was experiencing with her.

He realized at that moment he was feeling alive. This fire beginning to burn in his heart was more than just the simple attraction of a man to a woman. She made him feel like living again. He'd been dead to the world for so long with grief and depression, this woman was igniting a passion down deep inside his soul. A passion for life, love, and all the beauty the world had been waiting to share with him again.

"What did you say?" She asked in true confusion.

"I wrote that piece the other night when I could think of nothing but you."

He turned, their faces coming inches apart. He could almost feel his heart bursting out of his chest as he felt the warmth of her spreading over his body. Her breath played lightly over his cheek enticing him to taste the lips trembling before him in anticipation.

Not new to the feelings of love, he knew the physical signs of lust, but better yet knew his own signs of falling in love. What he was feeling here was more than lust. He wanted more, he wanted a woman by his side who could make him feel the way he did when he wrote this piece. He wanted someone who could understand his needs, physically, mentally and spiritually. He needed to know that this woman, who had sparked his need for life again, would want the same things.

Lauren pulled away from him, a rosy blush creeping up her cheeks as she shyly looked away. She didn't question him, though he could see in her eyes she didn't believe a word of what he'd said. He vowed to himself to show her what a truly amazing woman she was and help her to believe in herself.

Max reached up and framed her face with his hands. "You are beautiful when you blush." Placing a light kiss to her lips, he withdrew knowing he needed to slow down this burning feeling if he was going to continue to act like a gentleman.

"That was the most amazing thing I've ever heard. You are a genius. Why aren't you publishing your music?" Lauren asked leaping to her feet. "No, wait. You need to be performing. You have the most awesome delivery. You play like a professional. Why have you been hiding such a talent?" She placed her hands on her hips as if to accentuate her questions.

He wanted to tell her so badly all of the things he'd been keeping a secret. Secrets he'd been holding not just from her but from himself as well. But now was not the time. He would tell her as soon as he spoke with the inspector tomorrow. Then he would tell her all of the things she should know about him.

He rose from the bench and walked slowly down the steps into the living room. "I've dabbled at it a bit. I'm not hiding it so much as just haven't done much with it lately." He said lamely, not wanting to lie, but not able to tell the full truth.

"Max, you've got a talent that can't be pinned up. Don't you see? This is something to big to just keep hidden away. You could be bringing joy and happiness to the world. Your music is medicine to the heart and soul."

Enjoying the sound of her heartfelt joy from hearing his music, he could barely contain himself. He dropped his gaze so as not to show more than he could explain for the moment. "*Bella*, you are sweet. I appreciate your kindness."

He followed Lauren's gaze as it settled on an open drawer in a cabinet next to the fireplace. He'd left scores and scores of sheet music, just like the ones she'd found on the piano. Some were of his writing, some had been written by another hand. Lauren lifted her head and found the two framed documents on the wall above the mantle. She looked back at Max in excitement and shook her head.

He wasn't sure why he'd brought his two Master's degree diplomas, one in the Liberal Arts, the other in Music, other than the need to be reminded he'd accomplished something in his life.

"Max, you are not telling me something. What is all of this? This is not just something you idly do when you're bored. You've obviously spent a great deal of your life in mastering the art," she said pointing to the certificates. "You must work at this every chance you get. There are enough pieces here to fill several albums, let alone several performances like the one we saw tonight."

Suddenly, she turned to him. "Have you ever performed before? Do you have stage fright?"

Amused, he watched her process the questions in her mind. Ignoring her first question because it would only bring up more questions he wasn't ready to answer yet, he smiled shyly and said, "No, I don't believe I have stage fright." Wistfully thinking of all of the times he had performed, he came to stand beside Lauren and drape his arm around her shoulders.

"You have to promise me you will contact someone about your music. You have too much talent not to share with others. You could be the next contemporary Beethoven!" Lauren turned into his arms looking up into his face. "What, you don't believe me?"

In actuality, seeing her excitement like this, made him wonder what she would do when she found out what his life had been before he'd met her. Thoughts of how he was going to break the news he was an accomplished musician, with more time on stage than off, were running through his head. Would she accept it without question, or would she tell him what he could do with his lies and his stories?

But really, he'd never really lied to her, he just hadn't expounded on the truth. Would she see that? And would she accept what he had to tell her? Part of it could be proven with the newspaper clippings and articles, which had been written during the time after the murder of his wife, while the media was all aglow with the excitement of another celebrity's gruesome details, details that should have been kept hidden. He'd never wanted his lovely Anna's life to be exploited in the manner the tabloids had published, some truths, but most were untruths.

What would Lauren believe?

"I'm going to help you!" She exclaimed giving him a peck on the cheek. "Aunt Maggie knows everyone who is someone in the music business. She will know exactly who to talk to."

Knowing he had to stop this newfound excitement in helping him to find his mark in musical history, he did the only thing he could think of doing. He reached up and framed her face with his hands, looking into her exuberant eyes he smiled down at her with an almost knowing look of someone quieting a child who had discovered something new and exciting.

"Lauren, I promise to think about it. I don't know I am ready yet." *Oh, but I am more ready than you know*, he thought almost shamefully. Trying to buy some time he said, "Give me some time to think about it and I will let you know when I am ready."

"Promise you won't brush it off as being unimportant?" She questioned, the light still jumping through her beautiful green eyes.

"I promise."

Pulling her with him to the couch he sat down bringing her down next to him. Happy to see she was just as willing to snuggle up to him as continue talking, Lauren melded to his side and placed her head on his shoulder. Resting his cheek on her hair, he closed his eyes and drew in the scent which could now only be known as Lauren. There was no doubt he was beginning to fall in love with this woman. His heart began to pound a little harder at the realization.

Was this love? What he'd been feeling all night was more than just an attraction. She pulled him in ways he'd never felt before. Her pure excitement for his music had been what had tipped the weights over to love. She showed him the same excitement he felt inside for himself when he was playing his music. Her realization of his gift was so perfect it had made him realize he had also found a gift in her.

His arms tightened around her, bringing her closer to him. He needed her to know what he was feeling. *Soon*, he told himself. He would call the investigator in the morning to tell him what he was about to do. Maybe he could give him some pointers on what methods he should consider employing for their safety.

Suddenly his cell phone began ringing. Shaken by the unexpected sound, Lauren sat upright and turned to look at him. Raising his eyebrows in surprise, he shook his head and reached back to pick up the phone he'd laid on the credenza behind the couch.

After looking at the number displayed on the screen, his eyebrows came down in a frown. "Hello, Mamma? Is everything alright?" He paused listening to the voice on the other end of the phone. He listened briefly and said softly. " *Mamma, andrà tutto bene. Devi crederci. Sì, ci sarò la mattina. Non preoccuparti, Pappa andrà bene. Ti troverò. Voglio bene alla tua mamma.*"
He pulled the phone from his ear and stood up quickly.

"What's wrong? Is your mother alright? What about your father, is he alright?"

"Lauren, I have to go. I have to leave for Chicago right away." He pulled her to her feet and into an urgent hug.

"What is it, Max?"

"It's my father, they took him to the emergency room. He passed out and fell and hit his head. He's still there. I have to go."

"Of course," Lauren nodded and rushed to pick up her things.

"I'll drop you off at home and then I have to catch the next plane out. I have to find my mother, she can't do this alone."

Not even thinking to change his clothes from the suit he'd worn to the symphony, Max grabbed his keys and his cell phone and led Lauren out to the car.

As Lauren lifted her skirt to get out of the car, Max stood patiently, and gave her a quick kiss as she stood. "Thank you, *mia dolce*," he said as he started back around the car.

"For what?"

"Everything," he said from his heart.

Chapter 10

The next morning Lauren was more determined than ever to go through her morning workout. The night before, the strong yearnings from both she and Max to become closer physically meant the next step being taken in their relationship. But she couldn't allow it until she was absolutely sure she could take the chance he wouldn't be repelled by her appearance.

She'd gotten dressed early, before the sun had even broken through to the first morning light. Josh had stayed the night at Robert's so she'd been able to start her workout with a healthy aerobic exercise to the sound of her favorite CD turned up to a level which would have brought him grumbling out of bed wondering what all the racket was about. Stepping out onto the front porch the chill from the night shocked her senses. Early morning mists were swirling around the flowers leading up to her door, their bright beautiful heads shining with dewdrops, as they seemed to search for the sunlight.

Lauren smiled as she came down toward the display of flowers she'd so painstakingly picked out and planted earlier spring. They were now flourishing nicely in the rich dirt so prevalent in the area. Max had begun work on restoring the original porch. Boards had been replaced where once they'd been rotting and giving way to the weather. The railing had been restored to its original beauty. She'd hung potted fuchsias in an array of colors from the rafters of the porch. It was turning out to be quite beautiful.

As she ran, Lauren began thinking of the night before. Max was obviously an extraordinary man. He had obvious skill working in carpentry, which as she'd learned the night before, had been at the hands of his own accomplished father in the same field. He'd told her how he'd worked side by side with his father as a teen learning the craftsmanship and the art of woodworking. He'd told her he enjoyed the time he'd spent with his father, learning of life and of craft in his early years. He'd told her that he'd gone to the University of Chicago but the conversation never got around to what he'd majored in. Never would she have imagined he had studied music.

What she'd experienced last night was far beyond a taught skill from a learned professor from college. Max held the gift of music in his hands and in his heart. The emotion and passion pouring through him onto the keys of the piano were undoubtedly those of a true composer. And yet, there was something more than just the composition of the piece of music. As she'd tried to tell him, his delivery was that of an accomplished musician, one who was worthy of the most skilled orchestra backup available.

Lauren reached her mid-point marker of the house with the hand carved mailbox, looking like a cross between a goose and an odd swan, its left wing pointed in an upward position indicating there was mail for the postman to gather on his daily rounds. With a laugh she turned to continue her pace and return back home.

She continued to wonder about this man she was becoming involved with. Who was he, really? He seemed to have so many secrets, and yet she was not afraid of him. She could feel nothing but gentle compassion and kindness. He was not a critical man, treating her with cynicism like her previous relationships. And she could feel the passions stirring deep within his soul, passions which were not just of a physical nature, but the kind found in great achievers. Yet she could see he was not using his passions to their fullest potential.

Then there was the obvious stirring of something between them which could only be explained as sexual attraction, but there was more there, too. She could see it in his eyes when he looked at her, something she felt in the stirrings of her heart. He was something she thought she would never find in a man—ever. The combination of his knowledge and culture, beauty and brawn was almost overwhelming. He was not your usual pattern for a man. At least not she'd met so far.

But he was different in a lot of ways. He hadn't tried to push himself on her, like most of the other men she'd gone out with. Even her two husbands had been not so gentle in their sexual advances. Max had obviously been attracted to her, but not once did he try anything she'd not wanted, nor asked for her to do anything that made her uncomfortable.

He'd made her feel loved and cared for with his gentle warm touch and his obvious respect for her as a woman. He asked questions, and truly listened to her answers. Attending to any need she had, down to settling his jacket over her shoulders as they walked along the water in the night air, she'd felt like a queen all evening long. Chivalrous in all things, his holding her hand as they walked had given her a feeling she'd never known before. She felt protected and safe, even loved.

Throughout the night she'd realized what she felt for him was far beyond a simple attraction. She'd dreamt of the day when she would find someone who could make her feel this way. But, she needed to slow down. It was much too early to be having thoughts of love and happily ever after. She couldn't let herself fall so quickly for him and end up broken hearted in the end. There was not enough proof yet he would stick around after the first period of infatuation ended. But it felt too good not to enjoy it while it lasted. Maybe, just maybe, she could work hard enough on herself to be more of a woman he would want to hang onto.

The evergreen giants loomed over her as she continued on her run through the rising mists of the morning. Fresh scents of pine and clean air made Lauren realize just how lucky she was to be in such a beautiful place. There was no doubt in her mind this was where she needed to be. And who knows, maybe she was meant to find this wonderful hunk of a man, too. She smiled outwardly, shaking her head at her crazy thoughts.

As she ran past the Miller's house she heard Josh calling out to her.

"Hey Mom, wait up!"

Lauren turned and continued to run in place as she watched her son run out from the neighbor's house. His long legs carrying him quickly up the path. Happy to see him, she smiled bright.

"Whoa, what happened to you?" He exclaimed running circles around her as she began to continue down the path toward home.

"What do you mean?" Lauren continued to smile, knowing she was smiling from the inside out.

"Not that I want to know or anything, but either you got laid or you hit your head or something, cause you have this crazy looking grin on your face."

Josh lazily took up a stride beside his Mom as they came up to the spot where she'd started off earlier that morning. She began the slowing of her heart rate and cool down of her muscles in a stretching routine she enjoyed every morning at this time. Taking in deep breaths and filling her lungs with clean fresh air.

"Not that it's any of your business," she said rolling her eyes and shaking her head. "But neither are true. I'm just happy."

"Well, whatever it is, keep doing it!" He said giving her a quick kiss on the cheek. "Because you look amazing this morning. I'm going to take a quick shower and change my clothes. Robert and I are going to go down to BJ's this morning and see if we can catch some fish. He said he and his father caught some whoppers out by the old dock on the East Side."

"I'll keep the fires burning waiting for you to bring home dinner tonight. Catch a big one enough for both of us," she said looking up at him. He looked so happy and content with what he was doing. It meant so much to her to know he was having fun. Her heart filled with joy as she looked at his smiling face. For reasons she couldn't quite understand she was so full of happiness she couldn't have described it to anyone in words.

So, she just kept smiling.

****

Lauren rose from the kitchen table to bring her dishes to the sink. Light fresh fruit was all she ate in the mornings after her morning workout. It was the only thing she would allow herself to have. She'd found if she didn't eat something she would start to feel faint by mid-morning and not be able to concentrate on her work like she needed. The fruit seemed to be just enough to carry her through until she had time for a lunch.

Lauren moved down the hallway to her desk in the back room and stopped to look at the progress Max had made on what they'd planned for her office. The shelves he'd crafted for her were perfect. She couldn't have imagined this room to look like this when they'd first met. But he'd told her to trust him. And he'd been right. What she had now was a wonderfully rich and inviting room which called to her heart to write about the romances she imagined.

The desk she'd been given was accentuated by the simple yet beautiful shelving made from wrought iron braces intricately shaped into a rose like pattern. He'd somehow acquired a wood that matched her desk perfectly with the grain, the texture and the stain. He'd replaced the old window with a huge encased window overlooking the lake. Under which he had fashioned a window seat from something that looked like old polished stones. It reminded her of the medieval period in some of the books she'd propped on the shelves above her desk. She'd found cushions at a yard sale the weekend before which seemed to have been made especially for this seat. They fit perfectly in the space provided. She'd adorned the space with huge throw pillows in bright colors of red and blue making the space an inviting refuge when she needed to relax from her work or curl up with a book or take a quick catnap.

The work he'd done so far was amazing. She'd never seen anyone who had so many talents, far beyond the work he was doing on her home. Lauren sat down on the window seat with a pad and paper, settling herself into the cushions behind her.

Max was a very complicated man. Who was he really? Carpenter by day and musical genius by night. But not all the pieces were matching up to a full picture. Something was missing. What was he not telling her?

The phone rang disrupting any further thoughts of this man she found so interesting. Jumping up she reached for the phone on her desk beside the computer.

"Hello?" Lauren straightened up and walked to her chair at the desk. A smile radiated over her face when the caller was identified. "Aunt Maggie! How are you doing?"

"Well, honey, I'm just dandy. How is my little writer doing?" Lauren's aunt asked happily.

Lauren had always cherished the sweet and gentle countenance of her Godmother. Even though she may not have been her biological mother, Lauren felt as if they were as close and maybe even a little closer than her Aunt's own children. She could see her mother's face when she looked into Maggie's eyes. It was the only thing left of her mother, and she treasured their time together.

Maggie quietly listened as Lauren spoke of her endeavors with the newest novel.

"I am stuck right now on a scene between the two main characters. I think I need to go into a bit more historical background to make it work, but I'm not sure if I should end it where it is, or delve deeper into the character's psyche," Lauren said finishing her thoughts.

"Well, I'll just leave that up to you. I don't come anywhere close to being able to put things together in words like you do. How is that big handsome man of yours?"

Lauren stopped short, wondering how her Aunt could have known about Max. Then she laughed at herself when she realized she was talking about her son, Josh.

"He is doing so well Maggie, I am so proud of him. He finished out the school year with almost all straight A's. He didn't make the honor roll, but came so close. He told me he wants to come out and see you this summer if he can."

"Honey, he can come out any time he wants to. You need to come spend some time with the family, too. We all miss you so much. We miss seeing your bright and cheerful face every day." Maggie said with what Lauren knew was heartfelt emotion. "But you are where you need to be, and that is all that matters. How is your house coming along?"

"Actually quite well. We've got most of the major repair work done now. The water leak is finally taken care of and the windows have all been replaced where it was most needed. What Max is working on now is more cosmetic than anything else. I hope to get started on the deck here shortly. We're hoping to have it done by the 4th holiday. I really want to have you all out for one huge party."

"Sounds like this Max has really worked out for you."

Lauren smiled, thinking of the possible budding relationship. "Yes, more than you know." She stopped herself from letting out a long sigh. Both her Aunt and Uncle Dan had gone through so much with her before. She didn't really want to tell Aunt Maggie about Max just yet, but she'd never been able to hold anything back from her. Anytime something was on her mind she would end up talking with Aunt Maggie and somehow things would always work out.

"Do I hear something more than just the usual repair man story going on here?" Maggie asked with interest.

"Um, well maybe." Lauren smiled wistfully as she stroked a hand over the handiwork of the man she'd begun to think of as more than just a casual friend.

"Do tell, my dear. You know you can't keep these kind of things from me."

"Well, Maggie, there really isn't much to tell. He is a wonderful man, with many talents. He's handsome, debonair, kind and gentle. And he's built like a solid rock. Looks sort of like one of those swashbuckling types at the opera. Strong Italian features, and very much the gentleman. In fact I think he should be in the opera! He has a very impressive tenor voice and sings like it's second nature to him."

"We are talking about the carpenter here right?"

"Yes we are. Different isn't it. Not what I expected, either. Plays the piano too Maggie, and writes his own music. He is almost too good to be true."

"What did you say his name was again?"

"Max. Max DeAngelo. Why?"

"Hold on a minute. I recognize that name. Let me go get this article I kept from a couple years ago."

"Okay." Lauren's curiosity was peaked. Aunt Maggie's memory was astounding. If she'd seen his name before, she believed it. She heard the phone being put down, then silence. A few minutes later she heard her Aunt rustling through what she imagined as a huge stack of papers.

"I know I have it somewhere here," Maggie said. "Honey, what does he look like?"

"Well, he is really very handsome, dark in coloring. About six-foot tall with dark, almost black hair. He has this cute little mustache and goatee, makes him look like a swashbuckler. His eyes, oh Auntie, his eyes are so intense. They are smiling one minute and the next I feel like they can see right into me and know exactly what I am thinking."

"Here it is. '*DeAngelo—The Next Musical Virtuoso*,'" as Maggie read the title Lauren's heart thudded hard.

"Are you sure it is him?" Could this be Max? There must be other musicians with the name DeAngelo. Right?

"Well, I don't know for sure, but I kept this article as an example to show my students what a young gifted person can do for themselves if they applied their knowledge and did what they loved to do. By your description, sweetheart, that is no carpenter. That man is Maximilliano Geovani Deangelo. Says here he was a new and upcoming star of the Opera world about 4 years ago. I think this is your man. There are a number of performances they show he's been on stage as the lead tenor vocalist. Says here he writes his own music, too. "

Maggie continued on to read the article to Lauren, whose heart froze. Lauren remained silent.

Shuffling through her papers again, Maggie finished by saying, "I can't remember what happened to him, but I remember reading later for some reason he disappeared shortly after his debut."

Lauren sat silently listening to her Aunt. She felt as if the rug had been pulled out from beneath her. The name was what sealed it for her. It was the same on Max's certificates of graduation. He'd lied to her. He'd straight-faced lied to her. Why had he done that?

"Now of course we can't be totally sure it is him until you see this picture. I'll fax it over to you from the office tomorrow morning." After continued silence, Maggie asked, "Lauren honey, are you all right?"

Lauren had been contemplating the possibility he was just like the other lying, cheating men she'd gotten herself tangled up with before. Maggie's concerned tone brought her back into the present and she shook the sinking feelings away. She'd wait until she got the article to see for herself. No sense condemning the man until she had proof.

"Yes, I'm alright. Just a bit of a shock is all. Please fax it over as soon as you can. I'd appreciate it. You would think that if you have someone working in your home for a couple of months you would know more about them. You are right. We don't know for sure it is the same man. Could just be someone uncannily like him."

They spoke a few minutes longer on updating each other with the family and ended with Maggie's words of caution.

"Now Lauren sweetheart, please be careful. I know you can take care of yourself, but this world is made up of all sorts of bad people. I'm going to look into this a little more and find out about this DeAngelo. Maybe Officer Peters from the church can find out more about him for us. I'll call you as soon as I find out anything."

"Alright. Thank you. I love you Auntie. Give Uncle Dan a hug and a kiss for me." Lauren hung up the phone and placed her forehead on her folded arms.

What was this all about? Rethinking their conversations, there was no doubt he'd lied to her last night. She'd felt it then, and she knew it now. She didn't need to see the article to know the picture would be of Max's strikingly handsome profile. Maggie had said she remembered something had happened and he'd disappeared. It couldn't have been an injury or accident. Nothing on that man showed he'd ever been injured in his life. He was healthier than most people.

Even if he'd been sick or injured, why wouldn't he go back to his music? It was obvious, from the night before, he'd spent a good part of his life studying and he still loved to play. She'd heard him sing in that beautiful voice of his. What was holding him back?

She saw she didn't have much time before work, but she had to see if she could find out anything for herself. The computer started up slower than she'd wished, taking its time to update a million files it seemed. Finally, she was able to open up the Web to make a search on his name. Not much came up. An article from the Chicago Opera House archives showed he had performed for them several times. A string of images showing people with the same name came up as a possible match to her search, none of which were him. Another search had his name popping up in various cities and countries. The Chicago Times listed his name in several articles. The title that caught her eye was the one saying "Local Artist Named as Suspect in...." But, when she clicked on the link it would bring her to a page to subscribe for current newsfeeds.

"Damn," Lauren muttered looking down at her watch. She quickly shut down the computer and got up. She'd been at it longer than she'd thought. On her way upstairs to get ready for her class at the college she laughed. How fitting, today's subject was the art of deception, a prime subject for the foul mood she was in.

Chapter 11

Max watched his parents closely at the hospital. His father's weakened condition had not affected the strength of the love he had for his wife. She held his hand faithfully throughout the whole ordeal, never once allowing a negative word to be said in her husband's presence. The family doctor came into the room when his father had fallen asleep, and began to tell them of the condition of his heart. Celeste shook her head and pressed her finger to her lips motioning toward the door. She bent down and kissed her beloved Rudolfo on the forehead and laid his hand down beside him on the bed.

Max and his mother followed the doctor into the hallway outside the small room just off the nurse's station on the Medical/Surgical floor. The sleepless night and most of the morning had been spent in the emergency room with his father. They'd moved him from Intensive care to this floor for observation at lunchtime during the hustle and bustle of patients receiving their mid-day meal. This had been the first sign of relief for Max and his mother for over 24 hours.

Dr. Puccino put his hand on Celeste's shoulder. "Mrs. DeAngelo, your husband is going to be fine." Both Max and his mother sighed with obvious relief. "Rudolfo experienced a slight myocardial infarction of the left ventricle atrium. The chloroform fumes he inhaled caused him to pass out, not his heart. Although, at the time of heart activity it may seemed much worse than it really was. I think he will be back to his old self soon enough. This doesn't mean he can resume activity as usual though."

Celeste gave Max a giant hug. "When can we bring him home?"

"We will continue to monitor his heart through the night, and if there are no further signs of activity we will let him go home in the morning. He will need to refrain from working for a while until his rhythm gets back to normal and I have released him from medical leave. But there is no evidence this will require additional medical attention at this time." With a smile he continued, but this time with a bit of laughter in his voice.

"Knowing Rudolfo though, I know Celeste you will have to literally tie him down in order to stop him from moving. But you tell him if he even thinks of getting up and going into that shop of his, he will be right back here at the hospital, with no option of getting any of your good cooking until he decides to behave himself and go home again."

They all had a chuckle about this. Then turning to his mother, Max wrapped his arms around her in a loving hug. "Let's go give Papa the good news."

As Celeste turned to go back to the room, Dr. Puccino tapped Max on the arm and motioned him to stay back.

Max nodded. "Mama, I'll be there in a minute," he called out to his mother. After ensuring she'd gone back in to Rudolfo, he turned back to the doctor who gave him a sturdy pat on the back. He'd been Max's doctor since they'd moved to the states, nearly twenty-eight years before.

"Good to see you home son. Decided to come home for a while? Maybe you can talk some since into that father of yours."

Max gave a tired smile. "No, I won't be able to stay. I have to get back to my own jobs."

The doctor gave a knowing nod.

He'd been one of the few who knew what Max truly had gone through since the night of the murder. Dr. Puccino had been there when Max had fallen apart, not knowing which direction to turn. He'd given him support and a shoulder to lean on when all of the legalities had to be dealt with after Anna's death. From one of their conversations, Max had found one of the deciding factors he'd needed to leave until the threats stopped and things settled down.

"I wanted to make sure you know this situation with your father's heart may not have happened without the fumes he inhaled. By my calculation there is a much higher possibility this was no accident."

Max had already come to this understanding without knowing the chemistry facts of what had made the fumes. His father had done nothing more than his usual work, using the same materials he did all of the time. There was foul play here.

"I know."

"You are aware then there is much risk with your being here now," the doctor pointed out.

"I'm aware of that, also."

"I don't know where you've been, and don't need to know. I just hope you are keeping a close watch on what goes on around you. For your sake, and everyone else, this is nothing to play around with."

Max nodded. "I will be leaving in the next day or two, and will find a way to protect them while I'm gone. I appreciate you taking care of my Father."

"Not a problem. If you are here in the morning, perhaps you could drop by my office for a quick check up, or just a cup of coffee. I'm always here for you."

"Thanks, Doc. I'll see if I can squeeze in some time."

As promised, Rudolfo was allowed to go home the next morning. Max and his mother got his father back home and settled, with a bit of grumbling from him and some fussing from his mother.

"I don't know what all this fuss is about," Rudolfo mumbled. "I can't see lying around when there's plenty things to do around here."

At the stern look from his mother, Max leaned in to whisper, "I wouldn't try it if I was you." This got a chuckle from his father. They both knew all of the fuss just meant his wife loved him.

* * * *

"Absolutely not. You cannot discuss the details of the murder with anybody. In fact your involvement with this woman is not recommended until we can put a close on this case." Inspector Warner sat behind the worn and battered desk of a man who has seen it all. The severe look on his face told Max he meant what he was saying.

"As for my involvement, I don't think there is anything I can or will do about that now. You can't make me put me life on hold forever. I may have had to go into hiding because of a crazy person, but I will not allow this to run my life any longer. I am no longer living in the area, so what I do should have no affect."

Max sat directly in front of the inspector and gave him an equally stern look. He'd come to the realization he'd been living in fear and depression too long. It was time to stop this nonsense and get on with life.

He'd told the Inspector he was going to pursue his music again. Just saying this out loud had made his heart sing. There was no doubt this was what he needed to do. The whole plane ride back he'd begun to make plans to inquire from friends and acquaintances he'd known in the past of any interest in his talent, he needed to acquaint himself with the orchestras in the area, set up relationships, and ultimately perform on stage again. It would take some time, but he was confident this was meant to be.

"What happened to your father was no accident. The amount of bleach in acetone to make chloroform didn't come from a washed and bleached work rag, like the report said. Someone would have had to pour in at least a cup to make those types of fumes." Inspector Warner stated. "The length of time since the last contact would have indicated he'd lost interest and perhaps was pursuing other things. But this latest development shows that isn't the case. Unfortunately, there is no way to tell whether the events are connected in any way. My gut tells me it's the same person. I believe it was done on purpose to get you to come back."

"I know. That's why I'm hiring a security guard to watch over my parents. I can't have this type of thing happen again," Max affirmed his knowledge of the facts.

"They are not the only ones at risk."

Max narrowed his eyes at the Inspector. "Are you saying you think he will come to Washington to try it again?"

"We don't know how far this person will go to get you." The inspector looked thoughtfully across at Max. "Perhaps if you do show your face publicly again, he will make another move and we will be able to track him this time. But we won't know for sure until you come back out again."

"So, you think I will still be putting everyone at risk, wherever I go."

"Just be aware any involvement, especially with a woman, could be a potential problem. The indicators on the notes seemed to infer this anger and hatred toward you is specific to the relationship to your late wife. But transference is one of those unknown quantities. You never know when a whacko is going to move the object of his obsession to another source."

Max's stared into the file in front of the Inspector, as if he would burn a hole straight through the cover of the file—his wife's file.

"That's the problem. The not knowing." Taking a deep breath, he cleared his thoughts. He had to move on, that was all there was to it. If he continued with the way things were, he would surely either go crazy himself, or just shrivel and die.

He'd finally found something to shake him out of the depths of despair, something he could not bear to lose. If he continued to be vague and lie about his past to Lauren there would be nothing to hang onto. He wouldn't blame her if she hated him for it. As it was, he was taking a real chance telling her now. There was no guarantee she would understand. But he had to tell her now before things went any further astray than they already had.

He heard what the Inspector was trying to tell him, but he seriously had to consider if he was willing to chance losing Lauren's trust if he continued with the lies. There had to be a way he could do both. He would have to figure it out before he got back to Washington.

Rising he and the Inspector stood in silence for a moment. He reached out to shake the Inspector's hand. "I will let you know what I end up doing Inspector. Please let me know if anything more happens down here."

The Inspector placed his hand on Max's shoulder. "If you do decide to move on these plans of yours, call me. There may be some things we can put into place to catch him if he takes action. Take care son, and let me know if anything happens up there as well."

Max spent the drive back home in deep thought. He'd rented a small sedan from the airport the night he got into Chicago. As he drove the classical music playing from the radio was quietly reminding him of the decisions he needed to make. Pulling up into the driveway of his parents' house he looked at the serene scene of a well loved home, the home where he'd grown up.

This was where he'd watched his family go through all the stages families go through. Teenage siblings fighting with one another, pets coming and going, financial struggles, all through the emotional strength of their parents deep love for one another and their children. A life he'd loved and longed to experience on his own.

He'd been robbed of his life long enough. It was time to take control again. Lauren had to be told the truth. He had no intention of leaving her. He needed to face this head on. To run now would only destroy any of the possibilities he could see for them. If she stayed with him, it was meant to be.

His decision was final. Now all he had to do was figure out how to tell her.

As he got out of the car, he received a small nudge to take heed and look around him for safety. Not seeing anything to be wary of, he continued on into the house.

What he wasn't aware of was the figure of a man crouched among the bushes across the street. Watching and waiting—for the right time.

* * * *

Later that afternoon, Max sat at the breakfast bar watching his mother make his father's favorite dish for dinner. Her *scaloppine al limone* was the best. Her secret to the thinly sliced chicken breast, usually dredged in wheat flour was to add a bit of almond flour to give it a nutty flavor. Then of course served with her special caper and lemon sauce, it was a meal any Italian man would crave.

He smiled, raising the cup of coffee he held in his hands up to his lips. He'd never seen his mother or his father exchange harsh words together, remembering only the calm peace his mother conveyed to everyone she touched. He'd quietly been observing the exchange between the two of them ever since he'd flown in the other night.

Apparent to the outside observer, the love they showed each other could not be ignored. It always amazed him to see the light in his mother's eyes when she looked upon his father, returned without question by the pure joy in his father's words every time he spoke of his mother. After 43 years of marriage, they still seemed to have the same spark for each other from when they first fell in love.

"Why such a grin or your face?" Celeste turned her head in a knowing way and grinned back at him. "You haven't smiled like that in quite some time."

Wiping her hands on the bright blue apron tied around her waist, she walked over to the counter where he sat sipping his coffee. She patted his cheek with her hand, softly rubbing his face with the palm, like she used to when he was little. Max leaned into her hand and covered hers with his own, finding the same warmth and comfort he used to in the stroke of her hand.

"Nothing really, I was just thinking about you and Papa." He squeezed her hand as she dropped it back down to the countertop. He took a handful of nuts from the tray of snacks his mother had put out for him, and tossed a couple into his mouth. As he looked up, there was an inquisitive look on his mother's face.

"And what were you thinking, Binny?" She asked. He smiled at her use of her pet name for him. She'd always called him her little *bambino speciale*.

He leaned back in his chair, trying to phrase his questions in a way that wouldn't stir up too many questions. "Mama, how did you know Papa was the one for you? You know, what was the moment you knew you were meant to be together?"

Celeste stopped what she was doing and looked intently at Max, like when he was a child and she was assessing what he said about something he'd done. Surprised, he raised his eyebrows and stared back at her, unsure of what he should say next. It took her only a minute then the smile in her eyes told him she knew why he was asking.

"I knew it. You have so much light around you. You are happy. I can see it," she exclaimed, clapping her hands together lightly with joy. Max's heart gave a little patter of happiness to see her joy for him. But, maybe she hadn't guessed yet about Lauren.

"What?" he asked, to see how much she thought she knew.

"You can't fool me, Binny. A mother knows." She picked up the tomatoes for the salad, and began deftly slicing them as she always did. Stopping for a minute, she peered at him, and then went back to her work. "Who is she?"

Looking up quickly Max burst out laughing. There was no passing anything by his mother. "Someone I met back in Washington. Someone I care about very deeply."

"I can see that." Celeste reached out to take his hand in hers and held it warmly for a moment. "To answer your question, I don't know about a specific moment, I just knew when I was with Ruddy I didn't want to be without him, ever."

Max nodded. It was the same way he'd begun to feel about Lauren.

She picked up the knife again to start chopping the zucchini and lettuce. "You can't put this feeling into words," she said confirming she still felt this way about Rudolfo. "Happiness, joy, excitement? None of these are enough. Love is different for everyone. You have to find out what it is for you."

He stared into his empty cup. Was this love he was feeling for Lauren? He could see them, laughing and being together at the age of his parents. This description his mother gave of never wanting to be without her felt right.

"Do you love her?"

Max raised his head to see his mother looking back at him. He felt the love she had for him pouring out. All he could do was nod his head.

"Getting involved again would be a difficult thing. I'm not sure it's time yet." He wasn't sure how to tell his mother about Anna's spirit, but felt she would understand. She didn't need to know the details of when and where, but she should know his reluctance was not about how he felt about Lauren. "Mama, there are some things I haven't told you yet. I didn't want you to worry."

Celeste frowned. Lifting the lid to her *scaloppine* to make sure it looked right, she stirred the sauce and set the lid back down. Moving to the chair at the end of the counter, she sat down and faced her son. "What now is this all about?"

Max stared down at his hands, not sure how to start. Truth usually worked out well. "Anna has visited me several times since she passed."

He wasn't surprised by his mother's quick intake of air. "*Dio mio*," she whispered. "I wasn't sure about it at first. But I have no doubt now she is trying to tell me something."

"How do you know?"

"She's shown up as a bright light a couple of times when I needed her most. I feel her around me, giving me hints and pushing me to do things. She's the one who made me start the job I'm working on now for the woman I told you about. I really think she led me there to meet her."

"Yes, yes, I have heard of this kind of thing." Celeste's eyes were wide as she nodded. "It is said this is a great honor to be contacted by spirit."

"It scared me at first, but now I'm getting used to it," he said with a laugh.

"Have you seen her? Do you know for sure it is Anna?"

"I saw her just like I am looking at you now. She looked the same, only a little wispy. Her eyes were so sad," he said trailing off.

"It is said they stay back sometimes to help the ones they love." Celeste paused in thought. "Maybe she can't move on until she has done what she believes she is supposed to do. We know you are not safe yet. I believe she is here to help you?"

"Maybe," he replied softly. He'd come to the same conclusion. "She doesn't belong here now. I have to believe there is more to our lives than what is here on this Earth. I just wish I could help her to move on to a better place."

Celeste patted his hands. "I see now why you question your feelings about this woman."

Max held her gaze for a moment then looked away. "No, I know what I feel. I just don't know if I should tell her yet, Mama."

"You will know when it is the right time, Binny. There is a purpose for all great things, and there will be no question in your heart when you know."

* * * *

It had been pure luck Jeffery was able to book a flight on the same airline as Max. The only way he knew what flight to take was after Max had gone into the house Jeffery had gone to the car to see if there was anything he could find to help him in his next steps. He had to do this right this time. This was going to be his last chance to finally put an end to it all.

It was between the two of them now. He didn't want to hurt anyone else. He'd involved too many people as it was already. Max's parents weren't at fault for what their son had done. Jeffery had gone over it in his mind a million times. He needed to catch Max when the time was right. To strip him of his ability to enjoy life, just like his poor Anna. He didn't deserve to live.

To his surprise, the car door had been unlocked, and Max had left the car rental slips and his tickets for the flight back to Washington on the passenger seat. The only way this would work is if he could get on the same flight and follow him from there.

Jeffrey had the rest of the afternoon to prepare. He shipped what he needed through a Banner Mail-It-All to their location in Seattle, and planned to pick it up later. They guaranteed the package would get there for half the price, which was good because he only had so much money to spend. He figured they were small enough they would have the manpower to check every package. That way he wouldn't need to risk carrying it through security at the airport. In fact, he didn't even want to mess with a carry on bag. So, what he needed right away was in his pockets. His wallet and a small Vitamin D bottle holding his drugs was all he needed. The pain meds and the vitamins looked similar enough. Nobody would be able to tell the difference without doing tests.

The flight wasn't cheap, but he'd saved for a very long time for this trip. It would be the last one he would ever make. There had been plenty of time when he got to the airport, to get the tickets and wait to board the flight. So, when things didn't go as planned, he wasn't sure what he was going to do.

As he stood at the ticket counter, the customer service agent clucked his tongue.

"I just don't have anything available, sir."

"Not even for a Veteran?" he asked, showing his military ID. "I have to catch this flight."

"No, I'm sorry. We don't have any flights for Seattle until 2 pm this afternoon."

As his blood pressure rose, the pain in Jeffery's head threatened to start over again. He had to get on this flight. Staring at the agent, he froze not knowing what to do next. But by some magic the young man behind him cleared his throat and stepped forward.

He stood, military duffle bag slung over his shoulder, his regulation hair cut denoting his military status. "Excuse me sir, I can change my flight to Seattle to the later time. My buddies let me know they are on their way now. You can have my seat. I'll fly out with them."

Jeffery couldn't believe his luck.

"Thank you son, God bless you," he said truly thankful.

After averting that fiasco, Jeffery waited to board the flight, watchful for Max to arrive. He couldn't risk his recognizing him, so he'd worn a baseball cap and found some glasses to change his look. The rough, unshaven beard would probably help, too. But he reminded himself to keep his right side concealed, in case the scar running from scalp to chin gave him away.

He ducked behind a magazine as he saw Max walk up to the boarding gate to ask a question. Max stood there a moment then turned to find a seat in the waiting area, never looking over to where Jeffery sat against the back of the vending machines.

It didn't take long before the seats for boarding were called out. Jeffery had known Max would be boarding before him with a First Class ticket, so he had no worries he would see him on board. He sat against the window seat, grasping the arm rests, his knuckles white from the force of pressure he used. The pure pain of the change in air pressure as they took off was almost unbearable. He wished he'd been able to pop one of the pain pills before boarding. But he needed to remain cognizant of everything Max was doing.

Once they were in the air though it took some time before the pain leveled out and he was able to open his eyes. Vision blurred for a minute, he was finally able to make out the passenger's faces who were sitting in adjacent seats.

The woman beside him clasped her bright pink coat close around her body as she leaned as far away from his as she could. The color made his head swim. He stared back at her.

"Are you ok?" she asked hesitantly.

Not wanting conversation, he nodded his head and grunted, turning to the window. He didn't care if he scared her. As he stared out the window, his only hope was he wouldn't start hallucinating during the flight.

Chapter 12

Lauren sat on her front porch, the sun streaming through the morning mist. She'd been up since dawn. Her stomach was churning with nerves having been stirred up with this whole mess about Max. As promised, he'd called her as soon as he got back home the previous night. He'd sounded tired and their conversation had been short. She'd talked with him coolly, as if their only relationship was that of homeowner and hired carpenter. Her decision was until he told her the truth about everything she couldn't allow herself to believe there was anything more. He would have to tell her on his own though. She wouldn't force the issue. He would need to come clean without any prompting from her.

Aunt Maggie had faxed over the article, and as suspected there was no doubt it was Max. One picture showed a man in his thirties, standing on a stage wearing an extravagant costume, singing as if his life depended on it. The lower picture was a close up. Although still in costume and stage makeup, there was no mistaking his face, especially those intense eyes of his. This picture showed confidence and strength, a deep inner knowledge of who he was and where he was going.

Lauren's internet search hadn't turned up much. Like her Aunt had said, it seemed like everything about him stopped. She paid for the one month subscription to access articles from The Chicago Times, especially for the one article she'd seen about his being a suspect in something. But it had turned out to be a link pointing to a page which had been moved or was no longer valid.

Lauren didn't know the whole truth, but there was no doubt he had lied about his involvement in music. Still, even though she didn't feel anything bad about him, she had to remind herself, she'd been fooled before.

Her first husband, Ben, had convinced her he was her soul mate, the only man who would love her for the rest of her life. She'd been young and vulnerable, but there was no excuse for his taking advantage of her. She'd trusted him and he'd taken that trust and turned it into something which hurt beyond words. He'd turned what they had into a gaping hole, filled with greed and lust instead of the love she deserved.

Evan had also taken her loving and trusting heart and turned her inside out. She'd learned never to trust what a man would tell you. One minute you were the light of their life the next it was as if you didn't exist. It had taken many years to get past the pain of those relationships. She didn't believe in hate, and definitely didn't want to carry around mistrust and fear all of her life, so she'd chosen to forgive them both. The saying of what you focus on is what you attract made sense to her. Though, there were times more difficult than others to remember not to allow the fears to take hold again. She'd thought she was doing a pretty good job of releasing those pent up feelings. And yet, here again, she felt as if she was being used.

Since finding out about his involvement with music, she'd tried to figure out why he would lie about it to her. The only thing which made any sense was he obviously had money. She didn't have enough facts to know whether it was inherited or whether he'd made an excellent splash in the entertainment business with his music. No matter where it came from, it was obvious he hadn't wanted her to know about his wealth.

Was he afraid she would try to get too involved and try to take his money? Did he think she was just a money-grabbing floozy just after his money? But then, why would he have taken her to his house after the night at the symphony? Was he just trying to impress her to get her into bed?

Lauren stopped herself and shook the thoughts from her mind. No, she couldn't think of him in that way. She had to believe in the good she could see in him. She wouldn't be duped again into forging a relationship, to have it ripped into shreds without any thought of how she would be affected. She couldn't go through that again. It would kill her. But, she did believe Max should be allowed the chance to prove himself as being what he had previously showed himself to be, a straight, honest and caring human being. Maybe there were other reasons he hadn't said anything.

Her heart began pounding as she watched Max's truck pull into the driveway. He pulled his truck up along side her car, as if it was a daily occurrence. She watched as he got out, his body rippling against the tight fitting T-shirt tucked into his jeans. He strode across the grass and up the front steps. She hadn't realized it, but she'd stopped breathing. As quietly as she could, she took in a gasping breath as he bent to kiss her cheek.

"*La mia dolcezza.*"

Looking up, her heart gave an extra beat at the brush of his lips on her cheek. She closed her eyes for a moment, in an attempt to harden the shield around her heart, as she knew she must if she were to get through this unscathed.

"Hello, Max. How are you doing?" She kept her hands clasped around the mug of coffee in her hands. Her eyes cooling as she looked back into his face.

Max straightened abruptly and took a step back, his eyes narrowed.

"I am fine," he hesitated. The uncomfortable silence which followed, as he continued to stare at her, made Lauren want to squirm in her seat. But she needed to stay strong. "It was an unfortunate scare for all of us."

Remembering her manners, Lauren felt ashamed she hadn't asked about his father. Softening around the edges a bit, she asked softly, "How is your father doing?"

The returned look in Max's eyes softened a bit too. "There were...issues...he fell... and hit his head and had a mild heart attack. I had to go back to find out. Mamma needed me there."

She could see in his eyes he was still withholding something. Lauren began to feel herself tense up again. When was he going to tell her the truth? Was all of this a lie? Had he gone back to Chicago for some other reason?

Suddenly, Lauren had a horrible thought. She swallowed hard and took another sip of her now cold coffee. He'd said it had been four years since his last relationship. Surely he hadn't waited this long to get involved again. What if he was married? What if he'd gone back to Chicago to see a new wife who was pining away for his attentions? Why had he come here in the first place? She couldn't even look him in the eyes. Lauren moved her eyes away from his, not wanting to let him see the rush of emotions now crowding her thoughts.

"*Bella*, are you angry with me?" Max finally asked.

Reaching forward he softly rubbed her white knuckled fingers gripping the mug, urging her to relax and let go of the handle. She let her hand drop to her lap, unsure of what to do. Desperate to reach out and caress him back, she wanted only to feel the comfort of his warmth next to her body. She longed to have him look into her eyes the way only he could, and make her heart melt in his hands. Yet, she had to stay strong. Their unresolved issues were too big to ignore.

Glancing back up into his face, she all but crumbled when she saw the look of concern in his eyes. She darted her eyes away again, as she could feel the telltale sign of tears coming forward surrendering the strength she'd summoned to deal with the problem.

He reached down and picked up her hand in his. The warmth of his hand penetrated through the coldness, sending a spark of flames up her arms, as if the mere touch of his hand could ignite her very soul.

"Lauren, *mia dolce*, I am so sorry I had to leave you the other night. There was nothing I could do. Mamma was frantic. She didn't understand all the tests they were doing on Papa. She needed me to be there for her. Please, believe me I didn't want to leave you."

Lauren brought her gaze back to his as he spoke. She saw only despair. His dark brows were drawn together with a pained expression telling her he spoke the truth. She shook her head, dismissing her previous thoughts. He'd told the truth that night about needing to go at least. She'd seen the fear in his face.

"*Amore* you need to know you are a beautiful woman who draws me from my heart. When we were together last, I felt something precious happening for us. This I feel is much more than both of us can understand right now. Please, don't be angry with me."

Lauren felt the tears stinging at the backs of her eyes, straining to spill out and ruin her image of a woman with strength. How dare he talk of such things? He wasn't even telling her the truth half the time.

"Don't," Lauren whispered, the lump in her throat threatening to choke her. Flinging his hand back toward him, she rose quickly and turned with a whimper to rush into the house.

In the kitchen, she stood motionless, her heart about to burst. Picking up a knife she began brutally chopping fruit which was meant to end up as a fruit salad for her lunch, but was ending up to be nothing but mush. He'd been quick to follow. His energy rushed over her in waves as she stood with her back to him, furiously chopping the apple into a million pieces. She wouldn't allow him to see it, but the tears which had threatened her on the porch were now streaming down her face so thick she could barely make out what she was doing.

Max came up close behind her. She could feel his presence without a doubt. Trembling with the intense need to turn and throw herself into his arms, she wanted to beg him to tell her the truth about everything. He reached out and stroked the curve of her neck with his thumb, his touch causing a roll of tumultuous desire to seep into her being.

"Lauren, what is wrong? Why are you so upset?"

She stopped her chopping and laid the knife down before she ended up cutting herself with the sharp blade. She kept repeating the same words over to herself as if willing him to comply.

Just let him talk to you, he is going to tell you.

Slowly, he put his arm around her waist and turned her around to face him. "Ahh, *il mia amore*, no, no *bella!*" he declared drawing her to him. As if knowing what she needed, he brushed the long tendrils of her hair with his fingers, following the curve of her shoulders to her waist where she was sure the curls ended in an explosion of disarray. She'd dreamt of him stroking her like this, yet she wished the circumstance to be different.

Her body was the perfect fit for him, their bodies melding together as if one. She couldn't help herself as she snuggled closer to him, her eyes closed, when he began softly humming a soft lullaby of old times. Soon, she let the tears stop as she began to feel calmer. Max pulled away from her slightly, as she reached up to dry the dregs of the torrent of tears which had washed down her face moments before.

With great care, Max pulled her into the living room and led her to sit down on the couch in front of the big brick fireplace. She began to shiver in the early morning coldness, and he stood to pull the multicolored afghan, laying across the arm of the couch, around her shoulders.

"My sweet. Tell me what is wrong."

Oh my gosh, he has no idea, she thought huffing out a breath in disgust. Before she could stop herself, she blurted out the first of her questions.

"How could you? How could you just lie to me like that?"

Max bowed his head over his hands, remaining silent a moment. He glanced back up to her, pain and torment worrying his usual good natured expression.

"I am sorry," he answered in a soft reverent tone. "I can't tell you everything, but you have to know I didn't want to lie to you." He looked back up into her eyes.

"Why can't you tell me? What happened to make you treat a whole part of your life as if it never happened?"

He remained silent, his intense gaze making her feel as if she were the one being questioned. She knew without a doubt he was measuring what to tell her and what to hold back. Lauren returned his silent analysis.

"Lauren, you are right. Music is my whole life, it means everything to me and I have allowed events in my life to put it aside as if it meant nothing. I was very successful at one point and I was doing very well."

"Yes. I found that out from the articles I could dig up on you. One critic said your apparent versatility with music won you the notoriety of being the 'virtuoso of his time'," Lauren responded. Max glanced up at her, his eyes full of humility, and bowed his head.

"I don't know about that, but I have been given the gift."

"You'd sold two albums that climbed up the classical and instrumental charts to the top ten within days of coming out. And that wasn't all. You'd just signed with the Philharmonic Orchestra of Chicago to perform what they called 'a season of Operatic choices from Giuseppi Verdi's venue of stories'," she nodded, confirming his success.

Max smiled, though his despondent expression filled Lauren with the sadness he'd held onto having given up on his dreams.

"My second album was my favorite. A group of my friends from the University, all accomplished musicians in their own right, got together and recorded some classical favorites and several of my own scores. It was created in recognition of my Italian heritage, as well as a tribute to my mother for her support and guidance throughout the years." He stared out the window a moment as if gathering strength, and glanced back meeting her frowning gaze. "The music you saw in the sideboard was only a small part of what I've done, and intend to do now I realize again what it means to me."

"You are so talented. I can't understand why you would have left all of that behind you," Lauren restated, trying to get some type of clue to his secrecy.

A breeze came through the open window, blowing the curtains around. Both Max and she glanced over at the same time, and she wondered if he too saw the butterfly in the distance, flying above the bright purple irises. Lauren remembered what Kathryn had said about their connection with spirit.

"It was because of what happened to Anna, isn't it?"

Max paused before answering her, and continued to stare out of the window toward the fluttering butterfly. "Yes, it is. Her death still influences my decisions." Max glanced back at her, a question poised on his lips, curiosity in his eyes. "Do you...feel her, too?"

Lauren's hesitant nod was slow to come forth. It wasn't her imagination. He felt Anna there as well. Max gazed at her a moment, then nodded his head, as if he'd known she too felt Anna's spirit.

"We need to talk about her," Lauren prompted, hoping he would open up about what had happened. Max took in a deep breath, and she could feel he was still fighting over what to say.

"I promise we will soon. Not now," he finally said, lifting her hand to his lips. Suddenly Max swung himself off the couch onto his knees in front of her, his hands still covering hers. Looking into his eyes, Lauren sensed an intense need rushing from him. "Lauren, *amaroso*, you don't know how grateful I am to you for helping me see how important my music is to me."

"You've always known," Lauren whispered.

"Yes, but I'd forgotten." Max gazed into her eyes, his filled with deep emotion. Purposefully tuning into her inner self, Lauren felt happiness, joy, peace, and oddly enough a whole lot of love. "You've sparked the fire again. This fire burns deep within my soul and you are there to fuel it. I now know I must continue to write and someday soon share with those who would enjoy it the way you do. This is what I have been made to do. I need you to encourage me. You make the music come straight from my heart."

Not really comprehending what he was telling her, she leaned forward and placed her hands to frame his face, pulling him forward. She brushed her lips over his, in a tender kiss which sent sparks racing where their lips touched.

Quickly Max rose back onto the couch and engulfed her in an embrace filled with such energy he almost knocked her out of her seat. He held her for so long, all the cares and questions seemed to melt away. It felt right. She hoped he'd never let go. Interpreting his actions as that of a man having recognized what he was meant to do, Lauren laughed and returned the hug.

"I'm so glad you've finally come back to your senses." Drawing back from him, she could still see the utter joy written on his face.

Yet, there was something else in his eyes. She'd never experienced this before. It felt as if his joy wasn't just for himself. It was as if he'd drawn her intimately into his happiness. Nobody had ever shared with her this kind of joy. She felt unsure of whether she should accept it in the way he seemed to be offering it. No strings attached, just the pure happiness he was feeling. Taking her hands in his, he reverently brought each one to his lips. Lauren could not figure out what was going on inside his head, she only knew she felt a sudden overwhelming joy well up inside.

"*Ma Bella*, I have to work some things out first. When I do, there will be no more secrets. But you have to trust me. I know you have no reason right now to believe me, but I'm asking you to be patient and know I would never do anything to hurt you."

Lauren watched as Max said this, waiting for some indication as to what was going on in his head. She could see nothing but honest concern and truth about what he was asking. Her eyes had narrowed as he spoke, watching and analyzing everything he was saying. So, at least he admitted he did have some type of secret he wasn't sharing with her. She was going to find out, whether he wanted to tell her or not. If he was famous, as he'd said, there had to be more media about him and why he'd left so suddenly.

Lauren closed her eyes for a moment to ease the tension out of her face then looked up at him again and gave a slow nod of acceptance. "Alright, so I give you time to work these things out. But will you tell me one thing if I ask?"

With a deep sigh, Max nodded. "If I can I will answer anything you want to know, but if I don't it isn't because I don't want to, it's because I can't."

Considering what would be the best question to ask, she needed enough to get started on her search to find out what was really going on. Lauren took her hands from his and placed them in her lap. Her mind was working quickly, searching for the question.

"I know a person's death can be devastating. But, you couldn't have dropped the one thing you are destined to do. I know something else happened. What kind of event would be so catastrophic it would make a person give up on himself and his dreams?"

He hadn't told her yet how Anna died, and she hadn't told him yet she already knew at least a part of it. She knew his withdrawal from the public eye had something to do with the visions she'd had about Anna. Lauren had caught her son, Josh, in every lie he'd ever told. Surely, she would sense if Max held any connection to this horrible death she kept seeing other than his affection for the poor woman.

He was holding back a vital piece of information she hadn't figured out yet. Why did Anna show up now, and what was she trying to tell her?

Max got up and paced back and forth in front of the couch, frustration pouring off of him in waves. She knew before he even spoke he wouldn't tell her anything she didn't already know.

"Lauren, I can't answer you in a way you will be satisfied. It is very complicated. All I can say is, after she died and the events that followed, I began to believe there was no more life left to live. My heart and soul were so devastated by what happened, there was nothing for me to do but to leave what I loved the most. Even if I had wanted to, I don't think I could have made myself write one more aria, or play the music I love so much. There was nothing more I could do, but I see now I can't let this rule my life. If I'm going to have any life at all, I'm going to live it the way it is meant to be. I can't do anything about the past, but I can do something about the future."

"And there's nothing I can do to let you know you can talk with me—about anything?" she asked, reminding herself of the many conversations she'd had with her son.

Max shook his head. "No, I am so sorry."

At the moment, she couldn't tell if he was truthful in all he was saying or if he was just a very good liar. The only thing she could think was this man obviously had a problem. There was no denying the fact there was a definite pull physically, and she longed for the type of relationship he seemed to be offering.

But what kind of relationship would it turn out to be? He seemed to care for her, yet he couldn't tell her the truth about himself and his life. This didn't seem like an ideal situation to get involved in on a personal level, where she might find out he really didn't care at all.

Lauren rose and walked slowly over to the mantel of the big brick fireplace, reaching out to touch the glass ornament of a unicorn her Aunt had given her. She'd told her the figurine was a reminder all dreams can become reality if one wishes them to be true.

Turning, she watched Max a moment as he sat solemnly on the couch where she'd left him. A deep sadness had enveloped him in a wet blanket of suppression. Her heart went out to him for the anguish she saw in his dark eyes as he looked up to her.

"I'll give you some time, but I'm not going to wait forever. I need to know Max. You can't expect me to go on as if nothing has happened here. I don't know whether I can trust you or not. Without knowing the facts, you could be giving me a line that ends up to be something I don't want to get myself, or my son involved in. Can you understand?"

Standing Max walked to her side. "I do understand Lauren, and I promise you will know very shortly. Just keep believing in me the way you did the other night. It would be devastating if you gave up on me."

Tentatively he reached out to hold her. His arm came around to encircle her waist. At first she drew back, but then realized she needed the touch he offered as much as he seemed to need it. She came to him and he drew her into his arms. Her head lay softly on his chest, and her arms came up around his neck. He took in a deep breath and let it out slowly, and held her there in silence for quite some time. Without him needing to say anything, she felt gratitude pour into her from his warm embrace. All of the emotions she'd been holding onto seemed to rush up to the surface. She didn't know whether to laugh or cry. She could have stayed there forever, but knew there were many things still to be settled. So, she gently pushed away from him.

Stepping back, Max smiled. "If I am going to get the siding up on the side of the house, I'd better get started. I can't have you giving up on me as your contractor. That just would not be right."

Shaking her head, not understanding his sudden change, Lauren stepped away to head into the kitchen again. One minute, he was all emotion, the next all about business.

As if on impulse, Max turned back around. "Tell you what, I want to make it up to you for the other night. Why don't you let me make you dinner tonight?"

"Make me dinner?" She asked from the doorway. Would he ever stop surprising her? Not only was this man sensitive and handsome, he was educated and artistic, and he could cook, too.

"Yes, I'll throw together a little Italian dish for you, and we can spend some time together."

Max's smile was catching. Lauren couldn't help but smile back.

"Well, I think I just might take you up on that. Josh has plans to go out to the movies with his friends. Your offer sounds better than the leftovers in the fridge."

"It's a date." He said with a grin. Reaching down he picked up the tool belt he dropped on his way in. The thought had her stomach tightening again at the word. She stood perfectly still, her hands steadying herself on the edge of the kitchen counter, strengthening her will against the unseen enemy—herself.

She would think of it as two friends getting together for dinner—nothing more. Inwardly she shook off the nagging feeling of failure and came back to the present. Lauren took a moment to watch as Max stood fastening the belt around his waist, obviously unaware his profile was perfectly outlined by the morning sun streaming through the curtains. His dark hair waved seductively around his face, curling over the collar of his work shirt. When he glanced up to meet her gaze his smile spread warmly into his eyes where there was a hint of amusement gleaming through.

He tilted his head slightly. "Don't look so scared. I haven't killed anyone yet with my cooking!"

Odd choice of words, she thought shaking her head. Good thing she knew that wasn't how Anna had died.

Amazed he'd caught on to her inner demons, she returned the grin, bringing the light and warmth back into her face. "Of course not. I've just never had anyone offer to cook for me before. You sure this just isn't a ploy for me to come over and cook *you* dinner?"

"You offend me," he said with feigned vanity, tossing his head back in a dramatic gesture. Grinning again, he stepped toward her and pulled her into his arms. Bending slightly to brush his lips against hers he raised his eyebrows. "Just come hungry, for anything and everything."

Being led by the moment she assumed, his lips met hers in a crushing kiss, deepened by what seemed to be desire brewing just under the surface. After grabbing one last kiss from her, Lauren watched as Max almost skipped out of the room.

"I will," Lauren said laughing at his spontaneity. Yet she couldn't ignore the familiar fear seeping into her heart.

As she started into the kitchen, the sudden chill in the room made her stop as the unsettling cold drift of air swarmed over her, almost from the inside out. She'd been through it enough times to know something was about to happen. A bright flash of light blocked her sight, and in that instant she saw the same vision of the gruesome dark stain surrounding the body on the floor, the back of the crouched figure over her, and the grandfather clock in the distance at the strike of midnight. Then in an instant, as plain as could be, she saw Max standing at the doors edge of the empty room, fear and anguish surrounding him as he stared down at the ugly dark spot on the carpet.

He had been there. She knew it for sure now.

She was fairly certain he wasn't responsible for the murder. The question now seemed obvious. Who was?

Chapter 13

Max left work at the house earlier with claims he needed to prepare for dinner. He needed to stop by the grocery store, but in reality he intended to contact the investigator and tell him just what he was planning on doing so action could be taken. Lauren deserved the whole truth. He would answer all of her questions about everything after dinner.

There was one point in their discussion earlier he'd thought it was too late, and she was about to tell him she no longer wanted anything to do with him. But, mercifully she'd given him a chance. She was right. He couldn't expect her to want to have a relationship with him if she didn't know the truth. That was no way to start a relationship, especially one he hoped would last the rest of their lives.

Everything became so clear to him that morning. He'd realized what he was feeling for her was love—true love. Without a doubt they belonged together. Desperate to tell her what he was feeling, he knew he needed to tread lightly. She'd been hurt before. This he knew for sure. In reality, until this whole thing was cleared up about his wife's murder, he could be risking her safety. Tonight he would give her the chance to see the truth and decide if she wanted to be involved. He would do everything in his power to make things right.

As they spoke, he'd felt an explosion of joy filling his every thought and physical being. Barely able to contain himself, he'd held her just wanting to feel her in his arms, envisioning the union of their souls together in pure happiness. But he'd seen the confused look on her face, and realized she couldn't understand how he was feeling or what she truly meant to him yet.

When she'd asked her final question, it took everything he'd had not to lay it all on the line for her right then and there. He was so tired of covering up and not telling the truth, it was killing him. She'd looked unbearably weary, the remnants of tears staining her cheeks. His heart broke knowing his answer had done nothing to resolve the questions she had. One more time, he'd had no choice, except to withhold the truth until he and the investigator could put some safety measures into place.

When she'd agreed to give him one more opportunity to prove himself, he'd been filled with gratitude and even more love than he'd felt before. This woman knew nothing about him, yet was willing to trust him just on his word. His heart had been singing as he held her there in his arms. Not only had he discovered he'd found the love of his life, he was about to begin again his love affair with music.

Happiness washed over him in waves as he smiled almost giddily taking items out of the bags he'd set on the counter. The chicken needed to start marinating before he could make the call to the inspector again. Although, as excited as he was feeling, he'd tried earlier from his cell phone in the truck as he drove to the grocery store, but the connection had been lost and he'd had no success in calling back.

Eyeing the beginnings of what he considered his best dish, he wiped his hands on the dishcloth he'd tucked into his jeans and reached for the phone. Max dialed the number which seemed to be permanently imprinted in his memory. One he would much sooner forget than remember.

"Inspector Warner's office," the curt professional voice answered on the other end.

Max had met the woman many times in his visits to see Inspector Warner. He smiled picturing the grandmother of five grandchildren and two great grandchildren. He'd gotten to know Mrs. Petrovsky well while waiting endlessly for his weekly updates on his wife's case. Warner was terminally late for all of his meetings stating one reason or another for his tardiness.

"Well, *bene pomeriggio, Nonna.*"

"Max! How's my boy? I haven't seen you in ages. If you'd let me know you were coming into town I would have made sure I was here to see you."

"Nonsense. I understand your granddaughter was not feeling well and you needed to watch her. Family is much too important to forsake. We will get together soon, and you can tell me everything I have missed about those grandchildren of yours," he said hoping he would be able to bring Lauren back to meet her soon.

She'd been a delight to talk to while he was waiting for the Inspector, and she'd gladly been there for him when he needed support. She felt like his grandmother. His *nonna* had passed long before he'd been old enough to understand the special relationship they could have had together. Mrs. Petrovsky had fit so well in his vision of what a grandmother could be, so he'd adopted her as his own.

"Honey, you are family. And don't you forget it. There isn't anything I wouldn't do to help you out. You know that. Now what is it I can do for you?" She asked warmly.

" I need to speak to the Inspector. Is he in?"

"Honey, he went home earlier today. Sicker than a dog he was. Coughing and sneezing all over the place. I told him he needed to go home and tend to himself. There's no use in him spreading his germs all over the place, getting me sick, too. Sprayed the whole office down with disinfectant as soon as he left."

Max smiled as he pictured her spraying everything with a can of Lysol. "I thought he sounded a little under the weather when I saw him yesterday. Do you think he will be in tomorrow?"

"Knowing him, he will be. But don't count on it. Is there a message I can give him for you?"

Grimacing at the thought of not being able to talk to him until the next day, Max decided he was going to tell Lauren anyway. There was nothing the Inspector could do to change his mind anyway.

"Just tell him I need to speak with him right away. If he could call me as soon as he is in I would appreciate it."

After saying their goodbye's Max hung up the phone and turned toward the dinner he needed to get together. Catching the time on the clock above the stove, he realized it was quite a bit later than he'd thought it was.

The kitchen was not unknown to him. He'd spent many a dinner with his mother learning all the right spices and methods of a true Italian meal. Until he was old enough to lend a hand, she'd told him everything she was doing and the reasons why it was so important. When he'd been old enough to handle a knife and work alongside her, he'd taken well to transforming the raw ingredients set in front of him into dishes which made the mouth water just to smell them cooking.

He smiled as he remembered how he'd enjoyed every moment he'd spent with his mother in the kitchen and at the keys of the piano. There too, she'd taught him well, and although he was an excellent cook he'd excelled with the gift of music he'd been given.

Swift as he could, he set up the needed pans and utensils to make the dinner. Bringing his ingredients over to the main counter where he could work unhindered, he began pulling the vegetables out for the succulent dish he'd planned. In preparation for the main dish, he began chopping onions. Not having had enough time to light a candle nearby before starting, the fumes rose up into his face causing his eyes to tear up. Then if that was not enough the doorbell rang. It was too early for Lauren to show up. He'd figured he still had another half hour.

Max wiped his hands on the towel and tucked it into the front of his pants as he walked out of the kitchen toward the front door. A strange feeling of something slithering down his chest made him turn back and pull up his shirt to find out what had crawled down his belly in an oddly sensuous way. The gold chain he wore holding the wedding ring from his past dropped to the floor in a snake like manner, but the wedding band was not with the chain. He brought his hand up to his neck in search of the lingering memento. It wasn't there. A quick search around him turned up nothing. It was nowhere to be seen. Max bent and picked up the chain and stuffed it into his pocket. He would have to search the house later. Hopefully it wasn't laying anywhere Lauren would see before he had a chance to explain everything.

Through the burning tears in his eyes he opened the door to find Lauren.

"*Benvenuta*," he said with a genteel bow at the waist. As he rose, he tried brushing the tears with the back of his hand, only making things worse. "You are early, *amore*."

Lauren froze then stepped toward him lifting her hand to his face. Her closeness caused an immediate thrill to race up Max's spine, which had him wanting to bring her closer.

"What is it? Is everything all right? Has something happened to your father?" The immediate concern she showed touched his heart. *Such a sweet woman*, he thought.

"No, no. Everything is fine. I was just chopping onions in the kitchen," he said with a little sniffle. "But if tears is what it takes to get you to come close to me, perhaps I should cry more often." He smiled and bent to kiss her lightly on the lips.

As they moved into the front entry, Lauren held out the bottle of wine she held up for his inspection. "You said you had everything you needed, but I thought perhaps an extra bottle of wine is never wasted. If we don't need it tonight, perhaps you will invite me again sometime."

Nodding he took a look at the vintage Sauvignon. "You have good taste. We might just have to put this to good use tonight."

Max led the way into the kitchen, and caught sight of Lauren as she walked toward the glass exposure of the house. The sun's beams streamed through the scattered trees from the large window over the sink and the sliding glass doors leading to the back porch. It played gently off her silhouette, lighting her face in a mystical way, like the woods fairy he'd seen before.

"It's beautiful here isn't it," she said more as a statement than a question as she gazed out toward the lake.

The sudden urge to take her outside and make sweet love to her, with the sounds of the birds and the fluttering leaves, tore through him in an almost painful way. He knew when he was finally able to show her how she made him feel it would be better than either of them could imagine.

"Yes, it is beautiful, and so are you." He smiled at the confused look she shot him, and turned to start back on his chopping of vegetables. His incessant urge to take her in his arms and make her pained look go away was becoming too familiar. Soon, he hoped, there would be no pain for either of them to remember.

"I love the layout of this house. It makes me think of family," she said longingly. "One day, I hope my house will be the same."

"It already does, *amore*," Max said truthfully. "It isn't the house. It is the love and caring within the house which creates the feeling."

The smile she gave warmed his heart. Then she lifted her nose and sniffed. "Oh my goodness, what smells so glorious?" She walked over to lift the lid of his already steaming dinner. Looking over his shoulder, Max saw her raise her eyebrows as she set the lid back down. The look of surprise on her face was obvious as she turned toward him.

"I guess I owe you an apology," Lauren said stepping up beside him to peer over his arm at what he was doing. "Looks like you really do know what you are doing. I came early thinking I might need to give you a hand. But it looks like you have everything under control."

Laughing Max lifted his arm and pulled her against him, planting a kiss on top of her head, unable to resist any longer. The irresistible scent of her made his senses go wild.

"Yes, I think you do owe me that apology. But we will talk about how you can pay up a little later." He released her and turned to wash his hands in the sink. "Why don't you go find some music to put on while I put the rest of this together? It won't take long for this to be finished."

It had taken everything he had to let go of her. She was driving him crazy already, and she'd just gotten there. If he didn't know any better he might have thought this was purely a lust thing he had going on inside of him. But he knew it was so much more. He'd seen this woman in his dreams, long before he'd ever met her. She understood who he was, or at least the part he'd been able to tell her. It was tonight he would put to test whether she could understand all of who he was now and what he was behind the shadows of his past.

He'd never felt this way about a woman before. Even with his wife, there had never been the connection he felt with Lauren. His wife had never understood his relationship with his music. At one point, she'd described their marriage as if she was living with a man who had a mistress. Knowing there was something he loved more than he loved her was too much for her to handle. He'd done everything he knew to show Anna she meant the world to him. But she could never let go of the fact he was so drawn to the beauty of music he could get lost in it's rapture like the loving arms of another woman. He would never forget how she'd fought with him the night she'd died, claiming he should have stayed home with her in her time of need. He'd carried that guilt with him long enough.

    Max turned to check the status of the Chicken Marsala in the oven. The subtle tones of Mangione came wafting through the hall from the stereo in the living room. He smiled at her choice of music, it was perfect for the start to what he hoped would be a wonderful evening. From the cool marble counter behind him he poured two glasses of the Sauvignon which had been breathing since she'd arrived.

    With glasses in hand he headed toward the living room to find out what Lauren was doing. Max stepped into the living room and a sudden shrill of fear ripped through his heart when he saw what Lauren was doing.

    Lauren had found a wide spread of CD's and tapes neatly placed in a walnut cabinet below the stereo. She smiled at some of the same eclectic choices she would have chosen for herself. She selected one she thought would invite the mood for a warm romantic setting. Standing in the middle of the richly decorated room, she stood soaking up the ambiance of the room.

    Her eye caught the glint of something under the piano bench. It was definitely out of place and looked like something Max would not want to loose. She walked over and bent down to pick up the shining object. It was a gold ring, fairly simple but exquisitely crafted the size obviously for that of a man. It looked like a wedding band. Curious, Lauren rolled it between her fingers. Looking around the area her eyes settled on a well-worn scrapbook lying on top of the piano.

    Even more curious she opened the book to peek at some of the pages. She first saw some loose pages written in cursive tossed over a page full of pictures. Not wanting to barge into Max's personal life without him offering it up to her, she closed the book and started to turn away.

    Snap. Out of the corner of her eye she saw the pages of the book fly open by themselves.

Odd, she thought. *Maybe the spine is warped.*

Lauren picked up the book to inspect the spine. Everything looked normal. She closed the pages and placed it back on the top of the piano. The unusual coolness rippled through her on the inside, and she immediately knew she should pay attention.

Something was about to happen.

The scrapbook flew open again right in front of her eyes. Startled, Lauren's stomach lurched. Scenes from the pictures seemed to jump out at her. The wedding party had many guests, the bride dancing with an older gentleman, a table piled high with wedding gifts, and the most gorgeous wedding cake she'd ever seen. As she stepped closer, she gazed at the picture of the bride dancing. The facial features and stature of she and the older man were very similar. Must be father and daughter. Dressed in his military formals, she glanced at the medals he had on his upper chest. To small to see in detail, she had a vague feeling they looked familiar to her. Moving the loose hand written pages aside, Lauren uncovered pictures of the bride and groom. This must be Anna.

It didn't surprise her when she realized the man in the picture was the man who was in the kitchen cooking her dinner. The picture struck her as a couple who was very much in love. The glowing look on both of their faces drew a feeling of envy and unquestionable fear from the pit of her stomach. The ring in her hand felt as if it were burning in her palm as she picked up the pages she'd set aside. With fingers shaking she brought them closer to read what had been carefully written.

"Dearest Anna. You are and have always been my love. Sweetheart, please believe me when I say there is nothing that would ever take me away from you. You know my music is everything to me and it disheartens me to know you can feel such jealousy over an innate object which cannot return the love I have for it in the way we love each other..."

Reverently, Lauren placed the written letter back into the book. He must have loved his wife very much. To be loved in such a way was precious. The feeling in her heart dropped. How could she ever imagine he could love her in the same way? She knew she'd seen too much. If she were to find out any more Max was going to have to tell her.

Although he'd never said he'd been married, she'd guessed this might be the case. It still didn't explain all of her questions, but perhaps one of the reasons he couldn't talk with her about Anna was because he felt guilty.

The chill made her shiver again, and she looked around almost expecting to see a vision of Anna before her. Laughing at herself, Lauren began to step away when the pages of the scrapbook began to flap about in craziness, as if trying to get her attention. This way and that they fluttered until the book lay open to a newspaper article. Curious, she moved closer to read the tiny print. The title jumped out at her first, *"Local Musician Suspected in Wife's Grisly Murder."*

She stopped and stared without feeling at first. Then the words hit her like a brick. *Oh, my God.*

She reached out to spread the spine of the book to read further. The pages were suddenly ripped from her unsteady hand and started flipping again, this time stopping on a page filled with scribbled notes pasted all over. The notes were not clear as to whose handwriting they could be, but their intent was obvious from the words jumping out at her. Lauren didn't have time to look closer as the pages flipped all of a sudden to another article showing Max, handcuffed, being led up the steps of a Chicago precinct.

Lauren's heart began to thump in her chest. Was Anna trying to show her Max was responsible? Thoughts tumbled through her mind, and she started to wonder if she'd been mistaken this whole time. Maybe she needed to get out of here until she figured out who Max really was on her own. All of a sudden, the pages flipped back to the wedding scene. As if flipping pages wasn't enough, she couldn't believe what she saw. The photos looked as if they were being ripped from the book by an unseen force. One after another they were tossed into the air as if in frustration. The one of the bride and groom flew up and landed softly on the piano keyboard. Anna dancing with her father was jerked out of its place and slapped Lauren in the face.

She turned as she heard Max's approach, scared out of her wits at what to expect. She felt as if all the blood had drained from her face. Tears welled up into her eyes and began to spill down over her cheeks. She was frozen in shock as she looked up at him. Her mind had gone blank for the moment, not knowing what to do or what to say. She couldn't have moved if she'd wanted to.

Max surveyed the brevity of the situation. Immediately he took action. Setting down the glasses on the sideboard next to him he stepped toward her.

"Lauren, I can explain."

Fear of what he was about to tell her crept into her causing her body to gain motion. She had to get out of there. She had to think. Was this the big secret he had to tell her? Why had she trusted him?

The urge to flee welled up inside of her and she tossed the photo she held in her hand toward the scrapbook.

"Did you really murder your wife? Is that what your big secret?"

The stricken look on his face did nothing to quench her need to escape. As she moved quickly toward the door she realized she still held the ring in her hand and she turned to toss it at him. Finding he'd followed closely behind she stopped and gave him a look that would have stopped anyone dead in their tracks.

"Lauren. You have to let me explain. It isn't what you think." Max reached out to take her arm.

She jerked her arm away from him. "Don't. Just don't. I have to get out of here."

Turning she scooped up her purse and keys where she'd left them earlier, and opened the door only to have it slam shut. She jerked on the knob, the door felt as if it had been vacuum sealed shut.

Both she and Max stared at the door. As Max came toward her she tried the door again, this time with success. The door flew open with ease.

Stumbling down the steps, Lauren ran toward her car.

Max, stunned by her reaction, waited only a second to realize what she was doing. As he followed her out the door he realized that second had been one too long. His stride down the steps was not enough to catch up with the intent woman who had already reached her car and was climbing inside.

Starting the engine and throwing it into gear, Lauren stomped on the gas, obviously not caring what she ran over in the process. Her rear tires tore into the grass barely missing the flowers alongside the walkway.

"Damn it Lauren. Stop. Let me explain," Max yelled at her taillights.

Fully intending to follow her, he ran toward his truck and stopped. He didn't have his keys with him and would have to turn the stove off of the dinner he'd been preparing, or it would burn down the house.

A few minutes later he was barreling down the road at top speed on his way to Lauren's house. Those extra minutes had cost him, there was no sight of Lauren anywhere. Swearing, he took a corner too sharp and his back bumper barely missed the fender of a very alarmed woman sitting at a stop sign. He reached the familiar house in less than half the time it would have taken on his normal drive to work in the mornings.

As he leapt out of his truck he swore again, realizing Lauren's car was not in the driveway. He began pacing back and forth in front of his truck, the lights from the headlights glaring out at him as if in contempt for his omission of truth. A light rain began to sprinkle overhead.

Where is she? She should be here by now.

Chapter 14

Lauren sat in the parking lot of the shopping center, hot tears rolling down her face. She knew she couldn't go home. Max would have followed her there. Her first thought was to drive to her friend Rita's house, but she'd been forced to pull off of the road. The tears had come quickly blinding her ability to see. Questions were now speeding through her mind, anger welling up inside as she sat in her car giving in to the feeling of utter despair and helplessness.

Who was this man? Had he totally duped her into thinking she could trust him? Was he an escaped murderer, running for his life? Her mind skipped over all the Hollywood themes she'd seen with set ups just like the one she'd just experienced. He'd obviously wanted to seduce her tonight with his charm and good looks. Did he really think she would fall into his arms without a care for the fact he'd murdered his wife?

Her mind stumbled about in a fury of rage, not really taking the time to think through the questions. Anger filled her utterly with feelings of unjustness and a violation of every emotion a woman goes through in those first stages of caring about someone. She immediately connected the feeling with being used. How could he have used her like this? Why had she trusted in him like she had? How could he have no regard for her and what this meant to her? Of course, being a man, the only thing he really wanted was to get her into bed and use her until there was nothing left to give, then he would leave her just like everyone else had done in her life.

Not thinking clearly, the old feelings of total disgust with herself, and distrust of anyone who showed her anything more than a smile, reared its ugly head along with the old habit of feeling sorry for herself. A feeling she'd sworn she would never allow to come back, for as long as she lived. She'd sworn to herself she would never allow anyone to take advantage of her, nor would she let them use her for their own personal reasons. Becoming stronger in re-committing this same pact with herself, Lauren took a deep breath and centered herself, knowing there was no use in feeling sorry for oneself. The tears began to subside, yet she felt herself wilt with an almost forced exhaustion from the emotions running rampant through her.

Then the horrible thought hit her. Maybe Max had intended to kill her like he'd done his wife. Fear began to seep into every bone of her body.

Good Lord, get a grip, she thought.

Getting control of her thoughts, Lauren came to a realization. There was absolutely no proof any of this was true. She replayed in her mind what she'd seen and compared it to what she'd been feeling in her heart about Max, and the fear she'd felt moments before drifted away. The articles Anna had shown her were very concerning, but she hadn't had time to find out if the media's take on an exciting headline was even true. Perhaps what she'd seen was an unfortunate set of events which looked worse than real life. Though the pictures had startled her, she felt deep down it wasn't enough information to prove him guilty of anything.

It was obvious he wasn't hiding anything from her anymore. After all the pictures were set out in plain sight for anyone to see. He just hadn't told her about everything yet. Maybe he was going to tell her tonight. He was going to talk, and he was going to have to tell her everything now. No holding back, he was going to answer every question she had. No more covering up with 'it isn't the right time.'

Reaching for the tissues she'd stored in the glove compartment, Lauren took one and gave a good clearing of her head. It was clear now none of her answers would be found here in the parking lot. She was going to have to face Max and make him answer them himself. This would be the only way she would ever resolve her questions.

She closed her eyes, feeling the tremendous pounding of a headache coming to the surface from the intense shedding of tears. Leaning back, her head resting limply on the headrest, Lauren gave into the feeling of exhaustion and drifted weakly into a light sleep. Her brain drifting over thoughts and questions still lingering in her mind.

* * * *

Where the hell is she? Max sat in his truck outside of Lauren's house, chilled to the bone from his rain soaked shirt. He'd paced back and forth in the drizzling rain for an hour waiting for Lauren's return. Now he sat ignoring the chills running through his torso as he waited longer. *She should never have run off like that. What if something had happened to her? What if she'd gotten into an accident?* Well known feelings of guilt ripped through him as he imagined the worst. He would be totally at fault.

His stomach churned, partially from hunger, and partially from the unquestionable fear something had happened to Lauren and he would never have the chance to tell her how he felt about her. The look of mistrust and sadness in her beautiful green eyes before she'd run out the door had hit him like a steel fist in the gut. He hadn't even considered she would see the scrapbook before he was able to explain what was in those pages. Not knowing what all she'd seen, without explanation, she must have come to the wrong conclusion. He'd caused her to experience a pain he'd sworn never to allow her to feel again in her life.

Anger at himself coursed through him like a torrential flood pouring over him in a wave of emotion. Fears of what might have happened to her came to the surface as if he were re-living the horrible night of his wife's death, this time not just in his dreams, but in real life. He had to believe she was alright, or surely he would go insane.

He began shivering to the point his teeth were chattering, so he started the engine and turned the heat on high. The fogged windows started to clear and at the front of the truck illuminated by the parking lights, there in the mist stood Anna. She stood there, as if waiting for him to say something. Max's heart started beating so hard he heard it thundering in his ears. He had the sudden urge to talk to her. Feeling a little odd about it, he cleared his throat, but all that came out was a croak. Clearing his throat a second time, he tried again.

"I've never talked to a ghost before."

She smiled, and he felt as if she said back to him, "*Just talk to me like you always have.*"

"Should I come out there?" He asked, wondering if it would be better if he went out to join her.

Anna shook her head. *"No, stay where it's warm, I need to stay out here where you can see me."*

"Oh, okay," he said, with the sudden realization it must be easier for her. His mind went blank. What did you ask a ghost? Not able to think of anything of a spiritual nature, he went with what was on his heart. "I've really messed up this time, haven't I?"

"You should have told her."

"I know." She wasn't telling him anything he didn't already know. "Is it too late?"

"I tried to help."

He nodded then his head shot up. "What?"

Her form was beginning to fade. She remained for a moment, head tilted to the side as she used to do a sad smile on her face. Then she blew him a kiss and slowly disappeared.

Suddenly remembering the most important question he could ask, he yelled out, "Wait. No. Tell me who did this to you," ready to jump out of the truck as if chasing after someone who was walking away.

"You need to find Dad, he's sick," was the last thing he heard her say.

He sat staring into the mist, unable to comprehend what had just happened. Calmness settled over him, the warmth of the heater finally taking hold over his frigid bones.

In his silence he came to a realization. He'd seen her. Not in his dreams. Not in a state of exhaustion. She'd really been there. An odd feeling floated over him as if he knew everything was going to be alright. Anna had come back to show him to remain calm and think things through.

He desperately wanted to shield Lauren from the hurt he'd seen in her eyes. The pain he'd caused. To soothe her, and calm her fears. Fears he knew only he could answer. Her reaction was what he feared the most. Would she accept his answer or would she tell him to never show his face again? He shouldn't have waited so long to tell her. She deserved better than this.

If she would only come back, he could tell her everything about who he was and what he was hiding. Perhaps then they would have a chance to mend the damage that had already been done. Maybe she would hear him out. Then at least he would have the chance to tell her how he felt about her and what she meant to him.

It seemed like minutes melted into hours. Max sat and rubbed his hands over his face, trying to disperse the gloom which had settled over him once again. Through the windshield he peered out at the darkness cursing at himself for what he'd done. Or rather, hadn't done.

It was midnight and Lauren hadn't come home yet. She might have gone to see her friend Rita, or her Aunt in Seattle. But Max didn't know their addresses or phone numbers so he couldn't check to make sure she was safe. He sat for another two hours waiting impatiently for her return. She obviously had gone to someone's home and was staying the night. Nothing was going to happen tonight. He would just have to wait until morning and talk to her then. Pulling out of the drive he drove slowly home hoping to catch her on her way home. No such luck.

Back at Max's house, he roamed about in restless uncertainty. Stopping at the piano he saw some of what Lauren had been so upset over. The pictures lying open were of a very happy couple at the beginning of their lives together. The words from his letter to Anna jumped off the page at him. '*Love*' and '*never ending*' stuck out like a sword in an old wound. He sank down on the stool and laid his head on his arms. He couldn't take loosing his love again. Had he lost her, by his own doing this time?

His hand fell limply onto the piano keys, the notes making an odd musical tune. Straightening up he placed his hands on the keys and began gently picking out a melody. A sad tune came flowing from his fingers as the feelings from his heart poured out over the keys. Tears began to well up into his eyes as if the notes he played were pulling them out. His thoughts were not of the old love he'd once had, but of the new love that he longed for deep within his soul, yet may never be able to fulfill.

His heart crying out in despair, he gave up and settled in front of the fire, staring hopelessly into the flames. Soon he drifted off, though his intermittent sleep was filled with old nightmares and new ones conjured up by his imagination. The fear and chasing after evil enveloped a stage of new players—he and Lauren.

* * * *

Lauren awoke with a start. The rain pounding relentlessly on the roof of her car and windshield, sounded like a train coming down the track headed straight for her car. She'd fallen into a deep sleep, her neck stiffened by the awkward angle without much support. Shivering from the cold, she glanced at her watch and grimaced at the time. She'd been there for over six hours. Her face felt swollen from the tears she'd poured out straight from her heart. With a huge sigh, she realized her actions although warranted, were not going to solve anything. She needed to go back home and decide what she was going to tell Max in the morning. Starting up the car Lauren pulled out of the parking lot to head back home.

It seemed like it took forever to drive back. As she passed the turn off headed toward Max's place, she caught sight of taillights of a vehicle moving out of sight in the direction of his place. Was that Max? It might have been the lights of his truck. What would he be doing this time of night? Had he been up to her place checking on her? She didn't know whether to be touched by the sweetness of the thought or to still be wary of a man she really didn't know.

Anger was the answer, she had to be strong and cut all feelings for him off from her soft heart, which seemed to get her in trouble so many times. Why did she always have to fall for the wrong guys? Fall? What was she thinking? They really hadn't known each other long enough for her to fall in love with him.

Unlocking the door to the house Lauren dropped her purse on the floor beside the door. Flipping on the soft light of the living room, the image of Max and she earlier came back to her vividly. Tired she rubbed her hands over her face and dropped down on the couch. She'd felt something so deeply connected with him. But could she have fallen in love with him that quickly? Had she jumped too quickly at the circumstantial evidence being shown to her evening? Max had said he could explain.

    Maybe there was something more to the story than what she'd uncovered. She'd always prided herself in giving people the benefit of the doubt when things didn't seem right. And this definitely did not seem right to her. Beyond what her thoughts were telling her, she couldn't ignore the fact her intuition was still telling her he was a good man. There was no way she could believe he could do anything so horrible as to murder his wife. Especially if he loved her in the way the letter had stated. Lauren took another deep breath and tuned into her gut feelings. The look on his face when she left was not of a man whose secrets had been discovered. He'd looked as if he were loosing something very precious to him. It reminded her of her own shattered feeling when she'd found out her parents had died. A feeling so deep, there was no mistaking its presence.

    She decided in the morning she would bring the tools he'd left at the house back to him, and tell him she could not stand any relationship where trust was torn away, personal or business. If he didn't tell her what she wanted to hear, then both would be severed very quickly. It had to be done in that way. It couldn't continue on the way it had, with only half-truths and mistrust. He would either tell her the whole story or their relationship would end.

    Feeling good about her decision, she stood to her feet forgetting she hadn't eaten all day, and dragged her tired bones up the stairs for what she knew was going to be a very long night—with not much sleep.

* * * *

    It was half past seven when Lauren drove up to stop in front of Max's house. She had packed up his equipment as planned early that morning in hopes to catch him before he'd left to come back to her house. After waiting at the front door for several minutes for Max to answer her knock, she made her way toward the back of the house. He was home because his truck was parked outside. There was no doorbell on this rustic old home, and the front door was made out of what looked like a very heavy oak wood. She could barely hear her own knocks on the door, and it was possible Max was unable to hear her as well.

Coming around the side of the house Lauren heard Max's voice very clearly coming through the kitchen window. It sounded like he was on the phone. When she stepped onto the porch she could see him leaning against the sinks edge, his back toward the window.

"Inspector, I can't keep living like this. I've made up my mind. Lauren has made me realize how important my music really is to me and it's time she found out who I really am." Max paused a moment, listening to the response on the other end. "I've considered what we talked about, and fully accept there are risks. But at this point I'm already dead if I continue the way I've been going. If he's going to kill me, then let him try. I have a few things to show him now I didn't have before."

Lauren saw Max reach out and run a hand over the muscles bulging from underneath his T-shirt. She moved closer to the window so she could hear what he was saying more clearly. He turned slightly and she saw a quick view of concern in his furrowed eyebrows as he listened.

" I have to disagree. Lauren has nothing to do with any of this." After listening again to the response, Max shook his head. "I think he only wants me. The bottom line is, if nothing else, I have to tell her. I'm going forward with my plans to start performing again. When this comes closer we will discuss the possible options and decide what needs to be done. I'll take the needed precautions here in case he decides to make any other moves."

He'd begun to pace back and forth in front of the stove. "Make sure the security on my parent's place stays solid. I can't have anything else happen to them." Max paused and nodded his head. "Yes, of course, I will let you know right away."

Lauren heard him close the conversation up politely and he turned to hang the receiver up. There she stood in plain site in front of the open screen door. From what she'd overheard, all thoughts of anger and mistrust had swiftly left her, now replaced with concern and a growing respect for this man. She was finally beginning to see the answer to her questions.

Slowly Max came around the end of the counter to the door and opened it for her to enter. Thoughts swarmed through her head piecing all of what she already known about him with what she'd just learned. No longer afraid, Lauren moved through the opening to stand beside him. He seemed unsure of how to act with her. He looked deep into her eyes, almost pleading for her to stay. In answer, she nodded her acceptance, and he laid a hand on her waist to lead her into the living room to sit on the couch. Sitting down next to her, he turned to face her.

"*Bella*, I'm not sure all of what you heard, but please let me explain," Max implored. The scrapbook she'd seen the night before was laying on the coffee table, this time closed, its contents hiding from her inquisitive eyes. She looked back to find Max looking back intently into her eyes.

"Ok, but you'd better tell me everything this time."

"I promise. No more lies. I won't be told what I can and can't do any longer." He took a deep breath and let it out slow. "I'm not sure where to start."

"The beginning is always best," Lauren responded softly.

Max nodded. "Let me tell you I've never wanted to hurt you in any way. Do you believe me?" His eyes searched hers for answers he seemed to need to hear.

"I believe you," Lauren answered from her heart.

Max reached out to grasp her hands. "I don't know all of what you know or don't know, so I'll tell you everything. What I have to say may not be easy to hear, but I need you to be as open as you possibly can be."

She nodded in agreement and motioned for him to continue. He started telling her his life's story, filling in all those places where he'd left himself out of the picture. Thankfully, Lauren started putting together the puzzle pieces for her new view of this carpenter, artist, gentle-hearted man she knew named Max.

His mother had taught him everything she knew about music and performance values from an early age. He and his sisters were put through music classes since they were able to walk, but he'd been the one to inherit the gift of transferring heart and soul into the music which came from deep within his being. He laughed as he told her it was his deep expressive voice which had won him all the acclaim she'd read about in the papers.

"My mother was so delighted when I told her I'd chosen a selection from Verdi's Rigoletto for the University's annual music competition. My fellow musical comrades were so impressed they influenced my decision to begin performing in as many operatic venues as I could. But I soon realized that wasn't where my heart belonged. I needed to write the pieces roaming around in my head all the time."

Lauren smiled, understanding exactly what he meant.

"But I needed more experience. That's when I auditioned for the Philharmonic Orchestra of Chicago. It was my luck the Maestro had been present to hear my work. You couldn't imagine how surprised I was when Sturdivan walked onto the stage and shook my hand. He actually invited me to continue studying under his direction. I put everything I had into all of my performances. And things just exploded from there. " Max's expression said it all.

She almost felt as if she'd gone through his growth alongside him. Pride in his accomplishments drew a joy from her the same as when her son had won the soccer scholarship to be granted his graduating year.

. "It was at the University of Chicago where I met Anna," Max started. Lauren could see a change come over him. Sadness settled over him like a black cloud waiting to rain on his previous joy. But she knew he needed to get this out, or it would forever be hanging over his head ready to thunder down on him.

"Tell me about her."

He grasped her hand as if needing strength to go on. "Apparently she'd had a rough childhood. She doesn't remember much of the early years, but she told me when she was about three her mother dropped her off one day at a Veteran's hospital to meet her Dad, and never came back for her. She said he'd told her he didn't even know she'd existed up until that point. He did the best he could to take care of her. His injuries earned him a Purple Heart, but it didn't help his PTSD any. He suffered from stressful fits of depression, nightmares and hallucinations almost on a daily basis. They went to live with his parents for a time, but he never seemed to keep jobs for very long."

As he'd been describing this Lauren saw short little flashes of the young woman's demise, with the same backdrop and the man kneeling over her. She'd almost gotten used to seeing this, but now knew there was a reason. Wanting to let Max finish without interrupting, she remained silent with the intention of bringing it up later.

Max went on to explain how the relationship started and how they'd ended up marrying just before his debut on the music scene. "Anna was a fantastic artist. Her work seemed to jump off the page and become alive. She'd been working on a collection of butterflies she'd been contracted to display in a gallery when all this happened."

Now it all seemed to fit so well. The butterfly was an extension of her previous life. She'd been trying to tell her who she was and what she'd been doing. That was why Lauren kept drawing, and seeing the butterflies everywhere.

"My mom and I were scheduled to perform a medley of scores from different favorite operas as the entertainment to a charity function to raise money for the new pediatric wing at the Chicago Medical Center. It was a great honor to be invited to perform for this event." Max took in a deep breath and let it out slowly. "And that is the last time I've performed on stage since Anna's death."

Lauren leaned in and gave him a hug. He held her there for a long time, and she let him draw whatever strength he needed to go on. As she pulled back, a glassy sheen had begun to form in his eyes. He looked away, to gain control again.

"It's alright. Take your time," she encouraged.

"Anna was five months pregnant. I made her stay home that night because she wasn't feeling well. The only way I could get her to stay back was if I promised to bring home some of her favorite ice cream," he said with a sour laugh.

Lauren watched and listened as he expressed the remainder of his story with great sadness.

"The performance was such a success for the hospital, my spirits were flying high. I had to take my time though because the roads were icy. It hadn't snowed yet, but it felt cold enough to let loose that night. When I got home I knew something was wrong. The front door was open, which was really strange because Anna was cold-blooded. There was no way she would have opened the door for air, especially on a night like that one."

He struggled with the next part. Lauren's heart went out to him as she imagined he was reliving it all over again. "I rushed in, calling her name, but she didn't answer. I started searching every room in the house. Upstairs, downstairs, everywhere I expected to find her, but she wasn't there."

A single drop ran down the side of his face and he brushed it away with irritation. "It was obvious something was wrong. She hadn't told me she was going out anywhere. Then I started thinking something had happened and she'd had to go to the hospital. So I ran to my office to start calling around. The first thing I saw was the vault in the corner of the room was wide open, everything gone. At that point I knew something worse than what I'd imagined had happened. When I started toward the phone on the desk, that's when I saw her."

He had to get up at this point to pace the floor for a minute. Lauren remained silent, allowing him to finish in whatever manner he needed.

"She was on the floor in front of the sofa, lying peacefully as if she were asleep. Her arms were crossed over her chest, like someone had stopped to place them there. When I came around the end of the couch, I saw the pool of blood soaked into the carpet beneath her." He stared into the unlit fireplace a moment, with a deep sigh of resignation.

"After that everything was a blur. Policemen asked questions over and over. Finally the coroner came after an eternity to take her away. They let me leave, only to come back the next day to handcuff me and bring me back to the precinct, saying I was their prime suspect as the locks hadn't been broken and they couldn't substantiate my alibi from the time I'd left the charity event. I couldn't remember which damned store I'd gotten the ice cream. I think I must have stopped at three or four to find the Chunky Monkey she was craving."

He came back and sat down next to Lauren again. The sorrow in his eyes had almost broken her heart as she watched him recall that night.

"That explains the article I saw last night."

"If you'd just waited I would have explained it all to you," he sighed. "But I understand why you had to leave."

"Well, I was a little freaked out by everything by the time you came in. Anna chose to show me the wrong things at the wrong time."

Max frowned. "What?"

"Anna was here last night and she was flipping pages in that book," Lauren said pointing to the scrapbook. "Tearing pictures off of the pages and throwing them at me!"

"I thought you'd done that. You're saying Anna made the mess?" He rolled his eyes and shook his head, laughing. "Sounds like her. She always did go for the drama in everything." Max fell silent, looking down at his hands. Raising his head to gaze into Lauren's eyes, he spoke in hushed tones, "I saw her again last night, this time she spoke to me."

Lauren's eyes widened, chills running over her skin. "You saw her ghost? What happened?"

Max ran his hands over his arms as if he too had felt a chill. "When you hadn't come home for hours, I started to think maybe something had happened to you." He grasped her hand again, and raised it to his cheek, and gave her a quick kiss. "She came to me to tell me you were alright and not to worry. I remember now, she told me she'd tried to help," he said with knowing smile.

"I wouldn't say she was much help to me last night. What else happened?" Lauren asked wanting to know more.

"Not much. She didn't hang around very long. Oh, except she told me I needed to find her Dad. Apparently he's sick."

Lauren immediately thought of the times Anna had channeled through her. It seemed now Max had told her he'd seen her spirit, it wouldn't be such a bad thing to tell him what had come to her.

"I wasn't sure if I should tell you before, but Anna has come to me several times, too. I don't see her, but she's come to me through a method called automatic writing. I remember her saying something similar. She's worried about her Dad."

Max stared at her a moment before acceptance set in. "You weren't as clear about how, but you'd told me she'd somehow come through to you before. How is it you know how to do this automatic writing?"

"For a while now I've been learning more about spirit, energies, crystals, chakras and things from a place down in Tacoma that deals with the metaphysical side of our existence. It's pretty interesting how everything seems to make sense now," Lauren actually felt relieved by having told him about her own secrets. "While I've started to learn more I've experienced more, too."

"Like what?"

Lauren looked down to their joined hands. The warmth enveloped her in a safe and loving way. There was no need to hide anything anymore.

"Anna has shown me several times a vision of the night she was killed."

Max sat back, still gripping her hand. "What did you see?"

"It's too quick to make much out, but there is a figure of someone, I'm pretty sure it's a man. He's leaning over her, crossing her arms like you said when you'd found her."

"Can you see his face? Did she show you who did this?"

"I'm sorry, no, his back is turned to me and all I can see is the back of his head," Lauren shook her head wanting so badly to be able to tell him what he needed to hear. "Then I've gotten another one with you in the doorway, standing next to a Grandfather clock. It's beautifully ornate, but I noticed the pendulum isn't swinging, and the hands are pointed toward midnight." Lauren looked up to see a stricken look on Max's face and wondered if she's said too much.

Max closed his eyes and began nodding his head. When he opened them again Lauren felt a wash of relief flow over her. He was actually smiling. "That old clock is sitting in my office. She'd seen it in an antique store and fell in love with it, so I bought it for Anna as a surprise for our next anniversary. They told us it hadn't worked in years."

"Why are you smiling?" Lauren asked wondering what he was thinking.

"You just proved to me everything you've told me is true. Nobody else knew about the clock. It had just been delivered the night before. We didn't know where to put it just yet."

This whole conversation was proving things for her as well. Up until now she hadn't been sure if she were making things up in her mind. Now she believed it was true. She was actually communicating with the spirit world.

All of a sudden her stomach began to rumble, with a very loud growl. She frowned and put her hand over her stomach. Max smirked at her. "And that proves you're just as hungry as I am," he said standing to his feet.

"Wait, we aren't finished here," Lauren jumped up, feeling as if she'd only gotten half of the story. "You haven't told me who and what you were talking about on the phone this morning."

"You're right, we aren't. But there are some very important things we need to discuss, and it's going to take quite a while to answer your questions. So, if you let me fix you some breakfast, we can at least talk about the rest of this more comfortable."

She was feeling a little light headed. Looking at the clock she realized it had been over 20 hours since she'd last eaten anything. "Alright, I'll help you so we can get done quicker. But only because I'm starving."

Chapter 15

As they'd made breakfast, Max couldn't help the feeling of peace and contentment surrounding him. This was how life was supposed to be. They'd laughed and joked while eating, as if there wasn't a care in the world. Yet, until this building unease could be put to rest, he couldn't think everything would turn out right. The inspector had a very good point. There was no promise this madman wouldn't come to Washington to finish the job. The question was how could he be prepared enough to protect himself and Lauren from any impending danger?

He sat back and gazed at Lauren as she savored her last piece of bacon. In awe of this woman who was so willing to give her heart to him without knowing the whole story, he made the decision. He wouldn't let that go. He couldn't.

Lauren glanced back up at him and stopped chewing. "What?" she asked.

"You are so beautiful," he said from his heart.

She smiled as she blushed and looked away. Then turning back to him she said, "Don't think you're going to get past me with your compliments. I've still got a whole lot of questions."

Max stood and gathered up the plates and put them in the sink. While he poured another cup of coffee for them both, he nodded. "I know, *Bella*. Ask me all your questions. I have nothing but answers for you."

"I was thinking, you said they arrested you because your alibi wasn't solid. What happened?"

"It wasn't because the truth didn't work. They hadn't been able to track down which grocery store I'd gone to, so until they could I was their prime suspect. When they finally figured it out there were security tapes showing I really was there at the time of the murder. After verifying with the night clerk I was the one in the tapes they had to let me go. There was no way I could have gotten from the event and then to the store and back home in the amount of time needed to commit the crime. She'd been gone well over an hour before I found her." Max picked up his coffee cup and walked over to the window and watched as two Robins listened carefully for their morning breakfast.

He knew he needed to give as much detail to Lauren as he could, and he was more than willing to do so now. Not that he would ever forget, but would he ever stop needing to explain what happened that horrible night—probably not.

"So, you were proven innocent. I still don't understand how you ended up here. I have a feeling it has something to do with the phone conversation I heard this morning," Lauren sat back in her chair with her coffee cup in her hands.

"You're right. Let me explain first, after the ordeal with the police, it didn't end there. A few days after the murder I started receiving these anonymous messages. Threatening me and blaming me for Anna's death. The police thought they were coming from some whacko following the case through the media. It wouldn't have been so bad, except I started finding things in my house, and the notes were getting more demented, placing me where I went every day. This guy was watching me. He knew my every move."

Max watched Lauren carefully, unsure of how she would take this new information. At any point she could just tell him she didn't want anything more to do with him. She had a frown on her face, but other than that he couldn't figure out what she was thinking, so he went on.

"The reason I left and came here is because he started doing things to scare me. When he blew up the wall in front of me, I decided I needed to get away for a while."

Max thought for sure she would have made a beeline for the door once he started this part of the story, but she continued to sit and listen, with only a raised eyebrow at the whole blowing up thing.

"That's when I came here. I've been here for a little over a year."

Lauren took another sip of her coffee and set the cup back down. Max could see she was putting all the pieces together, contemplating what her next question should be. She stood and walked slowly back into the living room, looking around her as she went.

"Did you buy this house?"

"No. This is my Uncle Estevan's home. He went back to Italy for an extended stay, and was looking for someone to take care of it while he was gone. It just happened it was the same time I was in need of a place to stay for a while."

"I'll have to assume then, since you've been up here they haven't been able to find the killer?"

"The problem is, when I went into hiding the notes stopped. So they haven't been able to find out who was making the threats. The police have set this aside as an unsolved mystery and filed it away in their cold case files. They keep telling me they have some leads, but never enough to make any arrests. I've had an Investigator working on this from the start. He hasn't given up yet." Max sat on the couch and picked up the scrapbook. "If you don't believe any of this, here is all the proof you need."

With increased tension in his stomach he watched Lauren take hold of the book and gently open the cover, as if she too realized the contents were irreplaceable precious remnants of a time in Max's life. As she flipped through the beginning pages, he knew it seemed like the album of a couple whose relationship was meant to age into the golden years of life.

The next pages were covered in newspaper clippings from the Chicago Times showing titles like *'DeAngelo's Wife Killed in Own Home'*, *'Pregnant Woman Murdered'*, and *'Homicide in Chicago Suburbs'*. He'd kept these only to remind himself when things looked bad, they could always be worse. Lauren seemed to scan through these quickly. Though she stopped to read in detail the one titled, *'Flourishing Music Talent Suspected in Wife's Murder'*.

"This reminds me why I don't read the newspaper or look at the news very often," Lauren murmured shaking her head. "Media has such a fatalistic viewpoint on life. Incessant negativity isn't good for anyone."

Max had to agree. They had taken the horrid events of a time in his life and spread him out to the readers as a guilty murderous individual who didn't deserve to live. Once he'd been proven innocent, though, instead of an array of articles rejoicing in the positive result, he'd found only one short blurb a couple of paragraphs long stating the true facts. In reality, he wasn't even sure his audiences would forgive and forget the lies once told about him. He could only hope they would.

She looked curiously through the confirmation of his story, stopping to read some of the harassing notes he'd kept. When she set the scrapbook back on the coffee table she turned to face him. There were tears glistening in her eyes.

"*Bella*," he said reaching out to brush away the one starting its journey down her cheek.

"I'm so sorry you've had to go through all of this. You don't deserve to be treated this way." Lauren leaned forward and wrapped her arms around his neck. He held onto her like a life preserver. She had come into his life and anchored his heart in pure true love.

Sitting back she closed her eyes for a moment, Max waited as he was sure she still had questions, when she opened them again he saw curiosity more than concern. "I appreciate what I heard you say this morning about needing to tell me about everything. Is this the person who has kept you from talking this long?"

"Yes, the Inspector thought it best not to involve anyone as we are still unsure where the killer might be. He made me promise not to tell you," Max said looking down at his hands.

"So why does the Inspector think there would be any danger to me?"

Max shot a glance her way. He hadn't been sure if she'd heard that or not. This is what he needed to tell her, but feared the most. They hadn't formed any type of solid relationship yet. There was no reason for her to get involved further.

"By the patterns of this psycho, he thinks he might connect you and Anna together in some way. The notes keep relating to me as the money grubbing whore who stole away his beloved girl. The Inspector thinks this might be the killer, and he's placed his own act of violence on me, fixating on my success for some reason. He isn't 100% sure though, and neither am I. But if it comes down to it I can't risk either of our safety."

Lauren stared at him. "Wait a minute. What are you saying? You don't want to be involved with me, or you wouldn't reclaim your music?"

"*Amore,* you have brought back to me everything I hold close to my heart and you've opened up new possibilities I want to explore. I don't think I can give up either one. Yet, if there is danger, I may have to delay one for the other." He bowed his head for a moment and took in a deep breath, a sense of relief washing over him. Looking back up at her he smiled lightly trying to relieve the thickness in the air. "I don't know if you realize how much I needed to tell you all of this. I hope you understand why I couldn't tell you everything before. I've wanted so badly to open up and let you know about all of this."

Max sat restlessly waiting for a response—any response. His heart began to thump erratically in his chest as she sat still, watching every move he made. Unsure of what she might be deciding to do, he felt a light sweat begin to form and he rubbed his palms on the side of his pant legs.

Then Lauren reached out and took hold of his cold and clammy hand. Leaning forward she touched her lips ever so lightly against his, sending a warm tingling feeling through his lips. He felt a loving warmth pour over them in a rush. The true accepting nature of her was not something he'd seen very often. In his heart he knew she represented the purest image of love he could ever have imagined.

As she pulled back, she took a deep breath before she spoke. "Well, I tell you what. I'm not about to let you go now that I've found you. I don't know exactly where this relationship will end up, but I'm willing to at least give it a chance. And there is no way I will allow you to put aside your music again. We are just going to have to figure this thing out somehow."

An explosion of happiness settled over Max. Desperate to tell her he'd fallen in love with her, he realized she still questioned their relationship. With everything else happening this morning, it wasn't the time to express his everlasting love for her. He couldn't risk losing her by rushing things too quickly.

They spent the next hour discussing some of the options he had thought about. His connections with the music scene wouldn't be hard to start back up again, especially with some of the newest pieces he'd composed. There wasn't a label who wouldn't see the potential in the music he brought to the table. He'd always had extremely good luck with all of his demo material. Besides, after he contacted his friends and associates at the recording studio, the director at the Harmonic Symphony would be elated to hear from him again, he'd no doubt he would be back up and running shortly.

Lauren agreed with him, if at any time something were to happen involving danger to her or her son, they would have to reassess where their relationship was headed. In the meantime they would take things slowly, exploring each other in hopes to find what Max already knew he'd discovered. They agreed he couldn't live life hiding from the unknown. Fear had to be addressed head on, and the impact of the result would need to be dealt with when it happened.

They sat in silence, each in their own thoughts for a while. Max reached over to give her a hug. When she pulled back, she drew her brows together and asked, "Do you have any idea who could be doing this to you?"

An odd popping sound seemed to come through the walls toward them, as if all of a sudden the walls were about to crack. The temperature seemed to drop twenty degrees in a matter of seconds. A chill ran up Max's neck and he looked around the room expecting to see Anna. He looked at Lauren, who had brought her arms up around her against the chill. They almost said at the same time, "Something's going to happen."

The scrapbook cover flung itself open to the left, opening the pages from right to left, uncontrollably blowing around as if crazed. It finally stopped at the pages with the wedding photos.

"Why does she keep showing me this?" Lauren asked him. They both knew who was responsible for this activity. Max shook his head.

He'd looked at the picture a million times. He had no idea what was so special about it. "What are you trying to show us Anna? Just tell me."

The pages fluttered around again, this time stopping on the page with the harassing notes. It rested there a minute. Max and Lauren looked at each other again.

"I think she's trying to answer my question." The book was shoved to the edge of the table toward them. "Who is it Anna? Who is doing this to Max?" Lauren asked her face pointing to the air around them.

Max didn't know what to think. He hadn't experienced this type of activity yet. The pages started flipping back and forth until they stopped again on the wedding photos. There were at least fifty people standing in the groups of people. How was he going to find out who these people were? Most of them were Anna's family. He only knew a few of them.

A whirlwind of a breeze shot up and the pictures were torn out of their holders one by one. Max felt as if frost had started to form on his nose, so he reached up and found it to be ice cold. They watched as the photos began blowing about, then landing haphazardly all over the room. Just like he'd found them last night.

One of them gently floated down and landed in his lap. He picked it up and stared hard at the picture. He and Anna were standing in front, posing for the photographer. Not everyone gathered behind them had been ready for the picture, some looking down at their clothing, others helping to straighten a bow or a tie for their companion. Total, Max counted fifteen people, all of which he didn't know except his father in law.

Testing his luck in getting an answer from her, he looked up and asked, "Is the person who is threatening me in this photo?"

All of a sudden the scrapbook slammed shut.

"I guess you have your answer," Lauren said, staring at the closed book. "Wait!" she exclaimed. "Do you know who killed you?" The photo was jerked out of Max's hand and landed on the coffee table in front of her. "Is he in this photo?" Lauren questioned.

The brisk air didn't surprise them, but what did was what happened next. The photo flew up into the air and dangled in front of them in mid air a minute then slowly drifted down toward the floor. They both sat, staring at the picture, the room returning to its normal temperature.

Max reached down to pick it up. He looked at Lauren's wide eyed expression. "Looks like I've got some research to do."

She nodded her head. "Who are these people?"

"I have no idea."

Chapter 16

The next morning Max arrived at the house at 7:45 am, an ungodly time, if you asked Josh. The sound of hammers pounding on the side of the house annoyed him even though he knew he needed to be up and out the door in 15 minutes to catch the bus. Fruitlessly, he covered his head with the pillow trying to block out the noise. Choking out an oath he ripped the covers off and with a half hearted stretch rose to claim the day in front of him.

Downstairs Lauren sat at her desk going over her budget. Max had insisted he continue the work on the house. Staring at the numbers she realized the cost of this renovation had risen much higher than she'd expected. Max hadn't even been paid for his time yet. The way things were going it was obvious she wouldn't be able to finish the deck as she'd hoped by the beginning of July. They would just have to wait until she was able to either get an advance on her book, or she would have enough time to save from her job at the college to pay for the next phase of improvements.

With a sigh she pushed back from the desk. She would have to tell Max right away before he started work on her dream. Catching a glimpse of him through the window made her smile. He'd already gotten a covering of dirt and dust over his usual black T-shirt. He looked just as good in work clothes as he did in his classy Italian dinner suit. She paused for a moment to watch as he bent to pick up another handful of nails to finish putting up the siding on the back section of the house.

As he stood up he turned to face the window and caught sight of her. Looking straight up into her eyes, a mischievous grin spread across his face, and he stuck his tongue out at her. Since their talk he'd begun to smile more often, and burst out in song as he worked. Now the look in his eyes released a feeling in her Lauren couldn't pinpoint exactly. But recognized if she allowed herself to open up and trust him would be the beginning of her falling hard for him.

She smiled back and blushed at having been discovered staring at him. Turning she made her way out to the front of the house. She'd heard the rumblings of her son a few minutes earlier and wanted to make sure he was getting himself out on time.

She found him on the front porch, the remnants of an apple in his hand. Obviously, he'd wolfed down the first thing he'd seen on his way out the door.

"Hey Sweetie, don't I get a kiss before you leave?" She offered her cheek out for the expected kiss.

"Mom, really, don't you ever get tired of that?"

"Never! You will have to do it until I'm dead and gone, which won't be anytime soon."

"Oh, man! I can't get a break can I? You'll probably haunt me after that, too!" Smiling he turned and gave her a quick peck on the cheek. Leaping down the stairs by twos he yelled back at her. "I won't be home till late Mom, Robert and I are going to Katy's after school. She's got this kick ass Dad who works on classic cars. Thought maybe we could get some pointers from him for the Mustang." Waving back at her he disappeared through the trees at the edge of the driveway on his way to his friends house.

Shaking her head at the unbelievable luck of having such a wonderful son, she turned toward the noise she heard behind her. Max had come in through the back door and snuck up to grab her around the waist. She could feel his strong arms envelope her into a hug that seemed to be the substance of everything she needed in her life. Love and happiness was all she could picture at that moment. There was no feeling of mistrust or previous hurts. She only felt her heart opening just a little more, and could feel the truest feelings of love beginning to pour out for him.

Slowly she turned to face him, offering her lips for the kiss she was anticipating. Max lowered his lips to hers sending shock waves throughout her body. The impact was almost too much for her.

"I want you, *Ma Bella*," he said huskily. Lauren felt herself tense up a bit still in fear of what would happen when they did make love. As if sensing her thoughts, he paused and laid his cheek against hers. "I know it will take time. It isn't easy what you've been through with me so far. Believe me, I am willing to wait. Even though you make it so difficult," he grinned and gave her another kiss.

Lauren laughed, unsure of how to respond. If she encouraged him, it would only make things happen quicker for them. She wasn't ready yet, even though every time she came within a few feet of this man it was like every hormone in her body began to do somersaults. The tug she felt in anticipation toward a more physical connection scared her. Pulling away from him she smiled and gave him a quick hug.

"Max I have to tell you something I'm really not too happy about."

His brows came together with concern. "Tell me, *Bella*. What is it?"

"I've gone over the figures more times than I'd like to admit. There is just no way I will be able to start the work on the deck like I'd planned. Finances are just not stretching as far as I had expected. This means after you finish the siding, we are going to have to discontinue any further work until I can afford it."

Max seemed to considered what she was saying for a moment. What she didn't know was he'd already decided he was going to do the work for no labor cost. She'd mentioned several times throughout their discussions about how close she was running with her funds. On the plane back from Chicago he'd decided he would give this as a gift to her, hoping to show how he felt about her. Knowing she wouldn't accept it very willingly, he'd decided to offer to do the work for delayed payment, and then at the time of his final billing for the project he would surprise her with almost no cost involved.

"Tell you what I'm going to do. I am really in no need of any immediate payment for materials or time. Why don't I continue the work, and we can work out a plan of some sort later. It's just my way of being a nice guy."

Lauren took in a deep breath, contemplating how this made her feel. On the one hand, she was excited about the possibility of having everything finished in time for the party she'd planned for her family and friends on the 4th of July. On the other hand she didn't want to feel like she owed him in any kind of way. She'd seen relationships crumble under the pressure of financial disagreements.

"I don't know Max. It would only work if we were to write up a contract with terms of repayment. I won't have this become a subject of contention between us. But we'll have to delay for a bit until I can work the repayment figures into my budget."

Smiling at her strict business side, he held out his hand to her in a gentleman's agreement. "Agreed, with only one exception. I start the work now, and we write in a clause for delayed payment to begin let's say in six months."

She raised her eyebrows in disbelief. This was way too good to be true. "Are you sure this is what you want to do? You know I'm good for it, but you don't have to take such a risk. I would understand if you wanted to wait a while. In fact I don't think you should do anything until I have at least the cash saved up to pay you for your time."

She was feeling a bit uncomfortable with the arrangement. She'd dealt with issues around money in the past with her second husband. He'd had this strange sense of right and wrong when it came down to what belonged to each of them in the split up. There had been court battles around what little she'd owned going into the marriage and what they'd accumulated during their time together. Luckily the small amount of inheritance from her parents she had put in saving had been granted hers. That was all she had for Josh's college fund so far.

Although this was a totally different situation she couldn't help but feel her defenses going up. She didn't believe for one minute Max would act in the same way as Evan had. But she couldn't take the chance something could come up between the two of them over the matter.

She realized she must have shown her concern on her face when Max took her hand in his and said, "I don't know who you have dealt with in your past, but it is obvious they have not been the right kind of people. I would appreciate it if you would stop comparing me to them. What I say I mean and I stick by my word." Grateful for his words, she continued to waiver a bit on the arrangement. "I'm going to do the work and we will put it in writing only because I think you'd feel better about it."

Shaking her head, Lauren smiled up at him. "Well I guess I've been told." Reaching up she placed her hand on his cheek. She'd been blessed to have been given the opportunity to have met this man. She could almost say her faith in the good of people was coming back. "Okay, but you are definitely going to get more than you expect out of this."

"I already have, *Mia Bellezza*. I already have."

* * * *

Throwing her jacket on, Lauren scooped up the book by the door, and rushed out the front door to get to work. She'd been working on her book all afternoon and hadn't had a chance to throw anything together for Josh's dinner. That was the purpose of frozen dinners, right? She left him a note on the counter explaining what he should do, ending with her usual 'Love Ya Honey'. Most times she would find out he and his friends had stopped to get something at the local fast food joint anyway, so she wasn't too worried about him starving.

Turning around to lock the bolt on the front door the sound of a car coming down the driveway stopped her in the act. The sporty Z-28 was not one she recognized, but the man who stepped out was all too familiar. He sauntered up the walkway stopping at the bottom of the stairs. The smug smile on his face reminded her of all the reasons why she'd left him in the first place.

"Hello there, LuLu," he said using a nickname he'd given her when they'd first met. One she hated then and she despised even more now.

"Hello, Ben. To what do I owe this surprise visit?" Lauren asked wondering how he'd gotten her address.

Ben tilted his head to the side making a show of looking her up and down more than once. Running his hand over his overly greased hair, he looked around at the house behind her, and came back to her.

"What, don't you have anything else to say to the one you let get away?" Ben had always been self-centered, but this was going a little too far.

Lauren gave a huffing sound in retort and finished locking the door behind her.

"I'm on my way to work Ben, what do you want?"

"You offend me, my dear. What makes you think I want something?"

"Because you always do." Lauren walked down the steps and stopped in front of him. "There is nothing here for you Ben. I don't know what you have up your sleeve, but you won't get too far with it."

"LuLu, I just came by to see how my best girl is doing." The use of the nickname angered her, but not as much as the statement of her being his best girl. She made the mistake once to get involved with him, there wasn't a chance in hell she would make the same mistake twice.

"Go back to the world Ben you live in and leave me alone. Now if you would be on your way, I need to go." She pushed past him to put her belongings on the passenger side of her car.

"Well, I can see you don't have time to talk about old times right now, so I'll let you go. But I'll come back later to catch up with you. How does tomorrow around lunch sound?" He said watching her walk around the front of the car.

"Don't come back, Ben. Tomorrow is not a good day. Max is going to be working on the back porch and I am just too busy."

"Max, who's that, your new boyfriend? And what is this busy project you are working on? Have a new book in the works?" Ben asked, obviously trying to pump as much information as he could from her.

"He's a new friend and he's doing some work on the house for me," she said trying not to give him anything to work his evil ways around.

"Sounds great. I'll come over and make sure he's taking care of you right," he said wiggling his eyebrows at her with a sexual intonation. To her surprise he grabbed her around the waist and planted a kiss on her lips. Releasing her as quickly as he'd grabbed her, he turned and got into his car. Starting the engine up he blew a kiss to her through the window and drove off.

Recuperating from the surprise Lauren rubbed her lips in what looked to be the act of a pre-teen aged girl trying to get rid of the cooties from an unwanted admirer. She shook her head and got into her car to head off to class.

What in the world did Ben want with her now? She was going to have to keep an eye on him and head him off at the pass. It wasn't going to be good she could feel it.

* * * *

Max was there the next morning as promised. He'd gone earlier the day before to pick up materials at the hardware store. If he'd stayed working just a little longer he would have had the pleasure, or displeasure, of meeting Ben. Lauren watched from the front porch as he unloaded the materials and carted them to the back of the house. Taking a sip from her coffee cup she watched with delight as his muscles rippled under his shirt with his last trip to the truck. He'd thrown a load of lumber over his shoulder as if it weighed nothing.

How could a man like this be interested in me? Still not trusting her feelings about Max, she sat pondering whether this relationship would end up like the others. The visit from Ben had put her in a sour mood, one she didn't enjoy. It made her feel inept, unworthy and unloved.

When Max had greeted her this morning she'd tried not to pass her mood on to him. Although distracted by her thoughts, she'd tried to be pleasant and gave him a kiss. but she'd refused to meet his eyes with hers. If she had she knew he would see all the shame and guilt having been stirred up to a boiling point by Ben's surprise visit. Intending to brush Max aside as she was not in the mood to talk, Lauren had let him know she had too many things on her mind and wasn't meaning to be rude.

Max had looked at her skeptically, as if he knew something else was wrong. "Lauren, you know you can talk to me about anything, right? I'm here if you need someone to listen," he'd said giving her a kiss on the cheek.

Again, in awe of the compassion of this man, Lauren had returned the smile with a little shake of her head. "You are definitely different, Max. I appreciate your offer and may take you up on it later."

Truthfully, she felt as if she could tell him anything. She didn't question he would actually be there for her to support her in everything she did, which was totally unusual for the type of men she'd been involved with before. Most men wouldn't have recognized there was a problem in the first place, nor would they have cared or offered any comfort for her feelings. Not knowing really how to tell him what had dampened her outlook, she kept quiet wishing she had the ability to rid herself of all those feelings stored away in her subconscious. When she didn't offer anything up to be discussed, he'd left her in peace, not forcing the conversation.

A little later, he'd come back around to join her where she still sat on the front bench. "Feeling better after your morning coffee?" His beautiful dark eyes twinkled in the sunlight at her.

"Not really," she said honestly. "I think I'm going to work out. Then I need to get working on this section of my book that's been giving me problems."

"Will I be bothering you if I get started on the porch out back? I've got to get started if we plan on having it done by the 4th."

"No not at all. Do you think there's enough time to get it completed? I want to start sending out the invites soon. If it can't be done, I'll have to rethink my plans and whether I need to put it off to another time."

"We still have a couple of weeks, I don't see why I can't get this done by then. Go ahead and make your invitations out, I'll make sure what I don't get done won't affect your party."

Nodding, she looked wistfully out over the flower gardens which had started to take shape . "This is the perfect place for a party on the 4th. Fireworks over the lake. Barbecue on the back porch. Friends and family getting together. What could be better?"

"You are a woman after my heart. You know I wouldn't be true to the Italian in me if I didn't enjoy friends and family." His bright smile shadowed slightly with what Lauren imagined was a thought of the lost time with his own family because of his forced concealment.

"You miss your family don't you."

"Yes, I do. But that won't be forever," his smile was filled with something she didn't recognize. He was probably thinking of getting back to his own life again, to the friends and family he missed. A bit jealous of the thought, Lauren's heart pounded with uncertainty as she turned to go inside.

The workout she gave herself that morning was more than she'd ever done. Exhaustion of the body came first, and then of the mind. She knew she needed to stop, but thoughts of Ben and his smirking face kept popping up in her mind. She had to get in shape. How could anyone want or love her if she still looked like this? Sweat poured down her back in rivers. The towel she kept in her hand to wipe her face was drenched. Out of the corner of her eye she saw Max pass by the window, a load of lumber slung over his shoulder.

What she didn't know was he'd been watching her workout. He'd never seen her work so hard, and it was beginning to worry him she was doing too much. He didn't want her to know he was keeping an eye on her, so he kept passing by the window with various things in his hands as if he was working on the deck in the back. She'd been at it for over two hours and if she didn't stop soon he was going to have to go in and stop her himself.

Lauren lifted her hand to change the intensity of the stepping machine. Suddenly an odd dizziness hit her and made her stop. Grabbing hold of the handles she slowed her steps down, concentrating on keeping upright. She reached out and quickly turned the machine off and brought her exercise to a stop. A cold sweat broke out over her entire body and she felt suddenly sick to her stomach. Carefully stepping down to the floor she turned and sat down on the bench against the wall. Water, she needed water that was all. Opening the bottle she'd set on the floor she took a few big swigs and closed her eyes. Well, at least now she didn't feel like she was going to fall over.

Max had seen the progression and became concerned when she'd suddenly sat down and leaned her head against the wall. Taking the steps two at a time he came into the house straight back to where Lauren was now wiping her face and taking in deep breaths.

Surprised at his sudden entrance, she stood up quickly, which was the wrong thing to do. Knees weakening she dropped back down to the bench, embarrassed by this unexpected frailty. This was not like her at all, but then she'd never pushed herself this hard before either.

"You okay?" Taking her hand in his, he saw a deep flush had covered her face. He searched her eyes for signs of danger and fatigue.

"I'm fine really. Just needed to drink a little more water is all."

"What are you doing Lauren? You are pushing yourself like a madwoman."

"Nonsense. I'm just having a good workout." She knew he was right, but couldn't let him know it. She did feel a little like a madwoman. The only thing that mattered to her now was losing this ugly weight. It was either that, or loose any sense of being attractive to anyone ever again, least of all to a man like Max.

"What you are doing is killing yourself," Max said again, a little more forcefully.

Feeling more in control of herself she stood again. "Leave it alone Max. I'm a big girl, I know how to take care of myself." She knew she was being rude, but needed to stay in control of the situation, so she turned and went to the door saying, "Now, if you won't be following me into the bathroom, I'm going to go take a shower."

Stunned at her response, Max sat for a few moments before getting up to go back outside. It was obvious something was bothering her, he didn't know what it was yet, but he would find out soon enough.

"I think you contest a little too much," he muttered to himself. He wouldn't push it now, but she was doing this for some other reason than just loose some weight. Something was pushing her and he was going to find out what it was.

Chapter 17

After her shower, Lauren sat mindlessly at the kitchen table. She'd fixed herself some toast and a cup of coffee, her thoughts drifting aimlessly from one thing to another. Not realizing the time, she went back to her office to see if she could get some work done on her book. The deadline was coming up soon and she hadn't written more than two pages over the last couple of days. She got up from her desk and stretched. Grabbing her coffee cup she wandered into the kitchen to get a drink. Max had gone to pick up some items he needed from the hardware store and had said he would be back after he grabbed some lunch.

Hearing a car in the driveway, she took her cup with her to the front window to see who it was. It seemed way too early for Max to be back quite so soon. Before she even saw the car she remembered who had said he would stop by around lunch. Swearing under her breath she watched as the white Z came zipping into the space beside her car. Ben stepped out looking especially sleazy in his tight jeans and jungle print shirt, his hair slicked back as usual, gleaming in the sunlight. When he caught sight of her in the window he grinned egotistically. His assumption she'd been waiting for his arrival and couldn't keep her eyes off of him couldn't be further from the truth. In reality, she was trying to decide how best to handle the situation.

Their breakup had not been an amicable one. In fact in her short time with him she considered to be one of the worst decisions she'd ever made. At the time, her youth and inexperience with men, had a hand in wavering her better judgment. She and Ben had tied the knot after a wild weekend of drinking and fraternity party mayhem. It was an obvious mistake after the alcohol had worn off and the initial physical attraction had subsided.

Lauren had tried to make the best out of the situation for as long as she could. But when she found out Ben had not only taken advantage of her, but had been trying to needle his way into her family's finances, the only right decision was to break it off as quickly as possible. Though, before she'd acknowledged what he was doing, Ben had already done his damage.

He'd already told her his infidelity was to be expected when being married to someone of her size. But, when she found out he'd been secretly trying to work his way into a high position in her Uncle's firm using the same type of reasoning, that had been the end of it.

He'd told her Uncle, with obvious expectation, a position was owed to him because he'd taken her off of their hands. Uncle Dan had thrown him out of his office that day with the threat if he even thought about coming back he would have more to deal with than a bruised ego. She later found out he and Aunt Maggie had never approved of the marriage, and knew from the start Ben was a self-centered user of people, looking for ways to get whatever he could from everyone around him.

"Yeah, she wants me. I've got this one in the bag, again," Ben said to himself as he walked up the stairs toward the front door. He needed to find out everything he could so he could devise a way to get back in with her. He'd always known she would be a good one for the bucks. She couldn't hold a grudge that long. Besides, who could resist him?

Lauren's intentions were to not let him through the door, and to get him out of there as quickly as she could. She was in no mood to put up with his nonsense. As she watched him come up the stairs it brought back the awful sickening feeling she'd experienced while working out earlier. Furrowing her eyebrows she opened the door and took a step forward into the opening to keep him from entering uninvited.

"Hello sweet thing. Got some sugar for me?" He offered up his lips for a kiss.

In disgust Lauren made a noise that sounded more like a snort from a wild hog than a response from a human being. Surprised by the sound which had erupted from her, Ben backed off and raised his eyebrows at her in question.

"Ben, what do you want here? Frankly I'm not even sure how you found out where I live."

"Oh, I have my ways honey. You know I've always loved you." His use of the word her made her ill.

"Really. What happened to the bimbo you were sleeping with this last time?" She asked, not knowing exactly which one she was talking about, just knowing there would always be one.

"Jenny? Well, she didn't work out. She was too needy, always wanting something from me and nagging about money."

That's not what Lauren had heard. In actuality he'd started going out with Jenny because she had family money, and he'd thought he could get her to loosen up on her inheritance funds.

But she'd turned out to be a little more tightfisted than he'd thought. When she started insisting he get a job and help to support the relationship, that had been the end of that. Lauren had also heard he'd begun gambling again and was in deep trouble with the casino's money handlers. He was definitely one to stay far away from.

"LuLu, it's been a while. Why don't we go inside and get caught up on what's been happening?" Ben reached up to push the door open wider so he could get his foot in the door.

Lauren automatically reached out to push him back away from the door. Taking this as an invitation to get closer, Ben lowered his arm to wrap it around Lauren's shoulders. In self-defense she immediately ducked out of his grasp and brought her heel down on the toes of his right foot. Cursing he pulled away hopping up and down on his uninjured foot.

"What the hell did you do that for?" The look in his eyes was more from an injured ego than from an actual physical injury.

"Ben, I told you back then, and I'm telling you now, it was a mistake to ever have gotten involved with you. And I sure as hell am not going to make the same mistake twice. You are not welcome and you need to leave. Now, take your sleazy self and get out of here."

One of the things she'd been worried about was he'd always been forceful, and she wasn't sure how long she could hold him back once he got it in his head to get what he wanted.

"You fat bitch. What, you think you can do better than me?" Ben asked with a deep intimidating laugh, as he stepped toward her, his hands on his hips.

Lauren stood tall, not wanting to show how badly his words had hurt her. Thankfully, she looked past him to where Max had just pulled up in his truck with the supplies for the deck. Getting out she saw him look around to the white Z-28 that was pulled up beside her car, and made sure when he glanced up he looked straight into her eyes. When he did, it was as if she could feel he knew exactly what was happening.

A strength came over her from Max's presence, and Lauren was able to set her face in a cold, unfeeling stance. She brought her eyes back to Ben's face. He turned to look in the direction of Lauren's gaze o see Max coming toward them.

Seeing the obvious build and external attractiveness of this man Ben turned to Lauren again with a smirk on his face."You think someone like him is ever going to stick with you, Babe? You better just give it up and come back to me before you get yourself all worked up over nothing. That won't happen in a million years." Shaking his head he stepped toward Lauren intending to show her that he was the best thing for her.

Seeing the intent in his eyes, Lauren held up her hand blocking him from getting any closer. She was not going to allow Ben to think he could push her around again. This was going to be the end of this right now.

"Ben, I am asking you to leave right now. Get in your car and never come back here. I do not want to ever see you again, do you understand?"

"Look, you don't look any better now than you did when we were married. Do you really think someone like him will ever want to be with something like you?" Ben had stepped closer still, pressing up against her hand, thinking if he could just get her next to him she would feel the old tingle again.

Disgust and anger were the only things Lauren could feel at the moment. Controlling the words she found herself wanting to scream at him she took a deep breath and shook her head. He was probably right. Yet, instantly she knew it not to be true, and she wouldn't allow him to feel like he'd won.

What was it the counselors had told her? People deface others because of their own self-image. He was trying to hurt her in order to make himself look better.

"You are just as big and ugly now as you were then." He smirked, seeing her defenses weaken. "But see I know what you are like in the bed, so I'm willing to give up the looks for what you do to me up there," he said, nodding his head toward the direction of the upstairs bedrooms.

Without further thought Lauren's hand came up out of nowhere and landed square across his jaw in a slap that could be heard all the way down to where Max was quickly coming up the walkway.

"You little..." Ben's hand shot out to strike Lauren across the face in like manner. But his hand never reached its destination. He found himself suddenly lifted off of his feet and swung upside down like a sack of potatoes over Max's shoulder. With a few long strides he was down the steps and had Ben on his backside on the front lawn.

"What the hell..." He began as he leaped up to his feet defensively. "Get the hell out of here. This is none of your damned business." Ben raised himself up as tall as he could, hoping to show Max just who was in control.

"I believe the Lady asked you to leave," Max said getting a closer look at this guy. He could sense fear welling up into Ben's eyes as he positioned himself like a bulldog in front of him blocking any possible access to Lauren.

The blatant anger on Max's face made Ben take a step back. "Well, this isn't over until I say so. I'll go, but you are not going to keep me away from her." Ben looked behind Max to see Lauren looking back at him from the doorway. "I'll be back, Babe. You'll come to your senses and remember I'm the only good thing that has ever happened to you." He looked back at Max with the look of a kid having gotten away with something.

Max reached out and grabbed him by the shirt, lifting him up off the ground high enough to make Ben's knees weaken. "If I'm not mistaken I heard Lauren say she didn't want anything to do with you. Now if you don't know any better I'd be glad to wipe that look off your face with my fist."

Ben could see the muscles in Max's arms flexing, itching to let loose and flatten him to the ground. Struggling free from the death grip Max had put on him, he moved away backwards, not wanting to turn his back on him.

"All right man, no harm meant. I mean, I was just trying to get me a little lovin' from the slut," he said trying to make light of the situation, to ensure he wouldn't have any competition from this self imposed bodyguard. He held his hands up in a gesture of surrender.

Max was back in his face in a second, his arm swung back and his fist met Ben's face in a quick hard punch sending his small body flying across the ground. He landed with a thud in front of him. Ben's hand went up to his nose, which had begun to bleed profusely.

"What the hell did you do that for?" He said muffled through the palm of his hand.

"Next time you decide to ask for a lady's attentions, perhaps you won't try to force her into submission first," Max said reaching down and hauling Ben to his feet. "And if you ever show your face here again there will be more than a little blood coming from your nose. Now I suggest you get out of here before I have to hurt you some more."

Raising his voice so Lauren could hear him, Ben yelled back to her. "Fine, you aren't worth it anyway. But remember what I said. You won't ever be what he needs, not in a long shot." Ben moved to his car muttering curses under his breath. "The bitch isn't worth getting my face messed up over. I've got plenty of women to mooch off of." He'd just figured she was going to be an easy one this time.

Max stood with his hands on his hips and watched as Ben got into his car and drove off in fury, the wheels of his sports car flinging gravel into the air. He turned to find out if Lauren was okay, not knowing if he'd gotten there in time before this guy had hurt her. She was nowhere in sight.

He rushed up the front steps and into the front room, a knot forming in his stomach as he went in search of her. Lauren had a look of pure pain on her face when he'd arrived, one that was not the result of any type of physical contact. He was almost positive this guy had not laid a hand on her before he'd gotten there. But what he didn't know was the damage which had been inflicted was worse than any physical contact could have done.

When Max found her she was leaning over her dresser, her clammy palms supporting her on the edge, head bent down in an exhaustive state. He came to the bedroom door and stopped. He'd never seen her like this before. She looked so frail, almost beaten.

"Lauren. Are you alright?"

Her head came up swiftly, not wanting him to see the tears welling into her eyes. She turned and wiped them away with the brush of her hand.

"Yeah, I'm okay." Turning she saw him standing just inside of the doorway. She turned away from him and reached for the basket of clothes she'd brought up to be folded. Grabbing one of Josh's T-shirts she began to fold it neatly and put it in a stack on the bed. "Thanks for helping me out there. He can get out of hand sometimes."

Max was across the room in no time. Reaching up he took Lauren's shoulders in his hands and turned her gently around to face him. "Who was that?"

Lauren saw a look on his face she didn't want to even try to interpret. It was something between anger, compassion, and something she couldn't even try to figure out at the moment. His anger didn't frighten her, like Ben had. She felt compelled to look away and try not to anger him any more, fearing only the possibility of him withdrawing from her. If this were to happen it would be better at a later time on her terms. She needed to deal with what had just happened first. She looked toward the window and took a deep breath, knowing she was going to have to tell him about this ugly portion of her life.

"That was Ben, my first husband."

"First?" Max's eyebrows shot up.

"Yes, Ben and I were married a short time when I was in college. It didn't last long. We broke up after I found him in bed with a young college freshman along with his attempts to wheedle money out of my family. Then I met Evan, Josh's father. We met about a year after I had graduated. But that didn't last too long either. After Josh was born, Evan became disinterested in me, like Ben had. So I left him to his many girlfriends and decided I was better off raising Josh by myself. I couldn't handle watching him get into bed with every other girl that came around the corner. It seems I couldn't provide either one with what they needed."

She shrugged her shoulders and stepped away from Max, wanting to put some space between them. She didn't want to continue dragging up all of the pain from the past. But she wasn't sure if she could just let it alone now either. Anger was beginning to build again against the men who had treated her this way. If either one had just given her a chance she could have been a good wife to both of them, not that they deserved it.

Going back over to the basket of clothes she bent to get another article of clothing to fold. She gathered it in her hands and began folding it with an intensity that showed her feelings.

"Why did you let him talk to you that way?"

Not knowing how to answer his question Lauren silently folded another towel and laid it on the bed. Shrugging her shoulders again she could only feel the emotions stirring up inside of her. She couldn't let him see her cry. She had to be tough and resilient.

"I don't know, I guess because most of it was the truth. I mean, why would you want to hang around? You could get any number of women, who would be more than willing to satisfy all of your needs. And all of them would look much better than I do. No question."

Max had come around the end of the bed. Suddenly, he pulled her up against him. He turned her to face him, his arms encircling her waist. "But I don't want them, I want you." He bent his head and pressed his lips against her forehead.

Lauren shook her head again, not yet ready to believe what he was saying. "You won't for long, Max. You haven't seen me without my clothes yet. Once you do, I'd bet you won't be around too long."

As she spoke she felt the muscles in his arms tense up, yet not tighten against her. Again denying there could be anything but a physical thing between them, she pulled away from him and went back to folding clothes. Head bent, not wanting to show any more emotions than she had already, Lauren fought to keep the tears from spilling out.

Taking a deep breath she looked up and said first what she knew would be coming later. "Look, I know there is no way you would ever want to stay with someone like me. It's just this weird physical attraction right now men have for me at first. You'll get tired of me soon enough, and then you will leave like everyone else. They always do. Just do me the favor of not messing around on me while we are together. If nothing else that is the least you could do for me."

With a movement that surprised her he'd pulled her to him and brought her around to face the stand up mirror in the corner of the room.

"Tell me what you see." Max was behind her, his body pressed up against her back, forcing her to remain facing the mirror. She stood looking at herself in the mirror, but couldn't trust herself to say anything. She could feel the tears stinging the backs of her eyes threatening to tumble out in a torrent of emotion. She shook her head, looking away from the picture she imagined he saw.

Max's hands came up to frame her face. He turned her face back to look into the mirror. Looking straight into her eyes he brought his hands down to her shoulders. "Do you want to know what I see?"

Hearing a softness she longed to feel, and a kindness she wanted to believe, she nodded her head to silently agree in hearing what he had to say.

"I see a vivaciously beautiful woman who has had some very bad experiences. She is a strong woman who has done a wonderful job of raising a bright young boy into a man, and has outdone herself in every other area of her life. She is determined to make a life she can be proud of, and to experience the joys life has to offer.

But she won't allow herself to see the natural beauty exuding from her very soul. That beauty comes from your spirit, Lauren. It comes from inside of you, and shines out to everyone around you. Your body has been made for the tender attentions of a man. You are not now, nor will you ever be one of those stick women they call beautiful these days. You are, what they call voluptuous, full of desire, beauty and love."

Max's hands slowly moved down her arms and he was now holding her hands in his, simply giving the touch she needed as he expressed himself to her. "I know this world is so bent on physical perfection it misses out on the beauty each person holds uniquely within themselves. You shouldn't be shunned, but appreciated and loved as a woman should be loved. As far as I can see you are perfect just the way you are. Your passion has been hidden away to long under your inability to see your own beauty. Any man would be blessed to be given the chance to share with you this passion and sexuality."

The tears she'd wanted to keep hidden away sprang forward and began to spill out over her cheeks as he spoke. His words had moved her so deeply she was speechless. Emotions were whirling around in her head so fast she thought it would definitely fly off her shoulders. Max turned her against his chest and held her against him for a moment longer. Tilting her head back with his fingers he looked down into her face. Kissing away some of the tears flowing down her cheeks he held her even more tightly in his arms.

"Don't let anyone make you feel less of a woman than you are."

These tears were not in self-pity. They were of a different kind now. "No, that's not it at all." She lifted her lips to his for a kiss.

"Then what is it, *amore*, why do you cry?" Brushing his lips across hers, he rubbed his thumb down her cheek tracing the trail of her falling tears.

"No one has ever said anything like that to me before and meant it. I think you really meant that." She wanted to believe he could actually see in her the beauty he'd described.

"Then they are fools." Suddenly, he brought his lips down over hers possessively. He desperately wanted to show her how she made him feel. He felt her lips warm against his, and he deepened the kiss, his tongue instinctively searching for hers as her lips parted for him, the taste of her filling his senses. It wasn't enough. He needed to show her what she meant to him. It was as if there was some unexplained force that drew him to her, with a connection deeper than he'd ever experienced before. Maybe this was what his mother had been talking about. He just knew he needed to be **with** her in every sense of the word.

His hand came up to feel the curves of her body. Brushing lightly against her breast, it caused her to take a sudden breath as his fingers lingered to feel the incredulous pounding of her heart against his palm. Lifting his mouth from hers he trailed kisses down her cheek to find the irresistible warmth and curves of her neck, her womanly scent filling his senses to ecstatic point of no return.

"Let me love you, *Bella*. Let me love you like a real man should," he spoke in a heavy breath, a wave of unbelievable excitement through his body in an almost painful flame. "Give yourself to me and let me show you the wonders you have never experienced."

Raising his head he looked deep into the smoldering depths of Lauren's eyes. She reached up to bury her fingers in his curls, pulling his lips down again to hers. The heat passing through those few seconds was enough to start a fire. She wanted him and she knew he wanted her. She couldn't think. The only thing to come to her was the fact she desperately wanted him. Her body felt as if it had come alive under the slow caressing touch of his hands. Desperate to feel his body next to hers, she needed to know again what it felt like to be loved, if only for a moment in time.

From across the room, neither of them was aware of the butterfly sitting on the windowsill. It waited only a moment longer, then it fluttered away to leave them in peace.

"Lauren?" This time it came as a plea. He didn't know how long he could hold on. He needed her. As she became pliant in his hands, he knew he needed her to say yes. To have the sweet scent of her bare skin next to his would be glorious. The urgency of needing to be inside of her was beyond anything he'd ever known before. Yet he also knew he wanted nothing more than show to her the kind of tenderness he felt she'd never received from any previous lover.

Without hesitation Lauren brought his lips down for yet another kiss, her eyes melting into his as they pulled from each other the answer they both needed.

"Yes," she said softly before his lips came down to crush hers, the passion only beginning to build.

Her answer was exactly what he needed to hear. Keeping his eyes on hers he brought his fingers up to begin unbuttoning her shirt. As he began to push the cloth off of her shoulders he felt her tense up, and she brought her hands up to stop the shirt from falling.

"Don't…" Lauren began, a look of pure horror coming across her face. "Not yet. Leave the shirt on. Please…"

Max saw the self-doubt and a look very close to terror in her eyes and stopped momentarily to bring her close again into his arms to quiet the fears he felt she'd been hanging onto for much too long.

"You are beautiful, *Amore*. Look in my eyes and see I am in awe of what you have to give. Beauty is in the eyes of the beholder. Let me be the judge of what attractions you hold for me, sweetheart." All he could see was the love encircling his heart. "*Mio Dio, sei bellissima,*" he said with a tremor in his voice. Running his fingers through her long curls he bent to whisper in her ear. "You are gorgeous *mio dolce amore. La tua bellezza circonda la mia anima.*"

She nodded again slowly, as she gazed into his eyes through her lashes. Sensing the fears subside he brought his hands back up to brush against the white lace encasing her breasts. The shirt fell to the floor as he bent his head down to nuzzle the tip of her breast through the lace. A deep moan escaped from her lips as she pressed him closer against her breast, her hands in his hair.

Bending down he swept her into his arms, as if she weighed nothing, and gently laid her on the bed. As he ran his fingers down her torso it brought a trembling shiver out of her, enticing the need to feel her body next to his. He smiled at her as he pulled his black T-shirt over his head baring his chest. He stood for a moment enjoying the look of devouring passion she gave as she let her gaze wander down his muscled chest. She held her arms out to him as if not being able to wait to feel him against her skin.

Max put his hands in hers and brought them down to either side of her head, curling his fingers with hers. His need was so great he knew if he acted too quickly this would be over before they realized it. He had to make his desires hold steady. Nestling himself between her legs he bent again to trail his kisses between her breasts, his senses filled with her femininely unique scent of apricots and musk. It just about drove him mad as she arched her back bringing her body closer to his as his tongue traced lazy patterns down her belly. He reached behind her and released the hook on her bra and pulled it away. His gaze went down to the sumptuous curves of her breasts, the tips straining to be touched and fondled by the warmth of his fingers.

He reached out to caress the beautiful pink tip of one while he took the other in the palm of his hand. The softness of her skin was like satin beneath his fingers. The sound that came from deep down inside of Lauren brought his gaze back up to her face. Her hair had come down in a wave as he'd laid her on the bed. It now framed her glowing face, spread out like a fan beneath her. The curls were spread wildly about as if in celebration of things to come.

Her quick shallow breaths and flushed face with heavily lidded eyes showed him her aching passion was just as deep as his. Again she held out her hands to him in an urgency to complete their union. Shaking his head again, he trailed kisses down her belly.

As she moaned out his name, he swore to himself never to give what he imagined she'd experienced in the past. No longer would she have only the quick and impassioned brawl, leaving sheets tangled and covers thrown to the floor. She deserved much more. This was so much deeper, with emotions just below the boiling point it now became a dangerously enticing act of what could only be interpreted as love.

He needed to show her just what it felt like to be loved by a man who knew how to please a woman first before acting on his own need. Pleasing her was the most important thing to him now, even though banking his own needs became increasingly difficult as he felt her quiver beneath him. He wanted desperately to be the one to bring her to the point of release of those unbridled passions he felt lying just beneath the surface.

As he bent again over her, trailing soft gentle kisses over her stomach, she felt a sensation of lightening bolts shiver down her spine. His fingers came up to loosen the button on the waistband of her jeans. The warm kisses he left in anticipation only made her body ache for more. He grasped her hips, pressing his face where the unfastened opening allowed her flesh to be exposed, causing her to almost whimper with desperation. He raised his head up far enough to catch her eyes as he pulled her jeans over her hips and then down her thighs.

Now she lay completely open to him, but what she saw in his eyes was not what she'd feared. He let his gaze move up and down slowly in an appreciative way. The look in his eyes was not disgust, but one of passion, need, and reverence. She wanted to remember the look on his face forever.

He now unbuttoned his own jeans and let them fall to the floor and stepped out of them. As Lauren had been watching his every move, this one caught the air out of her lungs. He was so literally beautiful she couldn't even think past the amazement of how perfect he was, in his clothes and yet even more out of them. He was like a love God standing there, his essence permeating from the object of desire so proudly displayed. Bringing his knee up to the bed, he came down next to her, his mouth swiftly covering hers eradicating any and all fears she may have had.

His kisses were demandingly crushing, as his need became more intense. Reaching out once again with his attentions he stroked her breasts. Feeling the tautness of her brightly flushed nipples his palm glided slowly down until it reached her hip. His eyes on hers he brought his fingers over to touch the spot between her legs so heated with anticipation, her sudden intake of air showed him all he needed to see, as well as the wetness he found as her needs were welling up inside her. Wanting to bring her to a peak of satisfaction he let his fingers search again until they found the spot that would send her over the edge.

Gently he began rubbing back and forth and in circular motions testing for acceptance. Her kiss became almost as if she was pulling his very soul out from him. She took what she needed and gave in return. She began to stroke his muscles, searching his body desperately as if needing to feel every part of him. With an almost uncontrollable response to her touch he continued to reign in his own need to satisfy hers. Keeping himself fully held back from taking her with him in a demanding flurry of need was almost impossible.

His hardened body pressed up against hers screamed out for more as he felt her release come almost at once as he starting applying pressure to the aroused point of his attentions. He'd sent her into a culmination of erotic convulsions, with only his fingers. Max waited until the tremors coursing through her began to slowly abate. With her eyes now closed in a half state of elation, he began to stroke her again.

The warmth of his hands continued to spread small streaks of excitement through her thighs and belly, a growing tightness forming again as she imagined him inside of her. Then suddenly she felt a warm sensation between her legs which hadn't been there before and she opened her eyes to find he'd moved and was now nuzzling the same spot with his lips and tongue. The sensation was so wild she didn't know if she could take it. The heat from his tongue sent sensations through her body in a wave of building excitement. She could barely control the feelings spreading over her like a fire being fed by her own passions. Her body screamed for release again, her legs trembling from the jolts of pleasure spreading throughout her being. Deep moans came from her throat as she focused on the point of his attention. Again she came with a guttural sound escaping her lips, the muscles of her stomach and her thighs jumping with extreme satisfaction.

She lay almost lifeless, feeling the intensity of the orgasm spreading throughout her body. Max had lain down beside her, his own quickened senses begging for her to open herself to him and give him the same satisfaction. A grin crept across her face in the realization of what had just happened. She couldn't believe this feeling. She'd never experienced anything quite like this before. She'd always enjoyed sex before, but never had anyone made her feel the way Max did. He'd made her feel like she was precious and actually deserved to be given the best. She felt as if she were on top of the world and could handle anything that came her way.

 Lauren could feel the tautness of his body against hers as he began caressing a place on her neck with his tongue sending shivers down her spine. She didn't know if she could take any more, yet she did know what she wanted now. She craved the feeling of him filling her to the utmost with his own passions.

 Then it hit her like a bolt of lightening. She knew now he was what she'd been looking to find for so long, she'd been waiting for this her entire life. What she'd experienced before was mere child's play. His passion for life was what she'd been longing for. She needed him to want her and to love her in ways she'd only dreamed of before. Ways which would send her to places only he could send her. She'd never felt this way before, and deep down she knew she would never feel this way again with another man.

 What had lain dormant for so long had sprung up from her so quickly it was almost overpowering. At the mere touch of this man's hands there were feelings struggling for freedom, to indulge in the pure joy of physical sensation. And she wanted more. She needed to feel he too felt this need, this intoxicating desire to be held and to be loved.

 Grasping his shoulders she pulled him toward her. His warm quick panting breaths on her skin filled her with an extreme desire to fulfill all of his needs. As he hovered over her, she reached down to grasp him in her palm and the quick responsive reaction she received from him sent a stream of pleasure into her heart. Max gave a deep moan, and she smiled as she felt his body yearning for more than a touch. Lauren's stroking hand sent a shock wave over sensitized nerve endings revealing just how hard it was for him to hold himself back from her. He didn't ask, but his eyes had turned to a shade as black as coal from his obvious response to her touch and she saw the desperate plea for her to give him more. He needed and wanted her and she knew there was no question how much she needed him. She knew she had to have him now. There was no holding back anymore.

She would give herself to him now. It was too late to worry about the consequences. This was what she'd been missing, an unquestionable bond between two people. Passion, intimacy and a yearning for love had been gone for so long she'd almost forgotten what it felt like. But now that it was here, this was more than she'd ever experienced before in her life. The incredible power she felt as she looked up into his face, seeing the extremity of the deep sensations of pleasure flowing over him gave her such profound excitement.

"Now Max, I need you now." Lauren said in a deep throaty voice. It only took one look to see she meant what she'd said. He didn't hold back any longer, with as much force as there had been the previous gentle touches, he drove himself inside her making them both gasp with the deep sensation. He stayed motionless for only a moment and then began a rhythm of deep strokes, which finally sent them both into tumultuous eruption. They both fell into glorious abandon in each others arms.

Slowly drifting awake after what seemed like hours, the warmth of Max's body as her cheek lay against the strong heartbeat in his chest, sent happiness to dance in her heart. She smiled and nuzzled up against his shoulder, taking in the deep manly scent only he held.

How could she be so lucky to have attracted the attentions of such a man? And a better question was how could she keep the attraction going? This was not something she was going to give up willingly. From this point on she would start doing everything she could to keep this man of her dreams. This time was going to be different, she was not going to give him the chance to need or want any other woman.

Chapter 18

"What do you mean the package isn't here?"

"I'm sorry, sir, but the tracking number for your package has not arrived at this destination yet. I show it is currently being held at the San Francisco facility." The young shipping agent nervously tapped keys on the computer, glancing toward Jeffery with anxious eyes.

"What the hell is it doing in San Francisco?" Jeffery felt as if his head were about to explode. Sweat streamed down his face in little rivulets as he stood in the hot warehouse conditions. He wiped them away with a paper napkin from the last meal he'd had two days ago. "This guarantees the package will be delivered on time," he said stabbing a finger at the tracking slip in front of him.

"Yes, sir, we guarantee our packages. But when circumstances beyond our control happen, there are times these deliveries can't be met," the shipping agent said with a crack in his voice. "If you had accepted the insurance clause at the bottom of your form," he said pointing to the tiny box on the right hand corner, "we would gladly refund your shipping costs."

Jeffery had started pacing back and forth in front of the counter. What the hell was he going to do now? He stopped short, not caring about the line of people behind him, "I don't want the fucking shipping costs. I want the package."

Eyes wide with fear, the young man picked up the phone at the side of the computer and said quietly, "Code 11 at the front desk. Code 11," he stammered again.

Moving closer to the agent, Jeffery yelled out, "What the hell is a Code 11?"

Flashes from a red beacon light on the ceiling began travelling the walls of the room, and people began scattering as a burly muscled man in a shipping uniform came through the door. He stepped up to the counter arms crossed over his chest, and gave the young man a signal to leave.

"Sir, if you don't step back, we will need to call the authorities."

Jeffery stepped back, putting his hands up, he knew he'd crossed the line for losing his temper. "Alright, alright, don't get all Rambo on me."

The agent nodded his head, throwing a glance toward Jeffery to make sure he stayed put. After pressing a few keys on the keyboard, he wrote a phone number down on the edge of the tracking slip Jeffery had brought in.

"If you call this number you will be given instruction on when and where to pick up your package."

"So, you're not going to do anything? Can't you rush it, or resend it up here?"

Pointing at the tracking slip again, the man shook his head. He looked behind Jeffery at the only person who had remained in the office and said, "Next."

Jeffery turned, madder than hell. "I knew I should have used UPS."

* * * *

The work on the deck had fallen into place, just like Max had promised. It was exactly what Lauren had envisioned. She stood now surveying what was her dream of the perfect back yard. She'd gotten up early that morning to begin preparing for the arrival of her guests. The night before was spent doing as much prep work as she could on the salads and deserts for the gathering.

Josh had spent all day at the reservation fireworks stands, doing what young boys do best. Spending money and pouring over every possible legally explosive combination available with a passion only boys and men seem to have this time of year. His choices had met with a myriad of approving comments and discussions from both Max and his friend Robert who had accompanied him on his trip. They'd come back with much more than she'd expected, which told her Max had obviously contributed to the entertainment fund for the party.

The deck had turned out to be even better than she'd expected. Max had done an awesome job on the water garden separating the upper and lower decks. She sat now on one of the deck chairs Max had bought as a surprise. The morning mists hung lazily over the lake as if in anticipation of the day's excitement. Max had told her the chairs were a house warming gift, but she'd argued with him until he promised to add them to his bill. She'd turned on the pump to the waterfall, listening to the soothing trickle of water coming over the rocks. The early morning chatter of the birds talking with each other, she imagined as they were talking about the awesome beauty of this creation. She smiled and took another sip of her coffee.

Family and friends were scheduled to come over early in the afternoon, which meant she still had a couple of hours to finish what she needed to in the kitchen and clean up the remaining areas in the house she hadn't gotten completed yet. Josh would be busy planning the fireworks show with his friend all day, so she wouldn't need to worry about him. Max had said he would be over early to help with the preparations.

Smiling, she remembered how excited he'd seemed when they'd been talking about her family coming over for celebrations. She'd never experienced anyone who felt the same about family as she did. Her other relationships had always left her feeling like her family was an imposition on their life and they never understood her need to be so close to them. Here now she felt not only did he understand her need, but he also had the need to be close to them as well. He hadn't even met her family yet, but she could tell he would treat them as if they were his own.

Must just be his Italian nature, she thought.

Hearing the crunch of footsteps coming up the pathway surrounding the house, she got up to see who was coming around the corner. What she saw were two legs covered in black jeans, and two arms gathered around enough flowers to fill an entire room with their fragrant blossoms. Peaking through the leaves and stalks were the unmistakable eyes of Max.

"What on earth is this?" Lauren asked rushing forward to help him with his load.

"These, *Bella,* are the blossoms you were thinking of yesterday. You didn't say it, but I knew you wanted color everywhere to welcome your family."

"You are unbelievable. You know that don't you?" Lauren asked, in awe of the variety and colors she saw in his arms.

Irises and carnations, dahlias and mums—reds, purple, yellow, pink, orange—every flower to be imagined sprang forth in an array of glory. If the color was not enough, the fragrance from them all was intoxicating. Who else would have guessed the perfect addition to a perfect day?

"This isn't all. There's more in the truck," he said laying the stalks down on the deck tabletop.

From out of nowhere, the black and white butterfly fluttered into view and perched on the edge of the purple lily she held. Max and Lauren looked at each other and smiled.

"Anna approves. She would have wanted this for you." As if nodding its agreement, the butterfly turned and lifted its wings to drift toward the garden.

Lauren believed she would have. "You shouldn't have Max. It would have been alright."

"But, I should have. You deserve everything your heart desires. Flowers are just the beginning my love. You will have everything you want and more. This I can promise you." Max said this with such confidence it dazed her. If that wasn't enough he reached round to grab her around the waist, and swing her back over his arm in a pseudo dance dip. Running kisses up her neck, he ended up at her lips, sending flames up and down her spine.

She straightened, knees still a bit weak from the kiss, and smiled. Smoothing her hands over her hair, she tempted him by saying, "Well, if you do much more of those we may not be attending this party too long. The guests will have to fend for themselves."

"My thoughts exactly," he responded with a simple peck on her cheek and stepping away. "I'd better go get the rest of what's in my truck so you can tell me where to put them all."

She brought out as many vases as she had, but ran out of the conventionally acceptable kind. There were so many flowers flowing over the tables she resorted to coffee cans, buckets and watering cans. Now as she stood beside him watching his easy movements in arranging the flowers in beautiful arrays of color, she again couldn't believe the qualities of this man. He loved music, flowers, family and even appreciated the work of the written word, everything she held dear to her own heart.

"I was wondering what to expect today? Do they all know about my deep, dark secret?" Max asked glancing to the side where Lauren was arranging a coffee can full of pink carnations.

She shook her head. "No, the only one I told was Aunt Maggie, and she only knows your wife was the victim of a horrible crime, and you'd lost her. Your secret is safe with me."

"Thank you," he said softly with a slight bow to his head.

"As for what to expect, best thing to do is not expect anything and just go with the flow. There will be every type here. You never know what you'll get."

He nodded silently as he pulled a long stemmed purple Iris from a bunch of flowers. Lauren smiled appreciating another one of his qualities. As they stood working together, she began to daydream about the last time they'd made love. Every time was something new, more exciting and deeply exhilarating. She'd been filled with a feeling far beyond the physical act of sexual pleasure. It was physically, emotionally and almost spiritually satisfying. She'd never felt so complete in all of her life. If they hadn't been made for each other, she didn't know who had.

Max turned, and caught the smile which had crept onto her face as she was thinking about him. "What are you smiling at little girl? You look like you've been caught with your hand in the cookie jar."

"Just thinking about what you are going to get later on tonight is all. Josh has plans to spend the night at Robert's after the activities tonight. I thought it might be a good chance for me to show you how much I appreciate all of your hard work over the last couple of weeks...and what I've been thinking about this morning."

Max raised his hand to his heart, rubbing it in a calming motion. "Be still my heart." Then looking a little further down his body, he said with a smile, "Later boy, she said later."

Lauren sent a sexually mischievous glance over her shoulder at the object of his last comment. "If you are really good, you might get a little taste before everyone arrives."

With a groan Max reached out to pull her to him, but she avoided the hug by moving quickly to the side and grabbed the spray bottle she'd been using to moisten the petals of the flowers.

"But if you are bad, who knows what you will get!"

She turned and fled his grasp in a whimsical set of giggles and laughter springing from her heart, filling his with an unspeakable joy. Joining in her mischievous act, Max rushed after her making animalistic grunts and groans throwing her into another fit of laughter as they chased each other around the deck like kids. After receiving several hits with the water bottle, Max ended up pinning her against the side of the house, smothering her with kisses that made her heart soar. Max pulled back and gave her one of his gorgeous smiles.

She reached forward and put her arms around him pressing her face in his neck. Closing her eyes, she prayed a quick prayer she knew she was not worthy of having someone like Max, but hoping she could do whatever she needed to keep him in her life.

Receiving and returning the hug in the full intention of its meaning, Max ran his hands up and down her arms and murmured softly, "I know, Mia Bella. I know."

In that moment of time Lauren knew there was no turning around from this one. She loved him with all of her heart. There was no rejecting this one. She would love him from now until eternity. She didn't know how she was going to do it, but she had to figure out how to make him love her the same way. Then maybe, just maybe, they could have what she so desperately dreamed about.

She didn't know it, but his thoughts were the same. He loved her with all of his heart and intended she would be his from now until eternity. The only thing holding him back was he needed to put an end to this drama controlling his life, and then to figure out the when and how to ask her to become his wife. He couldn't ask her to be involved when he still had unknown murderers threatening him. But for now, there was a party to put on and he intended it to be the best party ever.

Squeezing her he backed away and said, "If we don't get working on this party of yours, there won't be anything but signs of a would-be party in the works for your guests to come see. Let's get these flowers finished up so we can get back to the kitchen and find out what needs to be done there."

"You are an amazing man, Max. I don't know what I would have done without you."

"The same goes for you Lauren. But that is going to have to wait till tonight," he said with the raising of his eyebrows up and down in the same suggestive manner she had earlier.

"Oh, you rat! Now we are both going to be thinking about the same thing all day long!"

"Exactly!" Max laughed as he received one last blast from the water bottle as they raced back toward the deck.

* * * *

Rita and her hoard had arrived first getting underfoot as soon as they had arrived. After a short intermission of appreciative glances, and mischievous advances toward Max, Rita settled in on the deck in one of the lounge chairs to soak up some sunrays. The twins were instructed to chase after their brother, and after some eye rolling and avid argument, just for the sake of argument, they happily set to playing hide and seek with him.

Her husband, David, had made sure she had everything she needed then turned his attentions on this new addition to Lauren's life. Strolling over to the barbecue pit where Max was tending the chicken and steaks, David peered over to see if the job was being done right.

"Do this often?" He asked just trying to start a conversation.

"Not as often as I would like, but I've had practice over the years," Max responded. He hadn't quite figured David out yet. He seemed to be the doting husband, and by the few interactions he'd caught with his children, looked to be a very good father. He'd given Lauren a big hug and kiss at the door when they'd arrived, and offered his hand for a simple handshake to Max when he was introduced. But something in his eyes showed he didn't trust him. Max waited for him to voice what was bothering him.

Looking over to where Lauren was laughing with the twins over something their brother was doing, Max thought David watched her as if analyzing her every move. Then he turned to Max for a moment and back to Lauren.

Stepping up to the grill, he said, "Where you from?"

David was not one for many words. You couldn't be if you lived with a character like Rita. The twins seemed to be just as bad. They seemed to be talking constantly.

"Originally from Italy, then we came here and settled in Chicago," Max replied in simple like terms. Reading this man he could tell he was not one for much detail, he wanted to know the facts and that was enough.

"Why did you come to Washington?"

"I needed a break from the direction my life had taken, was offered a place to stay here on the lake while my cousin is in Italy visiting family." Max almost felt guilty being so vague, but it definitely wasn't a lie.

"So are you a handyman by trade or do you do something else?"

Max paused and smiled inwardly for a moment. Yes, he was more, so much more than a handyman. He had music in his soul and it was screaming to come out for everyone to hear. Allowing a light smile to run across his face, he looked into David's eyes and said, "I'm a musician. Soon, because of Lauren's help, I will be back to doing what I've meant to do for a very long time."

David nodded. Max felt he somehow understood the untold story behind the simple statement.

"Yes, she is a wonderful woman isn't she?" He looked back to where his wife was talking with Lauren over the serving table holding the beginnings of the afternoon's snacks and meal fixings.

"There is no question about that," Max responded.

"Ever cheated on a woman?" David asked holding no punches.

The question didn't startle Max. He'd been expecting it. "No I have not, nor would I ever, especially with Lauren. I know what she's been through. I have too much respect for the opposite sex. What Lauren and I have is more than just a physical relationship. You don't have to worry. I won't do anything to hurt her," he said this straight from his heart.

Lightening the moment, David looked Max up and down a couple of times and said in his deepest voice possible, "Good because I wouldn't want to have to hurt you."

By the looks of him, David wouldn't have been able to hurt Max even if he tried. His small boned stature would be no match for Max's well toned body. He stood eight or nine inches over David's small frame.

Playing along with him, Max straightened his shirt looking down at the chicken sheepishly, "No, no. We wouldn't want that to happen." They both looked at each other and burst out in good-humored laughter.

"Just as long as we understand each other," David said in a more serious tone.

Testing the steaks with the barbecue fork, Max reached over to grab the serving platter they were to be placed on. He looked David in the eyes. "You have my word on it."

From across the deck Rita and Lauren were discussing the seriousness of the conversation David and Max seemed to be having.

"What do you think they are talking about?" Lauren asked her friend.

"You know the drill. Max is going to be given the third degree by everyone who loves you, honey. I'm sure he was expecting it."

Lauren looked across and found Max looking straight at her. The smile on his face told her he was holding his own. Then a little twinkle came into his eyes and he gave her a little mischievous wink, which told her his thoughts had turned to something else. She blushed slightly and nodded her head ever so slightly in agreement, to show him she knew exactly what he was thinking about. He laughed out loud then turned back to what David was telling him about.

"Okay, so spill the beans. How good is he? Does he do it for you?" Rita said with her usual straight to the point questions.

"I don't know what you are talking about," Lauren answered a bit embarrassed it was so obvious.

"Come on now, you know exactly what I am talking about. You two have a connection that doesn't come with just conversation and beating around the relationship bush. You've been going to bed with him. It's all over your face and his. So tell me all about it." Rita put her hand on her hip tapping her well-manicured fingers impatiently.

Lauren glanced up to make sure Max wouldn't see what they were discussing. She didn't want him to think she talked about their sexual relationship with everybody.

"Well I won't go into everything here, but I will tell you this, he does things to me nobody ever has. When we make love, there is something different about it. It's as if I've never been with anyone else in my life. I really think we were meant for each other in so many ways it's impossible to ignore."

"I knew it. He's the one. He is definitely the one for you. I could feel it was true love the first time I met him. So, tell me what makes his lovemaking different. Can you put it in words, and if not, just give me a hint and I'll figure it out for myself," Rita said with a throaty laugh that made her husband turn and look at her. Shaking his head as she blew him a kiss he caught it and put it to his lips. Then shaking his finger at her, he went back to talking to Max.

Lauren caught the little interlude and smiled because she knew she and Max had the same type of connection, but they were playing it down a bit today for the sake of family and friends not really knowing how close they had become yet. Rita obviously already knew.

"Rita, you are so bad, and you know it. You know I am not the kiss and tell kind of girl. But just to satisfy your question, I can say what is truly different about him is I really feel he's there for me. He's really thinking about my needs and not just wanting to satisfy his own needs. I feel so totally connected to him, it's as if we were one person. Does that make any sense at all?"

"True love, I tell you, true love," Rita agreed, nodding her head.

Lauren grinned, and added with a little mischief in her voice, "Besides, he is really good at what he does."

"I bet he is!" Rita burst out laughing. Moving closer, she whispered, "Tell me more."

All of a sudden the doorbell rang. "Saved by the bell," Lauren said leaping from her chair. Rita groaned as she swept past her at not getting to find out the details.

"Aunt Maggie!" Lauren reached forward to give her Aunt a huge hug. "Uncle Dan," she exclaimed returning the bear hug he bent down to give. "I'm so glad you could both make it."

"Hrmph!" The disgruntled voice came from behind Uncle Dan. Turning to see who was there, Lauren let out a little shout of joy.

"Amy! I didn't think you were going to be able to make it out. Oh my word, look at you!" Pushing Uncle Dan to the side lovingly, Lauren cleared the path for the abundantly pregnant and obviously uncomfortable cousin Amy.

"I wouldn't miss this for the world. Come give us a hug," she said spreading her arms in what would have been a bear hug with the same enthusiasm as Uncle Dan. But because of her size it ended up to be more a pressing of cheek to cheek with her lifelong best friend and cohort of earlier days. "Okay, where is he?" She asked peering into the room looking excitedly for the new and important person in Lauren's life.

"We are all out on the deck. Come on. Let me show you around a little on our way out."

Amy waddled in after her, trying not to show how desperately all she wanted to do was just sit down. Following her through the door, her husband James, looked bone tired. Lauren had heard how extremely inventive Amy's cravings had gotten, sending him on late night runs to the little 24-hour shopping mart for some of the strangest things.

Giving Lauren a quick brotherly hug, he gave her a noticeable double look over. "Lookin' good, Lauren. If Amy wasn't my angel from heaven I might have to snatch you up."

Lauren gave a laugh. Maybe after all she wasn't looking half bad. James was nothing to laugh at himself. He was definitely a looker. His blond mane curled nicely down his neck over softly bronzed skin. He had what is called the California surfer look. Tall, with plenty of muscle, and the pretty boy look that drove some women wild. His blue eyes laughed engagingly when he smiled. There was no question why Amy had fallen head over heels for him.

Taking both Maggie and Dan's arms in hers, Lauren squeezed them both, voicing again how glad she was they'd been able to come out for the party. She hadn't much of a chance to show them any of the improvements she'd been making before Max came in the back door meeting them as they came into the kitchen. He had a full platter of steaks in one hand and an empty bowl for barbecue sauce in the other.

His mouthwatering rogue like appearance seemed to fill the room with such masculinity there was no misjudging his presence by man or woman. Flashing one of his killer grins, he all but melted the hearts of the women in the room, especially Lauren's. She felt her heart flutter as her thoughts formed into, *'He is mine, all mine.'*

"Hello all, very nice to meet you. Sorry, can't stay. I've got dogs about to explode." Grabbing another bowl of his specially made barbecue sauce from the counter, he turned and flashed another smile just for Lauren, and strode out the back again to stop a disaster from happening to the hot dogs on the grill.

"Oh my," was all Aunt Maggie was able to let out after the full impact of his totally encompassing virile male presence had left the room. Uncle Dan just rolled his eyes.

"Damn!" came out of Amy's mouth with eyes widened. She stared after him in a greedy fashion, which earned a scowl by her husband. "Don't worry Jimmy, it doesn't hurt to look," she said giving his hand a healthy squeeze.

"Yes, well, that was Max. He is tending the grill and has to defend his honor. David has been out there trying to drill all his grilling secrets out of him," Lauren smiled as her heart did a double flip of its own.

"Let's see this house of yours," Dan said, obviously trying to change the subject.

"As you can see, I've been working real hard at getting the house rehabilitated. It's not really remodeled, because there really isn't going to be much change from what it looked like when it was built. I suppose the correct term would be renovated." She spread her arms out encompassing the kitchen and breakfast nook. "This however, is my addition to an already perfect house," she said as she led the way out onto the back deck.

"Oh honey, this is amazing!" Maggie exclaimed apparently awe struck by the beauty.

Sunlight filtered through the leaves of the maple tree at the side of the deck, giving a playful silent tune for the green dancers on the ends of its branches. The trickling waterfall seemed to fall into step with its musically rhythmic sounds. The lake view, through the trees, beyond the deck was sparkling with bright blues and iridescent whites that made you automatically think of reaching for your sunglasses. There were amazing smells coming from the fully brick-encased grill making the mouth water in anticipation of tastes yet to come. It was truly a sight of welcome and fulfillment. One had only to sit and listen to the sounds of nature and take in the sounds of laughter of friends and family to feel what Lauren had envisioned before she'd even started the project.

Uncle Dan stood nodding his head at every angle. "Good job, Lauren," he said pulling her into a hug. "So did your handyman do all of this?"

"Yes he did, with a little help from me and my dreams." She knew Dan was measuring Max up, and felt a little guilty about not warning him about the wolves who would be circling him with questions, wondering if he was going to fit the picture of what they thought she deserved. "Go easy on him, would you Uncle Dan. He's no where close to Ben or Evan." She lifted and gave a quick peck on his check to the lifted brow he raised to her.

"We shall see," he said gruffly pointing his direction to where Max stood with one eye on the grill, the other in conversation with David and James.

Lauren stood for a moment, watching the gathering of her family men around Max. He fit right in. She knew she didn't have anything to worry about. Then, from behind her, she suddenly got an intuitive feeling someone was watching them all. She turned and studied the trees as far back as she could, but there was nothing unusual. In the pit of her stomach, she felt she was right, so she continued to stare in the distance of the front tree line. A chill ran down her back when she thought she saw the outline of a person beyond clear sight. Then the form seemed to fade into the surrounding trees.

"What do you see?" asked Amy from behind Lauren.

Lauren shook her head. "Nothing, I thought I felt something though," she said shaking off the feeling of someone watching them.

"Uh-oh, you want me to have Jimmy take a look? We know there's truth to all your feelings."

Amy had always been receptive to her unique way of knowing things. In fact, she was the one who pointed her in the direction of Kathryn. Taking a last look, Lauren decided it must be the thrill of finally having everyone out to celebrate. "No. It must be all the excitement in the air."

"Well, there's a lot of that for sure," Amy agreed, looking around. "It looks to be a general meeting of the men over the grill. God, I hope it's ready soon, I'm famished!" They had both turned to watch the meeting take place over a swirl of fragrant smoke rising from the delicious and savory meats Max had prepared. She was beginning to feel rather famished herself.

Turning, Lauren smiled at little Amy, whose hand had been placed protectively over her protruding belly, stroking in smooth calming brushes.

"Where on earth did you find him, in the yellow pages?" Amy asked with a giggle. "Remind me to let my fingers do the walking next time I need something done around the house."

Giggling herself, Lauren sat to enjoy the view herself for a moment. This handsome man, every woman seemed to tremble at his rouged good looks and succulent manner, was hers. At least for now, she thought with a slight twinge of self-doubt sneaking its ugly head into her thoughts. How would someone like her be able to keep him for very long? Sex can only hold on to a man so long, and then they would be looking for something more—something for the long run. A furrow in Lauren's brow made Amy's radar go flying into alert.

"What's the matter? Isn't he treating you right? Jimmy and Dad will knock a little sense into him," she said with the already motherly protective field going into overdrive.

Coming back to the present, Lauren shook her head vehemently, realizing what Amy must have seen in her eyes. "No, no. That's not it at all. He is wonderful, I couldn't ask for better. He is so amazing, I just……I don't…." Lauren stumbled over the words to say.

Looking around she made sure nobody else was in hearing distance. Maggie had gone to say hello to Rita, who was brushing her fingers through the ringlets of her little boy sitting on her lap. Lauren turned to see her ever-attentive cousin eyeing her in speculation.

"I'm just not sure how to keep him," she said simply, knowing Amy would understand totally. Lauren glanced again toward Max as she heard his deep laugh at something James had said to him, her Uncle still standing off a bit watching him closely in his interaction with the others. "He's just so perfect, almost too perfect. I don't think I'm good enough for him."

Rolling her eyes in disapproval, Amy leaned forward and took Lauren's hand in hers. "What is it honey?"

Lauren hadn't wanted to let anything spoil the day, but the thoughts of what Ben had said kept haunting her. "Ben was here."

Amy made an exasperated sound. "What did he want? Is he bugging you again? You don't have to take that you know. Where is he? I'll send Jimmy over to take care of him."

With a laugh, Lauren realized just how silly it sounded and lightened up. "Actually, you don't have to do that, Max already took care of it for me. But he said some things that really have me thinking."

Looking back at Max she could hear Ben's taunting in the back of her mind. "What makes you think you are good enough for him...you'll never be able to keep someone like that...I'm the best you will ever have..." Shuddering, she looked up to see Amy glaring at her.

"You don't have to even tell me, I can just imagine what he said to you. Don't believe it. He is such an asshole, and you know it." Amy watched as Lauren's gaze had fixed on Max. "Lauren, if anything, you are too good for him. Those other two were just jerks. Don't let what happened in the past crowd out what you could have now. Just relax. If it was meant to be, it will happen. If he proves me wrong, then I'll send Jimmy after him, too." Amy reached out and stroked Lauren's hand as she'd done in calming the baby within. "Besides, even if it isn't meant to be, I sure as hell wouldn't pass him up. I'd be enjoying every little piece of him. A major piece of eye candy if you ask me."

Laughing, Lauren shook her head. Amy always had been the optimist of the family. "What are you talking about, James is no dud either. If he hadn't fallen so deep for you, I might have given him a taste myself."

They both fell into laughter, giggling over things only the two of them could hear with their heads close together in a conspiring manner. Max looked over and saw the joy and the laughter blooming over Lauren's face. He could feel another edge of uncertainty slip away as he could see so apparently her love of friends and family. He watched her for a moment, his heart melting a little more, before he began to turn the meat again for the slow cook method he loved so much. His eye caught the sharp gaze of her uncle who had made his way over to stand beside him at the grill.

"She is an amazing woman."

Dan stood silent a moment eyeing Max. "That she is," he said slowly.

"You don't trust me," Max said simply, making a statement of fact rather than questioning.

"Don't trust anyone with my little girl. You don't mince words. I like that," Dan said with an approving nod. "What are your intentions?"

Gauging the situation to be the very important pinnacle of family perception versus good grounded man-to-man judgment Max chose his words carefully. "Well sir, Lauren and I haven't discussed any permanent familial standing as of yet, however, you can be assured I am not one for unencumbered flings. My family is of good Italian stock, and as such my intentions are in pure standing with my upbringing."

Nodding his head methodically, he lifted his eyes up to find Max's unfaltering steadfast look of integrity.

"As long as we understand each other boy," Dan reached out and slapped him on the back in unspoken approval.

"Without question," Max returned. Smiling slightly, he wondered if Lauren knew he was going to be put under every family member's spyglass. If he'd been an ant he would have fried by now under the intense speculation.

He caught her swift glance as she shared words with her cousin Amy and Rita's little boy, Gavin, who had apparently been caught doing something he shouldn't have been. She gave him a soft innocently wistful smile, which made his heart skip a beat. She had no idea how beautiful she'd become to him. He needed to remember to tell her just how beautiful she was before the end of the day. Sneaking a quick suggestive glance up toward her bedroom window and back down, his thoughts clearly showed in the depths of his eyes. She blushed then brought herself back to the conversation with Amy.

Aunt Maggie caught the whole display which had been meant only for the two of them, and sighed deeply. She could only hope this would be what Lauren had been hoping for all of her life. Ever since she was a little girl, when she'd come to them as an orphan, she'd been a romantic at heart. The books she read, the stories she wrote, were all about love. Maggie's sister had been a romantic as well, and she'd won the heart of her prince charming. Lauren being the result of that love, it was only right she too would have the same characteristics of her parents.

Romantically inclined, like her mother, yet strong of heart like her father. She knew Lauren loved others with every fiber of her being. She loved so deeply, and she also hurt deeply when that love was let down or unmatched. Maggie had seen it happen to many times to her little girl. She saw the love lights in her eyes again. There was no question Lauren was in love again.

Chapter 19

Later, after good food and laughter had been shared, Dan, James and David had gone down to check out the fireworks being handled by the boys. Lauren, Rita and Amy had gathered the children together for a nap, and were talking quietly over them as mothers do. Max brought in another load of dishes to the kitchen sink where Maggie had decided to put a dent into them with some suds and steady effort.

She smiled gently as Max laid another layer of plates over the ones which already sat at the edge of the sink. He leaned back against the cupboard with a heavy sigh and closed his eyes for a momentary rest before going back out for another load.

"This day always seems longer than any other holiday. I think it must be because of the anticipation for the celebration at the end" he said slowly opening his eyes.

Maggie glanced at him with a smile and merely nodded in agreement.

"So, you haven't asked me any inquisitive questions yet. I'm not sure if I should be grateful or scared." Max laughed.

"You are good for her," Maggie said as she placed the last plate on the drying rack. Turning off the water, she turned to wipe her hands on the dishcloth hanging on the stove.

"I think that is the most impressively profound statement I've heard all day. Not quite a question, and yet had such deep meaning." Max sighed and took a seat at the kitchen table. "Join me for a minute, would you?"

Maggie complied with his request, sitting reservedly at the edge of the chair.

Being as straight as he had with Uncle Dan, Max leaned back and looked intently at Maggie. She was a beautiful woman. Her face had become flushed with the days outside activity. Just like Lauren, her Irish descent was obvious, with red hair streaked at the sides with a bit of graying. Her blue eyes were soft in color and looked at him just as intently, holding still a hint of reserved judgment.

"So what is the verdict?" He asked quietly.

Maggie looked down at her hands, then back up to meet his gaze. "I don't make a habit of placing judgment on someone I don't know well. However, I do know a little more about you than maybe some of the others here today. I am aware of what the media has put out about your past, and would like to know what your take on the situation is, before I make any of my own conclusions."

Nodding slowly Max showed his acceptance of her statement. As she'd been the one to discover his true identity before he'd been able to tell Lauren, he couldn't blame her for not trusting him yet at face value. If all he'd done were to read about someone in the news he would be doing the same thing.

"I can understand. I'm not sure we have the time to go into all the details right now. I do want to assure you, what happened was a very tragic thing. It's taken me some time to get past it all. My Anna was a gentle and loving woman. She didn't deserve to die like that. No one does."

The earnest statement entrusted him to Maggie's way of thinking more than any lengthy explanation ever would have. She could see in his eyes that he meant what he said, and trusting her instincts she believed him.

Maggie nodded slowly, keeping her gaze fixed on his. "My instincts tell me you are very trustworthy. So what happens from here?"

"Lauren has helped me to see I need to continue to enjoy life and to surround myself with those things which bring happiness. My music is one of those things. I have let it set for too long, it needs to come out again to be enjoyed."

"How are do you plan on making that happen? I understand from what Lauren has told me there are still some complications from the investigation. The murderer was never found."

"You're right. This won't be an easy thing to do. But I can't let this take over my life. I'm going to pursue my dreams," he said with determination.

Quietly Maggie got up from the table and moved over to where he still sat. She leaned over and gently gave him a hug and a light kiss on the cheek. "You are a very talented young man.

I've enjoyed your work tremendously. I'm sure you will do what is right." She brushed a hand across his brow. "Lauren is lucky to have found you. Remember to treasure the small things Max, sometimes they only come around once in a lifetime."

Catching her hand in his Max smiled up at her, knowing exactly what she was talking about. "Believe me Maggie when I say I'm the one who is lucky. She is a treasure and deserves the best. I plan on doing everything I can to see she gets it."

* * * *

Jeffrey wouldn't let Max go for long this time without making sure he was still where he'd followed a few weeks before. All afternoon, covered by the heavy brush, he'd crouched, watching the activities of family and friends at the lakeside.

Ever since the debacle with the shipping of his supplies, he'd been trying to figure out the best way to carry out his plans anyway. He'd been in contact with his friend who had gotten the C-4 bricks for him in the first place and was told it would take some time to round up some more for him. The potential cost to have him ship the stuff to Washington was too much for Jeffery to handle right now. He would just have to wait and see if his original box ever showed up. In the meantime, he would wait for another opportunity to carry out his last deeds.

He didn't want to hurt anyone else, but it seemed Max was never alone anymore. Until he figured it all out, he would keep watching to make sure he didn't disappear again.

Even though he'd taken some of the Hydrocodone from a source he'd found here, the pain was getting worse. Drifting between dozing to sleep, the blast of the fireworks caught him off guard. The darkness disoriented him, and he began to think he was in a field not unlike the one he'd run through so many years before. He felt himself again, at the east entrance of the compound, weighed down by the guns and ammo strapped across his belly. The shouts of his Sergeant to get down and move fast ran through his memory as the explosion of land mines and machine gun bullets flew past him. He began thrashing about as the branches of the underground bushes scraped against his face in his attempt to get clear of the incoming enemy. The smell of gun powder burnt his eyes, and he was partially blinded to his surroundings.

Pain. There was so much pain.

In the dark, Jeffery pushed to his feet, and stumbled out of the trees onto the driveway where he'd been hiding. He covered the side of his face pounding with phantom pain and could almost feel the blood dripping down his palm. Nothing looked familiar as he looked side to side, trying to find the C-130 plane which should have been there already to pick them all up. The trees standing tall on either side of him didn't look right. They were too tall to be the Melaleuca trees he was used to seeing. In the distance he saw an opening. The plane must be there.

Please, God, let it be there, he prayed toward the heavens, and he began running, barely able to pick his feet off the ground, in hopes to get there before it took off.

* * * *

Fireworks were flashing brightly in the sky, patriotic blues and reds and gold painted brilliant pictures in the darkness. They could be seen across the lakefront, winking in noisy competition attempting to outdo the others across the way. Lauren leaned against Max in the crook of his arms, his chin atop her head, gazing at the prolific show of lights across the water. Josh was having the time of his life, his friend Robert in like exuberance, choosing and lighting the next and best explosion for the evening. While Uncle Dan monitored from the side, making sure all safety precautions were being met, so as not to end up with an unfortunate accident. Everyone else settled back in comfort to enjoy the show.

Lauren felt as if she was on top of the world. Although unsaid, Max was feeling the same way. Here in his arms was a magnificent woman, whose apparent love for her family and the returned undoubted love from them all was a testament of her being the soulful, kind-hearted woman he desired. He felt with her anything could be accomplished. Squeezing her gently, he turned her around to face him.

He placed his hands on either side of her face and brought her lips to meet his. Murmuring as his lips brushed against hers, "You make me feel like a new man. Let me show you tonight *mia amono, leggera di mia mondo.*"

Emotion poured over them equally as the light kiss turned into one filled with need and urgency. Max felt his kiss had caused her breath to catch in her throat, and he tasted the desire and growing demand for satisfaction flowing through them both.

Drawing her away slightly, Max stayed his desires, knowing this was not the time or place to show anything further. "Will you be mine tonight, *Amore*?"

"Need you ask?" She asked.

The quickening of his heart welled up inside with the vivid thought of his hands and lips running over her flesh. But this was not just a physical need. His desire was to feel loved, and to feel a connection much deeper than one of physical demands. He sensed she felt the same. But he needed to show her how much he wanted her, needed her, and would do anything to have her. She ran her hands up his chest, encircling her arms around his neck and pulled his head down to hers again. The kiss she gave him almost brought him to his knees. Her taste and the potency from the heat pouring out from her lips was just a taste of what he knew would be coming to him.

"Darling, one more of those, and your guests are going to have to help themselves to the leftovers, and leave on their own," he said with a mixed race of anticipation and excitement travelling up his spine. Pulling her softly against him, he shifted slightly so they could both continue to watch the last of the fireworks from the water's edge.

Watching the embraced couple, Amy and Rita sat across from each other on the deck and caught each other's gaze.

"No doubt." Rita said with a little smile of satisfaction.

"None whatsoever," Amy said in agreement snuggling close in her husband's warm arms.

* * * *

Everyone said their "goodbyes", and Josh had happily gone off to Robert's for the rest of the evening. Lauren looked over the remaining disarray of her kitchen.

"This is just going to have to wait." Turning, she gave Max a seductively mischievous smile. "I have better things to do."

Max could feel his heart begin to pound ruthlessly in anticipation. He'd never felt this way about any other woman. This need to touch and to be touched, to lose oneself in desire and emotion, to feel as if nothing else mattered in the world except the two of them was a constant reminder of the love he had discovered. It built quickly, running through his veins like fire, where it had been simmering all afternoon. Just watching her, innocent of her beauty, the sexuality she exuded was enough to turn any man's head.

He grabbed her tightly around the waist and pulled her hard against him. *She is mine*, he thought, desperately wanting to show her just how much she affected him.

"*Mio dio*, I want you," he exclaimed, his body urging him on to take her quickly. His passion grew so quickly it was as if the only thing he could feel was the taste of her, the only thing he could see was the passion in her own eyes, the only thing he wanted was to be engulfed in her. He swung her around pressing her up against the counter.

An overwhelming passion came over her as he brought his lips down over hers. She'd only dreamt of this level of intensity in the past. Now it was here firmly in her hands. Passion, demand, urgency, and need all rolled up into one wonderfully sexy man.

Lauren's own heart thudded roughly against her chest as he deepened the kiss. His tongue probed for more, the intoxicating taste of his mouth filling her with desire. His hand came up to mold the contour of her breast in his palm as her hands came up to his shoulders. Kneading the muscles, she pressed him closer yet, as if to envelope this wonderful feeling inside of her.

Suddenly, and what seemed to be without effort, he whisked her off her feet and carried her up the stairs to the bedroom. As he set her down lightly on her feet, he surprised her by shoving her up against the door, his mouth devouring hers. The physical demands and need for satisfaction filled his senses, as they never had before. He couldn't get enough of her—and he knew he never would.

"*Mio Dio, sei una tentatrice,*" he exclaimed wrought with need. She returned the same urgency and desperate need as his. His lips now covering her throat left a heated trail wherever they sought the warm glow of her skin. Nuzzling the base of her throat, he murmured, "You are a temptress with your sweet enticing nectar."

Reaching down, his hands caressed her inner thighs, and she groaned as her body arched against his. In a quick movement, he pulled her clothes free following every curve of her body with his hands as he went. She was desperate to feel his flesh against hers. Lauren's breath came quick, with shallow pants, as she struggled with the button on his waistband. Without a care, Max tore his shirt from his shoulders, buttons flying everywhere. In no time he had all of his clothes thrown to the floor. He pressed his warm flesh against hers, his lips roving over her neck and shoulders, as if he was trying to taste every last bit of her.

Hungrily, Lauren brought his lips back to hers, eager to give freely what he drew from her. She nipped at his neck with her teeth, just below his ear to entice a deep moan from his throat.

"You are driving me crazy," he growled.

Turning her toward the bed, he all but threw her onto the comforter, his hardened body pressing deeply against her. She gave a throaty moan tempting him to go farther, and to take her. Max's heart was beating so hard in his chest, it was a wonder he was capable of movement. But move he did, and with a quick thrust, he was inside her. Her hot wet folds engulfed him with her own urgency. She arched against him, driving him deeper and deeper. The intensity of the feeling of power swam through her blood, empowering her to willingly give as much as she was receiving.

As he thrust upward he dropped his head to draw her breast into his mouth, sending almost blinding electric shock wave sensations throughout her entire body. She came with such force she thought her head would come off of her shoulders.

Stars danced through her head as she lost all thought and floated toward an almost unconscious state of mind. But Max had more interesting things in store for her. His continued long strokes brought her quickly back to the present, where the urgent need began to build again at her core.

The occasional brilliant flash of fireworks over the lake continued to sparkle through the open window, the explosiveness of what was going on inside this room outshining their impudent blasts. Her eyes fluttered open again, and she looked straight into his with an equally passionate ardor, sending him into overdrive. They began to move in unison, each bringing the other closer and closer until it felt as if they were one. It felt as if they'd floated up into another field of existence, one where energy sparked from the meeting of their bodies, and the atmosphere was filled with nothing but feelings and sensation. He began to drive quicker and deeper as her excitement built strong and quick around for him. As she gasped in with the powerful sense of ecstasy, she clasped around him building for yet another wave of release. Max lost control and they both dove into a place of unquestionable splendor.

Sometime during the night Lauren had stirred enough awake to find Max had pulled the comforter up over them to keep them warm, and now had his arm draped protectively around her in his sleep. Snuggling closer, she drew in his scent, knowing this was exactly where she wanted to be. Closing her eyes she drifted off to sleep again, comforted in the knowledge she truly could be loved.

*　*　*　*

"You think I should call someone?" The waitress said to the cook through the space separating the kitchen from the booths out front of the 24-hour cafe. She was indicating a customer who had come in not looking altogether well. He sat talking to himself in the corner booth, both hands on either side of his face as if holding in something threatening to explode.

He frequently looked around as if afraid of having been followed. When the waitress had gone to him to find out what he wanted to order he shook his head and only mumbled something at her which sounded like '*coffee*' and eyed her suspiciously.

Looking at him with experienced eyes, the cook shook his head.

"Naw, he's just coming down off something really hard. Let's just let him be for the time being. I've got something for him here if he wants to cause trouble." Holding up the end of the baseball bat, he nodded his head at the troubled customer, making sure he saw him.

This wasn't the first time Jeffery had gotten that look. It was getting harder for him to keep it together. When he'd looked at himself in the cracked mirror of his tiny room at the motel this morning, he'd looked like hell. As he brushed a hand over his head, the crackle of dried leaves and twigs caught in his hair fell to the floor, reminding him where he'd spent the last few hours.

He'd been thinking how he'd followed Max that day when he'd come back to Chicago. He hadn't understood when the police had called off the investigation of Max. Sure, they'd questioned him, but there was no forced entry. It was so obvious he was the one who had killed Anna. Max had driven to that no good, nosy investigator on the south side, the one who had pestered him incessantly for a time after Anna's death. He'd asked him over and over again where he had been that night. Truth was, he really didn't know. He thought he'd seen her that night when he'd gone to see Mongo, but couldn't be sure. All he knew was he'd been having horrible nightmares all night passed out on the couch.

There was no question in his mind Max had come to corroborate his story again with the asshole. So thoroughly convinced Max had killed her, he started imagining all the reasons for the murder. They couldn't fool him. They were in this together.

Today he'd watched as Max and the group of people had been outside having the time of their lives. Each time he'd seen Max wrap his arms around that woman, Jeffery's anger came rolling to the surface as he imagined she was his dear sweet Anna on her wedding day. When Max periodically lifted her fingers to his lips, memories came crashing down over him. He'd seen him do that before with his Kitten. Flashes of a bright and beautiful wedding day skimmed across his memory. The memories brought a pain shooting through Jeffery's head. Raising his hand to his temple he rubbed to make the pain go away.

When the fireworks started Jeffery travelled back in time to a place he prayed everyday he would forget. Unsure of how he'd ended up in the diner, he only knew he'd escaped again from the devastation he'd experienced in that mine field in 'Nam. It wasn't until the fireworks stopped had he been able to bring his focus back to the present time.

Another pain shot through his head like a jolt of lightening, clearing all lucid thought from his brain. He sucked in a jagged breath on the upswing of an agonizing sensation of a serrated knife piercing and sawing through his head. He groaned out in exasperation as the pain subsided.

Momentarily blank, he sat looking into his coffee as if the pursuit of life had come to its final destination. Visions flashed through his head of past, present and fantasized future. Anna's youthful figure swayed in front of him, her white wedding gown, in a wispy peasant style fluttering around her in the breeze. Her soft dark hair played wistfully around her flushed cheeks. She reached out for his hand, but it was not actually he who she reached to embrace. Max came into the picture, his manly virile presence permeating the peaceful scene. Jeffery had known Anna was lost to him the moment her dark eyes expressed the love she felt for this other man. Inciting the anger he felt so strongly against the injustice he felt for her being taken away from him, he began mumbling under his breath.

Suddenly, the vision changed. She was the same beautifully youthful girl from before, but now her hand covered in protection the prominent bulge of her third trimester. Her eyes this time filled with sadness as the tears streamed down her cheeks. She reached out to him as if she were to entice him to step away from his thoughts. Then her expression changed to extreme gut wrenching fear as she stepped back away from him crying out his name. Even now, somewhere in the distance he heard her calling out to him.

Then everything went black for a moment, when images came rushing back into view he lost sight briefly in his left eye as he struggled to gain control of himself. Sweat was pouring profusely down his forehead as he looked up to see the waitress standing over him with the coffeepot.

"Want anymore?" She asked tensely observing the distanced clarity of his actions.

Shoving the cup out toward her, he only mumbled again, and brought himself back to the present. Pouring quickly, coffee sloshing over the sides of the cup onto the table, the waitress hurried away to get as far as possible away from him.

Closing his eyes, he very clearly saw Max's face in front of him.

"You shouldn't have taken her away. She would still be mine if you hadn't taken her away. You'll pay. I promise you that."

Chapter 20

The work on the house was coming to an end. There were blinds to be ordered for the widows and some finish work to be done around the door jams and window encasements. Max had completed the finishing touches on the deck which needed his attention, and was currently working on the intricate placement of granite stones in the pathway leading to the house from the driveway. The stones would continue around each side of the house to the back deck to give a whimsical look of a moat encircling the rustic timbers of the porch. Low covering Irish moss between the flagstone, lined with pink and white evening primrose would encompass the nature around them.

Lauren sat at her laptop, fingers working over the keys as if her life depended upon it. Since she'd become intimately involved with Max it seemed as if the words could not be written fast enough. She was way ahead of schedule. Her agent had worked hard for her and was pleased to hear they could tell the publishers they could move the publication date at least three months prior to the original date.

She'd worked feverishly on completing the current book so she could begin work on the next one forming in her mind. It seemed as if creativity was flowing through her in a way she'd never experienced before. It was as though the excitement she experienced with Max was filtering through into all other areas of her life as well. Life was wonderful, and the old feelings of worthlessness had been brushed away, exposing only bright inspiring new ones.

Lauren took a brief pause in thought and heard the sound of notes being played reflectively on the piano in the front room. Curious she followed the beautifully wistful notes floating through the hallway. At the piano Max stood, tool belt slung low on his hips, his shirt nowhere to be seen as he'd discarded it earlier in the heat of the day. His well-toned muscles glistened in the sunlight streaming in the window, causing a flutter of excitement to pass through her belly. She watched as he became more involved in the notes flowing from his fingertips. It was such a thrill to become consumed by this man's talents. He held such sensitivity and magic in his hands, and still had an almost overpowering virility, strength and masculinity emanating from his being. It was almost as if he were at odds with himself, two worlds so totally apart from each other, yet entwined in so many ways.

Unable to stay back, Lauren moved forward, and he caught sight of her from the corner of his eye. He turned his head and gave her a sheepish grin, continuing to move his fingers across the keys playing the notes with ease. Notes which had never been played nor heard, and were no one else's to claim, flowed out from his very soul.

"Didn't mean to disturb you, I just couldn't keep this tune out of my head."

"No problem, I needed a break anyway."

Lauren hadn't pressed him about his music for some time. Though, she'd left it alone, hoping it would spring forth again on it's own, like the words now creatively jumping forward onto the pages in front of her.

Enjoying the view, she sat on the couch across from him, watching his muscles move sensuously with the movement of his arms his continued melody. "You are quite the picture. This makes me think of more strenuous types of music that can be made."

With a half laugh-half sigh, he stopped fingering the keys and stepped over to where she sat. Reaching out he pulled her to her feet so they stood face to face, only a breath away from each other.

"I wish I could listen to you forever." She lifted her face to his and looked deeply, searching for what she wanted to see. "You have such a gift Max. Have you thought more about performing again?"

Max's eyes darkened and he nodded. "I have something to tell you, *Bella*. But I don't want to do it here. Let me take you to dinner tonight." His dark eyes danced with bright excitement as he smiled into hers. Briefly brushing his lips across hers, she could feel the energy. It was something big. Something he could barely keep inside.

"Okay, I've got an English class early this afternoon. I could meet you down at Daisy's by the college. She's always got some really good food. Would that work?" Rubbing her lips against his again, she wondered what it was he had to tell her. Not wanting to put too much into it, she wouldn't let herself worry about what it could or could not be. That would only darken this wonderful feeling.

"That would be perfect." He nodded his assent. "I've got some things to take care of this afternoon—about six then?" Bending forward he enveloped her in a hug taking her breath away. He grinned at her as if knowing the suspense would be killing her the whole time.

"That works." Thoroughly curious now, her brows gathered in consideration. "Do I need to have her put a bottle of wine to chill for us?"

"Don't worry. I'll take care of it." And with that he went back out to finish up on the placement of rocks for the one side before he'd to go.

* * * *

Daisy's was a small quaint, off the beaten path café, with home-style cooking. With Daisy at the grill, and a couple of hard-working students working the tables, they spread cheer and welcome to all the guests.

Lauren stepped through the entry to be met with a handful of waves from some of her students who joyously ingested their evening meal with such gusto not many restaurants could claim to match. She spotted Max at a table in the corner, laughing whole-heartedly at something Cindy, the young waitress, had said to him. She giggled and blushed brightly as she stepped away from the table. Lauren met her halfway and gave her a quick squeeze. Cindy was one of her students, struggling to pay her way through journalism, on her way to become the next brightest spot on television.

Cindy sent Max another flirtatiously longing look. Glancing back at Lauren, she said, "Is that wonderful hunk yours Ms. Roberts?"

Lauren grinned on the inside and nodded. "It looks like he is."

"Oh my God, I can't believe it! He did some work at my Mom's house last summer. Made my hands sweat every time he came near me."

"Me too," Lauren murmured and smiled back.

"My Mom kept calling him back to do things just so we could get another look at him. Said he wasn't going to get away that easy! But that's Mom for you, always in search of Mister Right. But I have to agree with her on this one, if he's not right, I don't know who is. Go on, I'll be right on back to take your orders." Cindy moved away, an added rise in her step and a toss of her hips.

Laughing, Lauren gave Max a quick kiss and settled across from him at the table. "You have made yourself quite the reputation around here. If I'm not careful you are going to be whisked away by a group of women wanting to test your manly advantages."

"You must be talking about Mrs. Nelson. I had a hard time letting her down, but I don't think she is exactly my type," he said grimacing at the vision popping up of the overly endowed woman in her late forties, who thought the more colors you could spread on your face the better. Her bright blue emblazoned eyes had become a nightmarish vision in his head over that summer, constantly winking, trying to entice him with the come-hither look. Shaking away the memory, he turned his attentions to the beauty who sat across from him.

"I'm sure every woman on earth thinks they are your type. It's only a matter of who catches your eye first." Max followed her gaze across the room to see at least a half-dozen feminine eyes looking their way, some innocently dreaming, others calculating what type of relationship he had with Lauren and if there was a chance for them.

Max reached out and took her hand gently in his, reading the doubt which had begun to gather again in her eyes. He started by kissing the fingers, lightly caressing her palm with his thumb, bringing Lauren to full attention. Then with his eyes on hers he slowly turned her hand upward and pressed his warm lips to the middle of her palm. Her pulse began to beat rapidly at his fingertips. At first he thought he must have imagined the light moans of some of the onlookers, but as he brought his lips up a slow trail from her palm to her wrist the heavy sighs all around him were unmistakable.

He continued to look deep into her eyes. "But you are the only one I have eyes for, *amore*."

Lauren had been breathing so shallowly she suddenly took a deep inhale for more oxygen. "Yes, well, one of these days I am going to make you tell me what all of these beautiful sounding Italian phrases you say to me mean. I think you must know it drives the women crazy when you do that!"

As he reached up to brush a stray strand of hair which had fallen forward over her cheek, his hand rested momentarily. "*Sie molto bella, stasera*. You are so very beautiful, *Amore*. I have so much to tell you when you are ready."

Cindy came to the table, a bottle of chilled red wine in one hand, the two wineglasses she'd searched to unearth in the other.

"This is the best I could do. I hope it will be alright." She quickly set the glasses down and poured a little bit into one of the glasses. Giggling she handed it to Max to taste. "I've always wanted to do that! I saw it in a movie once, and it seemed so classy." Raising her eyebrows a bit, she waited for Max's approval.

"*Perfetto*," Max winked at her. "This will do just fine."

After Cindy took their orders, she went off to start rumors of possible proposals or other celebratory reasons for their 'best' wine. Max enjoyed watching Lauren nervously bring the glass to her lips for a slow sip, she gazed at him, the tart pungent taste of the wine causing the corners of her mouth to curve upward in an almost sensual manner. As he watched emotions play across her face, he knew the anticipation was getting the best of her imagination.

"So what do we owe the pleasure of enjoying the house's finest?"

He'd had a couple of final phone calls to make when he got home and would be ready to move forward with his music and his life. All of which had become tied into the makings of a beautiful relationship with this woman he adored. He almost wished this could be a proposal of sharing their lives with each other, to wake each morning to a new day to enjoy with each other. A proposal of that type had more riding on it than just the simple joining of two lives. It also carried with it a possibility of danger and of shattered lives.

Shaking mentally, he brushed the old fears away, not allowing them to control his actions any longer. Changes were about to happen, and he would make that proposal soon, but first things first.

Max took a long sip of his own and set his glass down firmly. Reaching out he laid his hand over hers, stroking the smooth skin with his thumb. As he turned her hand in his, he grasped her fingers and kept his eyes on hers.

"Let me just say you are beautiful, *mia amano. Tale bellezza, tu abbi presa mia luore sempre.* Such beauty, you have stolen my heart forever." He again raised her hand and brought it to his lips in a gallant manner. Laying it back down on the table, he covered it with his own. "First, I want to thank you for making me realize I've been sitting on my music long enough." A smile floated across his lips as he saw her grin. "And I wanted to let you know I've been looking into what it would take to get back into the music business."

"That is awesome Max!" He couldn't have asked for more as she smiled with joy and support

"And..." he paused, waiting to bring her full attention back to what he was saying. "My contacts I have in the field have been busy. I've been offered an opportunity to perform at the Fall Music Extravaganza with the Seattle Symphony."

"Oh my God, that is so wonderful." Jumping up she gave him a smack on the lips, and then settled back down in her seat. "I knew it. I knew you would be able to get back in the way you deserve to after all this time. Fall? That isn't much time. You are going to need to be practicing with them aren't you? When do you start? They must know your work. Who is the conductor?" She shot questions out faster than he could answer them. He could almost hear the wheels turning in her head, and then she started coming up with the answers before he'd answered them.

"That's it isn't it? You know the conductor? Who is it? Where did you work together?"

"Slow down there, you're going to hurt yourself," he said patting her hand. The excitement he felt pouring from her was not only energizing, but it was arousing as well. Because he'd experienced it first hand. This normally cool and calm person could on the drop of a dime turn into a whirlwind of energy, fire and power. He'd seen it in her work, in her need for accomplishment, and their sexual joining filled with passion and need.

"Mark and I go a long way back. We met at the Chicago Music Hall a few years back when my career was just taking off. He'd been working with the Chicago Symphony director in the back room when I came in to practice one day. You could say we formed a bond right away, the kind that doesn't go away with a little time. So when I found out he was coming in to do work with the Seattle Symphony for this extravaganza, I took the chance he hadn't forgotten my work."

Sliding his hand up the stem of his glass, he smiled remembering the conversation he'd recently had with the friend. It had been as if they'd seen each other only the other day, no references as to what had happened, or why he'd disappeared, just wanting to know when he would come play some music with him.

"I don't know anybody in their right mind who could forget *your* music. Tell me all about it Max, every last detail."

Neither of them had noticed the man who had entered into the dining area. He wore a cap over his unkempt hair, slung low over his eyes. His clothes were of fair quality but looked as if he'd slept in them. Jeffery slid into a corner booth at the far wall where he had a perfect view of both of them talking and laughing. Max's face was turned away from him, but he could see the woman clearly. Sinking into the corner he watched and waited.

Cindy brought Max and Lauren their plates of spaghetti and garlic bread, and was coming for the ice water to refill their glasses when she spotted him. She swished by his table to let him know she would be right back with him to drop off a menu.

As she did, she cheerfully said, "I'll be right back to get your order."

After brushing the annoyingly sunny waitress away with an order for coffee, and coffee only, he sat back to watch the interaction between the two across the room. It was obvious Max had deep feelings for this woman. He would need to watch him for a while to see if she was worth using as another point of anguish in his plot to pay Max back. Perhaps he could use this relationship as a way to hurt him as deep as he'd been hurt by Anna's death.

He twitched as jolts of pain stabbed again at his temple. The drugs were starting to wear off again. They weren't lasting long enough anymore. By switching to the Hydrocodone opiates off the street at least he wouldn't have to put up with doctors. A long time ago they'd begun to question his real need, and suggested other types of therapy, like psychotherapy. He was never going back through that again. Doctors were always plying God with your life only to get their hands on more of your money. Playing with your mind and trying to make you think you were crazy. There was nothing wrong with his mind.

No, he was going to have to leave it up to whatever luck he had in what little life he had left. Opiates weren't hard to come by, if you knew where to go. But because of the varied strengths he could get his hands on from different sources, he was taking more and more to dull the pain clawing stubbornly at his brain. Slipping a couple of pills out of his pocket he washed them down with some coffee leaving a bitter taste in his mouth. He knew it would be over soon enough, but it didn't really matter since there was nothing left to live for now anyway.

Now he'd found Max, he only had to hang on long enough to see his plans through. Sitting back he continued to watch the couple as they unknowingly were being sized up for the next steps to take in his vengeful plan. The pills began to take hold. But he wished he could take the others he'd been given which would push him over the edge, where he could collapse again into unconsciousness. Not yet, he had to hang on a little longer.

"So this is really just a pre-recording appearance for marketing purposes. I'm not sure I will be going full force into full-on performances yet. We will just have to play that by ear. We should probably take a look at other local possibilities first before jumping into anything too broad, test the market a bit and see what the response is before we go all out."

"Of course, but I have no doubt you won't have any trouble." Lauren's stomach had begun to churn as she'd listened to his excitement. When he spoke of 'we', she assumed he was speaking of the contacts and agents he had in the music business. Even though she was excited for him, the one fear she had was he would start to break away and go on his own. There were so many possibilities out there for him, so many other people, so many other women who would do whatever it took to be with him. He didn't need her weighing him down.

"We won't know what the response is to my own scores, I've had positive response some years back, but it doesn't mean it will be accepted by the music crowd now."

She smiled, as she saw the wistful look in his eyes as he spoke of his work. Everything was about to change, she didn't know how, but she knew it wasn't going to be the same. As she took in a deep breath, she knew she would just have to get used to the fact he wouldn't be with her too much longer. The thought had her insides churning with the old feeling of failure brushing hazily through her thoughts.

Max flashed a smile. "I'm going to go meet with them next week. Bring to the table what I think would fit into the theme of the evening. Since we don't have too much time for practice we talked about a couple of classic operatic pieces, ones fairly well known by the musicians already. But since my goal here is to break in again with my own pieces, Mark told me to bring something whimsical and yet passionate. On the personal side, I was thinking maybe the piece you heard the first time, the one I wrote with you in mind?"

There was silence for a few moments. Max was thinking of the pieces he'd written, and each time it came back to the ones he'd written with her in mind. Those were the ones with the most passion, the most love.

For Lauren, she imagined this was going to be the beginning of the end. She couldn't believe she'd thought for one minute they could have a relationship. He would move out of her life, back into the life he'd known before, with his music, as it should be. Even knowing this, it was not easy to comprehend what she'd hoped to start with him wouldn't have a chance. The realization hit her like a truck. Every part of her wanted to scream and reach out to hold on for dear life. But she would only embarrass them both, so she would keep calm. She wouldn't cry. No, she wouldn't. Unable to stop them, Lauren's eyes brimmed with tears, yet she forced a faint smile on her upturned lips

He'd been staring into the darkness of the red wine still in his glass, and then glanced up.

"I'm sorry. What did I do?" He leaned forward with his napkin to brush at the tears which began to slide down her cheeks.

That had done it. He'd apologized before he even knew what he'd done. It seemed like all of the feelings she had for him leaped out all at once to play havoc with her composure.

"*Mia amano*, don't cry. *Amore*." He laid his hand on her cheek in a manner which broke her heart even more. "Sweetheart, *amore*, what is the matter?"

Cursing herself for her outbreak of emotion, Lauren shook her head as she got up from the table. "I'm just happy for you. It's nothing. Don't worry about it, just a little too much wine. Excuse me for a moment I'm going to the ladies room."

As Lauren swiftly made her way to the restroom she passed Cindy with a pitcher of ice water. Cindy noted the tears in her eyes and the blushed redness in her cheeks as Lauren looked away not wanting to be noticed. Sloshing some water into the half empty glasses on the table, Cindy saw the dismay on Max's face as he looked toward the direction Lauren had taken.

"What on earth did you do to the poor girl?" Putting her hands on her hips, she looked at him in indignation.

"I have no idea." Disturbed by Lauren's sudden outbreak, he couldn't figure out what he'd done.

Cindy shook her head and patted him on the shoulder. "Well, whatever it was, maybe you should spring for the double chocolate fudge cake we have tonight, might cheer her up." She started to walk away from the table then patted her pocket. Turning back around, she handed Max a folded up napkin. "That guy over there wanted you to have this."

The blood rushed to his head as he took the napkin, his hand shaking. "What guy?"

Max looked past Cindy to where she indicated but nobody was there. As he turned back around, someone was leaving with his back turned. His graying hair was covered in a baseball cap, his jacket wrinkled and fraying slightly at the edges. He was of medium build, might have had more muscle in his younger years, but looked to have lost a lot of weight recently as his clothes hung loosely around him. The man turned briefly to shoot a quick look at Max. Their eyes met, and in that second Max knew he'd seen him before, in fact he swore he knew him. The brief glint of recognition and what looked to be pure hatred showed in the other man's eyes setting the hackles up on Max's neck. Then he was gone.

Cindy turned around and shrugged her shoulders. "Funny, he was there a minute ago. You must have just missed him."

Max jumped up from his seat and flew toward the door. Throwing it open he rushed out onto the cement slab. There was absolutely nobody in sight. He came back in and sat down, gripping the napkin in his hand. His heart thudding in his chest, he slowly opened the note and froze.

'She's a pretty thing. It would be a shame for anything to happen to her.'

The reality of what had just happened clamped down hard on Max's ability to think straight.

He is here.

Lauren came back out of the restroom and sat down. She'd been berating herself for how she was acting with Max. He deserved this chance to bring his music to the world. There was nothing she wanted more for him. She needed to take hold of her fears and keep doing whatever she could during the time she had left with him. Perhaps then she could somehow make him see they were meant to be together. Just maybe he would see they needed each other.

Max looked up at her with a blank look then quickly stuffed something into his pocket.

"Sorry about that," Lauren said in a light tone, "Must have had too much wine."

He nodded absently and looked toward the door. Lauren didn't know what had come over him, but he wasn't the same happy man she'd left a few minutes earlier.

"What's wrong?"

Max stared at her and dropped his gaze to the tabletop and shook his head. "Nothing."

Lauren was sure something was not right. "Tell me. What happened?" she encouraged.

"It's nothing," he muttered, picking up his glass he threw back the remaining wine into his throat and stood up. "Are you done here?"

She stared at him, unsure of what to say.

Cindy rushed forward with the two pieces of double fudge chocolate cake. "Hold on there, big guy. You haven't had your desert yet."

There was absolutely no emotion on Max's face, as he remained silent standing like a totem pole. The look in his eyes was as blank as a sheet of paper. No emotion, no feeling, nothing.

Both Lauren and Cindy looked at each other. Rage began to fill Lauren's thoughts as she imagined he must have decided she wasn't worth the trouble any longer. Staring him in the eyes, she slowly stood and reached for her purse. For a moment she thought she saw a twinge of regret in his eyes, but she interpreted it as his realization she was a waste of his time.

Then as a surprise to them all, he suddenly flashed one of his killer grins, and winked at Cindy making an indication he would call her with his hand to his ear.

"Later, babe," he said throwing a sideways look at Lauren.

Confusion on the faces of both women, they looked at each other as if he'd gone mad. Cindy's jaw had dropped and she gave her head a vigorous shake. Lauren narrowed her eyes at Max.

"That won't be necessary. We won't be having cake, or anything else," Lauren said firmly. "I'm leaving, don't bother coming over. In fact, I'll have Josh bring over your things in the morning." She would not cry, she told herself. She would not show him he was breaking her heart. Before he could do anymore damage, She threw a couple of twenty's on the table and rushed out of the restaurant and swiftly got into her car. Without so much as a glance back she pulled out of the lot, leaving a trail of dust behind her.

Damn it, she did care. She cared too much. This was not going to be an easy one to get over, she thought. In fact, she wasn't sure she would ever be able to get over it.

"Are you crazy?" Cindy asked Max as he stood staring at the door. "What were you thinking?"

Max turned to stare at Cindy, unable to answer. He must be crazy, he sure felt it. "I don't know." Second guessing his actions, he rushed out the door to try and explain, but was left with dust in his face.

He'd done the only thing he knew would work. The note brought every fear to the surface. Lauren could be the next victim of this madman's game. His only thought had been he needed to leave. There was too much risk of her being hurt if he stuck around. She was right. She shouldn't have anything more to do with him. He couldn't give her the chance to talk him out of leaving.

As he walked toward his truck, his heart began to ache, his stomach churning with the knowledge he would never see Lauren again. The only thing worse was he'd also just broken the heart of the woman he loved.

Chapter 21

Lauren waited at the counter of the little Quiki-Mart, with her milk and the bottle of White Zinfandel she'd decided to take up to her room after Josh was asleep. She knew she was going to break down, she just didn't know when. At the moment she was too angry to cry. She waited as the young man behind the counter counted out change for the cigarettes the man ahead of her in line had purchased.

She noticed the hand the customer held out was shaking so hard he almost dropped the change. He turned his head to look side to side as if looking for someone, and she realized he was the same man she'd seen sitting in the corner booth at the restaurant when she'd run off to the bathroom. Trying to be polite, she smiled at him as he turned from the counter to leave. He looked straight at her, discomforting her a bit with the demented glaze in his cloudy gray eyes. He laughed, with an almost childlike giggle, as he passed by her.

Whispering to himself, he shook his head like a wet dog, as if to clear it. "Not yet. Soon, soon," she heard him say then he was out the front entrance and seemed to disappear into the night.

Lauren watched for a moment, trying to recover from the unexpected uneasiness settling over her. Taking a long deep breath she turned to conduct her business at the counter.

"Think he's nuts?" The young man grinned as he bagged her items.

Forcing a grin herself, Lauren tried to brush it off, "Might be."

She'd parked off to the side of the building, out of view of the front exposure. Wishing now she'd parked where others could see her, she came out the door and threw a glance from side to side, making sure the crazy man was nowhere in sight. Quick to move toward her car she dug in her pocket for the keys to unlock the door. Then suddenly, as if appearing from nowhere, he was there standing between her and the car door.

Sliding to a stop, she tried to find her best option for escape. Looking up into eyes half crazed, yet partly sad, she tried to act as if nothing was wrong.

"Oh, you startled me," she said slipping her hand with the keys back into her pocket. Somewhere she remembered someone telling her to put the keys between her fingers and use them as a weapon to gouge at the eyes or throat.

He smiled then, just kind of staring at her, with those glassily clouded gray eyes. He was shaking too, shaking so hard she felt sorry for him.

"Not like Kitten," he said reaching up as if to touch her gently like a child. "No, not Kitten." His head shook and he stepped a little closer.

Tensing, and getting ready to strike if she needed to, Lauren took a step back. He pulled his hand out of his army jacket pocket and she heard the sound of metal hitting the pavement.

"No, no, can't lose this," he muttered, bending down to pick whatever it was up. He held it up for her to see and smiled. "You wanted me to have this, didn't you Kitten?"

In the faint light it appeared to be some type of medal hanging from a ribbon. As it dangled briefly in the air, it reminded her of the one she'd been channeling from Anna. He stuffed it back in his pocket, staring at her with demented curiosity.

He didn't look as if he wanted to rape or kill her, but he didn't look right at all. She decided her best step would be to try to get back into the store.

"Look, I think maybe I forgot something in the store. I'm going to go get it, alright?"

"It won't be long now Kitten and it'll be done. You can sleep when I'm done. Daddy will take care of it." He looked now as if he was a thousand miles away. It was obvious he didn't realize she'd slowly started to step backwards toward the front doors. He cradled his arms around an invisible child, rocking back and forth, singing softly as if to quiet a crying infant.

Watching for any type of aggressive behavior, Lauren stumbled up the curb and pulled the front door open with a violent whoosh, running toward the counter.

"Call the police. That man is out there by my car. He wouldn't let me go. I think he is crazy."

By the time the police had arrived, he'd vanished. No trace of him was to be found. All Lauren could do was give them a description, hope they would spot him and pick him up for some type of treatment, and pray that she never had to see him again.

* * * *

The whole evening had been one crazy thing after another. By the time Lauren got home she'd begun to try to convince herself she should be thanking Max for at least showing her he was a jerk before they'd gotten too involved with each other.

"Too, involved. Ha!" she exclaimed mockingly as she put the bag on the counter. "You've only fallen totally in love with him." But then she realized worse things could have happened. She could have ended up marrying him. Frustrated she'd allowed herself to fall into the same vulnerable place as before, she knew she would have to ride it out. Though, this time she felt as if there was no turning back to who she'd known herself to be before he'd shown up.

Tears were coming. She could feel them in the back of her throat. But she had to hold back until she was sure she would be alone. Then she would get them out and get on with it.

Turning to put the milk in the refrigerator she saw the note Josh had left her.

Don't worry about me, Robert's mom asked me to stay for dinner and help him hang out with his little sister while they go out for the night. You know where to get me if you need me. Love ya, he signed off with his usual creative doodle to his name.

That was all it took to start the tears rolling down her cheeks. Every emotion she'd been holding back jumped forward and came to the surface in a gale force wind which knocked her off her feet. Sitting down on the edge of breakfast nook bench, she wrapped her arms around herself, closing her eyes to let the tears come. Her body wracked with sobs, she sounded as if she were being brutally murdered. She let it come as hard and as long as she needed. There was no holding back.

Allowing herself to fall in love with Max, almost from the first day she'd set eyes on him, had been her fault. There was no blaming him. She'd allowed it, even though she'd known what would happen to her when she found out he was not going to be there with her in the end. This was different than from before though. The pain clawed at her heart.

Max had been different from the others. He'd shown a true compassion, and a kindness not many men knew existed. She'd thought a bond had been forming, the kind which came from true love. Something about him drew her spirit, which had begun to blossom into what she always knew was possible.

But again man's ego prevails. Ego, forever surrendering to the power of a greener grass within their reach had once again made a fool of her. Max had never claimed his everlasting love for her, though she thought she'd felt it from him. Every time their bodies met and their spirits became entwined, she could have sworn she felt him give himself over to her in ways no other man had done. She wished she could interpret the beautiful words flowing with such certainty and ease from his lips in the throws of passion. The words seemed to say he loved her and couldn't live without her. But then, her over active writer's imagination must have been creating the story she so longed to unfold in her life.

Her sobs had begun to subside to a whimper as she dried her tears with the fresh kitchen towel she'd taken on her way to the table. Reaching out she opened the bottle of Zinfandel and poured a good portion into the coffee mug hanging on the wall.

Well, tears are definitely not going to get me anywhere, she thought with a grimace. But she deserved to feel sorry for herself at least for one night. Tomorrow she would brush it aside and try to move on with her life as she had the other times. Strong enough to not let it ruin her life, she needed to come to grips with what had happened before she could put it to rest along with the other mistakes she'd made.

Bringing the bottle and her half-full mug out with her, she viewed the deck with a cynical eye. At least *this time* she'd gotten something from the whole relationship mess. Her house was to a point now where she could finish the rest of the small odds and ends herself. Her breath hitched when she spotted the soccer ball lying peacefully at the base of the maple tree.

No, that was not true at all. She'd gained something much more with Evan. Josh, would always be the one shining light she could depend on. He'd always been her saving grace, the one thing which made her move forward and continue on, even when it may have seemed impossible. She would always have him to love. Yet he was growing up so quickly. Soon he would be driving and moving on to college. He wouldn't be there to brighten her day, to let her know she was not alone. And then what would she have?

She could stand to be by herself, and actually enjoyed it. Needing it when she was deep in the creativity of a story unfolding onto her computer screen, she'd almost talked herself out of wanting someone to be in her life again. The one thing she definitely didn't need was the pain and stress caused by a relationship. At least, not with the type of men she seemed to attract. But there was something to be said about companionship and intimate friendship with a lover which blew that negative thought straight out of the water for her. She saw the proof of it in her own family. Why was it, other people could find love, yet all she could find was heartache? Maybe she just wasn't meant to be with anyone. Maybe God had other plans for her.

She looked around. The beauty surrounding her broke her heart even more. Now whom would she share this with? Was she to grow old and alone in this creation of her dreams? A creation which had been fulfilled through the hands of a man she loved deeply. Would it ever be possible to look out on her deck and not remember the feelings she'd had when she would watch Max at work? She could see him now, his muscles gleaming in the sunlight, his thick black hair blowing in the wind, his beautiful tenor voice singing out some Italian love song, and the gleam in his eye when he would catch her watching him.

He'd created feelings in her she'd never experienced before. Feelings, which were now wrenching her heart in two, with the knowledge she would no longer have them in her life. It felt the same as when she'd found out her parents had been brutally killed in an auto accident. One moment the things you cherished the most in life were there, happy and alive, the next they'd been torn from your existence without the chance to say goodbye. This time he was not dead, but nevertheless had been ripped from her world in the blink of an eye. She hated he'd done it, knowing it would tear her heart out, without a second thought. She couldn't get past the thought someone would do this intentionally.

She wouldn't be able to let this drag on like she had before. It would kill her to watch Max make excuses and try to make the relationship work out of guilt. And if they did try it again, when could she ever believe him? Would he always be looking for something better, regretting the choices he'd made? No, she wouldn't do that to herself. She had to end it quickly. Now all she'd to do was figure out how she would be able to pay him for the work he'd done on the house. She would go on Monday to the bank and get a loan. That was the only way to do it, quick and neat with no strings attaching them together any longer.

Before long she'd gone through the bottle of wine and was feeling quite belligerent about the whole thing. He wasn't going to get off free and clear thinking he'd gotten away with anything. She was going to tell him just what she thought about it.

Stumbling inside she grabbed the phone off the wall to call him and give him a piece of her mind. Feeling quite sure of herself she sat down to make the call.

* * * *

The inspector hadn't answered his phone when Max called first thing when he got back to his house. Hoping he would have an answer about what to do, he'd left a message with his answering service.

When he'd been handed the note, his thoughts had travelled back to the first time he'd received one. All he knew was the fear and the waiting had started again. Nobody deserved to go through that, least of all Lauren. Whether this madman would carry through with any threats toward Lauren, he couldn't be sure. He did know he couldn't risk her being hurt.

Max sat on the couch, despondent, and hating himself for what he'd had to do. At a second's notice, it was the only thing he'd felt would work. He had to take himself out of the picture in a real obvious way and hope this whacko would follow him. If she thought he'd changed his mind and wasn't interested in her, she wouldn't try to remain to figure things out with him.

His heart cried out for the love he'd discovered with her. It wasn't too late. He hadn't told her he was leaving her. Maybe he could go explain and beg Lauren for forgiveness. Almost convincing himself this is what he needed to do, his glance landed on the paper napkin lying on the coffee table. He groaned and rubbed his hands over his face.

Who the hell was that man? He knew him from somewhere. Quickly going through his mental notes of people he'd met, he still couldn't place him. Not here, but from where?

Just then the phone rang, startling Max out of his pondering thoughts.

"Hello," he said almost impatiently.

"Hello, yourself," Lauren responded.

"Lauren?"

"What if it is? Were you expecting someone else?" she said, slurring the S's in each word ever so slightly.

"Of course not," Max could hear there was something different in her speech. Bringing his attention directly on her, he knew he needed to at least try and apologize for what had happened earlier. "Are you alright?"

"What makes you think I'm not okay?" she said, this time stumbling over the words.

"Have you been drinking?" Max asked with a little concern. Why would she do that? That wasn't like Lauren.

"What if I have? Don't I have the right to do what I want? I'm a grown woman and can get drunk if I want to," her indignation at being questioned came out in her raised voice.

"Would you like me to come over?" He should go over and see what this was all about.

"How dare you? Don't you think I have feelings? Or am I just supposed to take whatever you have to give, with a smile?"

His heart sank. She'd done exactly what he'd wanted her to do, and now he wised he'd never wanted her to think these things of him at all. "Let me explain, *Bella*," he started out.

"Don't even...don't use your pretty little words on me. There is no explanation. You know exactly what you did, you...you egotistical male excuse for a... person," she said unable form her thoughts right.

"I'm coming over. Are you going to be all right? Stay where you are. I'll be there in a few minutes." Not waiting for her to answer he hung up the phone and grabbed his wallet and keys.

"The hell you will. I don't need you or your cheating lips..." Lauren said vehemently, only then realizing there was dial tone on the other end. "Just as well, I need to tell you it's over... face-to-face."

She'd started to feel the room tilt around her and tried to blink it away. It didn't work. It still tilted to the right. Maybe she should go lie down. Bringing the phone with her to the couch in the living room she lay down to wait for him and proceeded to close her eyes...just for a minute.

Max flew out the door of the cabin and down the steps to his truck. Grabbing the handle he saw the slip of paper wedged into the window between the weather stripping. Pulling it out he impatiently unfolded i, and then stopped as if in a daze. After reading it over several times he let it slip from his fingers to the ground. Closing his eyes he laid his head against his hand resting on the truck door.

When he opened his eyes, the words stared up at him from the paper below:

Thought you could escape. I found you.
You thought you could replace her.
You shouldn't have killed her.
You must die to pay for your sins and the pretty redhead too.

> *Not now, but soon, when you are least expecting it.*
> *Your life will be over just like hers was.*

It was happening again, the fear, the anguish and the anger. But this time it was different. The words '*and the pretty redhead too*' jumped up at him like a dagger to the heart. This time someone he loved was being threatened. He'd all but decided if it happened again he would wait it out until it stopped, or the tormentor come out of hiding, and he would deal with him in one way or another. But now he needed to figure out how to protect Lauren. She was in danger now. Slowly he bent down and picked up the paper, knowing he would need to keep it for evidence when he tried the inspector again in the morning.

He needed time to think. Time to reason out all the options he had. Going back into the cabin he took the phone with him to the table and laid both notes out in front of him. He couldn't go to Lauren now, he may still need to leave, and if he saw her now there was no way he wouldn't break down and tell her everything. Taking a deep breath he dialed her number.

The ringing of the phone woke Lauren out of her self-imposed slumber.

"Hmm?" She mumbled into the phone.

"Lauren, this is Max. I'm not going to be able to make it over. Are you going to be okay for tonight? I need to get something done."

Waking a bit more, she heard what he said but jumbled it around with the dream she'd been having of people coming out of the dark, reaching for her, talking nonsense about kittens and babies.

"Of course you won't. You don't care I was attacked and he could hurt me. You just don't care," she mumbled again in half sleep.

Instantly on alert Max sat up straight in the chair. "What do you mean you were attacked?"

"At the store, he came out of nowhere and…" She was so drowsy she almost fell asleep while she was talking.

"And what, what happened?"

"And then he was there in my dreams and he kept reaching for me. I don't know what he wanted," she said sleepily, a yawn interrupting her words halfway to the finish.

Relaxing a bit, Max realized she'd fallen asleep and had been having a bad dream. Feeling guilty already, Max felt sick to his stomach. He didn't know exactly what she was talking about, but he would find out when she was a little more coherent.

"Of course I care Lauren. I just can't come to you right now. I'll come see you in the morning."

"Sure. Whatever," she said mimicking her son's responses when he wanted her to think he didn't care. She hung up the phone and drifted off to sleep again.

Chapter 22

Through the night Max had struggled back and forth over what he could do. It was obvious the threatening note meant he was again in danger, and now Lauren was in danger, too. With every possible answer, it came back down to the fact the intimidator was really after him. Lauren had been included only because of her involvement with him. The only way to protect her was to cut the involvement away. And the only way he could do that would be to leave.

It was breaking his heart as he began packing the boxes through the night. Knowing the love he'd found with Lauren would be ripped away like it had been by the murder of his wife. Ripped away like some portentous event which kept occurring over and over again. He may not be able to save their love, but he could save her life. He would not be the cause of some maniac hurting or even possibly killing the woman he loved, again. That he couldn't take.

He would leave and take the danger away from her. And if it ever came to be this man was caught, he would try to make amends with her. It wouldn't be right to ask her to wait as there was no guarantee how long it would be. She was too good of a woman to be waiting around for him to work out his problems. She deserved to be loved and cared for.

That thought hit him in the gut like a punch from a heavy weight contender. What if she did find someone? What if she became involved with someone and the harassment came to an end? Could he live with himself, knowing some other man was caring for and loving the love of his life?

Doubts and confusion tripped through his mind as sweat began to run down his face, and his breaths cam in irrational bursts. What was he going to do? How can he leave her now?

He sat at the piano, where he'd been packing his music sheets away. The light of dawn came mistily through the trees to playfully dance around him. Slumping down he rested his head on his arm atop the piano. Bringing his free hand up to the keys he began to pick out the notes to one of the pieces he'd been working on. It was a score with deep emotion—his emotion—as the notes began lightly, teasingly, temptingly across the hearing senses. He'd begun to write this one the day after the party at Lauren's house. The day had started out playful, teasing his senses, Lauren unknowingly tempting him in ways only she could do. By the end she'd been tempting him to claim her as his own, with the blushes, and the laughter. She'd aroused him to proclaim his love for her with her soft and caring ways, luring him to take her mind, body and soul by the end of the evening with her sensuality.

Now, unafraid to show feelings, tears began to stream down his face onto the keys below, his heart showing him he would regret the actions he had to take to protect the one he loved. His heart jumped at the sudden banging on his front door. It was much too early in the morning for visitors. Wiping the tears from his face he quickly went to open the door. Surprised he found Josh walking back and forth on his porch, a look of determination and anger written all over his face. As soon as Max stepped outside onto the porch the fist which had been balled up at Josh's side came flying up to connect with his face. It caught him off guard and the boy was able to connect with the side of his chin by a millimeter as Max attempted to dodge out of the way.

Sidestepping the second approach of his wrathful visitor, he wrapped his arms around him from the back to keep him from coming at him again.

"Let me go. I warned you once not to mess with her. You better just take what's coming to you." Josh thrashed about like a snake almost causing Max to lose his grip on him. An elbow succeeded in ramming into his ribs evoking a sharp intake of breath.

"Josh. Wait. Let's talk this through. What do you think I've done?" Unsure of what the young man knew, Max continued to hold onto him, tightening the grip as Josh's efforts to escape were beginning to succeed.

"You don't even have the balls to admit it. You son-of-a-bitch, I thought you were different." Josh's words came out in gasps, almost in sobs. "I don't know what happened, all I know is it has something to do with you."

"Stop fighting me Josh, just calm down. Let's talk. If you still want to hit me after then have at it."

Max saw Josh considering this for a moment. He wasn't stupid. That would give him the advantage. Max knew Josh realized if he would let him go then he would have the opportunity to hit him again.

"Sure. Whatever," Josh said relaxing his attempt to get out of Max's hold.

Carefully, Max let go and stepped back from the angry young man and studied him cautiously. Seeing he was not going to swing at him again, just yet, Max scrubbed his hands over his tired eyes and stubble roughened face.

"I need to sit down," he said as he walked back into the cabin almost falling into the couch, making sure Josh had followed him back in. The young man began pacing back and forth in front of him. Max could see the emotions crashing around in Josh's head. Not just from the grim look on his face but from the fire that was dancing in his eyes.

"Why are you so angry, Josh?"

Josh looked around to see the half-filled boxes being packed. He started nodding his head. "Now it makes sense. You're just like the rest of them. You used her, got what you wanted, and now you're going to leave. She doesn't deserve this. I knew you were going to hurt her. I warned you, there'd be hell to pay if you did." Slamming his fist against the end table lamp, it flew across the room and smashed to the floor in a loud crash. It took him by surprise and he jumped back, fists up in the air.

Already riddled with guilt, Max wearily closed his eyes again. "Josh, I don't know what you think you know, but I haven't meant to hurt your mother. Sometimes things don't work out the way we would like them to."

"My mom's always told me, sometimes we just don't want them to," Josh retorted. "I would never do what you are doing to a woman. I would never be like you or…or my father." He said this with such vehemence Max flinched with the growing ache spreading in his heart.

Just then Max realized Lauren knew nothing of his plans to leave. Why would Josh think his mother knew about his leaving? Where had he come up with that? Obviously Josh assumed she knew. But what was the cause of this outbreak of anger on the boy's side?

"Josh, why do you think your mother is upset?" Max came forward to sit at the edge of the couch.

"Came home last night and she was passed out on the couch. She's never done that before. When I tried to wake her up she kept saying something about you and Cindy. I left her on the couch, but I was worried about her. When I came down this morning to check on her she'd been up for a while, but I could see she was crying. Now she's outside trying to kill herself by carting around those slabs of rock for the walkway, talking about she doesn't need anybody to help her, she can do it all herself." Having worn himself out, Josh sat down on the arm of the couch and gave a deep sigh. "I was really starting to like you Max."

Touched by his honesty, Max gave a sigh of his own. He really liked the young man in front of him, too. He just didn't know what to do about the whole ugly situation. He knew the best thing he could do was leave. This was the only way he could think of to protect them. Yet how could he let them go? What he felt for the boy and his mother was too deep to just brush away.

Shaking his head he looked over to where the boy sat sullenly at the end of the couch. "Josh, I assure you I never wanted to hurt your mother. I care very deeply for her, and for you, too." He paused long enough to have Josh raise his head to look at him. "There are some things I need to get straightened out first, but I intend to ask your mother to be my wife. I love her and want her to be with me."

Simply said, he knew it to be the truth. Whatever it took he needed to make this work. It was what was meant to be. He felt it as sure as he took breath into his body to live.

Josh looked at him, as if summing up his words. Narrowing his eyes, he looked at the boxes behind him. "You say you love her, but if it's true, why are you leaving?"

The boy had him there. How could he prove his words with the action he was about to take. There was only one answer to that. He couldn't.

And now he'd more to worry about than harassing notes. His actions the night before might have forced a wedge into the relationship too deep to dislodge.

"I can honestly say, I don't know. I guess I thought it might have been for the best. But I am going to straighten this out with your mother. You are right, she doesn't deserve this." Tentatively standing up he offered his hand to Josh.

Josh glared at him as he seemed to consider his words. Then on impulse he reached out to grasp Max's hand, with a bit more force than was necessary.

"Friends?" Max asked.

"We'll see."

* * * *

From the woods Jeffery watched the activity at Max's cabin. The drugs he'd taken were starting to make him loose sight of where he was and what he was doing half the time. They did that sometimes, especially if they were from a tainted batch. Now, carefully hidden in the brush he'd awaited the discovery of the note he'd left on his truck. It was almost a joyous feeling to see the reaction it evoked from Max. He'd wished he could have been closer to see if it brought forth tears.

Darkness had overtaken him and he'd passed out from the strain of the actions of the evening. Confronting the woman and escaping in the nick of time before getting caught had drained him of all energy. Now he would rest until the next step needed to be taken.

He'd awakened again at the sound of loud noises coming from the cabin. Inching up slowly on his belly, so as not to be seen, he peered out as the young boy seemed to be provoking a fight with Max. Unable to hear what they were saying he had to be content with the scene in front of him. After the quick struggle they had entered the house together, and when the young man had left shortly thereafter, he didn't seem as ruffled as he had been before. Jeffery recoiled into his hiding place as the boy was on foot, and could have easily uncovered his whereabouts when he headed back through the woods toward home.

Max hadn't come out of the house right away, but when he did he had his cell phone to his ear. Jeffery heard him say something about '*at the Hyatt in Seattle, next to the Paramount*' then he'd gotten into his truck and had driven off in a cloud of dust.

This was exactly what Jeffery had hoped to find out. These next steps were going to take some planning. If he could get an idea of what Max was going to be doing in the next few days, he would be able to take the necessary action to carry out his plans without a hitch. Creeping across the grass to the front door, it was incredulous luck he found it was unlocked. He slipped quietly inside, and went to work to find the information he needed.

* * * *

Lauren heard his truck pull up, and knew it was Max before seeing him. She lifted another of the pathway rocks and placing it on top of the other ten in the short wheelbarrow Max had been using to transport materials. She grabbed hold of the handles, lifted it carefully, and with some difficulty began to wheel it down the side of the house where Max had just begun the work the day before. Coming up behind her he we peered into the wheelbarrow as he started to walk alongside. .

"What are you trying to do? Kill yourself? That's about 150 pounds."

She'd expected him to try and come to her aid. Careful not to tip over she came to a stop at the point where she'd laid the last rock. Sweat poured down her face from the continued exertion since early that morning when she'd decided she was going to finish the job herself. She didn't need him or any man to do this, she was perfectly capable to do it alone. That was the way it was going to be, so why not start now. She'd impressed herself by already completing about twenty yards of pathway, and was almost finished with that side of the house.

Straightening up she brought the back of her hand and forearm across her forehead to keep the sweat from pouring into her eyes. She gave him a quick glance as she reached in to pull out the next rock to be set, and placed it along the pathway where she intended it to remain.

Max shook his head at her and reached in for a rock to place on the path.

"Stop, I can do it myself," she said briefly, lifting out another rock.

"Let's sit down and I'll go get you some lemonade. Lauren, we need to talk. "

As tempting as it sounded she stayed firm in her decision. "Don't want to talk to you and I don't want any lemonade."

She really did need to sit down though. The sun had come out and was beating down on that side of the house. If she stayed working at this pace in the sun much longer she might involuntarily need to sit down. But with a fierce need to show him she didn't need him, she went back for another rock.

She faltered slightly on the lifting of the next rock and Max went to her side and grabbed her at the shoulders.

"We are going to talk. I don't care if you want any damned lemonade. You are going to get some." With a stern look, one Lauren likened to that of a father with his child, he forcibly lead her around back to the deck where he sat her down in one of the lounge chairs under the maple tree.

"How dare you drag me around like some puppet? I said I don't want to talk to you," Lauren said attempting to get up, but found the strength she'd held onto all morning had suddenly gone, leaving her feeling limp and exhausted.

"Stay," he said pushing her back into the lounger. He brought her feet up so she was forced to lean against the back of the chair. Turning he went into the kitchen through the back door.

Feeling a bit faint, Lauren lay her head back and closed her eyes for a moment. The next thing she knew a cool cloth was being applied to her forehead where Max had brought up a chair next to hers and he sat facing her, a look of concerned anger noticeably fixed on his face.

"Drink this," he said pressing the glass of cool, refreshing lemonade to her lips.

Taking a few tentative sips, Lauren felt the faintness begin to fade away.

"You shouldn't let yourself get overheated in this sun. Even I know that. Haven't you ever noticed how I work on the side of the house with the shade, especially on a day like today?"

The sun had come out that morning in full force. It was going to be another one of those scorchers, not well tolerated by most Washingtonians. It would probably be in the nineties, and although early, it was well on its way on the upswing of the heat rise.

"I just wanted to get that side done, and then I was going to take a break," Lauren said defiantly, turning her head away from him so she didn't need to look into his eyes. "Besides, I'm sure you've got better things to be doing. You don't need to worry about coming back to finish anything. Just get your tools and make sure to send me a bill for all your time and expenses. I'll make sure it's taken care of right away."

She thought she'd remembered he had some things to take care of to prepare for his meeting with the symphony conductor, so she hadn't imagined she would have seen him until afternoon. By afternoon she would have had all of his tools and materials collected and waiting for him to pick up on the front porch, and they wouldn't have to be going though all this now.

Max leaped out of the chair in fury and began pacing back and forth in front of her. "So, that's the way it's going to be? Just get your things and get the hell out? You won't even give me a chance to explain why I did what I did yesterday. Had it ever crossed your mind I was acting strange?"

"I've never seen you out in public. How am I supposed to know what you're really like?" she retorted.

"I'm the same now as I've ever been."

Lauren raised an eyebrow at him in response. "Obviously it's not something I need."

A flash of anger crossed through his eyes. Taking her by the arms he gave her a slight shake. "I thought we had more. Do we have something here or was I just imagining it?" Seeing the sudden change in her face he dropped his hands and stepped away.

Surprised at the sudden outburst, Lauren's own emotions began to slip. She stiffened trying to take hold of herself. "It's for the best anyway." The words came out curtly, but her heart was slowly tearing more than it had already. "We both know it wouldn't work. Your interests are," she paused trying to find the right words. "Not here with me," she finished, trying not to allow this discussion to become a confrontational argument.

Stopping suddenly Max swung around to face her again.

"Not here with you?" He asked incredulously, with a raised voice. "My interests, as you put it, are nowhere but here. I've been so close I haven't been able to see the reality of what's going on." Rubbing his hand over his tired eyes, he came back to sit down on the chair next to her. "I have just spent a sleepless night doing nothing but think of you and how I can keep you out of all of this. You are in danger here with me, yet I want to keep you in my life. I finally came to the only answer there is to make. That is to take you out of my life."

Not yet hearing what he was really trying to say she heard only he wanted her out of his life. She continued to look at him grimly, the undercurrents of pain seeping up into her tired eyes.

With a deep sigh, Max stretched his neck and raised his gaze back to hers. "I shouldn't have tried to keep it from you. After I got the first note last night I spent a good portion of the night going over it all, then I got the second note and even though it tore me to shreds, I spent the rest of it packing to leave this morning. But then Josh showed up on my porch ready to punch my lights out."

"Wait." Lauren said holding up her hand, trying to process all of what he'd just said. First she needed to know, "What notes?"

Looking at him with the intensity only a mother possesses, he was not going to be able to just skim through it this time.

"When we were at the restaurant, the waitress gave me the first note. It scared me to death, that's why I tried to get you to see you would be better off without me. Then after we talked on the phone the first time I was going to tell you what had happened, but when I headed out to come talk to you, I found this," he said reaching into his shirt pocket and drew out a plastic sandwich bag with the notes scribbled on the back of what appeared to be a napkin.

He held out the bag for her and waited as she finished reading. Max had put the notes back-to-back, so she was able to study its contents without opening the seal. The letters of each word were capitalized and written with a shaky hand with a pen which looked as if it were running out of ink.

"You see why I was so torn up? I've been trying to figure out what to do. There is only one answer to this, Lauren, I have to leave."

Still unable to grasp the severity of the situation, gathering her thoughts Lauren went back to the one thing which hurt the most. "So, you are telling me your solution to this is to take me out of the picture. To leave me in the night and not tell me where you are going?"

The sheepish look he gave her told her he hadn't really thought this through. "Honestly, I was going to tell you, but I was going to wait until we caught this guy first. I knew you wouldn't understand. He's here, Lauren. And now he's threatening you."

She heard his slow intake of breath, seeing a spread of emotion across his face starting with anger and ending in fear. Lauren's inner sensors felt the emotions churning in his gut. He took her hand in his and made sure she was looking him in the eyes. "Don't you understand? I can't be responsible for another person I love to be hurt or even killed because of me. I couldn't bear it. That would kill me even if he didn't get to me first." Holding her hand to his cheek for a moment, he closed his eyes.

"So, if what your are saying is true, you pretended to act like an ass, no like Evan and Ben, to have me break it off with you before having to come to me with the truth." she questioned without a reaction to his obvious flinch. "Not much better, do you think?"

Max shook his head and lowered his eyes. "Not such a good idea."

She continued, "On one side you are telling me you love me, and then on the other side if my son hadn't found you out you were ready to pack up and leave me. I'm not sure what to believe." She brought her hands up to rub her face then realized they were covered in dirt so she dropped them back into her lap. "Just tell me the truth. Instead of fighting to stay with me, it's easier to let me go, right?"

"No, no, I was only trying to protect you."

"I appreciate the thought, but you should have told me the truth."

"I saw him, Lauren. I know what he looks like. If I could only remember where I've seen him we could bring this whole thing to an end," Max implored. This got Lauren's attention. "It was the craziest thing. After I got the first note, Cindy told me it came from the man in the corner. I looked up and he was leaving. He looked straight at me. I've seen him before, I just don't know where."

"Wait, you know that man who was sitting in the corner, the scraggly looking one, with the long hair wearing a gray jacket and a crazy look in his eyes? That was the man who attacked me last night."

"Attacked you?" Max's head shot up to meet her questioning look.

"I told you about it last night. You didn't seem very interested though."

"I thought you were out of it. It sounded like you had been dreaming and it wasn't anything to worry about."

"No, he definitely attacked me last night." Thinking over the events of the night, she reconsidered her words, wanting to be clear on what happened. "Well, maybe attacked is not quite the right word. He was inside the store when I went in, and he was mumbling something to himself when he left. Something about it wasn't time yet. It kind of freaked the cashier and me out. Then when I went to get into my car, it was like he appeared from nowhere. He was just there and wouldn't let me get into my car."

Max shook his head. "I am so sorry I didn't believe you. I should have known you wouldn't just come up with something like that out of the blue. He didn't hurt you?"

"No, but he seemed drawn to me for some reason. He reached out like he wanted to touch me. Kept looking at me strange, talking about his '*Kitten*' and how he was going to keep her safe."

Max stared at her, his eyes widening, a scowl forming on his forehead.

"What?"

"I know who he is." Bending down he placed a light kiss on her lips.

His actions softened her heart a bit, but she continued to be firm. "You aren't out of the danger zone yet. Tell me the rest of it. Who is this guy?"

"That's Anna's father."

Lauren frowned, "Does he live out here?"

"No, last time I heard he was living somewhere in Chicago."

"Why wouldn't he say something to you if he recognized you?"

"It's been a couple of years since I saw him last. Maybe it wasn't him. I need to dig up some pictures to make sure. That's the strange thing. There is no reason why he should be out here. But what you said confirms it's him. You said he kept talking to his '*Kitten*'? Anna's father used to call her that."

"You are telling me that your dead wife's father attacked me in a store parking lot, thousands of miles away from his home? What sense does that make?" Lauren frowned.

"I don't know. All I know is all this is happening now, and it seems to me it can't be coincidence. I'm going to make some calls back home and see what I can figure out."

A thought suddenly hit Lauren. "Maybe I have something to prove it was him." She jumped up and ran into the house, returning with her notepad. "Here, these are some of those strange drawings and things which come to me at strange times. That man dropped this last night," she said pointing to one of the medals she'd drawn a few weeks back.

Max took the notepad and stared at the medal.

"Is that his?"

"Yes, that's his medal of honor." Max continued to stare, then looked back up. "Even if it is him, it just proves he's here. We don't know for sure he's the one who's threatening us."

"True, but at least you've got somewhere to start."

Silent, he nodded and began to flip through the pages, stopping on the representation of the black and white butterfly. Raising his eyes, they glistened in the sunlight. "When did you draw this?"

Lauren thought a moment, "I think it was just after you started working here. I've seen them everywhere. Ever since we started the move from Seattle, they keep popping up. I'm pretty sure it's Anna."

"That's the same one she was working on before she died." He set the papers down and reached out for her hand. "She's drawn us together for a reason."

"Maybe she needed us to figure this out for you."

Max began to shake his head then knelt beside her. "There is more to it. I can feel it in my heart. *Mia amano*, you've got to believe me."

She looked away at his words, but he brought her face back level with his. Lauren's did know if she should budge from her mindset from the night before, but her contemplative look made him go on.

"*Bella,* you've brought me to my knees." She gave a slight smile at the literal meaning of his words. "Please forgive me for what I've done."

"I'm not ready just yet." She stated and saw the frustration on his face.

"I am so sorry I made a mess of everything. It truly was a big mistake."

So far he had stayed true to his word. "Didn't you say you were packing up to move?" Lauren asked pointedly. "What changed that?"

"Your son can be very persuasive in his own way," Max said rubbing the side of his jaw. "And we came to an understanding I couldn't keep running from my fears."

"I'm sorry. I'll have a talk with him. He shouldn't have been bothering you."

"No, don't. He should have, and he did what was right. I respect him for that. He is a fine young man who stands behind his word."

Not exactly knowing what he was talking about she let it go for the moment. "Well then, come inside and I'll fix you some breakfast and we'll just talk over what *you* believe we should do now," she said with emphasis as she rose up to stand before him.

"I was afraid you were going to say that. After I explain it to you, you'll see my leaving is the only way to do this."

After a moment's thought, Lauren said what she'd first thought when she'd read the note. "Did it ever occur to you, since he has already spotted me as a connection to you, he won't stop, even if you did leave?"

She saw the light bulb connect as she said the words.

"Jesus Lauren, what have I done?" Pacing back and forth a minute, Max grabbed her hand.

"Both you and Josh have to leave. You have to move away to where he can't find you—somewhere far away"

Lauren thought his eyes had begun to look a little wild, with no sleep and the thought of the possible danger. Feeling more in control, Lauren decided what they needed to do was to sit down, have some nutrition, and then talk about this logically without the drama.

"Table that thought for a bit. We are going inside to have some breakfast and we can work out the details. Maybe make some of those calls you were talking about."

Max simply nodded his head and followed her into the kitchen. "It's the only way. I don't see any other way around it."

Lauren had some other thoughts on the subject.

"We'll just see about that."

Chapter 23

They did agree on one point, the harasser, if it was his father-in-law, had stepped up the pace on his threats. After a long drawn out discussion, it was decided the plans Max and the Inspector had drafted would change for the safety and sanity of all involved. Lauren refused to be uprooted from her home because of the lunacy of some half-crazed man who couldn't be proven to be the actual murderer of poor Anna. It was critical however to keep everyone involved as safe as possible until the lunatic was brought to light.

After some convincing, Max agreed the only way to make sure they were both safe was for him to move in temporarily with Lauren so he could keep an eye on her. Lauren arranged for Josh to spend some time at his Great Aunt and Uncle's house in Seattle. This was a big relief for Lauren, as she knew he was always welcome there. She didn't need to worry about his safety too through this whole thing.

Max insisted he would get the best security money could find to do more than just check in periodically, they would be stationed, just out of sight of every entrance to the house, whether he was there or not. One of them would follow her back and forth from her school to her car every night she was in class. He wouldn't let anything happen to her. Every time he began to think it would be better if they were to go their separate ways, to split up the possibility of being linked together at one time, Lauren would prove him wrong and throw out the idea.

Investigator Warner was opposed to the arrangement at first, but then began to see the cleverness of the idea when he suggested his security be the ones used to watch the house. They would know what to be looking for, and what needed to be done in order to put this guy away. No matter what, there needed to be a witness to hear any acknowledgement of guilt from him, whether it was to Max or Lauren he didn't really care.

No exception would be made, however, for the night of the performance. It would not be changed whether the harassment had stopped or not. Lauren would not even consider staying away that night, besides his family was scheduled to be coming in for the evening and they would be in the watchful eye of the Investigator's security team. When they had talked with Inspector Warner again, he conceded this would be the best plan to take. If his hunch was right, the performance would draw this madman into action, and he intended to be there the whole step of the way.

Performance night had come up quicker than Lauren could have imagined. Here it was the beginning of September, just before school started up again for Josh. Lauren only hoped this whole thing would be over soon. Then maybe their lives could go back to normal.

Nothing had been discussed about what they would do beyond the night of the performance. Everything hinged around the fact they believed this would be the night the madman, whoever he was, would make his move. In the pit of her stomach, Lauren knew something was going to happen. Every intuitive nerve told her, of any other time, this would be the time it would happen.

By what she could gather from the various notes Max had received, this guy wanted revenge and he wanted it to be big. He wanted Max to hurt as he'd been hurt, and what better time than to do it during a time which was important to Max. Two other notes had been left at Max's cabin, saying the time was getting close and he would pay for what he'd done. The last of these notes said, "Hope your performance ends with a bang! You will hurt and the pain will be insufferable as is mine."

Security was doubled at the performance hall, and 24/7 coverage was arranged at the hotel. Max made sure there was no way anything could happen to him, Lauren, or his family.

While Max was getting ready for the trip into Seattle to meet his parents at SeaTac Airport, Lauren sat in the front room staring out at the beautiful colors outside the window. She felt a sadness come over her, the autumn greens and reds, yellows and orange, did nothing to take away this emerging feeling.

If everything worked out, and they were able to catch this crazy person, what was going to happen then? She and Max had never talked about the future. She was sure there would be offers for him to do more performances, and he would attract media attention based on his incredible story. He would obviously be travelling and making a name for himself again, as well he should. But, would he want her there by his side? Would there be any reason for him to want to spend the rest of his life with her?

She wanted so desperately for him to want her the same way she wanted him. There was no question in her mind she loved him with mind, body and soul. But she didn't know for sure he felt the same about her. He showed her in so many ways he loved her, but he'd never talked about what the future would bring.

"Ready to go?" Max asked from behind her.

Forcing a smile on her face, Lauren turned to meet Max's gaze. "I am if you are," she replied, unable to dispel the sadness in her tone.

Max narrowed his eyes at her a moment, then offered, "*Bella*, don't worry. My parents will love you." He pulled her up into his arms, his hug warming her, so she pushed the uncertainties out of her head.

"Of course, they will, silly. I'm just worried about what might happen tonight."

"Nothing can happen to you. Inspector Warner assured me you will be covered at all times." Giving her a quick squeeze, he let go to bend down and pick up her bags

"It's not me I am worried about."

A soft smile came into his eyes when he looked up. "Don't worry I can take care of myself, *amore*. All you need to do is take care of yourself. If anything looks strange to you, just point it out to the security, they won't be far away."

The drive into the city was a quiet one. Lauren was caught up in the thoughts still hanging over her like a black cloud. She knew exactly what she wanted to happen, but the odds were it was more fantasy than reality. The meeting of his family seemed to be more of a convenience than something he desired to happen. He spoke of it in generalities in the overall picture of what would be happening the next two days. She'd searched for any sign of eagerness when he spoke of the dinner plans with his parents. But he seemed distracted and not very interested in the upcoming plans.

What she didn't know was, Max sat quietly as they drove going over each note in his head for the upcoming performance. It had been so long since he'd been on stage. There had been so little time to practice with the orchestra. Was he ready to come out, so to speak, and present his own work to the world? With both parents and Lauren being there in the audience, he couldn't bear it if he were to make a mistake. Subconsciously he was worried about what the following evening would produce. If this crazed madman finally showed himself, would they be able to catch him? Had he done enough to protect Lauren from any harm? Would this finally be the end to his nightmare? In all reality, his stomach was tied in knots, his confidence wavering with the uncertainty of everything weighing heavily over him.

Lauren watched him out of the corner of her eye. She could see the frown on his face and the tensed muscles formed in his upper body. Time would only tell whether he was regretting his relationship with her. She wouldn't question it now. But she felt the need to comfort, so she did what came natural to her. Reaching for his hand, she wrapped her fingers with his, and stroked his forearm with her other hand.

"It's going to be alright," she said simply.

Looking into her beautiful green eyes, Max wanted only to draw from her the love she was so willing to give. For a moment there was no question. He had to believe. He couldn't get through the evening without believing they would come through it in the end fine. Squeezing her fingers he nodded silently, throwing up a prayer for safety and protection over the love of his life.

Dinner went well with his parents. They'd chosen Elliott's Oyster House restaurant directly on the water off Pier 56 in Seattle. Claiming to have the best seafood on the West Coast, Max had wanted to show his parents the best he could offer. Fresh seafood was almost unheard of in Chicago where they lived. Sure, you could get what had been shipped packed in dry ice, flown in from various parts of the world. But nothing could compare to what was served straight off the water.

Lauren didn't believe she could find herself loving two people as quickly as she did Celeste and Rudolfo. They were the cutest two people she'd ever met. Holding hands with each other, showing the love and commitment all married couples should have for each other. Max was no less attentive to her, holding her chair out, opening doors, including her in every part of the evening. She dreamed this was the start to a relationship as beautiful as his parents seemed to have.

Max's mother seemed to be the one with all the questions. She asked questions about how they'd met, and what they'd been doing together. She was delighted to find out Max had met her parents and that they seemed to like him. Her questions were polite, yet apparent to all she was getting as much information as she could about this young woman in her son's life.

"Binny said you have a son. I forget. How old is he? Tell me all about him," Celeste said with true interest as she spooned up another bite of Crème Brûlée, a favorite she didn't indulge in very often.

"Celeste, my dear, stop interrogating the poor woman. She hasn't had a chance to breathe between your questions." Rudolfo gave his wife's leg a loving pat.

Lauren smiled at the loving exchange. "That's okay, I don't mind, especially when it comes to my son." She shot Max a glance to find him watching her exchange of conversation and laughter with his mother. He seemed almost pleased with himself, she thought curiously. Approving, he lifted her fingers to his lips to give a light kiss, followed by his thumb sending sensuous sensations through her body as it drew slow circles over the top of her hand. Not realizing his effect on her, he continued with a slight smile on his lips, as if he had a secret he was not telling.

"Josh is 16 this year. Not being biased or anything, but he is truly the best son you could ever ask for. He is so smart. I can't believe sometimes I'm his mother! If he continues with the same grades as last year, it will set him up to get into any college he wants. That and his soccer skills, he is sure to land a scholarship somewhere." Smiling up at Max, she squeezed his hand. "He and Max have played a couple of times. They seem to have hit it off together."

"How does he feel about Max being his father?" Celeste asked pointedly.

Lauren's eyes widened. "Well, I..." she started, not knowing exactly what to say. Avoiding anyone's direct eye contact, she looked down at her plate and made a show of trying to gather up the last bite on her plate.

Max jumped in, "Mamma, Lauren and I have not yet discussed this possibility with him. We don't need to rush things just yet."

Lauren shot him a sideways glance. Was he trying to say he was unsure of what the future would hold for them as a couple? All her fears rushed forward, and she needed a few minutes to gather her composure. Standing, she said politely, "Pardon me. I'm needing to visit the ladies' room. I'll be right back."

At the mirror, Lauren straightened her hair and added a touch of lipstick to her lips. She berated herself for wanting too much too soon. It was obvious Max wasn't ready to give any commitments to her. He could profess his love for her, and show her things she never believed possible, but he could not see beyond the present.

Taking in a deep breath, she turned to go back out to the table, and Celeste came in through the door, a picture of beauty. She smiled at Lauren and turned to the mirror herself.

"Please stay a moment, dear. I want to apologize if my questions put you off." Reaching out she laid her hand on Lauren's arm.

The act of kindness suddenly brought tears to Lauren's eyes. She'd begun to feel so close to Max's family. His mother reminded her of her own. Politely mannered, yet pointed in her statements, she got to her point without any need to question why she wanted to know. Shaking her head, Lauren turned toward the mirror again to dab the glassy drops away.

"Dear, it's obvious you love my son. Try not to be impatient. He has suffered a great loss. It will take time for his heart to heal."

"I know, Celeste. Thank you. Sometimes I'm just not sure he feels the same as I do," Lauren answered truthfully.

"Max is a complicated man. He has such passion for what he loves. He loves you, too. I can see it in his eyes." Celeste drew Lauren into a hug. Releasing her slowly, she looked deep into Lauren's eyes, and paused for a moment. "I can see why he does. Give him time. I look forward to the time I can call you and your son family."

* * * *

Max paced back and forth backstage waiting for his queue to go onstage. Everything was going as planned so far. There hadn't been any sign of Jeffery, or any other intruder so far. They still had no proof Jeffery was the one to watch out for, other than his run in with Lauren at the store, and his unexplained appearance in Seattle. So, they really had no idea who they were looking to find. Inspector Warner was there, along with a large force of security, to trace all movement around Max and Lauren. Their hopes were to pick up on some unusual activity which would lead them to the person responsible for making Max's life a living hell, and hopefully close the unsolved murder at the same time.

The standing ovation for the last piece played by the Symphony clued Max to head out to the stage, where once again, he would be able to play his beloved music for fellow music lovers. He'd chosen several pieces they all felt were appropriate for the feel of the evening. Nothing too dramatic, all the pieces had a mellow flowing nature.

The words of the conductor could be heard as the crowd began to settle again for the next awaited performance.

"… and coming back, after his unexpected tragedy, here to present to you his own works…the musical genius of…Maximiliano DeAngelo!" The crowd burst out in a wave of applause, much stronger than Max had expected. As he walked out over the polished stage floor, he was overwhelmed at the response he was receiving. The spotlights temporarily blinded him from seeing what was happening. But as he reached the piano, looking out over the crowd, he could see one by one they'd risen from their seats to give him tribute to what he'd been through and what he meant to them as a musician.

In no way, had he imagined this to happen tonight. He'd expected to have a few people who knew him turn out, wanting to see what he'd been up to, and why he'd disappeared. But this showing of appreciation, and concern, far exceeded his expectations. Down on the front row he could see his parents, and Lauren who had been drawn to tears at the unexpected response. He connected his gaze with Lauren and his heart grew with love as he saw her bring her fingers to her lips to blow him a silent kiss.

All he could do was express a brief thank you for the audience's show of appreciation and sit down to begin his show of expertise at the ivories before him. The melodies which came forth were amazing, bringing out emotions people hadn't felt in years. Couples reached out to hold each other's hands as the music poured out from this man's heart. He sang with some of the tunes, his deep tenor voice drawing feelings of its own from everyone there. Memories of loves in the past, dreams of love in the future, and realization of loves of the present floated through everyone's mind.

With each piece he began with thoughts of Lauren. The way she made him feel when they were together. The laughter in her eyes, the soft kisses which brought him to his knees, came from his fingers and voice, as his feelings for her flowed vibrant and true in an explosion of emotion.

By the end, it was again apparent why this young man was considered a musical virtuoso. This time though there was something more behind his performance. Now there was not only the love for the music, but the vision of love behind it, which made it phenomenal. Everyone was on their feet again, this time the volume of hands clapping together was almost unbearable. From his viewpoint, Max could see the faces of the individuals in the front rows only. Each looked as if they were in awe of what they'd just experienced. Women were dabbing their eyes, while men were flushed with the effort in showing their admiration.

He bowed, again and again, wanting to show them his own appreciation. His heart overflowing from his own response to his music, but also to the extraordinary praise he was receiving. He motioned to the rest of the orchestra, who had accompanied him, and they all bowed a final time.

Overcome by emotion he turned to walk off stage. Out of the corner of his eye he saw what he believed to be Jeffery turning to exit the curtains on the left side of the stage. It was only a brief second, but Max would swear it was the old man he'd seen at the restaurant. As quick as it was, he saw the ratty coat he'd been wearing before, with the cap drawn low over his straggly hair. The old man was no doubt Anna's father.

His heart started pumping hard with fear now. As he tried to make it back to his dressing room fellow musicians were giving him high-fives, and various others who had made it backstage were shouting praises and patting him on the back. It all seemed to be happening in a silent movie, his thoughts on one thing and one thing only. He'd arranged with Lauren to meet with his parent in his dressing room after the performance. Then as he began to open the door a flood of media rushing forth to get his take on the performance and how the audience had responded. Reviews would be spreading like wildfire. Distracted by his need to make sure Lauren was alright, he reminded himself how he responded now was just as important to his upcoming success as the music itself. Turning to face the crowd, he saw Lauren looking particularly beautiful in her evening gown of dark jade green velvet which brought the firelight into the curls framing her face. His parents were beside her, but all he could see was the love which filled Lauren's eyes as she gazed at him. He smiled, desperately wanting to tell her how he was feeling at that very moment. But the group had surrounded him pressing for answers to their questions. Seeing she was safe made him calmer, and he turned to the demanding voices around him.

Chapter 24

It seemed the evening had drug on forever. Finally, they were back at the hotel waiting for the elevator. Nothing had happened at the theater. Max had been on pins and needles after he'd seen Jeffery. But, after a discussion with Inspector Warner, it was apparent they could do nothing but wait for some type of action. Precautions had been taken for any unusual activity around their room at the hotel. But that didn't stop Max from worrying. Something was going to happen tonight. He could feel it in the pit of his stomach.

Celeste and Rudolfo were to stay the night and fly out in the morning. It had been arranged their room would be on the same floor as Max and Lauren's so it would be easier to protect them all at the same time.

Punching the elevator for the eleventh floor, Max passed a hand over his face in exhaustion. Not wanting to talk about the possibilities he'd dreamed up might happen, he tried to lighten the mood.

"Well, I guess that was unexpected! I didn't realize I would get such a response." Smiling tiredly, he put his arm around his mother's shoulders. "Guess we'll just have to score it up to good genes."

Rudolfo patted his son on the shoulder and gave a hearty laugh. "That is exactly what it is, and don't you forget it!"

Walking down the hallway, they exchanged some more cheerfulness. As the came to Max and Lauren's room first, Lauren stopped in front of the door.

"If you don't mind, I'm going to head in and get myself ready to pass out. Today has been one heck of a day."

The look Max gave her told her she had better be ready for more than just passing out. She blushed sweetly as she unlocked the door.

"I'll be back in a minute. I'm just going to walk these two to their room." Kissing her swiftly on the cheek he waited for the door to close behind her.

Celeste took his arm as they headed down the hallway toward their room. "Have you asked her yet?" She asked quietly.

Knowing exactly what she was referring to, Max squeezed her hand and laughed softly. "Not yet, Mamma, you know I have to make sure everything is going to be okay before I ask her. It wouldn't be fair."

"You know she will say yes, no matter what the circumstances. Don't pass up the chance. She won't wait forever."

"I know, Mamma. I know." Max bent and gave his mother a kiss on the brow.

His father waited quietly as they exchanged goodnights. Grabbing him in a quiet hug, the two men came close together for a moment. "I agree, don't waste the chance. She reminds me of your mother. Asking her to marry me was the best thing I could have ever done. Lucky for me she said 'yes'."

"You are right Papa. It is time."

After making sure they got into their room safely Max sauntered down the hall to where Lauren would be waiting for him. Should he ask her tonight? He'd already decided he was not going to live his life in fear any longer. Why not ask her on the most important night of his life?

Quickening his pace, he turned the corner to ask the love of his life to join him for life in marriage. What he saw was unexpected. What he saw turned his blood cold.

Swarming around the hallway outside of the door to his and Lauren's room were six or eight police officers. They were all armed and looked like they were ready to draw at a moment's notice. Inspector Warner stood at the open doorway to the room next to theirs on the far end. Inside the room behind Warner, Max could see all sorts of equipment, lights blinking furiously, set up on tables, along the wall, and on the beds.

"What the hell is going on here?" He asked nobody in particular. Grabbing his keycard, he went to open the door to their room.

Inspector Warner, came forward, and quickly grabbed it out of his hand. "You can't go in, son," he said quietly.

"What do you mean I can't go in?"

"He's in there with her."

Every emotion he'd been holding back came exploding out. "You let him go in there? How did you let him slip by?" He questioned in hushed tones, though the fear mixed with confusion was a potent combination, as his blood rose up to the surface.

"We knew he was already in the room when she entered. It's the only way, Max. Calm down, we are monitoring what's going on now."

Angered by his words, Max came at him with everything he had. Expecting this reaction, the older man stepped aside. Two security guards caught Max off guard and held him captive as he fumed and cursed. Realizing he wouldn't be able to escape their hold, he calmed himself down, only enough to make them let go of him. Warner pulled him into the adjacent room.

"What the hell do you mean you knew he was already in there? And you let her go in? How is that called protection?"

"Max, let me explain. This is actually the best possible situation. He doesn't really want to harm her. He wants you. While he's waiting for you to show she might be able to get him to admit to your wife's murder."

* * * *

Lauren entered the room, the events of the evening still swimming around in her head. Groaning she removed the shoes from her feet. Sitting on the edge of the bed she raised one foot to her lap and began massaging the toes.

A noise coming from behind her alerted her to the fact she wasn't alone. She placed her foot back on the floor looking for the possibilities of getting out of the room alive. Glancing quickly behind her she could see the bulge in the curtains overlooking the balcony. Someone was there, and she had a good idea exactly who.

She stood quietly intending to move toward the door, but the skirt folds of her long velvet dress made a swooshing sound, wrapping around her legs like tentacles. Fear jumped into her throat as she realized the person behind the curtain had come out, and she may not make it to the door.

An arm came around her waist as she reached for the doorknob, jerking her back toward the center of the room. She could feel the man behind her, as her back pressed up against him.

"Not so fast, little lady," he said whispering in her ear. "You can't leave. I'm not finished with you yet." The arm not wrapped around her waist came into view and she clearly saw the 9-millimeter revolver he held in his hand. "Don't do anything stupid, or I'll have to use this on you."

"What do you want?" She asked breathlessly. Afraid she was going to faint, she breathed as deeply as she could to get more oxygen into her system. His arm tightened around her, in reaction to her movement. Moving backward, he brought her up against the edge of the bed again and shoved her down.

"It's not what I want, but who I want that is the question."

She could see now this was the same man who had stopped her from getting into her car at the Quiki-Mart. His hair, now falling forward into his face, looked as if he hadn't combed it in days. Sweat poured off his brow causing him to wipe at it furiously with the sleeve of his shirt. He'd taken off his jacket and discarded it on the floor as he paced back in forth in front of her.

"Where is he? Why didn't he come in with you?"

Cautiously, Lauren moved to a more comfortable position, watching his every movement. She remembered what Max had told her earlier and realized the room must have been fitted with listening devices. She wasn't sure, but she thought she'd heard scuffling and talking outside of the door. Surely by now Max would have come back and they would have determined this man was here with her.

She had to get him to talk. That must be what they were waiting on. There was no other explanation. On one hand she hoped someone would come busting through the door to save her from this, but then on the other she realized this might be the only chance to get this man to admit to his wrongdoing. She glanced nervously at the door, half expecting Max to come crashing through, like the strong warrior she imagined.

"Who are we talking about?" She asked innocently.

"That piano player. He thinks he can get away with it, but he can't. I've been waiting for him." Brushing again at the sweat pouring into his eyes, his vision blurred by the salty liquid. "I wanted to get to him at the music hall, but there were too many people. Doesn't matter now I've got you. He's going to pay for what he did."

"What is his name? And tell me what he did," she said, thinking of all the ways she could get him to talk about what had happened. She wanted him to say as many specific things she could think of, and hopefully they would be recording it by now.

"That good for nothing Max, he stole her away from me, then he killed her. He killed her just as sure as I'm standing here. Took my baby away," he stumbled with his words, his eye twitching and shutting as if in pain. He shook his head as if trying to get the pain to move somewhere else.

She could see he was struggling. "Who did he steal from you? Tell me all about it." She said again trying to lull him with her calming voice.

"I don't want to talk about it. Where the fuck is he?" Nervously he started moving again, walking back and forth between her and the door. The gun was limp in his hand, as he tried to regain control. For a moment Lauren wondered if she should try to take it from him. Then she saw it, and was struck to stillness, realizing what she was seeing. The bag was half open, sitting beside the bed. She could see gray chunks of clay formed around what looked to be wires leading to an electric box of some sort.

Explosives! He meant to blow them up!

"I said where the fuck is he?"

Swallowing the fear back, she brought her attention back to the man in front of her. "I'm not sure. He said he was going to be back in a few minutes. Maybe he went down to get something from the bar," she said, trying to come up with an excuse that sounded plausible.

She began to think about what would happen if he became agitated. If Max were to come in, there would be no excuse for this man not to just blow them all up. She needed to figure out how to get him to tell her where he'd placed the detonation button. But then how was she going to stop him from using it?

"Why are you holding me here? What have I ever done to hurt you?" Lauren asked, trying to get conversation going again. Maybe she could talk him into letting her go. Quickly dismissing that thought, she realized she couldn't help Max if they didn't get this man to admit to killing Anna.

"You are the only reason he's going to come back here for sure. He tried to replace my Anna with someone else. Thought you could take the place of my beautiful little girl?" To make his point he grabbed her and pushed her toward the mirror on the wall. "You think you are prettier than her? You think you could ever replace my Kitten?"

Not even waiting for an answer he pushed her back against the bed and began pacing again. "Nobody could replace her. She was my little girl, my baby." Tears filled his eyes as he got up close to study Lauren.

Tentatively, Lauren pushed herself back into a sitting position. "Sir, I would never try to take the place of your little girl." Wanting to try to get on a more personal level, she tried again. "May I ask your name? I don't know your name."

Quickly he rattled off his name, rank and serial number, as if he'd practiced it countless times. He stood hands at his sides, a blank look on his face. Then almost as if shaking himself out of the self-imposed attention, he sat for a moment in the chair across from her.

Lauren took advantage of the moment of weakness. She had to get close to him. Close enough for him to feel comfortable in telling her what happened the night of Anna's death.

"Jeffery, tell me about your daughter. She sounds like such a wonderful girl."

Pride washed across his face as he thought about his little girl. "I am so proud of her. She has done so well in school. She had a geography project in school today. Had me up half the night, helping her cut out the map of the Western Hemisphere. She just had to have every single country and island you can think of."

Switching back and forth between past and present, he went on to tell her about her school years and all the scruffs and scrimmages she seemed to get herself into. His mind kept going back to where he was most happy. Those years he'd spent as a parent had been his saving grace. Now he could only wander between images and memories, fond and ugly. Sometimes he didn't know what was real.

In the other room Max sat stiffly in one of the chairs, listening to the conversation. Inspector Warner had explained to him it would do no good for him to go into the room, because then Jeffery would have no reason to keep any of them alive. It would only escalate the situation into action. An action none of them wanted to see.

They followed the intermittent conversation closely. Muffled movements could be made out, but they could only guess as to what was happening. At one point it was all Inspector Warner could do to hold Max back, when they heard the tiny whimper as Jeffery had grabbed Lauren by the arm to shove her toward the mirror.

"Just let me in there. I'll make him talk. If he hurts Lauren, he's going to do more than talk." Max paced back and forth in front of Inspector Warner. Lauren shouldn't be the one in there with him. He was supposed to have protected her from any and all harm, but the only thing he had done was hand her over to the madman without so much as a fight.

"Look, I realize how difficult this is for you. But I think this was the best way to do this. Listen to them. She's got him talking, reminiscing about the past. She just might be able to get him to say something without even realizing it."

"If it sounds like he is getting rough with her, not you or any one of your guards will be able to hold me back. I will get in there and show him what pain is."

Max began flexing his fist, wishing he could get in there to save Lauren. He had to save her. He couldn't let her get hurt. He couldn't let her die. Not like before. Sweat was running down his back, his white shirt sticking to him annoyingly. He had long before discarded his Tuxedo jacket. The cummerbund followed not long after. He was ready. Ready to put an end to this nightmare started more than five years ago. Put an end to the fear of the unknown, to bring justice to the needless death of Anna, and get on with this new life he could see ahead of him.

"Let's hope it doesn't come to that."

Inspector Warner turned to approve the entry of two men into the room. Both wore suits, obviously cops. The older and taller one wore a gray, somewhat clean and pressed suit, the creases still apparent in the pant leg. The other man's suit had seen better days, in fact you might even change the side of the street you were walking on, based on the looks of him.

Nodding toward the two men, Inspector Warner held out his hand to the better dressed of the two. "Captain, I wasn't expecting to see you down here." He acknowledged the other man and held his hand out just the same. "Detective Ross, I appreciate your coming down."

"Being this is our precinct we need to keep tabs on what's happening. Thank you for stopping by earlier to get approval for your set up and monitoring of the situation. My team is ready when you give the word."

"I've been ready for this for the last five years. Nothing could stop me from following through to take this guy down. I appreciate your being here though. Everything will be done by the book, no reason to throw this one out for a technicality."

They all paused for a moment as raised voices could be heard coming from the other room.

"She shouldn't have married that guy. He was no good for her. Nobody was good enough for my Kitten."

"Jeffery, she loved Max. You can't keep two people who love each other apart." Lauren's soothing tones came forth.

"I loved her too. I was a good father. She didn't need anyone else." You could hear the inner pain coming with each word he spoke. "He took her from me. And now she's gone."

"Your little girl didn't leave you forever. She loved you very much, and she wanted to see you get better." Lauren was scrambling, trying to remember everything she could about what Max had told her about their lives. "She took care of you and made sure you were alright. You can never take the love of a child away from her father. That kind of love can never be replaced."

"Yes, she loved me," he admitted, seeming more settled.

Looking over to the bag, she realized she needed to let them know what he had brought into the room. If they were to rush in on them, they may not get to him before he was able to set off the detonation. Nervously licking her lips, she tried to think of all the ways she could bring it up without making him agitated.

"Um, Jeffery, I don't recognize that bag. Did you bring it in with you?"

Next door Max stiffened, waiting, for the answer.

"That's mine all right." Jeffery said, quickly coming back to the present. "Do you want to know what I'm going to do with what's inside the bag?" He asked with a hint of glee in his voice. Lauren saw his hand instinctively go to his right pocket.

"Yes…yes, I do."

"See, I used to be in the army, and I know all about things that go 'boom'." He'd begun to stare off in the distance as if seeing flashes from the past. "You want to know the worst death a man can have? It's being blown up. Blown up into little bitsy pieces."

Back in the adjoining room they all looked at each other, dumbfounded by the knowledge.

"He's got explosives. He's got fucking explosives!" Max exclaimed, breaking the silence.

Chapter 25

Lauren had begun to sweat. She knew all too well what was in the bag, and she'd also seen Jeffery's hand go to his side front pocket. Now she knew where the trigger was, she'd to let them know where it was without him knowing she was trying to tell someone listening.

"That would be horrible." Seeing the expression of total inner destruction come down around Jeffery, Lauren tried another angle. "Someone close to you died that way. You must have been devastated."

"You have no idea what devastation is until you've just seen your best friend in the world blown up, and all you can do is pick up the pieces to try and put him together."

She could see his thoughts had drifted off again. Then he shook his head again, as if warding off an invisible intruder. He placed his hands on his knees and looked at Lauren intently.

"I'm not going to think about that right now. The only thing that matters is I will finally get to pay him back for what he did to my little girl. He deserves to suffer, deserves to die. And you just happen to give me more to torture him with. If he sees what I am doing to you, he will suffer. He will die a thousand times before he actually gets to die."

Lauren's skin began to crawl as she imagined what he had in mind. But she knew she couldn't focus on what he was saying. She needed to keep calm and use every possible chance to get the information they needed to put this poor man away. Thinking quickly, she tried to assess what was the best thing to do. She had to tell them which pocket he had the trigger in.

"That probably would do it." Perhaps agreeing with him would help him to talk about it. "I suppose you would need to keep the trigger to those things real close, like in your pocket so you have access to it at all times."

"Pretty smart, aren't you. What are you, a teacher or something?"

"I teach English Literature."

"I never had much use for that kind of stuff. Bunch of useless words if you ask me, just like that art my little girl was studying. Couldn't understand why she wanted to have anything to do with it. She could have been a doctor or something."

Trying to continue the conversation, Lauren realized how to tell them which side the trigger was on. She could only hope they were listening close enough to figure out what she was doing.

"No, you look like a real man. Looks like you are good with your hands, too. You're right-handed, that makes you able to handle all sorts of things. Like those electronics in the bag over there by the bed. Looks pretty complicated to me."

He took the compliment without a second thought. What he didn't realize was she'd just told the police the explosives were by the bed, an electronic device was to be used to ignite the fuse, and the trigger was in his right-hand pocket.

* * * *

In the other room, Inspector Warner smiled. "Good girl. Keep him talking. You know what you're doing. Just keep going." Turning he grabbed his pad and wrote down the specifics he'd just picked up.

"What are you talking about? It sounds like a bunch of nonsense to me," Max said pacing back and forth in front of the Inspector.

"You didn't just hear the treasure she got him to tell us?"

"No. All I know is she's being held against her will and they're talking about what they do for a living. How is that going to help?"

"She's a smart one. If you had been really listening you would now know, like the rest of us, the location of the explosives, the device being used to ignite them, and which hand he will be using if he should be reaching for the trigger. All of that is information we, in the law enforcement business, treasure. Most of the time we go in blind sighted, not knowing what or where to be looking for the danger. This way we can protect her better by knowing how to take those dangers out of the picture."

Another knock on the door brought their attention to the person entering. Rudolfo poked his head in, finding Max he motioned for him to come to the door.

"Son, they are telling me I can't come in. Come out here and tell me what is going on."

Looking toward Inspector Warner, and Captain Delaney, Max got their approval for him to step out.

They worked their way past the security and police activity directly outside the door, toward the left and slipped into the snack and soda machine area just before the elevators.

Rudolfo waited impatiently for Max to tell him what had happened. As quickly as he could, Max told him all that he knew, from the moment he'd left them at their door.

"Poppa, I don't know what to do. They are telling me I can't do anything right now. Just wait and listen. Warner said if they go in now, they might be able to put him up for a short time for kidnapping and holding Lauren against her will. But because he hasn't done anything yet, it would only be temporary. Bail would be set, and he would get away with minimal time, if any. Maybe some medical or psychiatric help, but he hasn't given any reason for them to hold him."

"You said Lauren was getting him to talk. Maybe she can get him to admit to Anna's murder."

"I know, but at this point I just want her out of harms way. I couldn't take it if anything happened to her. Poppa, you were right. I do love her, and she should be my wife. But she doesn't even know it."

"I know son. Have faith. Pray for God's mercy. I need to go tell Celeste what is going on. I'll be back to check on you in a little while."

"Why did you come down to the room in the first place?"

"Mamma and I decided to change our flight reservations. We will be staying for a couple of extra days. We haven't had any time away for a long time."

Distracted by some added movement in the hallway Max nodded absently then turned to leave. A thought made him turn back to say, "Poppa, I don't know what is going to end up happening tonight. But above all, just remember I love you both."

Rudolfo accepted the words in the truth they were given. "Take care of yourself Max. Don't do anything rash, but if it were my Celeste in there, I don't think any army could keep me out." With a quick hug, he left Max there to ponder his words.

* * * *

"He's taking too long. What the hell is taking so long?" Jeffery muttered walking over to the door. Listening he didn't hear anything. Frustrated, he walked over to the balcony and opened the sliding glass door. Looking quickly from left to right, he saw nothing that concerned him. Closing the door again he came back to where Lauren sat tensely on the edge of the bed.

She had to keep him talking. Every time there was a lapse in conversation he got annoyed again and started looking like he might do something aggressive. Jeffery stopped in front of her. He closed his eye below the long-jagged scar running along the side of his face, and rubbed at the temple with his free hand.

"That looks like it hurts," Lauren said with sincere compassion. "Did that happen when you were in the service?"

Jeffery stared at her a moment, as if not knowing how to answer. "Yeah, damned Viet Cong tried to take my head off." Suddenly he sat down in the chair across from her, his hand at the back of his neck. "Hurts so bad sometimes I wish they had."

"Have you seen a doctor?"

"So many times, you'd think I was one," he chuckled then rubbed again at the side of his head. "Those damn quacks can't do anymore for me. Said this thing I've got lodged in my head is inoperable."

Lauren watched as he moved in agitation again. "Can you take anything to help the pain?"

"Doctors won't prescribe anything anymore, so I get some stuff that sometimes works, but not all the time."

"Maybe you should take some now," she said half for the sake of not wanting to see anyone in pain, and the other half thinking maybe it would knock him out.

He pulled out a small sandwich bag with one pill in it, and set it on the table. "Can't take it until I take care of Max, then I won't need it anymore." Jeffery stared at the pill as if he hated the sight of it.

"Why don't you tell me why you think Max is responsible for Anna's death?" There was no better time than the present to get him talking about the murder. It was obvious this was what they were waiting to hear, otherwise, they would have made a move to enter the room to take him down.

"I suppose he wouldn't have told you anything about it, would he."

"No. Max hasn't said anything. Why don't you tell me all about it? I would think, if I'm going to pay for something he's done, I should know why."

"She said he was going to some performance that night, and he left her there at the house, by herself. All I know is the police said someone had entered the house without force, made it look like it was an attempted burglary, and then killed my angel. It only makes sense it was him."

"Why do you say that?"

"He must not have wanted the baby. His career was more important to him. And he must have come back early to get them out of the way. I can see his hands……." Stopping abruptly, Jeffery didn't continue with the thought.

"What can you see Jeffery?"

"I have nightmares…hallucinations, sometimes. I can see the gun in his hands, and I try to stop him, but he always shoots her—right in front of me. Then he laughs and says, 'the bitch was in the way anyway.' It only makes sense. He never loved her as much as I did."

"That might be so, but that doesn't make him a killer."

"Police never found the killer. They call it an unsolved murder. But I know that Detective helped to cover up the evidence. That's the only way he got away with it."

Jeffery groaned and got up to start pacing back and forth again, his hand at the back of his neck.

"You know Jeffery, sometimes our dreams are only an image of reality. The nightmares do not show us the actual picture, only a snapshot of what we fear the most." Lauren wasn't sure where that had come from, but she was sure she'd heard it somewhere.

Jeffery winced at his pain and narrowed his eyes. He looked at her with new interest.

"What are you saying?"

"Perhaps you see Max in your dreams because by marrying your daughter he took her away from you. In your mind that was just as bad as outright shooting her."

Lauren could see he was in pain. His left eye was closing in defense to the light coming from the lamp at the side of the bed. She could also see he'd been favoring his left side. Movements were not as fluid, or responsive, as were the ones on the right side of his body. She wasn't sure what happened with his type of injury combined with PTSD, but she was certain she needed to try and get an answer out of him soon.

"It had to be him. There is no other answer." Wiping the sweat from his brow, he bent forward as if trying to keep his wits about him.

"But we both know they proved it was not possible for him to be there the time of the shooting. He was on the road coming home from the performance. Then he stopped at the little food mart about 11:05 that night. Logistically there is no way he could have left the hospital at 10:45, gotten all the way home in Brinnon 35 minutes later, killed your daughter and then been back at the food mart within 10 minutes. It's just not possible."

"That time of death records must have been fooled with. Besides they're never accurate."

"It's a proven fact the time stated is usually within half an hour of the actual death. They quoted your daughters death to be at 11:15pm. Half hour before he was just finishing up the performance with his mother. Half hour later he was at the food mart picking up ice cream."

"I don't know how, but he did it somehow." Jeffery had been standing in front of her, but as he started to get frustrated, he began pacing again. He ran his free hand through his hair, brows furrowed in concentration.

"I keep seeing her standing there, and I'm reaching out to comfort her, and then it happens. He shoots her, right there in front of me. There was nothing I could do about it."

"Where were you that night Jeffery?"

Not realizing she was setting him up, he answered honestly. "I'm not exactly sure. I know when they came to tell me about my baby, I was face first on my couch. I think I met with Mongo that night to pick up some more OP. But I can't remember."

Bingo! Lauren immediately remembered the word 'Mongo' from the channeled words from Anna. It was a person. He must have had something to do with her murder. God, she hoped Max would remember her telling him about this.

She could see the confusion in his eyes, and it suddenly dawned on Lauren, the truth of the matter was, Jeffery had no idea he was there the night of the murder. Somehow, he must have blanked it out. He'd made up in his own mind this story about Max being there because he couldn't accept the true facts. He was the one responsible for his daughter's death. She had to figure out how to get him to remember.

"Who is Mongo?"

"Lopez. He's a dealer on the eastside. Everyone knows him. He's the one you go to when you need something quick. You got the cash he's got the goods."

Lauren closed her eyes a moment. *Please, Anna, help me. I need you to show me how to find out what happened that night*, Lauren implored silently.

As simple as just asking the right question, Lauren felt as if the scenario was getting much clearer, at least in her mind's eye. The jittery feeling she would get before connecting with Anna settled over her, and flashes of the familiar image from before weaved in and out of her thoughts, like a tapestry being woven into its final form. This time the pictures changed as if she were looking through the viewpoint of the man she'd previously seen leaning over Anna's body. Like a video clip, he was yelling at someone holding his hands out then swerved around in time to catch Anna who'd begun to crumple to the floor, a bright red stain spreading across her chest. He lay her down gently and crossed his angel's hands over her chest. Then he stood and twirled around toward a man, who was crouched with a bag in his hands, in front of what looked to be a small safe in the corner of the room. They were shouting something at each other, but she couldn't make out the words, but she could feel anguish pouring over her in waves as she experienced this man's point of view.

As the vision faded, Lauren felt a little light headed and pressed the back of her hand to her forehead. "You went to see Anna that night, didn't you? She let you come in to talk. Try to remember for me Jeffery. Did Mongo go with you?"

His pain must have been getting to be excruciating. But she said this in such a calm, matter of fact way it seemed to lull him into a state of remembering.

"When I think about how she died I start feeling as if I was really there." His eyes were glazed over with pain, physically and emotionally. "I see it over and over again in my hallucinations.'

"Tell me about your hallucinations. What happened that night?"

"It usually starts out with me heading out from my place with Mongo. He's talking about how he knew I had a real need for the stuff he got for me. But he said the price just went up, and I had to come up with more cash—a lot more cash." Rubbing his eyes wearily, Jeffery set the gun down next to him on the table. The weight of it seemed to be more than he could bear at the moment.

Seeing this as a step forward in the right direction, Lauren continued to prompt him to go on. "How were you going to get more cash?"

"I needed the stuff bad. I'd run out and the pain wouldn't stop with just alcohol. It was late at night and I'd already drained my accounts for the month. So maybe Anna would loan me some more money. She'd done it before, a couple of times. Said they had enough to help me out, and not to worry about paying it back, she would deal with Max."

"So you and Mongo went to see Anna that night?"

Slowly nodding his head, Lauren could see the true memories begin to unfold for him. "I told Mongo to stay in the car, but he said he needed to use the bathroom. So we went up to the door and knocked."

"What happened then Jeffery?"

"Anna comes to the door, surprised I would be out of the house so late. She lets us in and then I tell her we need talk. Then Mongo asks her if he could use the bathroom. She tells him to go to the front entry when he is done. So we leave him in the bathroom and she and I go to the back office."

* * * *

Inspector Warner kept his ear to the audio coming from the next room, while watching Max as he seemed to be measuring up the possibility of overpowering his obstacles from getting to Lauren. It would be different if he was the only one to deal with—that would be no problem. He couldn't stop the strength of that young man if he tried. The problem was the Police Captain and his Detective inside the room, and all the armed officers outside in the hallway ready to act on a moments notice.

Warner understood the hopelessness Max was feeling. He'd seen it happen time and again throughout his career, in the force and in private practice. Kidnappers, ransom holders, bank robbers, they were all the same, using innocent people's lives to negotiate their personal gain. This was no different. Holding someone, against his or her will resulting in a planned loss of life, was just as bad—or even worse. It was not an unplanned accident. They had actually planned for their own death as well as their victims.

Placing his hand on Max's shoulder, Inspector Warner tried to console him, knowing it would really do no good. "We are going to get her out of there. Don't worry son, she's going to be alright."

"You don't know that," Max responded curtly. "I can't go through this again Bob. I can't let it happen again." The anxiousness growing, he swiped his fingers through his hair and turned, but the Inspector caught the glistening eyes as tears were threatening to form.

"Listen, that is one smart lady in there, she's got him talking. He's going to stumble and admit to it, I can feel it. Just be patient, a little while longer."

"I'm not sure how much longer I can take this."

"I know. It's hard to wait when the one you love is in danger. Max, as soon as..."

The Inspector stopped in mid sentence. Waving his hand he motioned for silence from the others.

"What?"

"Listen." Warner had picked up on Lauren's questioning of what had happened that night. Jeffery was responding, just like he was talking to an old friend.

After a few moments Max was ready to bust in there. "He's admitted to being there and bringing his buddy Mongo with him. That's enough. Let's go get her out of there." Jumping up from his seat he looked ready to bust down the door. Warner made a gesture and a hand came down firmly on Max's arm from the officer stationed inside their room.

"Hold it Max. He still thinks he is talking about his hallucinations. He has to admit to actually being there."

Max closed his eyes and breathed slowly and nodded his head.

"You're right." Resigned, he returned to sit down next to the Inspector to wait it out. "We've come this far, we need to get it finished once and for all."

* * * *

"What happened when you went back to the office?" Lauren was trying to stay calm, she knew she was getting close to the truth, and wanted to shout for joy.

"I asked her for the money. But she tells me she doesn't have that kind of cash sitting around. So she goes to the safe and gets one of her bracelets. It was a pretty little thing, with diamonds and emeralds, said it was worth over four grand. So I took it. But this is where it gets all fuzzy...I just don't know what happened from there." Jeffery started to shut it out again. "I don't know. It's just these damned hallucinations."

"But you do know what happened. Try to tell me what happened next." She couldn't tell him what Anna had shown her, he wouldn't believe it if she did. He needed to tell her in his own way.

Jeffery began pacing again.

"Mongo came in to see what was taking so long. Anna and I were standing at the couch because she said she needed to sit down. I'd put them in my pocket. Mongo had heard everything, and he went over to the safe and started pulling all the jewelry and stuff out. I told him to stop, but he just kept doing it. Anna told him she was going to call the police if he didn't get out of her house. That's when…" Jeffery stopped, as if something wasn't right. All of a sudden a look of sheer horror came over Jeffery's face. "Oh, my God!"

Dropping to his knees, Jeffery grabbed his chest, tears rolling down his face as he looked up into Lauren's eyes. "That's when he shot her. Said she was just in the way. Mongo shot my little girl, and I couldn't do anything about it. Oh God, I was there and couldn't save my baby."

Lauren wasn't surprised to feel the familiar chill setting over the room. Jeffery's labored breaths came out in little fog bursts which hung in the air a moment before dissipating. She wasn't sure what to expect, things flying in the air, bright lights swirling around the room?

She heard a thunderous noise at every door in the room. A variety of voices were barking out orders to break them down. She could hear Max shouting for people to get out of the way. Jeffery, sobbing with the realization of what had truly happened, sat motionless on the floor, his head drooping against his chest. But, the doors held firm, just like the time she'd tried to leave Max's house. She knew nobody would be allowed to enter until it was time.

Then she saw her, a thin, wispy formation of light against the moisture particles in the air. Anna floated in front of Lauren a moment and smiled, bowing her head toward her as if in appreciation. She drifted toward her father, who was sobbing with his eyes closed. Without any warning, the detonator flew out of his pocket and hovered in front of Lauren then dropped gently in the palm of her hand.

Jeffery jerked up his head and stared straight at his daughter's image. "Kitten?"

Lauren couldn't hear what was being said, but she could see Jeffery was listening intently.

"I'm so sorry," he moaned. He nodded his head a few times and Anna reached out to touch his quivering face. "Don't go. Don't leave me again," he cried out as she slowly disappeared. It was all too much for him. All of a sudden he grabbed the side of his head and silently slithered to the floor unconscious.

At that moment doors seemed to burst open from all sides. Not realizing he was passed out, guns were trained on Jeffery's still body making sure he wouldn't grab for the explosives.

Bomb squad was already at the bag beside the bed examining explosion protocol. Lauren motioned to one of the officers and placed the detonator in his hand as she was whisked away into the strong loving arms of Max.

Finally, Lauren and Max were in each other's arms again, holding on for life.

Chapter 26

Lauren sat on her front porch sipping on her first cup of coffee for the weekend. It had started to get chilly now in the early evening, with a light frost first thing in the morning. Most days it didn't seem to warm up until noon. It was going to be a mild winter this year, she could just tell. It didn't matter to her much, just meant she needed to put on a warm coat before going outside.

The birds, not yet gone south, were out chirping their songs in the early morning mist. The bright sun burned through the light clouds in an effort to reveal its glory to the world. The wind the night before had blown down some broken branches and dead needles and pine cones from the trees in the distance. They littered the yard with their early winter carpet.

She sat enjoying the time alone, thinking of what the future might bring. Max had called every single night since they'd been apart. Each time they spoke he would profess his love for her and tell her how anxious he was to get back to her. But there were still things he needed to clear up with the treatments for his father-in-law, and the now solved murder case back in Chicago. He promised they would be together again soon, and they would make plans for what would come next.

It had been two months since they'd seen each other. They'd been literally torn apart by all of the police activity surrounding Jeffery and his realization of what had happened the night of Anna's death. Under police escort he'd been taken to the nearest hospital where they discovered the small shard of shrapnel in his brain on the left side. Up until now none of the tests had shown anything wrong. The last time Jeffery had been in to see the doctors at the Veterans Administration about ten years before, and he'd been told him the pain he was feeling was psychosomatic, and regulations had changed so they could no longer prescribe the painkillers for him without physical evidence of medical need. That was when he'd gone elsewhere to find the opiate drugs he needed.

Antonio 'Mongo' Lopez had been picked up for the murder of Anna DeAngelo. His extensive police record showed this was not the first time he'd been suspected in a murder, shooting, or burglary case. By luck they also found the weapon used, stashed in his closet, awaiting the need to be used again. Signatures from his gun matched the ones found on the bullet pulled from Anna. He was booked for second degree murder with a $5 million dollar bail. The judge obviously didn't want him to be let out for any reason.

Treatments for Jeffery had been working well. The medications given to reduce the swelling in his brain were giving him tremendous relief already. They were planning on going in to take out the piece of metal causing most of his troubles the next week. Luckily the shard had worked its way to an area where it would only necessitate a small entry hole where it would be removed by a small suction device.

Due to his fragile condition, and his involvement in the murder case, the judge left it up to Max to press charges, for accessory to the murder, or at the very least harassment. Lauren had made it very clear, when asked that night after it was all over, she was not going to press charges for the willful hostage situation. She felt he needed psychiatric help, and didn't think he would have hurt her if he'd been in his right mind.

At first Max had been unwilling to let Jeffery off so easily. The pain he'd caused over the last few years was unforgivable. But as bits and pieces of the story began to unfold, Max realized in Jeffery's confused state of mind, he'd blanked out the whole event with the added trauma of his daughter's death. Mongo had made sure he'd been given enough opium to haze over the whole night, so all he could do was grab onto the first logical explanation, and that was to blame Max.

It had been hard for Max to make the decision not to press charges. But when he'd told her Jeffery had asked for his forgiveness, with tears in his eyes, and sadness in his heart, Max could do nothing more than to accept his apology and assure him he would be getting the best medical and psychiatric help for his conditions. Newer legislation had allowed for extended psychiatric monitoring and treatment for post-war veterans, and he made sure Jeffery was going to get what he needed to become a better person. That was the least he could do. He knew it was what Anna would have wanted for her father.

Max was scheduled to be back in two weeks. He'd sold the house in Brinnon, and was planning to come back to Washington. In their last conversation he told Lauren he'd been doing a lot of thinking and had something to tell her, but it couldn't be done over the phone. Begging him not to make her wait too long, Lauren couldn't imagine what it could be. They'd never talked about any type of permanent plans, only that they wanted to be together.

Maybe he wanted her to move in with him. That would be a big step. Looking around her yard, she already missed its peacefulness, if that was what he was going to ask her. She didn't if she was ready to move yet. Josh was doing so well in school. He only had two years left. Surely they could work something out. But then, perhaps this wasn't what he needed to tell her at all.

Shaking her head, she stood and stretched. She felt good. It seemed as if all of the old feelings of unworthiness had slipped away. She was feeling like a new woman. She continued teaching in the mornings, leaving her afternoons free for whatever activities Josh had in store for her. She was now in the middle of her second Regency novel, the British forever squabbling over their regalia. She felt whole again. And she was in love. Life couldn't get any better than this.

Setting her cup in the kitchen sink, Lauren started back toward her office when the phone rang. Picking up the extension by the kitchen table, she saw it was her best friend Rita.

"Well hello there!" she said brightly.

"Hello yourself, what are you so happy about?" Rita responded.

"Nothing much, just woke up in a good mood."

"That's more than I can say for myself. I can't remember the last time I stayed fresh and happy for more than ten minutes after getting out of bed."

"Twins at it again?"

"The twins won't leave each other alone, and that little skunk of a boy of mine seems to be getting into trouble every time I turn around."

"Sounds like you need to get out of the house for a while," Lauren suggested, not knowing she was being set up to fall into the neatly laid plans of her deviously smiling friend.

"Exactly! Come with me Lauren. Let's just go have fun today. We'll go shopping and go to the parlor to get our nails done. Let's get the works. I'm so desperate I'll pay for everything. Just come with me, please."

"Well…I don't have much to do today. Josh went to Robert's for the weekend. Some big car project they seem to be working all the time."

"Then it's settled. You're coming with me. There is no question about it. I'll be over to pick you up by 10am. See ya!"

* * * *

With that Rita hung up and just about jumped out of her chair in glee. What Lauren didn't know was the previous evening Max had contacted Rita to set the whole thing up. He said he couldn't tell her what it was, because that would be unfair to Lauren. But it was something big. He arranged to pay for everything, for both girls. Knowing what he did about Rita so far, he knew she wouldn't turn that offer down at all. What he needed her to do was to get Lauren to buy an evening dress she loved, get her hair done up, and spend a day at the spa pampering herself. If anybody could do it, he knew Rita would.

With a deep heartfelt moan, Rita lifted her head up from the massage table across the room from Lauren. "This has got to be the best thing we've ever done."

"Can't argue with that," Lauren responded as she could feel what tension she may have had slip away with no intention of returning.

Later, Lauren sat back in the soft luxurious lounge chair to relax a moment before putting on her sandals. She was sad to see the day end. But figured there was really nothing left to do. They'd just spent the whole day trying on evening gowns, because as Rita put it, she needed to spice up her wardrobe to be seen with not only a gorgeous hunk of a man, but a famous one too. Then they ended up here at the spa for the full works. She couldn't remember a time when she'd indulged in everything in the same day—including nails, pedicures, facials, massages and hair.

"You are going to look awesome in that dress. It looked as if it was made just for you."

"I can't believe I bought it."

"No worries honey, it's on me."

"Rita, you can't do that. It's almost a whole house payment! I'll have to figure out how to pay you back. I can't allow you, but you tricked me."

Snickering, Rita agreed. "That I did! You should have seen the look on your face when I came back out of the store with your dress in my hands. I couldn't tell if you were going to smack me or hug me!"

Lauren had really wanted the dress. The sea green silken taffeta was the perfect color to set off the beautiful natural red highlights in her hair, matching the color of her eyes. The sloping sweetheart neckline of the bodice clung in just the right way to showcase the beautiful curves of her breasts. Its skirt, not as full as she'd needed in the past, seemed to embrace her as a lover would from waist to mid-thigh and then flaring out from the knee. It was as if it was the frame for her now curvaceously delicious body. She knew it looked good, but hadn't even considered actually purchasing it when she saw the price tag.

"I don't know yet, I haven't decided. Your husband is going to skin you alive when he sees how much you've spent today."

"Not going to happen." Rita said joyously, giving Lauren a smile as if she had a secret.

Looking up at the clock, Rita gave a shriek. "We've got to get home. No more pampering, it's time for some action now."

Action - what does that mean? Lauren never questioned Rita. When she was on a roll, all you could do was hang on for dear life and hope to come out in the end.

When they'd gotten back to Rita's house she'd insisted on bringing all of their purchased goods in with them. Lauren suggested she leave her items in the car, as she would just need to pack them back in the car when Rita was ready to bring her home. But, Rita absolutely refused, and began pulling all of the packages out of the trunk herself.

"Rita, what has gotten into you? You are acting really strange. Stranger than normal," Lauren said clarifying her statement.

Looking around her, as if seeing nobody was around to hear her, Rita made a sound of resignation. "Alright, you've got me. It was supposed to be a surprise. But we are going out tonight."

"Out?" Lauren asked reservedly.

"Yes, well, I've got tickets to see M......Rigoletto. You know the opera," Rita said excitedly with a little grin of a satisfied cat.

"The opera?" This was definitely not the Rita she knew. Something was definitely going on. She just couldn't figure it out. Rita would never in a million years be caught dead going to an opera. It just wasn't her style.

"Yeah, I thought I should introduce some classical music into my life. So why not opera? Who better to go with than you?"

Well, that explained the determination Rita had been showing all day in making sure she had everything she needed to get dressed up. But, the opera? She knew something fishy was going on, but at this point she was ready just to go see what Rita had in store for her.

"We have to be ready to go right at 6pm. It's already five, so let's get going sister. Here...take your dress and shoes and stuff and go up to the guest room."

Shooing her into action, like she would have with her twins, Lauren couldn't imagine what was going to happen next.

Precisely at 6pm they were both dressed and ready to go. Rita wearing a sparkling evening gown in an unusual lemon yellow color. Most would not have been able to pull that particular shade off, but with Rita, it was expected. And she did amazingly well, plumed headdress and all.

Lauren took one last look in the mirror. She looked good, real good. The only downside was she'd hoped to wear this particular dress for Max. She could almost see the reaction he would give when she walked into the room. His eyes would sparkle and his lips would curve into one of his knowing grins. Knowing that she knew what she did to him every time he saw her. Tonight would be fun, but it just wouldn't be the same without him.

"Let's go, let's go!" Rita yelled from the bottom of the stairs.

"Coming, Mom!" Lauren yelled back as she came to the top. She stopped and smiled down at her friend.

For a moment they just looked at each other. Tears began to form in Rita's eyes and she batted them away. "You are gorgeous, always have been. But tonight you are especially beautiful."

Slowly coming down the steps, Lauren laughed shyly. "Too bad Max won't be coming home until the 12th. I wish he were here."

At that point Rita almost let it out. Smashing her lips together, all she could do was say, "Umm hmm." Inside she was dancing with joy. *You got your wish honey.*

As Rita opened the door Lauren gave a big gasp. There in the driveway was a black limousine, the chauffeur holding the back door open for the ladies to enter. To her added surprise, there in the back of the limo was Rita's husband, David, looking just as dapper as could be expected in his tuxedo. If she'd been surprised at Rita's announcement of attending the opera, she was no less astounded to see David dressed to the hilt, and going with them. Now she knew something was happening.

After settling themselves against the plush leather seats, David brought out a bottle of champagne to toast the evening. Watching her two best friends warily, she decided to give it one last try. If they didn't answer this time, then she would just have to wait and find out.

"What are the two of you up to? Something is going on, and I want to know what it is."

The two of them looked at each other, looking as if they were going to explode with excitement. With a giggle Rita leaned forward and gave David a cute little Eskimo kiss.

Rubbing their noses together was enough to send them into gales of laughter.

Recovering sooner than his wife, David turned to Lauren and gave an innocent look, "I don't know what you are talking about. My snuggle bunny and I just wanted to take you out on the town tonight. Is that so bad?"

She'd never been known to give up, but she had to admit they were good. It all seemed to make sense. Or did it?

They drove downtown Seattle where shop windows were already beginning to be dressed for the Christmas Holiday. It seemed like every year retailers were bringing the holiday out earlier and earlier, in order to get a few more days of buying power under their corporate belts. Lauren looked out the window listlessly as she tried not to stare at her friends cooing at each other.

"Lauren. We have been so rude. I am so sorry. We don't get out by ourselves very often." Rita said reaching out to touch Lauren's hand. "Can you forgive us?"

"Yeah, sure, but maybe you two should get a room."

"That would be wonderful! David, don't you think that sounds like fun?"

Lauren didn't want to spoil the evening, but she couldn't help feeling a bit down. She saw David shake his head firmly then tried to get Rita's attention with a twitch of his head in her direction.

"I'm not exactly sure why you brought me along anyway. I feel like I should just leave you two alone. Only you didn't let me drive today, so I don't even have my car to get back home."

"No worries. Just stick with us. Everything is being taken care of. Oh look, we are almost there!" Rita said turning this way and that in her seat trying to get a better view out the window.

The chauffeur pulled up outside the Paramount Theater. As they got out of the limo Lauren could see other people entering the building. She could swear she'd seen some of them before, but couldn't place their faces with names, or even a time when they may have met. Looking around she couldn't see an event banner, or any type of handout or performance schedule being handed out. Just as they came to the performance hall entrance, there was a small reader board with the simple statement, "Private Performance".

When they entered the seating area, there were not too many people there yet. She could see a group near the front of maybe fifty people. As they got closer toward the front her heart began to pound and she began looking around to see if she recognized any more faces. To her surprise her whole family was there. Uncle Dan stood to one side talking to James and her son Josh, while Aunt Maggie was talking quite animatedly to Celeste and Rudolpho. Cousin Amy was seated, holding her sweet baby in her arms, asleep against his mamma's chest.

She knew it then. Max was here. He was responsible for this whole thing. But why had he done this? They'd talked about his coming back on the 12th. What on earth had prompted him to go to all this trouble?

Aunt Maggie caught her eye, and rushed forward to greet her.

"Lauren, sweetheart, are you as surprised as you look?" Smiling, she gave her a quick hug.

Just then the lights began to dim, and everyone rushed to find a seat. Lauren found herself sitting between Maggie and Celeste. Both reached out to pat her hand as she fussed in her seat.

From behind the curtains Max came out, looking more handsome than she'd remembered. Although the number of people were few the applause as he stepped out to the front was unanimous. Dressed in his tux, her heart exploded with pride as she remembered the response from the audience the last time he'd performed. His eyes searched the crowd until they found her there, tears brimmed her eyes as she gazed up at him. The smile which came to his lips was unmistakable.

Motioning everyone to sit, Max raised the microphone up to speak.

"Thank you so much everyone. I am so blessed with your presence. I'm sure you are all wondering why I have called you out tonight. There is something I would like to share with you all, and will be a bit of a surprise for someone very special to me."

He brought his gaze back down to Lauren, and held it there for a few silent moments. She could almost feel the love coming down to her, enveloping her in a warm embrace. She wished she could go to him and tell him how badly she'd missed him. Just as she'd done the night of his last performance, she raised her fingers to her lips and blew him a kiss, knowing she would love him forever.

The curtain behind him swung open to reveal the beautiful grand piano, gleaming with pride in the stage lights.

"I'm going to be playing for you some of my most favorite selections, a compilation of some pieces I have written in the last few months. What I would like you to know is all of these pieces were written for my precious Lauren, *mia amano.*"

Sitting at the keyboard Max began playing the most amazing pieces of music Lauren had ever heard. At some points the notes flowed together in a way reminding her of the gentle sounds of a stream in the springtime, at others they were filled with so much emotion it brought tears to her eyes. She knew exactly what he'd been thinking of when he'd written each piece, she could feel what he'd been feeling. There was no question he was the master of his own music, and his feelings were deep true emotions of the heart.

The last piece was ending in a very smooth and light twinkling of the keys. Max turned to the microphone and spoke the words Lauren would never forget in a thousand lifetimes.

"Lauren, my love, you have stolen my heart. *Tu sei l'amore della mia vita.* You are the love of my life. *Non ho mai amato nessuno come te.* I have loved no other like you. *Sei la luce del mio mondo.* You are the light of my world."

Standing he came to the edge of the stage again and held out his hands to her. "Come, join me, I must look into your beautiful eyes for this."

Lauren heard Rita sniffling into David's shoulder as she rose slowly to join Max on the stage.

As she reached him, he took her into his arms and held her close. In her ear he whispered, *"Tu sei molto bella stasera, amore mio.* You hold such beauty my love, inside and out. *La tua bellezza ha preso il mio cuore per sempre.* Your beauty has taken my heart for always."

Pulling away from her was the hardest thing he could have done at that moment. But what he had to say next was the most important thing he would ever say, and he wanted everyone to hear. Her green eyes looked into his with such a strong love he almost forgot what it was he needed to say.

Kneeling to one knee, he kept her hand in his as he reached into his pocket. "I am so in love with you. Come be with me on this journey through life. Let me show you all the ways that I love you, accept you, support you, and are thankful that you've come into my life." Out came his hand, and in it was the most beautiful ring she'd ever seen. He brought her hand to his lips and said, *"Sposare mi e viviere per sempre insieme nell amore.* Marry me and let us share our life together, in love always."

Lauren was so filled with emotion all she could do was nod her head in acceptance. She tried to speak, but nothing came out. Tears began to spill down her cheeks as Max placed the ring on her finger.

Rising to his feet applause came forth from the audience in a wave of approval. Back in Max's embrace Lauren could see her family, and most importantly her son, were all smiling and exchanging hugs. This had to be the most important night of her life. She'd never experienced so much love at one time.

She heard an exclamation of awe from the audience and looked around to find out what they had seen. In the overhead lights a grouping of butterflies swirled about as if dancing with joy. One of them fluttered down to land on the joined hands of Max and Lauren, as if saying its congratulations. A bright glowing light brimming with a stunning gold essence came from beyond, brighter than any stage light could ever be, and shone over them in its glory. Then the beautiful butterfly danced away on wings of love and disappeared into the light.

"She's crossed over," Lauren whispered.

Max nodded and smiled down at Lauren.

"*Ti voglio qui con me per sempre amore mio. Qui tra le mie braccia per sempre.* I want you here with me forever my love. Here in my arms forever."

"I love you too," she said simply and lifted her lips to his.

The love she'd dreamt of all of her life was now hers to keep.

The End

Author Bio

Analiesa Adams is an author who enjoys reading and writing about the many nuances of life, and romance through her insight from both personal experience and careful observation. Her lifelong dream to express the intrigue and revelation of her many interests, using contemporary romance, suspense, and paranormal themes, has motivated the creation of over 100 plots. Though challenged by her professional occupation, she will never give up the freedom of creating through writing.

Bookkeeper by day, writer by night, Analiesa Adams' heart belongs in the stories she creates. Author of *In Desperate Search of Peace,* and *The G.L.O.V.E.S. Series,* about all things metaphysical, starting with *The Healing Touch – Book 1* and soon to come *Ethereal Images – Book 2*. Her discoveries into the spiritual and metaphysical can be found in her ***blog*** and shared in the spicy tales of romance entwined with the uniquely mysterious order of life.

When not delving into her newest creation, she enjoys spending time with the light of her life, undeniably her son. His smile and humor have brought her through many tough times, and he continues to be her inspiration. Currently, the two loves of her life are two kitties named Loca and Cali. Though they keep her laughing, they both are a constant bother to her writing.

To keep updated on the next adventure in the writings of Analiesa Adams, visit my website at: AAdamsBooks.com. Drop me a note on the contact page and let me know if you would like to be added to my E-mail list for updates.
Follow me on Twitter at: https:/twitter.com/aadamsbooks
Favorite me at Smashwords at:
https://www.smashwords.com/profile/view/aadams999

Made in the USA
Columbia, SC
18 July 2022